THE
SUGAR
THIEF

NANCY MAURO

THE SUGAR THIEF

A NOVEL

RANDOM HOUSE CANADA

PUBLISHED BY RANDOM HOUSE CANADA

www.penguinrandomhouse.ca

Random House Canada and colophon are registered trademarks.

LIBRARY AND ARCHIVES CANADA CATALOGUING IN PUBLICATION

Title: The sugar thief / Nancy Mauro.
Names: Mauro, Nancy.
Identifiers: Canadiana (print) 20210398302 |
Canadiana (ebook) 20210398310 | ISBN 9780307359759 (softcover) |
ISBN 9780307359773 (EPUB)
Classification: LCC PS8626.A88455 S84 2022 | DDC C813/.6—dc23

Text design: Andrew Roberts
Cover design: Andrew Roberts
Image credits: (baker) prostooleh / Getty Images; (chalkboard) Peshkova / Shutterstock; (chalkboard font) Epifantsev / Shutterstock

Printed in the United States of America

1st Printing

Penguin
Random House
RANDOM HOUSE CANADA

For Lola and Sasha

And for Josh

One

Wanda

The passengers on Flight 908 fear death, but after an hour of sitting in the non-reclining seat by the toilet, I'm warming up to the idea. The man beside me has dropped his head down to his lap, his tender pink scalp visible through his hair. Everyone else seems to have resigned themselves to that eerie, heart-pounding silence that precedes catastrophe. Outside, turbulent winds batter the plane, and a bouncing wing-tip light is the only indication that anything exists in the grey sky. But when I turn from the window I spot something even more terrifying.

I see her. Sunglasses on, hair wrapped in a gold lamé turban. She's charging down the aisle like one of the Four Horsemen of the Apocalypse. Turbulence shuttles us back and forth but Sabine grabs whatever's in reach to steady herself: a seat back, the overhead bin, a ponytail. I've got my phone out anyway, so I just tap the record button and then shrink down in my seat.

Because she wasn't keen on paying extra to choose seats in advance, we've been split up. She's in the front, I'm in the back, and Paul is a few rows ahead of me in the window. She stops at his row and I watch her lean across some poor woman in the aisle seat to shake him. I can tell by the force she's using that he's asleep. Of course he's asleep, Paul isn't bothered by things like our impending death over Lake Superior.

In addition to the side-to-side beating we're enduring, the twin-prop plane suddenly loses altitude. My backside rises right out of the seat by the inch or so of easement the seat belt allows. Shouts of nervous laughter fill the pressurized space. I manage to hold on to the phone as the pilot says something in a garbled baritone over the intercom. Sabine is still on her feet. But a flight attendant is making her way down the aisle toward her, gripping headrests as she goes, her face screwed into an angry knot.

"Ma'am, you absolutely have to sit down!"

Sabine ignores her.

I can see the top of Paul's head now as he straightens up.

"Are you kidding me? You're asleep?" Sabine says to him. "Get a camera on me now."

I mean, she's right. As her social media director, I know she's right. This experience has viral potential. And it's kind of my job to find the viral potential in everything Sabine does. I angle my phone between the seats. Five million YouTube subscribers aren't checking in just for her pastry recipes. They want behind-the-scenes content. And what better content than Sabine Rose, the dark-eyed knockout, perennial bad girl and pastry chef prodigy saying her last goodbyes, convinced she's about to go down in a fiery plane crash?

Except she doesn't seem the least bit frightened.

"You need to return to your seat, immediately." The flight attendant has reached her now, slightly out of breath. "This is highly dangerous."

Sabine turns to her. The turban makes her a full foot taller than the other woman. "What *I'm* doing is highly dangerous?"

The flight attendant nods her head. "That's right, now please—"

"What's highly dangerous is what the two fucking morons in the cockpit are doing!"

I grit my teeth. Swearing doesn't play well.

Not that I'm going to use this footage. This will definitely go in the Not for Public Consumption file. It's important to have boundaries.

Although.

The job at hand *is* to turn some of her emotional volatility into content. And there's plenty of instability to choose from. Sabine is prone to blow-ups and breakdowns. She overreacts, can't multitask, won't just grin and bear it. It's my job to keep her on track, and it turns out I might have been doing this job too well.

I try not to go there constantly, but my thoughts keep winding back to it. The Deal. Well, the pending deal. These thoughts are often illogical. For instance, right now I'm wondering, will a plane crash help our deal go through?

"Come, there's an empty seat beside me." Sabine has turned back to Paul. "Don't bring your phone—I could have done that myself. Get the camera out!"

Like I said, Sabine's right. It's the reason we're on this plane in the first place. She hasn't been home in close to ten years, but we decided she should attend this big family celebration weekend. Get on camera with her father, a local baking legend. She needs to appear sympathetic, rooted, legitimate, a scion of culinary genius.

And us?

Where Sabine goes, Paul and I go.

I see him grip his video camera and try to get out of his seat. It's a cramped little plane and he hits his head on the overhead bin. The good thing about this display is that it's diverted many people's attention from the turbulence. Sabine is already making her way back to the front of the plane, grabbing onto passengers' shoulders as she goes.

Things have gotten intense since we reached critical mass online. We're on the cusp of taking this internet fame and translating it into hit streaming series fame. From the minute I walked into the new Toronto corporate Netflix lobby, a Times Square–esque experience of oversized screens streaming endless content, I've weighed every move as though it were a cog in the complex machine-learned equation that decides whether our show will be green-lit. Will they make an offer?

It depends. Sabine's not perfect, but they've given us notes on how to get her there. How to make her ironclad, so that when she gets uploaded to the big Netflix algorithm their investment pays off. They like Sabine. They like her stats. But the show was my idea. I wrote it, pitched it, sweated over it. Yes, it relies on her celebrity status, but I scripted that too.

My worry is the Netflix people don't like *me*.

It's the way they address me as an afterthought. In the pitch meeting, they brought Sabine her sparkling water and gave me the same, assuming I wanted what she wanted. This is not just petty observation; in any workplace it's hard to become autonomous when your main role is viewed as that of support staff.

This is also not paranoia, although no one could fault me for it if it was. Some ugly things have happened to me. I'll admit, I've been to the bad place. Nearly didn't come back.

So barring pettiness and paranoia, what I'm left with is plausible concern. Concern that the development team is subconsciously taking their cue from Sabine. I'm a vehicle of sorts for her. A necessary evil in ways that are not obvious to anyone outside our little huddle of three. I didn't set out to be indispensable, but for the past three years that's exactly what I've been. What we've been to each other.

And Sabine may have had enough of it. That makes me panic. More than any turbulence.

"Sir, you can't leave your seat!" The flight attendant, having lost one battle, now tries to step in front of Paul.

For a moment I think he's going to sit back down. Instead, he tugs down his T-shirt, which reads *Dim Sum and Then Some* and features a dancing dumpling, then squeezes past the woman. "She paid for my ticket," he says, because he knows which side his bread is buttered on.

We both do.

INT. AIRPLANE – DAY
SABINE BUCKLED IN DURING HEAVY TURBULENCE.
COOKIE PACKET OPEN ON TRAY IN FRONT OF HER.

SABINE
Welcome back to *Sweet Rush* where we are on board a pretty rough flight over Lake Superior! I'm just praying that after devoting my life to great baking, these terrible airline cookies are not the last thing I ever eat!

CU: SABINE GRIPS ARMREST AS PLANE SHUDDERS.

SABINE (CONT'D)
We're on our way from Toronto to Thunder Bay, Ontario—that's way up north for our American friends—to celebrate the fortieth anniversary of

my family's bakery! Check in with us at *Sweet Rush*
throughout the weekend. We'll bring you some of
the best pastries in the world, made by my own
father, including the legendary Persian.

PLANE BANKS AT STEEP ANGLE—HER DRINK SPILLS.

SABINE (CONT'D)
That is if we survive! (NERVOUS LAUGHTER)
Now, if you're thinking—*Persian? Is that even
something I should be eating?*—stick with us.
We'll take you behind the scenes of my father's
top-secret recipe . . .

ANOTHER BOUT OF TURBULENCE, CAMERA DROPS.
SCREAMING FROM PASSENGERS. PAN ACROSS SEATS
AS PEOPLE TRY TO REGAIN CONTROL BEFORE WE
RETURN TO SABINE.

SABINE (CONT'D)
. . . and learn how the strangely named Persian
pastry put my family's bakery on the map. So, roll
up your sleeves and get sweet!

Two

Sabine

Back at the three million mark, my agent, Collette, warned me that there was no end to the number of people willing to debase themselves online, and that whenever I turned the camera away from baking and pointed it at myself, I needed to make it count.

Coming from one of the most successful people in the business, these are words I've tried to take to heart. Last month I stood sideways in a mirror and, wearing a pair of tube socks and not much else, got some good, three-quarter shots of myself. I then cropped them down to the curve of my hip and the dark green whisk I'd had inked on it. And voila—forty-seven thousand reactions on Instagram. Cropping is what separates art from pornography.

These tattoo reveals have turned out to be some of my most successful posts. The image of the gingerbread man climbing out of my cleavage scored an all-time high in terms of unique impressions. And the blackbirds streaming out of a vented pie crust on my lower back sent my analytics app into a tailspin (especially after someone observed that the clothesline where a handful of the birds are perched is actually the string of my thong).

But Collette just pulled a face, like I had completely misinterpreted her. She told me to drop the clickbait tactics. The goal is a softer me. A relatable, genuine me. More rounded and grounded. She wanted me to limit what I post to Instagram (too easy, too curated, too fake) and focus on my YouTube channel. Camera presence and real emotion. Which is more relevant to the show we've pitched Netflix.

To that end, Paul got some good footage of me panicking and gripping the armrest while I riffed on Wanda's intro script. I even threw in some rapid Breaths of Fire that I'd learned in a yoga class, but honestly, I wasn't scared. This might have had something to do with the two Xanax I swallowed in the airport bar before boarding.

In the seat beside me, Paul's already watching playback on the camera display. That's when I notice the turbulence has passed.

"Guess we're not going to die today," I say.

Paul nods. He's a cameraman of few words, which I appreciate.

I look out the window. Shoreline begins to appear through the dirty grey clouds below and I feel a sinking sensation that has nothing to do with the plane's changing altitude. It's not like I had some dramatic falling out with my family years ago—there was no clear hurt inflicted on me—just your typical absent parent bullshit. I'm hoping we'll gloss over all that when my father and I actually come face to face. This is a celebration, after all.

The mandate now is to cut a few episodes during this visit and provide fans with a deeper dive, a tactic which I am reluctantly on board with. Wanda reminded me that there will be no product to review, no logo to ghost. I make my money flogging Robin Hood baking flour and Wilton candy melts on YouTube. People can smell when I'm overselling, and they aren't shy about pointing it out. The problem is, the more successful I become, the more sponsors I get, the more products I have to integrate into my baking channel, the more my viewers notice. All it takes is one semi-articulate commentator to sabotage a post that's taken us an entire week to script, shoot and edit.

Which is why the Netflix deal has got to go through. It's the kind of thing they tell you not to hang your hat on, but after nearly a year of Collette and her agency muscle chasing the producers on my behalf, there's no way to pretend it doesn't matter. Having my own show would be the great leap to on-demand television that every YouTuber dreams of.

Last week we got our chance. Collette, Wanda and I spent three days pitching our competition show, *What's in Your Pantry*, to the joint heads of unscripted development at Netflix (which sounds impressive but consisted of sitting in various boardrooms with three thirty-somethings named Brie, Britt and Brett). Our show features Wanda and myself issuing surprise challenges to amateur bakers. But after three days of shaking hands and high-energy smiles, it seems that it's the Netflix people who've issued us a final challenge.

Our last meet with the development team happened around a garden table at L'Élan in Yorkville. The cocktails had arrived and we'd somehow reached that stage of familiarity where Brie, Britt and Brett, the Three-Headed Cerberus, as Collette calls them, had started offering their origin stories. Mostly boring ones about growing up in Toronto suburbs. I watched Wanda pull one of her braids over her shoulder and stroke it. At twenty-eight, she still lives at home and looks it. As is my habit, I quickly scanned her hands, her fingernails, the condition of her cuticles (they are dry, she tends to bite them). Every week or so we go for a manicure, my treat. She has strong baker's hands. That's why I hired her as my assistant.

Wanda was staring at the Cerberus with large, unblinking eyes. I could tell she desperately wanted in on the conversation, but no one was wiggling over to make room. I was not prepared for what came out of her mouth right then.

"Sabine's from Thunder Bay," she offered. "She comes from bona fide baking nobility."

Britt looked over to her end of the table as though surprised to find her there. "Well, here I thought she was born in a clamshell from sea foam."

Wanda pushed her glasses up her nose. She does this not with her finger, but by scrunching up her face and contorting her upper lip until, magically and grotesquely, the clear-rimmed glasses inch back up into place right beneath her bangs. "Her father makes this pastry called the Persian from a secret recipe. It's kind of famous."

I took a big sip from my second blood-orange martini to keep myself from telling Wanda to zip it. But the producers' attention was caught. There was a waft of gender-neutral fragrance as all three joint heads swivelled in Wanda's direction. She sat up a little straighter, encouraged. It was the first time during any of our meets that the Cerberus appeared interested in what she had to say.

"*Persian?*" Britt rolled her wine glass stem between long brown fingers. "As in the cat? Or the rug?"

"Or the Middle Eastern empire," Wanda supplied, pulling out her phone. "Its origins are a mystery."

"How exotic," Brett said, readjusting his earth-tone linen tunic.

In fact, it's the complete opposite of exotic. The Persian is a frosted confection invented in Northwestern Ontario, and the name is something my uncle made up and fed to reporters.

"I can't believe you've never heard of it." Wanda was tapping away on her screen. "People line up for Persians every day. I've got the *New York Times* article right here."

From the far end of the table Collette glared at me as if to say, *get her under control*. She has it out for Wanda, who, in that moment, was drawing us further away from the purpose of the luncheon—to get these people to commit to our show. Also, Collette's old-school instincts were telling her to avoid associating me with a pink, deep-fried pastry from some one-horse town, no matter how Instagrammable it was.

But the producers were leaning over Wanda's phone to get a better look at the bun.

"What is it, exactly? A doughnut?"

"Laminated viennoiserie," Wanda said excitedly, swiping through various photos of people shoving Persians in their mouths. "Sort of like a puff pastry doughnut without the hole. Not even Sabine knows the secret recipe."

"It's just a silly local thing," I said, finally, placing my empty glass down squarely on a napkin. "For tourists, really."

She shot me a look. "Tell that to the Food Hall of Fame."

The thing about Wanda is that while she's a natural craftsman (I discovered her making showstopper pastries in a dirty little bakery on Dundas West), she also has this knack for becoming whatever you need her to be—cheerleader, public relations expert—before you even know you need it. In short, there is an unhealthy amount of entanglement between us that I don't like to think about too deeply.

"'Francis Rose celebrates forty years in business'—how nice!" Brie chirped, looking up from the phone. "Is that your father?"

I nodded. I knew about the anniversary. I'm not exactly estranged from my family. Life has just taken me a thousand miles away. Zia Stella, however, still calls once a month to comment on my videos, my weight and my recipes.

"Looks like a party," Brett plucked the phone from Wanda's hand. "I hope you're going?"

"Not a chance." I picked up my empty glass and signalled to the server.

Collette gave me another withering look. I guess it had to do with martini number three, but she's one to talk. I know what's in that travel coffee mug she carries everywhere.

"Oh, but you should." Brett returned the phone to Wanda. "We were just talking about that, weren't we?" He looked around at his colleagues.

"You have such a great story, Sabine," Brie said. "So, *of the times*. But there's something . . ."

"Missing." Britt supplied. Britt was clearly the boss lady.

I sat back, folded my fingers together and allowed myself to feel deeply irritated despite the slow warmth of the gin. Missing how? My life is an open book. You don't get the kind of following that I have on social media for being a recluse. Add to that my two *New York Times* bestselling cookbooks (we won't count the third, overdue one), a regular appearance on the CTV morning show *Wake Up Canada*, the pile of Streamy Awards I've won, the cookware line I launched in conjunction with the Food Network, all the articles in *Food & Wine*, *Toronto Life* magazine, the *Globe and Mail*—the list goes on. I think I've covered more public ground in five years than most people do in a lifetime.

Wanda frowned. She was the one who opened this stinking can of worms. "*Sweet Rush* is one of the most popular baking shows on YouTube. Sabine's consistently ranked among the top three YouTubers in the country—ever since the gay wedding cake story broke five years ago. She's not a flash in the pan."

"Sure," Brie smiled. It seemed to me they were taking turns wearing the same brittle grin. "But this isn't about a PR packet. We know all about the gay wedding cake, the affair with Reynolds Whitaker, the woman who single-handedly brought down the city's most vaunted Michelin-star chef."

"Her Forbes designation," Wanda added.

"Top food influencer." Brett nodded. "We get the narrative."

At the end of the table, I spotted Collette's agenting instincts twitch to life. She slipped a pen and notebook out of her purse. This was the actual conversation we'd spent a year preparing for, and the week dancing around. The producers were about to air their reservations with me.

"You're a tough cookie," Britt said. Her tone implied that this was a good but incomplete way of being. "But you lack vulnerability."

"Vulnerability, yes!" Brett snapped his fingers. It was a judgy, conclusive sound. "On any given episode of *What's in Your Pantry* people are making themselves vulnerable. They're inviting you into their homes, into their kitchens, letting you film their children, their dogs, their deep desire to be a professional pastry chef. They're competing for a chance to be the next TV baking star. But what are you giving them in return?"

"The chance to be the next TV baking star," I said flatly.

Because that's how *What's in Your Pantry* will work. Wanda and I visit, unannounced, two different amateur bakers in their homes and issue them a baking challenge with only the ingredients they

happen to have on hand. Then we bring them face to face and
judge their bakes. The unannounced part is real. Sort of. The contestants have obviously agreed to the challenge but aren't told
when we'll show up. Once they invite us in, they get two hours
to prove their authentic baking talent. This means something.
Viewers get to see them sweat. Meanwhile we go behind the scenes
and compare their homes, their lifestyles, their children. Will you
root for the single mom of two keeping it real in suburbia? Or
the failed actor sharing a downtown studio apartment? Each chef
gets one buzzer shot per episode. Which means we stop the clock
and they get to make a special request for some ingredient they're
missing. More butter or granulated sugar, which we will provide.
They also get an assistance request, in which Wanda will roll up
her sleeves and whisk eggs and sugar into a Swiss meringue, or
do whatever's needed.

We wrote the pilot—well, Wanda wrote the pilot—to fit neatly
in the template of reality TV. It has a formulaic structure with just
enough openings to make people lose sight of the formula.

"I'm the judge," I told the Cerberus. "That's all that matters
about me."

They looked at me as if seeing me for the first time. Which is to
say they were assessing. Thirty-five and holding. Former model—
I won't deny it, looks have gotten me my shots. Dark hair, black
eyes, olive skin and a wide mouth. Straight white teeth, which are a
prerequisite for any on-camera eating. I haven't been skinny since
I stopped doing coke every waking moment, but what good baker
is skinny? Still, my clothing hangs off me effortlessly or clings to
me provocatively. I am always camera-ready. They can see this.

"But are you likable?"

My eyebrows must have shot up into my hairline because Brie quickly gestured around the table. "Obviously, you are in this context. But an audience is a different thing."

"Let's ask the algorithm," I said. Or else the gin said. I happen to know that everything these people do, every chance they take is based on some fucking machine. I turned to Wanda, who was busy tonguing at ice chips in her glass. Now was the time for her to do her job as keeper of my social media empire and share some hard-won stats. This moment relied on accuracy.

True to her purpose, Wanda put her glass down and leaned forward in her seat. "Sabine has over six million followers across her social media platforms, so I'd say, yeah."

But Britt was looking at me. "Empathy is different on television."

"It's so much easier for men," Brie said sympathetically.

"You'll be judge and jury here," Brett added. "Bad cop."

"If only you had a child," Britt sighed.

"Or a dog," Brie offered. "Dogs equal empathy."

"I'm allergic," I told them. "Dogs and children." What was the point of this courting we'd been doing all week, all year really, if they had no intention of green-lighting our show? My chair rocked slightly on the garden gravel. I brought my hand down on the table to steady myself, but I used too much force and sent the silverware into a noisy clatter.

Collette started clicking her pen rapidly with one hand. She reached across the table with the other and placed it on mine. It was meant to look kind, but it felt like an iron vice grip. "So, what I'm hearing," she said in an encouraging tone, "is that you have some notes for us."

The clicking of the mechanical pen worked. All eyes went to Collette's hand. Just like that, the brainstorm cloud broke and the three producers sat back in their chairs, no longer sharing the same neural pathway.

Collette smiled the shark smile for which I pay her 15 percent of my commissioned earnings. She knew there was the TV series we were pitching, and that there was everything around it that would inform whether that TV series would get made.

"We brought you *What's in Your Pantry* in the spirit of collaboration. So, if you think there's anything Sabine should be doing to support her public persona, you can bet we're all ears."

The server came to take our orders, but Britt waved her away. The gesture is one that I despise, having worked in restaurants for ten years. But it woke me to a certain fact. We weren't there to collaborate. The Cerberus had a vision in their three heads and we either filled it or we didn't.

"Let's start with this Persian that Wanda mentioned."

Three

Wanda

Sabine's walking so slowly I'm starting to suspect she's drugged out of her mind and that we're going to have to carry her up the jetway and into the terminal.

It wouldn't be the first time.

"Get ready for a mob scene," she says sarcastically as she steadies herself on my arm. "They haven't seen me in nine years. Maybe ten. They'll probably fight over who carries my suitcase."

I smile at Paul. We'd be grateful to anyone who wants to carry her luggage.

"I want you two to lay low this weekend," she continues. "These aren't showy people. Keep out of sight, but make sure you get everything in the can."

She doesn't have to tell Paul that. He's always got his camera out and balanced on one shoulder. He's had it there for the past three years so that it's become part of his face. I'm always surprised when he lowers it to reveal hazel eyes and a soft chin. Paul's your basic silent type. A tech-college grad who bounced around commercial production houses as a grip before Sabine snagged him and let him actually drive the camera. Now he films exclusively for our YouTube channel while I write, produce and edit.

He's already sent me the footage of Sabine pretending to panic during the turbulence. We're a well-oiled machine.

Because she's walking so slowly, I barely realize it when Sabine stops. The walls of the jetway are lined with advertisements for local businesses. She's looking at one with an illustration of a girl sitting cross-legged on a flying carpet which happens to be hovering over a modern-looking bakery. I take a step back. The girl in the poster is dressed like a genie with a high ponytail and kohl-rimmed eyes. She holds a pastry with one hand and kisses the tips of her bunched-up fingers of the other hand. A puff of pink smoke encircles her and the carpet and trails off to form words: *Bennett's Bakery! Forty Years of the World-Famous Persian!*

There is a lot going on in this ad, but I say nothing because Paul's filming over her shoulder. I tell myself again that my instincts were right in getting us up here for a long weekend. This secret recipe business and quirky small-town success story is totally ownable.

By the time we're out of the jetway and into the small terminal building, the rest of the passengers are no longer in sight. A yellow sign indicates arrivals, baggage and the taxi stand all in the same direction, down one flight. Sabine stops under the sign for a moment, as if orienting herself. Then I see her throw back her shoulders, straighten her Norma Desmond turban, and charge toward the escalator. I follow a step behind; Paul lags even farther. We're letting her feel like she's doing her own thing. She is crazily nervous to see her father. He is a successful baker who she never talks about and rarely talks to.

Which sounds like an ideal situation as far as I'm concerned.

My father calls me at least twice a day despite the fact that I live at home. Neither he nor my mother can manage money to save their lives, and if it wasn't for my help with the down payment, we wouldn't own the roof over our heads. Even though my father immigrated from the Philippines thirty years ago, his English tends to fail him whenever he has to do anything even vaguely official, like renew his driver's licence, pay the mortgage or deal with the neighbours. Never mind that my seventeen-year-old brother, Manny, is perfectly capable of handling any of these tasks. But I'm the oldest of four kids and the only girl so you can bet it's always *Wanda this* and *Wanda that*. At my age, I'm supposed to be doing beach vacations and buying nice clothes. Instead, I go to the twins' parent-teacher interviews, do regular drug searches through Manny's drawers, and monitor my father's email to make sure he isn't offering relatives in the old country a place to stay in the new.

In this respect, I'm happy to be on this extended weekend trip. I wasn't sorry when Sabine got muscled into it during the luncheon with the Cerberus. They want to see her roots. And I kind of want to see them too.

Sabine has carefully curated the story of her rise to success. This part holds no mystery for me. The steps are simple: be beautiful, pick an industry, sleep with the guy in charge, then wait for the right moment to crush that guy and profit off his downfall. I don't feel bad for Reynolds in the slightest. Old shits like him should know by now that it's the price you pay for getting to sleep with hot young women. There's always been a price; recently it's just shifted dramatically toward public edification. If people are stupid enough to do it, I say, let the heads roll. No, the unknown part of Sabine's story is those years spent here in this isolated northern town. And I'm not a hundred percent sure that she herself knows what they mean.

Four

Sabine

Only after the crowd around the baggage carousel thins out do I realize that no one's here to pick us up.

"You sure they got the right flight number?" Wanda asks, frowning as she scrolls through her phone. She's sitting beneath a large birchbark canoe that's suspended from the ceiling. I wonder what would happen if the cords snapped and the boat fell on her. Then I wonder why I have this thought.

"They're running late," I say, though I have no way of knowing.

"I'm out of the city for exactly two hours and already calls from my father, my brother, one from my mother." She shakes her head.

There's always something wrong in Wanda's family that she must attend to, usually to do with the house they own in Parkdale. The Victorian's got to be worth two million since the neighbourhood finally succumbed to Toronto property wars, but it's a dump from the outside. This afternoon when I stopped to pick her up on the way to the airport, I could tell the Uber driver thought I was there to buy drugs. I've only been inside a handful of times and the crumbling foyer is always dim and smells of Bengay, sticky rice and gym shoes. The living and dining rooms have been turned, rent-free, into bedrooms for various branches of the Ocampo family that have overstayed their tourist visas while looking for a better life. By Wanda's account, her father is a bleeding heart. A while back he sent twenty grand to a fourth cousin whose house blew away in a hurricane. I sort of understand the "better life" thing since my family did it too. Only mine did it years ago and with a lot more self-interest. The men came first while the women and children followed with explicit directions not to leave a forwarding address.

The sliding glass doors open for the last of the passengers and allow in late evening air that's scented with jet fuel and pine sap and, faintly, behind it, the sumpy cabbage smell of paper mill smokestacks. In summer, the days here last forever. I take off my sunglasses and look around the arrivals area, which also serves as the baggage and check-in areas. It's been modernized, but it's the same tiny airport of my childhood. When you leave home and don't come back for years, you forfeit the constant references against which to test the accuracy of your memory. I don't have siblings to challenge my ideas, or photo albums where history retains colour and nuance. I have a handful of memories I believe are genuine at root. But they have taken their own shape and colour over time.

One of those is of the day I arrived here from Italy with my grandmother when I was a child. My father, Francesco Rosetti, had already been in Thunder Bay for five years. He'd learned English, dropped the Italian name and made himself into a successful pastry chef and co-owner of a thriving bakery business. I have a vague memory of him coming to collect us, and it takes place in this same airport. It's my immigrant-ship-sliding-into-the-harbour moment, and in my mind, just as cinematic. I was a little over four years old, which means my father had never actually seen me. For some reason I disappointed from the start.

My grandmother had been talking about him non-stop since we got on the plane in Naples. I was told that he was a baker, and so I expected him to be wearing a white apron. Instead, he looked more like a prince, elegant in a spring wool coat and a shirt spun of Egyptian cotton. At six feet, he had shoulders like the square frame of a house, his dark eyes alert, his brow placid. Handsome. When he saw my grandmother his smile fully engaged his broad jaw and white teeth. Later I'd learn that he used that smile sparingly. He had a fine ridge of nose, strong without the typically hawkish bent of his countrymen. His dark hair had been cut neatly around a skull that could have been scrolled on a lathe. In Canada, he called himself Francis. Or, rather, other people called him Francis because he wasn't the sort of person to talk about himself. My grandmother would never call him that. At age four, my ear had picked up some English from the TV in the abbey school lounge. Francis sounded feminine, which he was not.

He didn't know how to be a father yet, and so when he saw me, despite his best efforts to look happy, he looked, well, shocked. His body went stiff. If there was a chair nearby, someone would try to bend him into it. He looked at me like he was trying to figure out where I came from and how to put me back before anyone noticed. This had not been my experience with adults. I was a beautiful child, moulded like a Renaissance cherub; the nuns used to argue over who got to brush my hair. But he hadn't even brought me a toy or anything to break the ice, and as a result I could not be persuaded to kiss him or even look him in the eye.

I was tall for my age, sturdy as a wood stove and unwilling to keep still. As the porters unloaded our belongings from the baggage carousel, I clambered between suitcases, making every effort to be a nuisance. "Maybe if she gets a foot trapped she'll learn her lesson," my grandmother said wistfully in Italian.

My father knelt down, put a hand on my arm and took a good, unsmiling look at my face. For some reason I was sure he didn't like what he saw. To show him I didn't care what he thought I wrenched free and swung my legs over a trunk, exposing my bum to the entire airport.

"Yes, you looked just like that," my grandmother said, as though reading his thoughts. "*Un diavolo in bicicletta.*"

A devil on a bicycle. That was me.

⌇

"What's your cousin's name?" Ten more minutes of waiting and Wanda grabs my phone, starts scrolling through my contacts.

"Enzo," I tell her.

"Enzo what?"

"Take a guess," I say flatly. "How many Enzos are in my contacts?"

Wanda dials and crosses her legs, tilts her head to one side. I can tell when Enzo picks up because she sits up straight and smiles. She always does this on the phone.

"No, it's her assistant, Wanda. We're waiting at the airport." She pauses and nods vigorously. "In Thunder Bay."

I know the Xanax has faded because I feel a rash of annoyance at Enzo for forgetting to pick us up.

"When?" Wanda gets to her feet. She paces toward Paul who's leaning against a pillar fiddling with his camera. She says something to him that I can't make out.

Then she spins and walks toward me, her face strange. "When?" She asks again, biting the corner of her mouth. "We're at the airport. Sabine is at the airport. Waiting. For you."

I don't get why she's saying everything twice. But maybe I'm only hearing it twice because that's easier than what I'm about to hear. She lowers the phone.

"That was your cousin," she says.

"I know!" I drop my carry-on bag. We're going to be here a while.

"He did forget."

"That little shit."

"Sabine." She swallows. "Your father died."

Five

Wanda

As we're bending into the back seat of Enzo's SUV, it occurs to me that our celebratory homecoming narrative has taken a sudden left-hand turn and, from a PR perspective, I'm not sure how to salvage the script.

Enzo's boyfriend, Marcus, is driving. He's pretty quiet but Enzo more than makes up for it. Even though we're barrelling down the highway he's eschewed his seat belt so that he can turn around and address us in the back seat.

"I can't believe you brought a camera crew to your father's funeral." Enzo tweaks the end of his moustache with a pinky finger. He's a small man with a gymnastic physique and swift gestures that lead me to believe he has a short fuse. He has brown eyes and sharp features and looks like he might very well bite your hand.

"I didn't know he was going to be dead." Sabine is crammed in between Paul and me. Her turban has begun to unravel but she doesn't notice. "Nobody thought to call me before I got on the plane?"

Enzo looks genuinely surprised. "Call you? I didn't even remember to pick you up. My mind is blown. It's nothing but crying and wailing at my mother's house. I can't even imagine what's going to happen at the bakery. We have a tent and a hundred folding chairs in the parking lot for the anniversary party. An Italian band is driving in from Winnipeg. My father's just like he was when you left—the most impossible human to ever walk the earth. Your pops was the only thing holding that place together . . ." Enzo's mouth twitches. He turns and slumps back in his seat.

Sabine stares past Paul and out the window where the boreal forest whizzes past. "What happened?"

Enzo turns again and grips the headrest. "He wasn't sick or nothing. Yesterday he was at the bakery as usual—arguing with my father, doing inventory, talking to customers. They were going to shoot fireworks off the roof at the end of the weekend. Everything like normal. He goes home for dinner and—poof!"

"He didn't disappear, Enzo," Marcus interjects. "He had a massive coronary."

"It happened at home?"

Enzo studies his cousin's face for a moment. "He didn't suffer."

Sabine nods. She hasn't taken her eyes off the window.

"Another thing? You know that my mother hasn't gotten any less dramatic these last nine years, right? She's going to drill you to the wall."

Sabine groans and reaches for her purse. We are both wearing the same deep russet nail polish, Burn Baby Burn. Her hands are shaking as she digs through the bag.

"Enzo, she doesn't need to hear that right now." Marcus shifts into the right lane. "Remember the little chat we had about sensitivity?"

Sabine finds the bottle of pills but can't get the lid off. I take it from her and twist it open. "How many?" I ask.

"A lot."

I give her two.

Sabine is naïve this way. She thinks she can just pop her pills or snort a line—employ whatever chemical adjustment is called for—and things will just fall into place as they have in the past. That's because she never really sees the work I have to do in the background.

"I'm not saying anything she doesn't already know," Enzo is telling Marcus. "She hasn't even visited in almost a decade. You can bet her Italian family is going to have something to say about that. You of all people should know what I mean."

"Keep our situation out of it." Marcus signals and veers sharply onto the short highway off-ramp so that the three of us in the back seat get pressed to one side. "It's ironic that you think your father is impossible."

I need to think straight, for the both of us, because the reason we're here is to help shove this Netflix deal through the very last wicket with some cheerful father-daughter footage. That's not going to happen. And nobody wants to watch a funeral.

Sabine looks up as the trees thin out and we enter a residential neighbourhood. Her eyes are glassy, her lips swollen, and there are tears streaming down her face. Sometimes I stop seeing it, but she is beautiful. I turn to Paul. The camera's resting on his lap casually, but I can tell that he's watching the little LCD screen carefully.

"Where are you taking me?" she asks.

"To my mother. You should just deal with it now." Enzo looks at me and Paul this time. "Also, I wouldn't march in there with a crew in tow."

"I know it's strange," I say with the little brightness I can manage, "but we're kind of like emotional support dogs." I pick up Sabine's hand and squeeze it. I'm not expecting anything in return. I'm here to support her. But Sabine returns the pressure. Ever so lightly, but it's there.

"Wherever she goes," I say, "we go."

Six

Sabine

I am the little girl on the flying carpet. My face is on every pastry box, plastic bag and TV commercial that comes out of that bakery. Between the ages of eight and twelve I put on the pink satin genie costume with its gauzy midriff and exposed shoulders and make appearances at carwashes, little league games and church bazaars. Any event that the bakery sponsors, I'm there clacking my finger cymbals and waving to the crowd while we distribute cartons of Persians. Though aesthetically I'm a cross between a harem girl and belly dancer, I am called the Persian Princess. My face gives me entry to this world and, even though I'm only eight years old, I know intuitively it is a chance to be useful to my father.

The family business is doing well as it is, so it takes my uncle Dante years to convince my father to advertise the Persian pastry. His rationale is, if it's already popular, why put advertising dollars behind it? Mr. Bennett, who used to own the bakery before us, hadn't even bothered to put a sign up outside! When Dante points out that Mr. Bennett had nearly driven the business to bankruptcy (which is the reason two immigrant cousins were able to purchase it), my father finally agrees.

When the men go to sign an advertising contract with the *Chronicle Journal*, it's one of the rare occasions when my father takes me with him. I sit on a mushy leather sofa at the back of the room while my father and uncle watch the sales manager frown at the proposed headline they've brought him.

BENNETT'S BAKERY. HOME OF THE PERSIAN PASTRY!

He looks up at them. "What the devil is that?"

"The advertisement—to go in your newspaper." Zio Dante leans forward on the desk, the rounded shoulders of his suit jacket threatening violence along the seams. "Why you think we're here for?"

"I get it. But why should I care?"

My father glares at the sales manager. Dante is in charge of dealmaking and the hot mechanical toil that is bread. But Francis is a pastry artist and explaining his work is beneath him. "This is our bestseller, the Persian. A risen-dough cinnamon bun." He goes on to describe the little pastry's volute shape and the way in which the grain melts on the tongue.

"Still don't care and you've spent five minutes describing it." The sales manager taps his pencil on the desk. "You need to give it a personality to match its name. Tell people it's gonna make them feel like Lawrence of Arabia. 'Open sesame' and all that. The thing to do is—" He stops suddenly, spying something in the crack between the two mountains that are my father and uncle.

"Well, hello gorgeous."

My father and uncle turn around, expecting to see some knockout in the doorway, but it's only me on the sofa. "That is just my daughter," my father waves his hand impatiently. "She won't bother us, finish what you say."

But the man slides open his desk drawer. He takes his time hunting through the contents. Finally he produces a lollipop that he gets up to bring to me.

"You're a pretty little thing, aren't you?"

He stands over me offering me the candy. At eight years old I am used to being looked at this way. People do it all the time, but usually from a safe distance. At this proximity it feels like I am being inhaled, and I know enough to know I don't like it.

"Go ahead, honey," he murmurs.

But I take the creep's lollipop anyway. And I do so without looking up at my father for permission. Even though I've been living in his house for four years, I don't know him well enough to predict whether he'll allow it. I am already transacting on my own here, always have, always will. So when the man leans down and pats my head, I flinch, but I let him do it.

He returns to his desk but is still looking at me as he picks up a pad of paper. "The thing to do is put a face to it." He points a pencil between the men. "That face in particular."

They both turn again to follow the pencil's imaginary laser trajectory to where I sit sucking a lollipop. The sales manager begins scribbling something on the pad.

"You've seen the Aladdin movie, hon?" he asks me. "You know how the princess flies on the magic carpet? Well, how would you like to be the princess on that flying carpet?"

I nod, although I haven't seen *Aladdin*. It wouldn't have occurred to anyone in my family to give up the single precious Sunday afternoon when the bakery is closed to bring me to the movies.

The man turns back to his drawing. I slide off the couch and approach the desk, fighting the impulse to sit on my father's lap. Instead, I hang off his shoulder watching the man sketch a rough approximation of the Persian pastry. Then, holding this pastry, he draws a little girl with a heart-shaped face, a ponytail and made-up eyes. With her free hand she grasps onto the upturned edge of a carpet that floats on the page. Though it is crude, I understand immediately that it's me, soaring through the sky on a tasselled rug.

"What we're doing here is giving the bakery a visual identity." He fills in my eyebrows, shades my non-existent hips with the flat side of his pencil. "Just like cereal—kids see the cartoons they like on the box and mums buy it." He picks up the pad, holds it at arm's length and squints. "You've got your very own spokesperson right here."

He puts the sheets back down and scribbles a headline under the picture:

THERE'S NOTHING AS MAGICAL AS A PERSIAN!

My father is mortified. But Dante is the one with the marketing prowess.

"There's nothing more ordinary than salt," my uncle says that evening at his house, stabbing his finger against the sketch as though he's crushing ants. "But Stella pays more every single time just to buy the one with the little girl and the umbrella."

"It's true, Francesco." Zia Stella also calls my father by his real name. She slides the drawing out from under her husband's hand. "What's the harm in it?"

My father crosses his arms at his chest. "I don't want her face all over the newspapers."

I sit up a little straighter. It isn't often that I hear my father talk about me like a real, living thing. Most days he regards me with that same puzzled face, as though he has no clue where I've come from.

"But it's a beautiful face," Stella tells him. "And we don't know how long it lasts. We should make the most of it now!"

"It's a dog face," Enzo says from his seat. At age six, Enzo's the one who looks like a schnauzer. He's small and wiry, yelps non-stop and functions as my best friend. I kick him hard to shut him up.

My father leans back in his chair, fishes a toothpick out of his shirt pocket. "I don't have time for this, Stella. I have a bakery full of people to manage."

"I'll sew the costume!" Stella presses the drawing to her chest. "I can do it, right, Sabine?"

I nod vigorously. "Let me do it, Papà," I beg. "I'll be really good at it."

But my father's face is stern, shut down. "It's a waste of time for you, Stella. The kids are older now. We need you behind the counter full-time, not playing make-believe."

"Playing?" Her eyebrows shoot up. "Is that what I do?" My aunt is an Italian housewife and offended that my father thinks raising children is a shirking of her duty to the bakery.

"I mean, if you do the work, we don't have to pay a counter girl."

"So, who's going to feed the kids? Bring them to school and pick them up?" Stella taps her upper lip sarcastically. "Oh, wait, Francesco. You have someone you want to volunteer?"

"Stella." Dante pushes back his chair.

She spins around. "Why can't I say it? It's what we are all thinking."

My uncle stands up. "Enough!"

"Dante, it's okay." My father raises his hand, but he's looking at my aunt. I suppose in that moment he understands that he's not going to win the most nurturing parent award. And that a young girl like me needs a willing female influence. He jabs his gums with the toothpick. "You'll take care of it?"

Stella has recovered. "We'll just get some pictures taken for the advertisement. It's no big deal, Francesco."

It is, in fact, my aunt's humble entry into a brief and glorious career of talent management. She hires a seamstress and commissions a satin costume, complete with a ruffled neckline and hems and elastic straps that have to dig ever so slightly into my shoulders if they are to stay in place. We watch endless reruns of *I Dream of Jeannie* and practise until we get my hair and make-up right. In the end Stella turns her nose up at the Sears photography studio and hires the best wedding photographer in town to shoot me sitting cross-legged, holding a Persian. It's a smart move. The advertisements are so well-liked that within a year they are turned into illustrations, embellished with a flying carpet, and printed on every carton, cake box and napkin that goes out of the bakery. Two years later we start doing television commercials at the local station and at the end of each I appear, pastry in hand, and deliver my famous line, "There's nothing as magical as a Persian!"

I like being a local celebrity. The kids at school forget I was the girl who couldn't speak English in kindergarten. I am now the girl who's on TV. I like not being around my grandmother, who spends more and more time in her bedroom watching

100 Huntley Street, even though she can't understand a word of it. I like not being in the house in general. More importantly, I like that I am helping my father by helping the business that means everything to him.

"She's doing so good, Franchi," my aunt tells him when we return to the bakery after an appearance at the curling club's annual bonspiel, the metal Persian trays emptied. "The owner liked her so much they ordered a dozen cookie trays for their Christmas party."

Zia Stella and I make a good team. Each year she sews my costumes a little larger. She arranges for me to present cheques at telethons, sing at the Italian Ladies' Benefit Society dinners, and walk out into the crowd at sporting events, bells tinkling, to sign autographs for kids and give out free Persians. Within three years the bakery's overall orders have doubled. The pastry counter sees line-ups every day, but more importantly than that, our bread is in demand. It's impossible to say that the bakery's success is a direct corollary of my efforts, but my father has started to notice me. Other kids have dads who drop them off at school and teach them to ride bikes. Mine is a ghost who's gone by the time I wake up in the morning and comes home exhausted in a fine dusting of flour. Now he is seeing me, giving me the occasional thumbs up or a pat on the shoulder. Over dinner he'll ask me to estimate how many people turned out at an event, making an impressed face no matter how many I claim showed up. By the time I'm twelve years old we've won wholesale bread contracts with the school board, then the hospitals, paper mill and grain elevator cafeterias. These are the bedrock industries in our town and suddenly this quaint, immigrant-run bakery is churning out their daily bread.

As for Stella, she's kept her promise to "manage" me. But her star is on the rise too. She is elected president of the Italian Ladies' Benefit Society around the time that the crowds get to be too much for us. At our last appearance she'd been swarmed before she could even get the dozen cartons of pastry out of the delivery van.

"This is not a job for a woman," my father tells her, examining the dent to the rear door caused by the swell of a hungry mob. My aunt is basking in her post-election results and doesn't argue.

"I'll take over on the weekends," he tells her. "Sabine and me together."

I am nervous the entire week leading up to my first Persian Princess appearance with my father, a little league game at George Burke Park. What if no one comes for the free Persians? He'll be disappointed in me and hand me back to my aunt. But the bleachers are full, and as I walk onto the infield ahead of him with a carton of pastries, I can already sense the crowd's enthusiasm.

The kids are supposed to form a line while my father sets up the folding table. Instead, the children acquire a sort of prescient swarm mentality. They come at me, reaching for the oversized cardboard carton. At first it's just the little ones, so I raise the box over my head. But then the players themselves hop out of the dugouts. Some are ten or twelve years old and bigger than me. I am knocked over immediately. The carton flies from my grasp. I feel the crushing weight of children and then nothing else. I see nothing. My ears are full of their shouts and cheers, but not a single word of it is articulate. Someone kicks me in the chest. I can't even scream; the air is crushed out of me. I am being buried alive by my own fans. Just as my arms and legs grow numb, the load begins to lift. A patch of sunlight appears, and then another, as children are miraculously torn off of me and hurled into space. My father reaches down and picks me up off the ground. He pulls the straps of my costume back onto my shoulders. His face is the colour of dishwater. He rubs something off my forehead and then stands with me in his arms. He carries me off the field.

In the van I press a napkin to the cut on my forehead. My costume is torn, and dirt is ground into my elbows and knees. Later we'll learn I have a cracked rib. But I am no longer shaken. I'm with him and safe. Even if I am an afterthought, he stepped in when it mattered.

"We are finished with this business, right Sabine?" he says quietly as we turn down John Street. "Done with the Persian."

I nod.

"Good. Because I never liked it. It was a mistake from the beginning."

My stomach drops. That's not true. I don't want to argue with him as I sit bleeding into the upholstery, but I've spent four years contributing to the business. Most of it has been fun.

"I like a lot of it. I like being on TV. I like helping with the business."

He looks at me for a moment. "I'm talking about the Persian. It's a mistake." He turns onto our street. "A mistake that began a long time ago."

I feel the heaviness of the words, the loneliness of our house as we pull into the driveway, and part of me doesn't believe him. The mistake he's talking about is me.

"Can I come work at the bakery then?"

"Doing what?"

"Baking."

He laughs. "You don't know how to bake, Sabine."

"I could learn. You could teach me."

He shakes his head. "I don't have time. I have a business to run."

"Then let me keep doing the Persian Princess. I want to help."

"You can help by going to school, doing your homework and keeping your grandmother company. This business *è finito*." He waves a hand in my direction. "I will tell Stella myself."

My aunt doesn't rally hard to save the Persian Princess after seeing my injuries. Besides, the novelty of my childhood has passed. At age twelve, my body has started to change. To imagine me floating on a carpet is no longer a simple suspension of disbelief. I have shot up and grown wider as breasts and hips emerge. Satin stretches over my buttocks. The gauzy midriff is no longer decent even before it was torn and soiled by infield dirt. Now come the dark years of teenhood, the betrayal of the body, the overcharged emotions. Stella's done what she could to offset it, but I imagine she is tired of my handsome father's tendency to wash his hands of things. She's foisted me back onto him. And he doesn't want me either.

Seven

Wanda

In the living room, the aunt rises to her full Lilliputian height as Sabine is brought forward. "You," the grande dame says and starts to cry.

As Sabine bends to hug the petite woman I can tell the pills I gave her have kicked in. Her eyes have acquired the slow-blinking, glassy perspective of a collectible doll. I once had to walk her onto the set of *Wake Up Canada* like this. Luckily everything had been measured and staged as per our agreement. She just had to be reminded to keep talking for her five-minute segment.

"We are ruined, Sabi!" The aunt clutches her and sobs. "Such a hard worker and an artist. Now what are we left with but your uncle!"

"Ma, it's too late in the day for this." Enzo removes his sneakers in the doorway, so Paul and I do the same. He ushers us over the plush cerulean wall-to-wall carpet toward a French provincial–style loveseat. The vinyl layer that covers the sofa has been custom cut with sartorial accuracy to accommodate ruched cushions and the sweeping wood cornices of the armrest. When we sit down the plastic sheathing makes the sound of farts.

The aunt has broken from the hug but still has Sabine's wrists in her hands. You can tell that once she'd been handsome but now her features have softened into pearl foil. "With Francesco gone, we are *finito*. I feel it in my bones. Oh, *figlia mia*, if only the Lord had taken me instead. At least everyone would be provided for."

The room falls silent and it's obvious she's waiting for something from Sabine. A daughter who feels nothing at the death of her father is gruesome. I telepathically urge her to reach around the Xanax haze for sorrow, something normal.

"You look good, Zia," she offers, backing away and perching on the edge of a sofa.

Sabine's useless this way. Whenever she leans on the pills, or vodka for that matter, I have to script everything that comes out of her mouth. So I sneeze loudly into the crook of my elbow.

It works. Zia Stella's eyes dart around the room until she spots Paul and me on the Louis XV–style loveseat.

"Who's this?"

Sabine looks at us like she's never seen us before.

I smile but without teeth. "Mrs. Vasco, we're Sabine's assistants, Wanda and Paul? From Toronto? We're so sorry for your loss."

Stella's lips twist in displeasure as she looks at the equipment Paul's holding. "Sabine, you bring a cameraman to your father's funeral?"

"She didn't know he was going to be dead." Enzo dumps himself in a chair whose gilded, cabriole legs give it the appearance of a man genuflecting in golden breeches. "Marcus and I even forgot to pick her up at the airport. That's the kind of day it is."

"Where is Marcus?" I ask, realizing he hasn't followed us inside.

"Oh." Enzo looks at his mother. His mother, in turn, looks at the crown moulding. "He's not allowed in this house."

We all sit around this statement for a moment.

"Marco is a good boy," Stella finally says. "I am just keeping peace."

"My father is a Neanderthal," Enzo tells me. "Even though he hasn't lived here in, what is it, Ma? Five years?"

"Three." Stella looks at her son. "What does this mean, 'Neanderthal'?"

"A caveman."

"Oh, yes," the woman winces. "Enzo is dead to him. And for why? Because he is a gay."

Paul and I shake our heads.

"Francesco, the father of Sabine, he is like a father to Enzo. *Grazia Dio*. He teaches him everything in the bakery. Now Enzo is a better baker than even me."

"Thanks, Ma."

"My husband? Forget it. I tell him, there is nothing a parent will not do for their child. But does he want to hear it? For Dante, all Enzo is good for is to slave in that bakery. Not once does he come with me to the meeting for the gay parents."

"LGBTQ parents," Enzo corrects her.

"I try to tell him, 'be grateful the gays get married now.'" Stella picks up an iPad from a marble side table and swipes it awake. "How else do we have grandchildren? You know what he says?"

She's looking at me. I wait for it.

"He says, 'First let me tie a rope around my neck in the garage. Then you have all the weddings you want.'"

Stella holds up the iPad. I recognize the article, Sabine standing in bakery whites behind an elegant wedding cake, arms folded, giving her best "fuck you" smile to the establishment.

"When Sabine is on the news with the wedding cake, I record it on the VCR. Dante doesn't let me show it to no one."

"Listen, Ma," Enzo says, sounding tired of the subject. "I'm hungry, can you make me something?"

Stella sighs heavily. She returns the iPad to the side table and waves vaguely in the direction of the kitchen. "Go make yourself a plate. *Comare* Anna next door already brought over a lasagna—who's going to eat all that? Paulo and Wander—you are hungry?"

I smile again. "No thank you, Mrs. Vasco, we're fine."

She nods. "Enzo will fix you a plate."

The wedding cake story is what launched Sabine's career. She has a tattoo of it on her shoulder. It happened while she was still living with Reynolds, doing her nightly mix of booze and drugs, and wasting away working front of house at his restaurant, Along Came a Blackbird. One day, she happened to be seating a couple who were complaining that the bakery down the street had rejected their wedding cake commission. The baker didn't "do" gay weddings.

Right then and there, without consulting Reynolds or the pastry chef, she volunteered the restaurant's pastry services for free. And took the commission on herself.

There's no denying the move was driven by personal gains. More than anything, Sabine wanted to be a pastry chef. She'd gone to culinary school but found herself trapped in this front-of-house lifestyle. Reynolds had promised to intern her to his patissier years ago, and he'd yet to make good on it. She'd been given that face for a reason, he'd tell her, and that was to greet customers as they entered Along Came a Blackbird, which happened to be the hottest Michelin-starred restaurant in the city.

"But something inside awoke that day. For me as well as for the grooms-to-be, Gregory and Max," we wrote in the foreword of her second cookbook/memoir, *Chaos Kitchen: Dessert at the Sixes and Sevens*. "It was our collective sense of justice. For too long we'd been kept from the people and things we loved because it didn't suit someone else's narrow idea of universal order."

The cake was a decadent, three-tiered affair filled with balsamic-soaked strawberries, crushed pistachios and finished with a semi-naked rose buttercream application that was ahead of its time. The cake crushed it on Instagram, and when Gregory and Max sued the first bakery in civil court for discrimination, the story set off a series of blasts across the national news outlets. Sabine, portrayed as the RBG of the cake world, got her first one hundred thousand Instagram followers overnight. A three-book deal followed along with a weekly baking segment on *Wake Up Canada*. When Gregory and Max landed a six-part TV documentary on Bravo, *My Big Fat Gay Wedding*, Sabine was featured prominently.

More important were the tiny explosions that took place in her personal life. She dropped the coke (pretty much), launched her YouTube channel, and quit both Along Came a Blackbird and Reynolds. It's worth noting that Reynolds did not go quietly; after all, he'd left his wife of twenty years and their three teenage children for Sabine. He launched a flame war on social media, calling Sabine a "talentless, opportunistic climber." Nobody believed him. He was the one who'd let conditions at the restaurant deteriorate, but he blamed Sabine for the loss of his Michelin star and the restaurant's eventual shuttering by the Department of Health.

I still, from time to time, find his sad-sack replies on our posts and have to delete them.

Enzo comes back in the room with plates of food. He gives us each a wedge of lasagna, its cross-section of latticework revealing a generous studding of small meatballs.

Sabine sits hunched, looking like the guest of honour at a pity party while Enzo puts the frilled noodle down in front of her.

"Was he complaining of anything?"

"Nothing," Aunt Stella tells her. "But you know Francesco, he wouldn't tell us if he was. Who knows what goes on in that head! You talk to him recently?"

"A couple months ago? His birthday, I think. He didn't like to talk on the phone, he was always in a big rush to get off, so . . ." her sentence drifts away. She looks down at the lasagna but doesn't even pick up the fork. "When is the funeral?"

There's a dramatic silence before Stella answers. "There is no funeral."

"There's a memorial tomorrow night, Ma. It's the same thing."

"The same thing?" Darkness breaks over the woman's face. "How will the Lord know to come and take Francesco to his eternal rest if there is no funeral? No body to show? No church? You think Gesù Cristo comes looking for him at a memorial service in his living room?"

"Maybe that's the way he wanted it," Sabine says quietly.

The aunt stares. "No, this is not his idea. I know where it comes from. It was the same with Mr. Bennett. He dies and we sit in that house looking at each other like idiots."

"*Basta*, Mamma," Enzo warns as he hatchets through the complex layers of pasta with a fork.

"God rest his soul, but your father, Sabine, he is always too easily led. He lets you go off to the cooking school and we never see you again." Stella pulls her black cardigan around her. "If you had a mother—a real mother watching you—none of this happens. You could be married now like a normal woman, having babies. Everybody would be so much happier. But look at our family—not a single bambino, nothing but snakes that swallow our own tails!"

I know Sabine, so I'm waiting for her to open her mouth and use it. But she says nothing.

The aunt's eyes move over her, the dishevelled hair, the hollow under her cheekbones, and the untouched lasagna in front of her. I get the feeling that Sabine didn't grow up with much in the way of a support system.

"And all those tattoos, Sabine!" The aunt raises her head and delivers a terrifying ululation into the popcorn spray ceiling. "I see them on the videos sometimes. On the Instagram. I don't know why you ruin yourself this way."

"Jesus Christ, Ma." Enzo drops his fork against his plate. A fleck of parmesan trembles on his moustache.

Sabine curls her fingers into the mahogany scrolls of her armrest. I am holding my breath. I see Paul's toes dig into the deep nap of the carpet. The rococo is closing in tightly.

"You think it's *bella*, eh? But a couple years from now it's going to look ugly. When you're forty and by yourself, covered with the tattoos, it's an ugly life."

Sabine stands up and walks out of the room.

The aunt watches her go, shaking her head. "Just like her father. When it's something they don't want to hear, it's goodbye."

"She's in shock," I say, although my documentarian instincts tell me I'm not supposed to interfere. "No one even bothered to call her yesterday. Her father died and you let her get on a plane without telling her."

Stella looks at me as though I'm truly stupid. It's amazingly effective. "We don't tell her," she says, "because we know she will not come."

I follow the deep blue pile in the direction that Sabine disappeared. At the kitchen entrance the carpet transforms into a marble tile. Inside, she stands with hands planted on either side of the sink staring out of the window into the backyard.

"Everything okay?"

She spins around. "Oh, it's you."

"Should we leave?"

Sabine rubs her nose vigorously and nods. "Call an Uber." She slides her phone over the kitchen counter toward me.

"Do they have Ubers here?" The phone recognizes my face and unlocks.

"They have taxis. Call one of those."

"Okay, which hotel is it?"

"No. No hotel. Back to the airport. Back home."

I lift my finger from the screen. I need to think. I've been turning this over in my head since the minute Enzo delivered the bad news. My instincts tell me it's not time to leave.

"She's a real character, your aunt. But you've got trolls who are a thousand times worse." The woman does have Sabine's cookbooks displayed prominently on the buffet.

"It was a mistake to come here." Sabine turns back to the window. "And I blame you."

I lean against the scrolled marble countertop. Its scalloped edges dig into my lower back. Didn't Mark Twain say something about the impossibility of talking reason to an idiot? Not that Sabine's an idiot, but she's a tad myopic.

"You can't just *not* go to your father's funeral."

"It's not a funeral. It's a memorial." She tosses her head. "Plus, he won't know any differently."

"It's just, well, have you thought this through? I mean, what about the show?"

Sabine narrows her eyes. "What about it?"

I hook my thumbs around the straps of my overalls to keep myself from wrapping them around her throat. Was she not sitting at the same table at L'Élan when the Netflix people finally got down to brass tacks? When they folded up their pleasant exteriors and transformed into efficient, cast-metal bots? Even the smiley one, Brie, lost the casual, collaborative spirit she so charmingly brought to their three-headed enterprise.

"We don't mind telling you this," she'd said while building an elaborate scaffold with her fingers and resting it on her knee, "because it's a business mission we believe in. As joint heads of unscripted development we've been tasked to tell stories of 'compelling characters, both relatable and empathetic.'"

I took this criticism to heart. I was her writer, her editor and her public voice. If someone was saying that Sabine was not real—relatable—they were saying I wasn't doing my job.

Except I do know what I'm doing.

I am the keeper of the production bible. I can rewrite; I have the material. I saw her face in the airport when I had to tell her that her father passed away. That it was sudden, that no one saw it coming. Her face had collapsed, but not into expressionless shock. Her head tipped sideways; her eyes brimmed. I was aware that

I had dealt a fatal blow. Her face told me that I'd unlocked some fundamental hurt she'd carried her entire life.

It was perfect. And we got it on video.

"You know what I've realized in the two short hours we've been here?" I ask now in an even tone. "It's that you *already* have the character and relatability those assholes are after. You've got those fundamentals baked in. Look at your aunt, your cousin— your reaction to them all. Why are you afraid to show it?"

She looks up.

"You know there's five million people out there who tune into you two-point-seven times a week, right? Do you really think it's just recipes and baking ideas they're after?"

You see, this is the missing storyline of Sabine's life. What the three-headed Cerberus needs to see before they sign off on our deal. It's the thing we came here for—but on grief-stricken, blue-carpeted, pink-frosted steroids. And I can't let her run away from it because she's uncomfortable. I've put too much into this.

"People like baking because it's a break from their own lives. But they follow *you* because you're a real, flawed, beautiful person. Now is the time to let them in." I spread my arms out as if to encompass her personal space, her aunt's kitchen, the entire town. "Because Sabine, you know this opportunity is not coming around again, right?"

There was a time, a few short years ago, when I was sitting on a windfall so massive that, when the vultures came, I simply folded. I was too young, too stupid to handle it. And by the time I realized what had happened, even the bones had been swept away. That's when I tried to commit suicide.

You would have, too, if you'd lost what I had lost.

All this to say, you look at your prospects differently after great failure. I'm not being heartless; I created this opportunity. I drew its outline and breathed life into it.

Sabine looks at me, she looks at my hands. She knows we're both in this together. "Okay," she says. "We'll stay."

I smile, but not too much. This is death, after all.

INT. *SWEET RUSH* KITCHEN – DAY
SABINE RAISES A PLATTER OF CANNOLI TO CAMERA.

> SABINE
>
> *"Leave the gun, take the cannoli."* Wiser words
> have never been uttered. And today I'm going to
> show you how to make this famous Italian pastry
> at home. We'll follow one of the first recipes I
> created for crispy, chocolate-drizzled cannoli filled
> with sheep's milk ricotta. A cannolo so good it was
> featured on the front page of the *Toronto Star's*
> Food & Drink section.

CUT TO OVERHEAD-MOUNTED CAMERA B FOR
MONTAGE SCENES. CLOSE-UP OF SABINE'S HANDS AS
SHE USES FRILLED-EDGE SLICER ON PASTRY SHEETS.

> SABINE CONT'D
>
> In today's episode I'll teach you how to mix, roll and
> trim your dough . . .

CUT TO CU OF GREASED PASTRY HORNS. SABINE
WRAPS DOUGH, JOINING EDGES IN DECORATIVE CRIMP.

SABINE CONT'D

We'll learn the best method to mold the cannoli
shells . . .

CUT TO SILKY RIBBON OF CREAM FILLING BEING PIPED
THROUGH PASTRY BAG NIB INTO CANNOLI.

SABINE CONT'D

And we'll practise steady control of the pastry bag
to get a professionally piped cream centre.

CUT BACK TO CAMERA A: SABINE SEATED WITH PLATE
OF CANNOLI.

SABINE CONT'D

These cannoli are making you an offer you can't
refuse. So, roll up your sleeves and prepare to
get sweet!

Eight

Sabine

The Mayfield Hotel, once a safehouse for vagrants and drunks, girls on the striptease or on the road to better things has, since my last visit, been bought up by the InterContinental group. The parking lot has been excavated to accommodate a saltwater pool and spa, the lobby bar turned into a Smith & Wollensky, the rooms upstairs stripped of carpet and wallpaper and rewrapped in 800 thread count cotton, tossed with duck down pillows, and beamed through with Wi-Fi.

Downstairs I stretch out naked in the eucalyptus-scented sauna. Somewhere in my mind I'm aware that this is a co-ed facility and that I'm supposed to be wearing my towel instead of lying on top of it, but I have that drowsy lack of inhibition that comes with downing the contents of one's minibar.

I raise my phone above my head to check my messages.

jesus, sabine, i'm sooooo sorry it's taken a tragedy to get this kind of footage. looks like ur views are through the roof. call me if you want to talk. i'm thinking of you. xoxo Collette

While I appreciate the flowers she'd had sent to the room, "tragedy" seems like an overstatement. Tragedy is a Tibetan schoolhouse buried in an avalanche, not an aged father passing away. Collette seems unnaturally excited by this turn of events. I swipe away the analytics app with its bar graph and pulsating arrows signalling an upwardly trending post and click through to the airport video.

It's hard to watch myself without being incredibly critical of my voice, my delivery and my posture, but this clip is almost obscene in its truth. My face goes from moderately irritated to skeptical before it crumples like a jack-o'-lantern someone's kicked in. Wanda places both hands on my arms. Then I start to cry, which just barely saves the whole thing.

I hardly ever scroll down into the YouTube comments or reply to subscribers—this is something Wanda takes care of. I'll never be comfortable with the familiarity that fans assume in their messages, but I'm curious about what people are making of my display. There are plenty of crying emojis, brief words of condolence, fans who use my grief as a base to spin off into their own stories of loss. Also the usual requisite insults.

Conway Witty 92   2 hours ago
serves u rite stupid bizatch hate this channel.

Mila Bakes at Home   1 hour ago
Aww, so sorry for you. Heaven got another angel xoxox

ChompChomp   1 hour ago
You are so beautiful when you cry

And then this one:

ReynoldsWhitakerII 1 hour ago
If only this woman was half as good at baking as she is acting. Watch her video for pineapple upside down cake—she doesn't even caramelize the sugar.

This, of course, is followed by a barrage of demands that ReynoldsWhitakerII get the fuck off social media. Several subscribers support my decision not to caramelize the sugar since it can cause browning issues with the fruit. But a handful of people are with him, festooning his comment with a set of clapping hands or a thumbs-up emoji. And I suppose this display of solidarity is all Reynolds needs to feel he's still in the game. It's for this smattering of validation that he's willing to use his real name instead of trolling me anonymously. You see, people either take this shit literally, or recognize the entertainment value.

I'm not sure who's more annoying.

According to Wanda, Reynolds has been popping up on my feed with some frequency as of late—that is, until she deletes him. I suspect it's because he's got a book coming out next year, a memoir about the rise and fall of the country's most decorated chef and restaurateur. According to the blurb on his website it's a "gritty and acerbic portrayal of his substance abuse and subsequent mental breakdown." My guess is he'll fill chapters with details from our relationship.

The substance abuse part is definitely true. It's true of most service industry types. I was with Reynolds for nearly eight years, many of them in secret until he got the balls to leave his wife. Living together was decidedly not as exciting as our illicit nighttime affair, which consisted of sex in his car or the pantry, or in hotels while accompanying him on business trips. When we lived together—well, that was some reality check. Or I should say, it was an exercise in staving off reality. He was twenty years older than me when we met, and he just kept getting older. We did coke all the time, although in my case, I had good reason. I realized I was basically married to an old man I was no longer attracted to but who held the keys to my career.

I was already a "thing" when I walked into Along Came a Blackbird to interview Reynolds Whitaker. I'd been at the best culinary school in the city but was getting a steady stream of modelling and acting gigs that everyone told me to pursue while I "still had the face." I'd landed the role of host on *Foodie Confidential* (I cringe now at the name), where I interviewed top city chefs as they prepared their signature dishes. The whole thing was boiled down to ninety-second content to run between advertisements on taxicab television. I never intended to be a bystander, a reporter of other people's creative processes—I wanted to be a pastry chef—but I was doing well in industries that were brutal to most. And for a long time it seemed that my face kept a lot of disappointment at bay.

At the end of his interview, Reynolds grabbed my arm and pulled me around the butcher block prep table in his back room. He wasn't physically impressive, but he had sharp, intelligent eyes. He pushed my three-quarter sleeve up to fully reveal the fluted cake pan tattooed on the inside of my arm just above the elbow. I remember being surprised by the intimacy of his grip, the way he traced the ring-shaped kugelhopf, looked at me with absolute confidence, and offered me a front-of-house job at Along Came a Blackbird.

I laughed and declined. "I went to Marcon," I told him. "For pastry."

His silver-threaded eyebrows shot up. "So what the hell are you doing this interview bullshit for?" He was still holding my arm with one hand, stroking it with the other. "At least here you'll be one step closer to the kitchen."

None of the men in the kitchen even blinked in our direction. It didn't occur to me at age twenty-three that his behaviour was so commonplace that his staff had quit noticing.

"Are you offering me a path to pastry chef?"

"It's certainly a possibility," he said quietly, rolling down my sleeve and patting my arm.

While I couldn't ignore the petting, what I didn't foresee was that shortly after taking the job we'd be fucking in supply closets. That in a couple months he'd be paying my rent, that he'd have a key made for himself. I wasn't cognizant of any of that in the moment. All I registered was that he was offering me a job— basically as a pastry chef.

I was stupid. No kid walks into the best restaurant in the city and becomes a pastry chef. Even the ones who are raised in bakeries. These positions are bled over, killed for. To be fair, I didn't think he'd make me a chef, fait accompli. But I did think sous-sous-sous chef was certainly in my future.

The first day I reported for duty, the maître d' told me, "You stack menus here, you stand here, and you smile in this direction."

"I was really hoping to work in the kitchen. Clean up duty, whatever you have."

He laughed. "With that face? You're joking." He took me by the shoulders and steered me to the hostess stand. "Reynolds would put you in a glass box and display you on the sidewalk if he could, sweetheart. Kitchen's for ugly folk."

I was flattered. You weren't being objectified if you liked it, right?

"You start front of house and you work your way to the back," Reynolds said a week later when, instead of driving me home, he pulled into a deserted warehouse parking lot and started unzipping my skirt. I was kissing him back, for the record. From time to time a single, plangent note would sound in the back of my head, alerting me to the fact that what I was engaging in was career suicide. But then, what sort of career did I have?

"Okay," I agreed without knowing what I was agreeing to. "But I really want to bake."

"Then work for it," he said, pulling my blouse up over my head. "Now shut up and let me see that kugelhopf."

By the time the gay wedding cake came around seven years later, a flight from the coop was long overdue. How and why it took that long is tough to explain without sounding like a pathetic opportunist. On the one hand I was used to men not giving me a chance. On the other, I had been orbiting greatness for so long that the laws of physics dictated I'd be sucked into the sun sooner or later. And that's exactly what happened.

Reynolds didn't like how my single, small success with a balsamic-soaked strawberry and pistachio cake went viral. He was distrustful of social media, refusing to acknowledge its power. He became old and odious overnight and would follow me around the apartment asking me whether I would leave him now that I was famous. For the first few months I told him not to be silly.

I even put him to work collecting thematically linked wedding cake recipes for my first book, *Big Gay Wedding Cake Bakes*. But the idea of leaving had taken root. And it certainly wasn't unwarranted. At thirty I was still only his head hostess. He had not let me into the kitchen at Along Came a Blackbird, though plenty of male chefs had come and gone. I myself had done a good job of making enemies of the pastry chef by taking the wedding cake commission without his consent. But that old French patissier could shove it up his ass. I was owed that commission after years of fucking Reynolds Whitaker.

To be clear, I didn't set out to bring down his empire. But once it started to crumble, I had to either ride the rock slide or get crushed by it. I needed a way out from under the man who paid my rent and my wage. But more importantly I needed to ensure there was no way back in. One thing I knew about myself back then was that I had an unhealthy level of dependency. Sure, I could leave Reynolds, but the first hardship I hit and back I'd go. And at fifty-one, divorced with two adult children who barely spoke to him, I knew he'd be a more than receptive taker. No, if I was going to walk through that portal, I had to seal it behind me.

In the end it was a simple, quick transaction, almost an accident. Everyone on staff had seen the rats. Two of them, chasing each other playfully around the kitchen. Everyone had taken videos. I just happened to be the one to post it. And the only one with enough of a following to attract attention. To go viral.

I did a female-empowerment themed interview after that with a staff writer at the *Guardian* who followed my posts. It wasn't my intention to set a journalistic agenda, but she saw me as someone using social media to expose what it was like to toil anonymously in a top-heavy, predominantly male industry. Once it was out there, my story became a platform from which the media began prying apart the brutal masculine seams of the food-service industry.

I wrote all about it in *Chaos Kitchen*:

"Once the pie was open the birds began to sing." Yet again this child's song proved a spot-on metaphor for what happened after the Department of Health finally shuttered Along Came a Blackbird. It was as if we were all freed from the hold of Reynolds Whitaker. Many of us, the women especially, went on to successful new ventures and prestigious teaching appointments. Some of us stepped into the media spotlight, mentoring young women in a spirit of entreprencurship and support. It's hard to say how long I would have persisted if those two rats hadn't made their way into our kitchen.

"Great tattoos."

I jolt awake, realizing I'm still in the sauna, still naked. Not alone. On the bottom bench, across the heater, a man in bathing trunks leans back on his elbows, a towel over his head.

"Jesus Christ!" I stand, snap my towel open and wrap it around my body. "How long have you been there?"

He slides the towel off his head, revealing hair the colour of sheet metal. "It's a co-ed sauna. Says so right on the door."

"Goddamn pervert!" I hop down from the top bench and nearly lose my footing on the cedar planks.

"Easy there." He sits up. "You okay?"

"Fine!" Then I nearly lose the towel. I'm dehydrated, dizzy, drunk. I struggle to wrap my body without falling either into his lap or onto the sauna rocks. When I push open the door, I'm unprepared for the room-temperature air that hits me squarely in the face and funnels down my lungs. I haven't even been back here for twenty-four hours and I'm already a mess. Some places just bring out the worst in a person.

Get it the fuck together, I tell myself as I follow the modern, geometric carpet past the exercise room and into the lobby where I drop into a deep leather club chair. The truth is, I haven't even been home yet. Meaning, *home-home*, the house where I was raised.

What would it be like now, almost ten years since I last saw it? My father had chosen the house, and everything in it, over his old life in Naples, leaving my mother, tethered by the enormous weight of her belly, behind. Had it been the right choice?

I look at the little spa pouch dangling from my wrist. It contains my phone, hotel card and keys to the rental car. Then I look at the towel I'm wearing along with the disposable spa flip-flops. They will have to do.

Nine

Sabine

My nonna Maria always talked about my unusual upbringing as though it were somehow preferrable to the kind of life normal North American families led. Children were a female devotion, she maintained, and I was lucky to have her and Zia Stella. For a female child, a father was not a necessary daily influence within the household. In fact, the best fathers were those who kept the whole enterprise running from a calm distance, like any good CEO.

My father had come to Canada in the first place on the invitation of his cousin, Dante, and his wife, Stella. They had, years earlier, settled in Thunder Bay, a small city in Northwestern Ontario with plenty of industry and a good job forecast. Zio Dante had written that if a man could handle the isolation and merciless winters along the north shore of Lake Superior, this was the place to be. In the big cities like Toronto or Winnipeg, the best an immigrant labourer could hope for was a job washing dishes, a one-room apartment in a bad neighbourhood and a pocketful of bus tokens to take him between the two. But in Thunder Bay a man could raise a family in a house with a backyard, park his car out front and have his pick of work in forestry, shipping or rail. And if those options didn't suit, the bakery where Dante worked as a deliveryman was hiring. That was good enough for my father, who was already a talented baker. It was the mid-eighties when he left his pregnant wife, Lucia, in his mother's care and took his leave of the impoverished Italian south in order to make a new life for the family. My mother must have really bought into this scheme because let me tell you, living with my grandmother could not have been a walk in the park. The plan was, he would save enough to bring the rest of us over, a feat which took five years to accomplish.

Also, we hit a major glitch along the way.

When I was two my mother got sick. Like sick-sick with cancer. She was in and out of a hospital for two more years before she died. Between accompanying my mother to and from her treatments and her job as a caretaker, my grandmother had no time left to raise me. They decided to send me to an abbey school near Salerno, an hour north of our village of Palatino. I've been told that my mother insisted on this. I assume she didn't want me to watch her die. It strikes me as an incredibly old-fashioned idea, but perhaps not a terrible one. Instead of sick room smells and IV drips, I have memories of the leafy medieval abbey with a courtyard and jungle gym, and the pleasant Ursuline sisters who dressed in civilian clothes and let me watch television with them twice a week.

On the downside, I have no memories of my mother.

My grandmother came often. My first memories of her are as a stooped, black-shrouded figure bringing a sack of wax paper cones to distribute to the children, each filled with honey from the beehives she tended for a living. I knew she was my grandmother, although the sisters didn't explicitly address the little woman with the spun-sugar bun of hair as my nonna. It was too painful a word for the girls in the school who were from broken families, who'd lost a parent, who still cried in the night. We just called her the Honey Mother. When she approached the abbey on Saturday mornings, the girls would flock to the iron gates, jockeying for position. I stood back, waited. My grandmother always reserved the largest cone of honey for me.

Actually, I do have one memory I like to attribute to my mother. A woman came to collect me from the abbey for the day and brought me by taxi to an outdoor fabric market. She wore a coral suit and high heels that clacked on the cobbles and she held my hand as we walked between the merchant stalls. She told me she was having a dress made, and I remember how she gasped with pleasure as bolt after bolt of colourful fabric was unfurled before her.

I told my grandmother this story once near the end of her own life. She shook her head. "It must have been one of the sisters that took you on an outing," she said. "Your mother was in bed, dying of uterine cancer before you could even walk."

But it was Zia Stella that I went to as I grew older and my questions got more complicated, as I began to understand the nuances of family life and observe the relationship between husband and wife. "Why didn't Papà come back to Italy when my mother got cancer?"

Stella's jaw set into a knot, but she didn't back away from the question. "You remember what your grandmother was like." Then she looked around her living room warily, as if to make sure the old woman wasn't still alive and hovering in a corner. "She didn't want to worry your father unnecessarily."

"My mother was dying. There was reason to worry."

"I think Nonna Maria was waiting to see how things went. They still had hope with the chemo treatments. And then when those didn't work, it was too late." Stella breathed deeply, her nostrils fluttering. "There was no point in Francesco returning to Italy after she had died."

This last sentence was like a slap to the face. "He could have come back for me."

Stella clucked her tongue. I had been brought to *him*, hadn't I? So what difference did it make? "What you don't understand, Sabine, is that for a hundred years immigrants and their families lived and died apart. If your father had fifty dollars in his pocket, he would have put that fifty dollars back into his business. English people always throw their money around. But for us, even a plane ticket was a luxury we could not afford."

Satisfied with her explanation, Stella sat back in her room of blue upholstered splendour.

Ten

Sabine

I grip the steering wheel at ten and two, as if proper hand positioning might offset the fact that I'm wearing nothing but a hotel towel and that my blood alcohol content is ticking well above the .05 percent threshold. I'm parked on the same side of the street as the house, but yards away. Close enough to see but not to be seen.

The house itself is a boxy grey structure built on the American Foursquare plan. It rises three stories over Summit Avenue and nearly all of the east-facing windows have sweeping views of Lake Superior. There is a rose window punched through the façade, surely an after-market addition, that lends it some charm. Still, with its hipped roof and protruding dormers, the house has a greedy look at odds with its plain exterior.

It's the house I grew up in. It's the house that my father brought us to after my grandmother and I arrived in Thunder Bay. Funny enough, it's the only house I have ever lived in and I am a stranger to it.

Oh, and inside it is his wife.

I remember the porch lights were on. I remember my father bounding up the front steps ahead of us to prepare the way.

Inside was dark wood panelling and heavy furniture that was not so different than that of the school I'd just come from. But there was none of the feminine needlepoint, doilies or plants that the Ursulines used to enliven their crumbling stone abbey.

There were rooms to the left and right of the foyer and a wide staircase straight up the centre. There was a grandfather clock at the base of the stairs. I went to it, mesmerized by the sway of the massive brass pendulum. I reached out and placed five grubby fingers on the glass that protected the clock's perpetual motion.

That's when I heard the sound above me. A rush of wind or the sharp intake of breath. I pulled my hand away, preparing for my grandmother to yank me by the ear. But she wasn't even looking at me. She was looking up the staircase. I looked up as well.

On the landing stood the Madonna from the nativity crèche that the sisters had set up in the abbey last Christmas. She had the same blonde hair swept back to reveal a face of classic proportions. Blue eyes, thick brows and a full mouth painted a nearly shameful rose. But instead of the billowing robes and mantle, this Madonna wore a wool skirt and sweater, beige with tiny seed pearls embroidered along the neckline. Instead of being a ten-inch statuette, this was a real live woman.

I stared at her. She stared back at me. But it wasn't the way I was used to being looked at. This way made me nervous. She took a single step down, her foot making a heavy thud. My father moved at the same time and for a second I thought he was rushing forward to catch her. But she went no further, her grip on the banister tight.

"Julia," he said. Then he gestured to me as I cowered in the shadow of the grandfather clock. "This is my daughter."

He said that. I'm sure he did.

—

Repeated enough, my aunt Stella's argument for the immigrant work habit and lack of sentimentality was sound, so I'm not sure how old I was when I started putting it all together.

My father didn't come back for his dying wife in the old country because he already had a very alive, very beautiful one in the new.

It's not pleasant realizing the framework of your house is rotten. That your entire life has been structured around the decisions of someone to whom you are a postscript. My grandmother and I had uprooted our lives to come here. I went to school, became a Canadian, learned the language, lost the old one. Took on a whole new identity based on nothing but this man's sense of duty to an afterthought.

I suppose things may have been different if she had been different. But Julia was, from the moment we set foot in her house, a woman invaded. She made it all the way down the staircase that first night, not knowing where to look first. The four-year-old with greasy hands on the glass panel of her grandfather clock, or the old woman with thinning white hair dressed like a folkloric hag.

My grandmother stood behind me and put both hands on my shoulders. I felt the first rumble, then, in my stomach. It was a mix of hunger and anxiety. Nonna was not one to spend money on exorbitantly priced airport sandwiches and so had fed me nothing but peanuts since we boarded our flight in Naples.

Julia came over to us. She wasn't as tall as she first appeared, but she was every bit as beautiful. Her nostrils were as delicately carved as a violin scroll and her eyes were the clearest, most unnatural blue. I wondered if it was a hindrance to go through life with such transparency. Could people look right into your thoughts? She stared down at me and my stomach really started to grind.

My grandmother was still holding me in place by the shoulders. In Italian she said to me, "This woman will be your mother, Sabine. Say hello before she thinks you are deaf and dumb."

I opened my mouth. I intended to say something to prove I was every bit as charming as the Ursuline sisters told me I was. But the machinery of my stomach backfired and what came out instead was a rush of peanut vomit. The hot spray hit Julia right in the chest, soaked through the delicate knit sweater, drenched the pearls and pooled on the Persian carpet underfoot.

I mean, it was not an auspicious beginning. Julia shrieked and my father yanked her away from me protectively. My grandmother cupped her hands around my mouth at first, trying to catch the puke. Then using her body as a shield to spare the carpet.

Julia hobbled back to the staircase, my father guiding her half of the way. Then he came back and kicked open the door to a powder room. My grandmother pulled me in and held my head over the sink. After I was spent, we huddled together in peanut-scented vomit. I was sure she was going to let me have it. Instead, she splashed water gently on my forehead,

"It's okay," she said, looking at me in the mirror. "It could have been worse. At least now it's done." Then she did something I'd never seen her do before. She smiled.

⟲

A light goes on at the side of the house and I instinctively shrink down behind the wheel, sure that I've been spotted. A figure emerges, backlit by the floodlight, and makes its way down the drive. It's dragging something that makes a loud scraping sound in the calm summer night.

A moment later Julia steps out of the shadows. She is white, almost spectral in the streetlight. I see she's grown old, finally. The sculpted planes of her face have fallen. Her hair is pulled back tight and she wears a long cardigan over what appears to be a nightgown. This is surprising since I've never seen her anything but fully dressed and made-up. I've never even seen her without earrings. She's taking out the garbage, I notice with relief. She reaches the curb, sets the bin upright, then turns to stare down the street in the opposite direction.

After I threw up on her it seemed like it was days until we saw her again. She didn't eat meals with us, she didn't watch television. She went out, came in and ascended to the third floor of the impassive house. The rational side of me knows it must be difficult to be a stepmother. But I was a motherless child, and she made no effort. My father always rushed to excuse her, and in my mind that made them a single, untouchable unit. I thought I hated her growing up, but maybe what I hated was how she took him away before I had a chance to claim him.

She's still staring down the street. I wonder if she's senile, if she's waiting for my father to come home. She must be in her seventies now. It's bound to be difficult for her to carry on without the shelter of a husband. Moonlight falls through the bower of old trees above, then through the windshield and casts stenciled shadows on my hands. I think of how easy it would be to put her out of her misery. Just slide the car into drive, hit the accelerator, rapidly close the distance between us, jump the curb, watch in the rear-view mirror as her white cardigan sails through the air, her slippers landing on the neighbour's lawn. She'd never see it coming.

She wasn't a simple, cruel stepmother, just completely absent. As he was. And you can't just plow into someone for not loving you, right?

Except that I'm not just playing it out in my mind. There's an unfortunate synchrony between fantasy and my nervous system. My headlights are off, and I have one hotel flip-flop firmly on the accelerator. It's one of those silent, hybrid cars and I can feel it moving. My hands are on the wheel. My trembling, useless hands. I'm exhaling Chardonnay fumes as the shrouded white figure grows closer. All that's left to do now is to yank the wheel hard right, summit the curb and make contact.

Eleven

Wanda

Light is already breaking when I dig my bra out from the sheets and climb out of Paul's bed. He's fast asleep in his usual position, on his back with an arm draped across his eyes. I lean over him for a moment, studying his nose. It's the perky, ski ramp type and it always strikes me as strangely at odds with his personality (which, having known him for three years, is definitely a pot set on simmer). Don't ask what I'm trying to divine from a nose. The point is, this is how these silent types work. They give you nothing to go on. You have to lead your own investigation into character and loyalty, draw your own conclusions, then look like an asshole when you misjudge them.

I get dressed and sit at the desk by the window to pull on my socks. The purple cast of morning stretches across Lake Superior and the Sibley Peninsula anchored in its bay. The peninsula is a raised monolith of land almost a kilometre out from the harbour. It's known as the Sleeping Giant for the profile it cuts in sheared rock. Look it up; it's famous. The Ojibway legend, which is printed on every T-shirt and coffee mug in the hotel gift shop, claims the giant was once a spirit who walked into the bay, lay on his back and turned to stone to protect the location of a secret silver mine from the white man.

What we do to cover our secrets.

Last night Paul and I combed through the footage shot in Stella's living room. I assembled a pretty rough but powerful follow-up to Sabine's in-flight turbulence video and airport reveal. While *Sweet Rush* errs on the side of light and fluffy, this dash of gritty reality has sent our views soaring. From the living room footage, I chose a segment that would flatter the aunt's sensibilities and highlight Sabine's vulnerability. The teary reunion, the aunt's grasp, Sabine's blanched face as she sank into the plastic-covered furniture. She still looks beautiful; Paul always makes sure of that. I included the aunt's amazing exposition in favour of LGBTQ rights as she paced the blue carpeting, then capped it with her lamenting the fact that there will be no funeral, just a shitty memorial in someone's living room.

What I can't post is the really good stuff. The aunt excoriating Sabine, predicting she will grow old and ugly alone, that her skin will sag and her tattoos blur. That stuff I put away in the Not for Public Consumption file.

Certainly, our weekly baking videos require a ton of careful set-ups, professional lighting and numerous takes. But the trick to these behind-the-scenes posts is authenticity. Quick and dirty. Which is good news for us. I can get these videos live, gauge reaction before Sabine even wakes up, and decide her next public move for her. I know it sounds slightly manipulative but it's always been the way we've functioned. She believes things just happen to her and I work behind the scenes to make those things so.

When we first met, we were both in a bind and it didn't occur to us to set boundaries. Her career was taking off and she needed a fully formed public persona—quick. Me, I'd been robbed blind and had nothing left to draw a ring around and call my own.

I was, from the start, what you'd call intrepid. I'd gone to an arts high school, done an undergrad degree in political science and had just received a master's degree in business and technology. My thesis was an app that used publicly available but overlooked data to predict agricultural shortages and bumper crops around the world. If you've never given much thought to agricultural patterns, you're not alone. Back when the app was still in wireframe form I had no idea what sort of information I wanted to aggregate. I just knew that when I found some interesting stats I would have the framework to crunch them. A while later I happened across a discarded book, *Aerial Views of the Earth, 1955,* in the study carrels at Robarts Library. It was a volume of colour photographs taken from commercial aircraft, but it struck me as post-war America's bounty on display. Golden wheat, lush tobacco, snowy cotton. Cameras have always lied, but the grand scale of these quilt-work fields made health and robustness easy to spot, just as it made fallowness and decay difficult to hide. I looked into it and, as with any great idea, the pieces fell into place. With satellite photography, drought and wildfire records, weather patterns, pestilence levels, labour union minutes, and reports of social unrest—all things publicly available, all things that affect agricultural output—I was able to assemble a database of surplus and deficit crops nearly any-where in the world. I called the app Wheat Bump and spent the next two years compiling enough data to make the program run.

It was my thesis advisor who put me in touch with Odin, a development company in Montreal that could help make my prototype more sophisticated. "Saleable," I think was the word they used. When the Odin reps came to Toronto to meet with me, they talked about how Wheat Bump could be used to help social reform and the distribution of food and aid ahead of disaster.

All things, they said, that a progressively minded student like me cared about.

I think I told them something stupid, like I was just after truth in a time when it had never been easier to obfuscate it. They smiled at this and casually mentioned that they were slated to open a Toronto headquarters in the newly renovated Ping-Pong Factory building. That I should come by for Bar Cart Fridays, free snacks and, of course, ping-pong. A month later they called me up to make good on their invitation. They'd hired a small staff to ostensibly manage a handful of worthy projects they were incubating. Funny thing, not once did I hear mention of any venture other than Wheat Bump.

I should have known when Odin started courting me that I was more than their typical student development project. I should have known that Odin didn't care about redistributing wheat surplus to third world countries. Above all, I should have known better than to sell them the Wheat Bump prototype for $200,000.

But that's what I did. I gave my dad half of that money to put toward a down payment on the house. Then I left for Europe. Six months later I had blown through most of what was left when my thesis advisor messaged me. Odin was in the news. They'd developed a promising betting tool for the stock market called Wheat Bump. The proprietary software could help traders gauge real risks—like whether they should dump Eurasian semolina crops or invest heavily in Korean soy. And Odin had just sold it to Microsoft for $42 million.

Twelve

Sabine

When the hotel phone pierces my consciousness, I have no idea where I am. It takes a dozen agonizing rings before I am able to heave myself to the side of the bed and make it stop.

"Don't tell me you're still asleep. What kind of baker are you?"

Zio Dante is not being jovial or avuncular. He means business, always. He is on the attack, always. In a foul mood, always. Overall, a real pleasure at eight in the morning while my head and stomach churn from the low weather system of drugs and alcohol.

"Hi Zio." I'm pretty sure I haven't spoken to him since he and my aunt split.

"Hi yourself," he shouts. "I hear that you come to your father's funeral with a camera crew."

"It was supposed to be an anniversary party." I swing my legs to the side of the bed and stand up, testing my intestinal resolve.

"You don't gotta tell me. I got a hundred rental chairs and a marquis tent waiting for someone to fold 'em up and take 'em away. I send back the fireworks, but the Italian band makes it all the way to Upsala before they get my call. Now I gotta pay them for at least a day."

I hear him break, then snort back a mass in his sinuses. I'm so busy judging whether or not I can make it to the bathroom that I barely realize that Dante has started crying.

"Are you okay, Zio?"

"Gesù Cristo, I can't believe it. Forty years we work together, side by side. Like brothers. And now he's gone." My uncle gives his nose a trumpeting blow. "The last thing he says to me Thursday? Make sure that order for Creekside goes out by five o'clock."

I hobble over to the bathroom, put the phone on speaker and set it beside the sink. I look incredibly bad. My hair is flattened on one side, matted on the other. There is a good chance that I puked on my pillow and then rolled over it in my sleep. My skin is puffy and grey. My eyes desiccated, two prunes weighing down a soufflé.

And then I remember the really bad thing I did last night.

"Anyway, I got fifteen minutes free this morning." My uncle clears his throat. "Meet me at the bakery in half an hour."

Oh no. Last night. What happened last night? I grab the phone but can't figure out how to get it off speaker, so I just talk into it. "Zio, do you know how Julia is?"

"What do you mean, how she is?"

I mean, is she alive? Or is she plastered to the front grill of my rental car? My breathing is so heavy I can feel it dividing down the separate channels of my nostrils leaving two contrails in the air.

"Your father is dead. She is not good."

"But when did you see her? Last, I mean." I feel my way blindly down the bathroom cabinet. On the floor I press one side of my face against the cool tile.

"You're wasting time with these questions. Now you only have twenty minutes to get here." The eggshell fragility of his voice has vanished. In its place, metal plates sliding over one another.

"I can't. I don't have a car," I lie.

"Your cousin will be there in fifteen." And he hangs up.

I haven't yet unpacked my suitcase, which makes gathering up my shit a lot easier. I'm in the middle of doing just that when Wanda shows up. She stands in the doorway in denim coveralls and rolls excitedly on the balls of her feet. You can tell the sort of girl she was from this single gesture carried into adulthood. Her inability to contain or mask feelings, to play her cards close to her chest.

When she sees my face her own face collapses. Like she's reflecting the ugly. "I thought you were going to get to sleep early," she says, her eyes running over the bed, which is a mess, the suitcase open on the floor. "It really smells in here, Sabine."

"Then don't get too comfortable," I tell her, nearly toppling over as I struggle into a pair of pants. "I need you to change our flight home. To this morning."

Wanda rushes forward to help me, but I wave her off. "I thought you decided to stay?"

"And now I've decided to leave." I fling off my robe and start searching for a shirt in the suitcase. "I've got to go to the bakery, but I'll be back in an hour."

"Have you even looked at the comments from last night? Your views are going through the roof."

I glance in the mirror above the dresser as I try to pull my shirt on. I swear there's a hatchet buried in the right side of my head. "I'll meet you in the lobby. One hour. An hour and a half, max. We can return the rental car at the airport."

"I did some quick editing and already the video with your aunt has over thirty-two thousand views!"

"What video with my aunt?"

"Don't worry—not the whole thing. Just the part that plays out the story of your father's unexpected passing, what he meant to other people." Wanda's wide brows fan out encouragingly. "It's really touching, Sabine."

"What the fuck, Wanda!" I can't find the armholes of my shirt. For a moment I'm trapped inside of it which just adds to my panic. "You can't just do that without her permission."

"Normally I wouldn't," she says, folding her arms across her chest in a smug way that makes me want to slap her. "She's your aunt. She's not going to sue you. In fact, I think she's going to be flattered."

My left arm finds purchase and pops through the sleeve. I raise my hand as a signal to shut up, which she should know by now. Then I fold down all the fingers except three. "Book three seats home. Meet me in the lobby. Do nothing else."

Thirteen

Sabine

"You look like shit," Enzo says when he pulls up in the SUV. He's listening to Journey's *Greatest Hits* at high volume.

I heave my purse in the passenger seat ahead of me. "Really? I didn't even notice."

"I called your room last night but no answer."

I forego the seat belt. I want to lower the volume on the stereo, but my hands are shaking too hard to make the connection. "I need you to do something. See that grey Nissan by the lamp post? Drive past it."

He shrugs and eases the accelerator. "So where were you last night?"

I bite a flake off of my chapped lips. "I think I killed Julia."

Enzo nods as if this is the most natural thing in the world. "Okay. Is she in the trunk?" He pulls up behind the Nissan which is banked crookedly and straddling two parking spots.

"No, circle around. The front—I need to see the front."

"Sabine, what's going on? Are you making me an accessory?"

Before the SUV even comes to a stop, I swing the door open and hop out, my feet skidding on the pavement. I get down on all fours in front of the rental. The metal and polymer grill looks intact. No blood, no hair, no dent. No scrap of nightgown. I think it's okay. Enzo gets out and stands beside me combing his moustache with his fingers. "You're kidding, right?"

I remember parking outside the house last night. I remember Julia dragging the garbage can down the driveway and setting it at the curb. I can still feel the gas pedal under the cheap foam flip-flop. Then suddenly I was back in the hotel parking lot, clutching a towel around my body.

I look up at him, nodding. "Yes. I am most definitely kidding."

He reaches out and helps me to my feet. "Then let's go. You're already late."

"Sabine! Wait!"

Enzo and I both turn to the hotel entrance where Wanda and Paul are standing, the former waving frantically. "Take Paul with you!" she shouts and gives him a shove forward. "You can't come all this way and not show people the Persian."

Enzo drives like a maniac through the downtown business district, giving me a sped-up tour of the quaint, low-rise buildings of my childhood. Some of them have been revitalized by their cupcake café and bistro interiors. Others front smoke shops and tattoo parlors. The original art deco Eaton's building is now a tele-marketing centre. A casino looms behind it.

"You're not helping my hangover." I grab the handle above the window.

Enzo bites his lip and, by extension, his moustache. "Like I said, we're late."

I get it. He's still afraid of his father.

"So, Marcus seems nice." I look at Paul in the back seat but instead of filming he's holding on to the door handle to steady himself.

"Marcus is great."

"But?"

"But he's over it," Enzo skips the mirror check as he switches lanes. "He's sick of pretending. He wants to get married. He's talking to a recruitment firm in Vancouver."

"What's getting married have to do with Vancouver?"

"He's issued an ultimatum. Either we get married or he goes. I've got to quit throwing a good life after a bad one, he says."

I can't argue with that. "It's not like your father doesn't know you're gay, right?"

"There's knowing and then there's *knowing*." Enzo eyes the yellow stoplight ahead, then rams his foot on the accelerator so that we barrel through. "Last year Marcus came to drop something off at the bakery. He kissed me on his way out—we weren't even thinking. But it was right in front of the guys."

"Ah. Your father lost his shit?"

"To say the least." Enzo takes his hands off the wheel, rolls up his right sleeve and shows me the scar running across his bicep. "The old man and I really got into it. He had my head over the blades of a standing mixer."

"Jesus Christ, Enzo!" I grab the wheel to keep us from plowing into a mailbox. "Why are you still working there?"

"Where else would I be?" He looks at me as though I've asked the most absurd question imaginable. "You know I hung around here to learn from your father." Enzo takes the wheel back and slows the vehicle. "Besides, Dante doesn't run that place. I do."

No, he just owns it. But I say nothing. I am one hundred percent not interested in coming between Enzo and his father. Besides, we've arrived.

I'll admit to a little kick of nostalgia as we pull into the parking lot. Bennett's Bakery still occupies an entire city block. High above the corner, the bakery sign rotates slowly, just as it always has. Its swollen outline suggests a distressed zeppelin, something that might descend on Memorial Avenue traffic on a particularly windy day. The side that is moving away from us simply says, *Bennett's Bakery.* When the other side of the board faces us directly, we read:

THERE'S NOTHING AS MAGICAL AS A PERSIAN!

Above the lettering is my eight-year-old self as a genie, cross-legged and levitating while holding the pink bun.

But the sign doesn't hold my attention for long. The building itself, once a simple red brick structure built on a shoebox's dimensions of length, width and height, has had a dramatic facelift. The entire front of the building has been cut away and replaced with plate glass walls and a ceiling worthy of an Apple store.

"Wow." It's the first word Paul has uttered since getting in the vehicle.

"I know, right?" Enzo turns to look at me. "We made some changes."

Inside the glass box, spanning the width of the building and in full view, is the entire Persian assembly line. Each piece of chrome machinery has been taken from the back room, polished until gleaming and put on display.

Paul slides down his window and raises the camera.

There had always been a morning queue for the Persian, but the one today snakes from the front entrance, across the façade and wraps around to the back parking lot.

"You get this kind of turnout every Saturday?" I ask, impressed.

Enzo's moustache twitches. "They're here out of respect. For your father. Or have you forgotten that he's dead?"

I stare back at him. "How could I forget that?" But his words are a sock to the gut. A reminder that I am now, as I always was, an outsider. Unwanted, unnecessary.

Fourteen

Sabine, 1990

I am mildly astonished by my surroundings. The clatter and whiz of machinery is ominous, and the men tending to it are loud-talking apes. They aren't charmed by me like the women in the bake shop up front were. My father sits me at the end of the long worktable.

"Roll up your sleeves, Sabi." He points to the mound of flour on the table.

I don't understand what my sleeves have got to do with baking, but I obey. My best guess is that magic—the ability to turn wet dough to hot spongy bread—must reside somewhere in the sleeves of my little blue corduroy jumper.

It's my grandmother's idea to take me to the bakery. To get me out of Julia's house. I have been eating less since our arrival, which, any Italian grandmother will tell you, is a symptom of terminal illness. But what do they expect? I've gone from the loud, communal table of girls and young novices at the abbey to a wood-panelled dining room where dinner is eaten on Royal Crown Derby porcelain. Where my father begins the meal by telling us why Julia won't be joining. My grandmother never comments, just leans over my plate and cuts up the rubbery meat that she's broiled. She rarely says a word for or against Julia.

Now in the bakery workroom he opens a shallow hole in the centre of the heap of flour and slowly pours in milk. *"Facciamo un pozzo."* Making a well. It is the bread-making method from the old country, before the mixers took over the duty. I lean across the table, watching as he avalanches some of the sides into the well so that the hole grows wider.

"Now hand me that." My father points and I fetch him a bowl that contains the innards of a single egg floating in oil. He helps me tip the bowl over the flour.

I look up, my eyes framed by thick waves of hair that my grandmother had attempted to pin back over my ears. I don't know what to make of him. He's not exactly smiling but he seems relaxed for once. Like he's pleased to stand by me watching the bright yolk slip into the centre of the flour.

"I think it's a mountain with a lake in the centre," I tell him in Italian. "And the egg is the sun."

"I like your idea better," he says. *"Facciamo una montagna."*

My father picks up a fork and begins whisking at the inside walls until the anticline collapses into the lake and sunshine. Topography disappears as flour, milk and egg turn into a ball of dough. It's the first pleasure of the baker, to take a small mound of powder and create a pliable structure.

"Are you ready to knead?"

He sprinkles the work surface with flour and shows me how to use the heel of my hands to press and flatten the ball away from me. My tiny hands make only the slightest impression in the dough, and I have to kneel on the stool to reach the entire surface. My father assists me; after each revolution he folds the far edge of dough back toward me, rolling the mound together again.

"You know when it's ready?" he asks. "You pinch a little between your fingers and it feels like an earlobe, then it's done."

I look up at him, eyes full of delight at such a repulsive prospect.

Then he says, "You will start school soon, Sabine. Would you like that?"

I stop rolling. "No."

"Still," he says. "You will have to go. Enzo is two and speaks better English than you. You want to learn English, don't you?"

"No," I tell him again and fold my hands under the table. Why is he ruining everything with this talk of school? Somehow, I intuit that Julia is behind the idea. His blonde Madonna wife who lives up on the third floor doesn't like me. But because she is always upstairs, I can sometimes pretend she doesn't exist. Besides, she doesn't behave like a wife. Zia Stella cooks every meal, vacuums her house, does laundry and sits down to feed Enzo. I only see Julia when she comes down the grand wooden staircase on her way out, beautifully dressed and trailing perfume. I see her when she returns and ascends to the third floor. Somehow, she manages not to occupy the space in between.

My father realizes he's said something wrong. He gathers up the dough now and begins showing me how to form it into a loaf. "How about after Christmas, okay? We'll worry about school then."

I brighten, grateful for the reprieve. I am four and the space between now and "after Christmas" might be a month, or a year. We can go on making mountains until then.

"Can I work here with you?" I ask him, following his demonstration by attempting to pat the dough into a round. "I won't have to go to school. You can teach me."

But his face has lost some light. I watch as he untangles my fingers from the mound. I am aware that now I've said or done something wrong. He picks up the loaf and places it on a tray. "This is no place for you, Sabine."

I am only four, but he doesn't have to tell me the lesson is over.

⌣⌐

"Electric hearts. This is what makes the machine better than the man." Zio Dante, docent and salesman, stands among the Persian assembly line in his white plastic bonnet. He is actually my father's cousin but, as is Italian tradition, I grew up calling him Zio, or Uncle. It was Zio's idea to tear away the brick-and-beam façade structure of the bakery and replace it with this glass box. His idea to get rid of the café tables and chairs that filled the front room in my day and bring the machinery out of hiding, to house it in the open atrium. His brilliant notion to force customers to pass through this atrium on their way into the store that is now located in the centre of the building.

Within the atrium, the Persian equipment is cleverly divided by an internal glass wall so patrons can get close, but not too close. Enzo, Paul and I stand in the line-up of worshippers. Behind the partition, Dante is leading a tour. I guess this is why he's called me at eight o'clock in the morning. To bear witness. The head baker is dead; long live the head baker.

"It takes many years to perfect the method you are about to see," he says, gesturing to the Moline machine, as intricately scrolled and the approximate length of a vintage Cadillac. "You won't find a Persian anywhere else in the world—so pay attention."

My uncle holds up a package of Persian dough and feeds it under the Moline rollers. Around me the crowd makes an excited sound as a flattened sheet emerges from the other side. I have to smile, watching as the dough engages the machine's torpedo attachment to spin itself into a tight spool. It looks like a rolled-up carpet when Dante picks it up. From this angle there is no evidence that a proprietary pink butter paste had been placed inside the dough envelope and folded six times over twelve hours. We watch my uncle switch on the guillotine blade that's mounted overtop the Moline's conveyor belt. As he feeds the long scroll of dough into the mill, the blade snaps to life, producing one ratchet-fast slam of the blade every second.

"Exactly one inch thick." Dante holds up a resulting bun to demonstrate. A faint pink spiral is visible now and will develop once it's proofed and cooked. "This is how we ensure the Persian you enjoy today is exactly the same fifteen years from now."

"Fifteen more years of this? I hope you've got it in you, Enzo," I joke. But when I turn, my cousin is gone. The acolytes begin to shuffle sideways as Dante moves down the production line, and Paul and I have no choice but to follow. My uncle stops before the glass proofing cabinet.

"Here, the Persians are benched for three-quarters of an hour." He peers into the incubator roughly the length of a mini-bus, where rows of plump yeast buns sit rising. Each rests on its own metal plate, and these plates rotate slowly across the length of the machine. "We make two hundred and fifty Persians each run."

The glass walls of the proofing cabinet reflect the customers' spellbound faces.

"There are two runs per day, five days a week. That's twenty-five hundred Persians produced each week," Dante tabulates for them. "And every single one sells out within the hour."

Dante activates the proofing cabinet carousel and takes a position behind the deep fryer to wait. Herein lies the secret of the Persian. Wanda was correct when she told the Netflix team that it's a type of viennoiserie dough, with the same flaky layers as puff pastry. But an enriched dough like that could never be placed inside a deep fryer. It would fall apart in seconds. My father had created a spectacular workaround; he managed to make the dough light and airy, the texture crisp, and keep the laminated layers intact throughout the deep-frying process.

We watch as inside the proofer, a dozen buns are lowered. They travel five feet on a metal drum then roll into a shielded trough of bubbling clear oil. Dante picks up a light wooden rod and, like a maestro, conducts this final symphonic movement of Persians. In the oil, the pastries perform an energetic minuet, their undersides turning a rich, honeyed hue while inside, they will blossom pink. They have intuition; Dante has only to touch each lightly with the balsa dowel and the coils flip for him, their raw sides succumbing to the oil.

"Save your applause," Dante says as his visitors clap with delight, "and put your money where your mouth is."

This batch will have to be transferred to the drying racks to cool before the pastries are capped with a delicate whip of pink icing. But the crowd loves the anticipation. They push around us to join the line-up in the shop, sure they'd seen a little more than they actually had. I nudge Paul. "That was something, huh?"

He holds the camera at arm's length and squints at the view-finder. "Even better if he'll give us a private tour."

"I look like garbage."

"You shouldn't look perfect considering what's happened. But I won't let you look bad."

This is why I keep Paul close. He has a storyteller's intuition that I can get behind.

Dante fishes out the last Persian from the oil and looks at me for the first time, his asymmetrical eyebrows tipping in recognition. His demonstration implies that he's just made the dough fresh when, in reality, my father or Enzo, the only ones with the recipe, would have prepared it in advance and frozen it. Last year on *Sweet Rush* we posted a video showing the lengthy and labour-intensive process of making the perfect croissant. Like the Persian, it involves flattening and folding the dough six times in order to give it its flaky, light layers, and refrigerating it for an hour between each fold. But these long-format instructional posts don't perform well, and hardly anyone commented on the perfectly lacquered tray of croissants we produced.

My uncle gets this. That's why, for the most part, we both do our grunt work off camera. You see, Dante is an illusionist. Just like me.

Fifteen

Sabine

It was the forest fires of the mid-eighties that ignited the national infatuation with the Persian. The north was burning. It took one particularly withering summer to dry the sodden muskeg until it crackled like old wash on a rack, and to wick the dense underbrush. The fires fanned in an impressive arc north of Highway 11, scorching the lid off the towns of Longlac, Geraldton, Jellicoe and Beardmore, skimming under the brow of Lake Nipigon and cascading west. Ash fell in Bemidji, Minnesota. *How incredible*, people said about the Persian, *that something so good could come from such disaster*.

The National Reserve flew in, water-bombing elliptical trails across thousands of acres of incinerated forests. Firefighter recruits from southern Ontario and Manitoba were trucked in and housed dormitory-style in the Port Arthur Armoury. It was Dante's idea to deliver fresh bread and Persians to these men every day. The big city papers came, their reporters broadcasting live from rooms in the Prince Arthur Hotel, and then meeting for steak dinners. It was an exciting time and it hardly mattered that the industry of the day was disaster.

Each morning the journalists went to the armoury to track the waggling stole of fire, to conduct interviews with squadrons returning from the blaze or to feature desolate First Nations chiefs coaxing their people into town from reservations that lay in the path of the fires. It was Dante who understood that what he had was a captive audience. The armoury line-up for Persians and hot coffee was longer than the line for the dinner buffet. A photograph of a young Dante crowned in firefighter's regalia hung in the bakery office my entire childhood. Smokejumpers, who'd been summoned by the northern forestry minister, had set a parachute helmet on his head and thrown arms around him like a brother who'd come through fire himself. Dante's brazen eye is on the camera; with one hand he holds the winged fireman's cap in place, with the other he toasts the viewer with a Persian.

"It is an ancient recipe from Persia," Dante told reporters, eyes twinkling. "A treasure from the cave of the Forty Thieves."

One by one the Canadian papers, searching for a square footage of levity amid the destruction, picked up the story of the pink pastry and its colourful origins. West it went with the *Winnipeg Free Press*, the *Calgary Herald*. Word of the Persian carried all the way to the edge of the continental shelf on the back of the *Vancouver Sun*. In Toronto, the *Globe and Mail*, already saturated with the chronic doom of the megalopolis, swallowed the Persian greedily. *Saturday Night* magazine said, "As the north burns, a pink doughnut rises like a phoenix from the ash." The pastry even reached the east coast by way of Halifax's *Chronicle Herald*, burning its own high-calorie path across the landscape as it went.

The International Mesopotamian Society wrote a letter to the bakery thanking them for honouring the ancient Persian Empire, and in 1987 the Royal Dominion Commission in Ottawa ordered a thousand Persians for the Canada Day celebrations in the nation's capital. These were delivered airmail. Queen Elizabeth, on a royal tour with Prince Philip, cut a towering birthday cake in front of 25,000 onlookers. But she was also photographed holding a Persian. "Let them eat cake," the CBC reported. "Her Majesty passes on the vanilla slab in favour of the Persian."

My father balked at what he called "this nonsense." Years later, when my uncle would retell the story or bring out the press clippings, he would dismiss it with the wave of a hand. He either feared the easy glamour of the Persian or refused to understand the value of a public life. See how we were nothing alike?

Dante is bulging and stout, a round roast stood on end. He carries his mastery of English on his shoulder like a parrot. The way I remember him, he was always smacking things—a good cuff to the kitchen table if his pasta bristled too stiffly al dente, a spank to the Chrysler's dashboard when the engine wouldn't turn in winter. A whack that once sent his mailbox into the neighbour's yard. It was an aspect of his attention-seeking nature, rather than simple brutality. As children, Enzo and I were often charged with creating two stacks of cinderblocks in the backyard, each the height of a toddler, over which his father would place a sawed-off section of two-by-four for his "karate" practice. Dante never once cracked the lumber. But he never walked away howling in pain either.

"We are open six days a week, twelve hours a day—"

"Sir, face Sabine while you talk," Paul interrupts him. "It'll look more like a news interview that you see on TV."

"Like TV, eh?" Dante's face lights up as he swivels forty-five degrees. "Every night we close at six, rest the machines and the shift ends. Six hours later it starts all over again."

Paul and I follow him into the pastry shop in the centre of the building. The walls are painted a rich brown and, twice a day, a run of Persians fills the sliding rack system lining the walls. There are two glass-topped display cases, each ten feet long, equipped with a cash register and a counter girl in a pink apron. You may very well miss out on a Persian, but there is still something for everyone in those pastry cases. In addition to the venerable favourites—éclairs, maple tarts, Danishes and turnovers—the bakery caters to the tastes of the town's sizable Italian community. Here, one can find the fluted, cream-filled cannolo, the delicate amaretto cookie and the frivolous sfogliatella, of which the *Chronicle Journal* has said, "It is as beautifully complicated as a peony and must be depetalled before consuming."

The most powerful thing about the place is, of course, the way it smells. They could flatten the building tomorrow, stand me blindfolded in its rubble and I'd know exactly where I was. Bennett's Bakery, a place of immutable quality, riding a great wave of confectioner's sugar, grade-A milk and eggs, Madagascar vanilla, lemon essence and a Ceylon cinnamon powder so fine its rust-coloured residue could be coughed into a tissue.

Dante doesn't let us linger. He beckons us through the metal doors into the workroom, a cigarette tucked behind one ear and his peacock feathers sweeping a wide arc. This is where shit gets done. The configuration of racks and work stations is the same, the floor mixers are arranged in a paramilitary formation of straight lines. These were the soldiers of my father's regime, and I remember the herculean effort that went into maintaining his standards. There are at least twenty men and women at work here, smocked and netted. An organized hierarchy of runners, wrappers and prep-bakers bent in those eternal positions of lifting, carrying, tipping and pouring.

"The bread we make here supplies all the major industry in Thunder Bay. We are in all of the supermarkets. Why?" My uncle picks up a pan from the cooling rack, knocks the loaf out and holds it up as if it's the baby Jesus. "Our bread has no parallel. It's soft, has no holes and lasts for a week."

In Toronto, Paul, Wanda and I film all our videos in a studio in Liberty Village. We carry our ingredients into the camera-ready kitchen and then carry them out so the room can be professionally cleaned at night. We pay dearly for the service but it's a must. The camera captures everything. Almost everything. But here, in a real bakery, you can see remnants of the old life. It's an environment of residue and the actions performed within it are repeated daily, leaving evidence. Egg paste, invisible when splashed on a wall tile, hardens to a yellow, lacquered sheen. Sacks of flour spurt fine mists from seams each time they're hoisted and stacked. Flour is airborne and impossible to control, an element of the baker's existence.

My uncle draws us toward the twin ovens, each rotating 180 fancy rolls for the Rotary Club's annual Daffodil Tea. He checks the oven thermostat then opens one of the great metal doors to show us how the buns have been slashed with the double-edged *lame* blade so that they will bloom like flowers in the oven.

"You ever make something like that? For these little videos of yours?" he smirks.

I shake my head.

"You never learn to make bread, eh?" Dante smirks. "I am not surprised."

Paul lowers the camera without me having to ask. Sometimes it's best not to fan the embers of my uncle's convictions. Instead,

I look around for Enzo. I haven't changed my mind. I may not have killed Julia, but I'm still going back to the hotel, grabbing my bags and getting out of here.

Dante is watching me. "Your father, when was the last time you talk to him?"

That question again. I shrug and look up at the egg and cream beaters that hang from pegs like ornamental cages. "A couple of months ago?"

"He say anything? About the Persian?"

"What about the Persian?"

"The recipe. He ever tell you the recipe?"

I laugh. "That's between him and Enzo. I don't ask about that."

Dante looks at me through narrowed eyes. "The position your father leaves us in—you think it's a good joke, eh?"

"I don't think he planned it," I say carefully. "Where is Enzo anyway?"

"Why you say it's between your father and Enzo? The recipe?"

I feel a tingle of pain in my skull where the hatchet is still lodged. I'm not ready for trick questions this morning. "Because Enzo's his baker."

"Your father never gives the Persian recipe to Enzo."

I'm confused. "So, who did he give it to?"

Dante inches a finger under the elastic of his hair bonnet and scratches vigorously at the whorls of still-black hair. "I don't know. Maybe you. You're the Miss TV baker now. Maybe he thinks you deserve it."

I look at my uncle. As usual he's dead serious. "You really think that's true?" My father gave very little of himself, least of all the recipe that he prized.

Dante shrugs. "I don't have it. Enzo says no. We have a week worth of dough in the freezers, then it's goodbye Persian."

"What about Julia?"

"What is she going to do with it, the old witch?" He waves his hand dismissively. "But tonight you will ask her, just in case. She and I are not simpatico."

I shake my head. "I won't be there for the memorial. My flight leaves at noon."

"Of course you will be there." Dante cocks a startled face. "You are his daughter."

"I'm right in the middle of a deal for a TV show and it just can't wait. Besides, it's not even a real funeral."

When Dante hears this his mouth flips open like a bivalve, cleaving his head in half and leaving the tongue to waggle monstrously between the hinged parts. "You must have grown crazy all these years. What are you, some kind of *disgraziata* just like your cousin?"

My phone starts to ring somewhere in my bag. I start pawing around for it.

"Are you listening, Sabine?" He wags a finger at me. "I expect you there tonight like a good daughter. Forget yourself for once and think of the family you left behind."

I slip the phone out of my handbag and realize I've missed three calls from Collette. All before nine o'clock.

"This is work," I say, interrupting my uncle's diatribe. "But Zio, thank you for the tour."

"Don't even think about getting on no airplane, Sabine."

"You're a natural on camera, you know that?"

—

Though the bakery still carries his name, we never knew Mr. Bennett. I was still in Italy and Enzo hadn't even been born yet when my father and uncle rose from the ranks of labourers, pooled their savings and bought the business from the old man's widow. I suppose we imagined Bennett as young and moustachioed, a bull with arms developed through his trade. It was only later in life that we realized this was a more accurate description of our own fathers than of the man whose business our family had eclipsed.

Our fathers decided to keep the name Bennett's Bakery for a couple of reasons. In the eighties it was still preferable to have an English-sounding business. And second, Bennett was apparently a mentor to my father.

The bakery attic, where my father set up his office, once also served as Bennett's office, though the old man was, by my aunt's account, a hoarder. After taking over the business, my father cleared out a jumble of expired ingredients and burnt-out bits of equipment. He swept the wide-plank floors that had been scoured by sugar crystals ground underfoot. Once the floor was resurfaced and oiled, it gleamed like the sandy-blonde shell of a crème brûlée, reflecting the Swiss slant of trusses overhead. Beneath the apex of beams, my father placed a double pedestal tanker desk made of heavy-gauge steel, with rounded corners and a black leather blotter surface. At home, his burled desk was a decorative item over which to greet men from the Italian community. But for work, he chose a militaristic model with peg legs and a blocky body. Across its five-foot span, vendors pitched everything from cardboard boxes to walk-in refrigerators. It was a place of negotiation, his least favourite part of the job. He matched the desk with a rolling chair of unyielding leather chosen for its stiff discomfort. A reminder that the work of a bakery was not accomplished on one's ass. There's a modern, multi-line office phone on the desk, but as a child I remember it being a handset model from the sixties. It shone like a black patent boot and rang steadily throughout the day.

I sit at my father's desk now and tap Collette's number on my phone. She must be waiting for my call, finger ready to deliver the slightest of haptic touches to the screen, because suddenly her deep, whisky-drenched voice fills my ear.

"They're in," she says in a hushed scream.

"What? Why are you whispering?"

"I'm having breakfast at their offices. I've barricaded myself in a toilet to bring you the news. Netflix is green-lighting your show."

I grab the arm of my father's chair.

"They're going to promote the shit out of it, Sabine. Jesus Christ, you convinced them you can carry this show! All it took was you getting on a plane and receiving some bad news! Sabine? Are you there?"

I nod wildly, but Collette can't hear this.

"There's one big caveat, okay?"

"Yes," I breathe. "Anything."

"I was watching you at lunch last week. You had three martinis *before* the food even arrived. I need you to sober the fuck up."

Collette is the shit-talking mamma I never had. "Easy," I promise her. "Done."

"That's not the caveat," she says. "Now listen."

Sixteen

Sabine

When I get back to the hotel Wanda's in the lobby with her carry-on bag at her feet arguing with someone on the phone. She hasn't seen me yet, which is good, because I'm having trouble controlling my face. The muscles have suddenly acquired a complicated sense of articulation, rigs and pulleys controlled by both excitement and dread.

When she spots me, Wanda scrunches up her face to readjust her glasses. She says something into the phone, hangs up and gets to her feet.

"Everything okay?" I ask. My voice sounds tinny and unnatural in my ear.

She nods. "My father missed an appointment with the bank. Again."

I don't pay her enough. It's not the first time this thought has flashed at me in all caps. Sometimes I combat the guilt by reminding myself that she hasn't asked for more. Or that I'm rewarding Wanda in other ways. But today I don't even bother.

She can tell something's up, so I can't deflect for long. She's looking at me with those Disney Princess eyes made even crazier through her magnified lenses.

"What is it?" she asks. "Did something happen at the bakery?"

I calculate, then recalculate. "Paul got a lot of good stuff."

"And that's it?"

This is a delicate situation. I shouldn't just lay it on her in a hotel lobby. "I'm really going to need you to focus on the edit. We got my uncle making the Persian, then giving us a tour. Then Paul shot a bit of me outside that we can use as an intro. Although I look like shit."

"I thought maybe you'd heard from Collette," Wanda examines her hands. "I actually tried calling her earlier, but she didn't pick up. Big surprise."

A pained expression crosses my face. "Why?"

Wanda raises a hand to her mouth. My instincts tell me she's about to bite the cuticle of her index finger, so I reach up and slap her fingers away for her.

"Sorry," she says shoving her hands into the pockets of her coveralls. "I was only calling for a check-in. Collette's very slow to respond to text messages, and by the time she does, the question is irrelevant."

"She's busy."

"You think so? Because, actually, her Outlook calendar is full of these spa days? She has every single Tuesday and Thursday blocked off and labelled 'self-care.'"

"Why were you on her Outlook calendar?"

Wanda smiles over the question. Her teeth look sharp in the dim lobby light. "My point, Sabine, is that sometimes I feel you put too much trust in her."

⌒

"We can't just push her out,"

"We're hardly doing that!" Collette's voice was weighty and urgent considering she was calling from a toilet stall. "They just don't think Wanda is co-star material. They want you, Sabine.

Solo host. Your face, your personality, your expertise, your one-on-one with the contestants. Wanda will still be on the show. Only as an assistant. Just like real life."

I got to my feet and circled my father's desk in the bakery attic. "I just don't think it's going to work. She wants to be half of this thing."

"She'll be a producer, get production credit. She should be over the moon. How many young women have their TV concepts attract the attention of Netflix?"

"Last week they weren't even sure they wanted me."

"Exactly! Think about how lucky we are."

I shook my head. "Wanda wrote the show that she wants to be in."

"But you're the one that caught their attention, Sabine. Wanda's pitch was just a vehicle. Look, you listened to the dev team's creative input, you travelled home, ten seconds after touching down you're already creating new content—powerful videos—that are tracking well *and* proving to the Cerberus that you're going to be a creative partner."

I sat back down on my father's chair and stared up at the rafters. I could feel myself balanced on the edge of Collette's argument. I wanted to fall into her camp, but I also knew Collette was persuading me from a place of ignorance.

Which is when I started thinking that I should have managed Wanda's expectations better from the start. Right when we heard that Netflix was interested in making us reality stars. Clearly managing people is not my strong suit.

"Let me ask you something, Sabine." I heard a toilet flush and Collette lowered her voice. "Do you *want* Wanda to co-star with you?"

I hesitated.

"You hesitated. My God, Sabine! You're scared of her."

"I just think we need to acknowledge this is her show as much as mine." It sounded weak but it was all I could commit to.

"Sabine, you're letting some emotional shit betray your naïveté, okay?" I could hear Collette's breath whistling through clenched veneers. "I've been doing this a long time. When Netflix knocks, you don't ask them to take their shoes off before they come in. Just now, over breakfast that bitchy one, Britt, pitched me their comp. '*The Great British Baking Show* meets *Property Brothers*.' I mean, do you need me to get you the fucking metrics?" Collette's voice rose higher than what was acceptable toilet confidential.

That's when I knew the real, actionable part of the caveat was coming. And it wasn't going to be pretty.

"Look, I'm not trying to be an asshole, but this isn't negotiable. They've given me a sneak peek at their response document and revised offer, but they'll be sending it out officially tomorrow. You need to sign right away. Also, Wanda will get a copy."

And you're going to make me break the news.

"My advice, Sabine? Break the news to her today. Before the dev team sends out their letter. It'll be much ... easier coming from you."

"So, did you hear from Collette or not?" In the lobby Wanda's got me trapped in her wide-eyed stare.

Do I want to host my own show? Of course I do. Do I think Wanda will back away gracefully? Not a chance. But Collette is right; she should be told the news in advance.

"No, I haven't," I tell her. What Collette is wrong about is that the news should come from me. "But Wanda, you changed the plane tickets, right?"

She nods.

"Okay, I want you and Paul to take that flight back home. I'll follow tomorrow."

Wanda raises an eyebrow; it arches right over the frame of her eyeglasses. "You're staying? For the memorial?"

I nod. Staying behind is legit. If it also means I get to avoid telling Wanda she's out in the cold, so be it. If Wanda charges into Collette's office tomorrow when she hears about the demotion, well, she won't be the first artist to freak out on an agent. Breaking this sort of news is what Collette does for a living.

"I'll stay with you!" Wanda says. "For support."

"No," I say quickly. "This is something I have to do on my own. For my family." My eyes flicker down to the phone she's still clutching in her hand. "And judging by that call, you have some things to take care of for *your* family."

It's opportunistic but I'm going for it.

EXT. BENNETT'S BAKERY – DAY

SABINE STANDS IN FRONT OF BAKERY. WE SEE ROTATING SIGN. LINE-UP VISIBLE BEHIND HER.

SABINE

I want to start off today's video with a big thank you for the heartfelt condolences that you've sent my way. I came up here to celebrate a milestone . . .

SHE GESTURES TO BUILDING BEHIND HER.

SABINE CONT'D

. . . and instead, was met with tragedy. One of the things getting me through this is my promise to bring you an exclusive, behind-the-scenes look at my family's bakery. Specifically, this little guy here . . .

CU: SABINE HOLDS UP PERSIAN PASTRY.

SABINE CONT'D

Looks like a cinnamon bun, but this is the Persian pastry that's even been featured in the *New York Times*. And behind me, the only place you can get it.

CUT TO CLIP FROM SEASON 2 DEMONSTRATING ROLL-IN METHOD.

SABINE (V.O.)

Back in Season 2 we showed you the process of making laminated dough from scratch—not for the faint of heart. The Persian seems to be made of this laminated dough which we know as the basic architecture of the croissant.

BACK TO SABINE IN FRONT OF BAKERY.

SABINE

That's right—I said "seems to be" because, the truth is, we just don't know. The recipe is secret. My father guarded it with his life.

SABINE PAUSES, WIPES AT EYES WITH SLEEVE.

> **SABINE CONT'D**
> What makes it secret? Well, the Persian is deep-
> fried. But if you take regular croissant dough and
> put it in the fryer . . .

CUT TO STOCK CLIP OF BURNT LUMP OF DOUGH
FISHED OUT OF DEEP FRYER. GIANT, RED "X"
GRAPHIC FLASHES OVER TOP.

> **SABINE (V.O.)**
> Well, it simply can't stand the heat. Adjustments
> were made in order to help the dough hold up in
> the fryer. What those adjustments were—even I
> am in the dark.

BACK TO SABINE. CU ON PERSIAN AS SHE PULLS
IT APART.

> **SABINE**
> Okay, some more magic here, when we tear the
> Persian apart. It's pink! That is no simple cinnamon
> bun. Again, this is all speculation, but I'd wager
> that the initial square of butter, the *beurrage*, has
> been infused with cinnamon and a berry compote,
> giving it this surprising hue inside.

CU: SABINE TASTING.

SABINE CONT'D

Mmm! Exactly as I remember from childhood.
Now we're going to take you past this massive
line-up and inside the bakery. But I know what
you're asking: Sabine, who has the recipe now?
And the answer is, we don't know. We just don't.
It may very well be gone for good.

If that's the case, I know people will be
disappointed. You can imagine—

SABINE LOOKS AWAY, FACE DISTRAUGHT.

SABINE CONT'D

Well, you can imagine how irreplaceable my
father is. The man who created all this behind me.
The man who taught me to roll up my sleeves and
get sweet.

Seventeen

Sabine, 1999

I am no longer the Persian Princess. I sit in the dead cold in my
father's new Buick and listen to the radio. The low winter sun
slants across the parking lot where my father and uncle stare up
at the bakery sign.

"Sometimes your business knowledge falls short, I've noticed,"
Dante is telling him. I can follow most of their conversation without rolling down the window.

My father takes his gloves from his pocket. Studies the embroidered leather. "I never said it was forever. It's time we change it."

"This is how people know the bakery."

It's been six months since I was deposed of my official duties
as the Persian Princess, but now I see my father wants to take it
further. He wants to get rid of the sign. I twist the radio volume
down low and lean closer to the window.

"Four years ago, I tell you and Stella I don't like this business.
But you insist and we put her face all over the place." He gestures
up to my image rotating steadily on its pedestal.

"It does good for us."

"Does it do good for her? With a broken rib? What if I wasn't
there that day?"

"Franchi, what's done is done." Dante drops his cigarette
underfoot and blows hot air into the bowl of his hands. "But it

doesn't mean we gotta go change every napkin and cake box we got printed."

My father turns to glance at the brick building behind us. He says something quietly that I can't hear. But as a result, my uncle storms off a few yards, spins on his heel and comes back. Over his bakery whites, his unbuttoned coat tacks like a loose jib in a sudden gust of wind.

"You and your ghosts! Everywhere you look you see them!"

I sit up, forgetting my own hurt for a moment. My father sees ghosts?

"They're in the attic, they're in the basement—"

"*Basta*, Dante."

But my uncle takes a step deeper into my father's inner radius. "What do you think is going to happen from eight thousand kilometres away?"

"Enough!" For a moment my father is lost in the exhaust of his breath. He looks like he might punch my uncle. Instead, he bends down and gathers two handfuls of dirty snow from the parking lot. He mashes them together tight, winds back his arm and hurls it up at the sign.

He hits the levitating genie in the knee. From the car I watch the lump of snow slide down over the word *Magical*. Then I shove my own hands, which are hardened to balls of ice, into my pockets.

My uncle is unfazed by the display. He even smiles as he fishes out his key fob and points the auto starter in the direction of his Chrysler. "Take it easy, *cugino.*" The car coughs awake and starts humming in the cold. "We wouldn't get along so well if we were all saints."

Eighteen

Wanda

You know how someone can just change your life overnight, but you fail to recognize the magnitude of that change until later? That's what happened to me when Sabine walked into my godmother's bakery, threw her mink jacket across the counter, spun around and lowered her leather tights until her butt crack showed.

But let me back up. If I hadn't tried to take my life, it's quite likely that I would never have been working at my godmother's bakery in the first place. Which means we never would have met, and I never would have had occasion to write *What's in Your Pantry*. Which, in a peculiar, circular way, has become the single most important thing in my life. My one and only shot to recoup the past and the opportunity I sold away years ago.

As far as suicide attempts go, mine wasn't well planned or executed. That's because I'd never considered doing it before I'd been cheated out of $42 million. Naturally, I imagined the thing to do was to get a sleeping pill prescription from a walk-in clinic, swallow the entire bottle and hope to lose consciousness before throwing it all up. But if I was thinking more clearly—or if I'd really wanted it to work—I would have done it in a hotel room. Instead, I amateurishly attempted it at home and was discovered face down in a pool of vomit by my five-year-old twin brothers. As I understand it, there was a lot of yelling and screaming and people rushing in and out of my room—my parents, my aunt and uncle, the paramedics. When I came to in the ER there was a rubber hose taped to my nostril. It led all the way down my throat, into my stomach and was pumping the contents up into a plastic bin. A nurse was standing by, ready to hold down my arms if I tried to pull the tube out. At the end of the stretcher my mother sat crying and repeating the same thing over and over. "Why, Wanda? Why?"

"Forty-two million," was all I could croak.

My family did all the right things. They lit candles at the church, took me for rides in the car and traded shifts so that for months I was never left alone. They also hired a lawyer they could not afford. To his credit, he didn't take them for a ride. After a thorough examination of my contract with Odin he explained that I had been cheated out of my share of millions in a completely fair and square manner. While Odin had, in their dealings with me, grossly understated the potential of Wheat Bump, there was no evidence of that in writing. The contract that I signed clearly stated there was no way of estimating the software's future value after I transferred ownership and their development team took over. Should I have made a case against them, all Odin had to do was argue that they made proprietary changes to the programming which resulted in a significantly higher valuation.

So, I was fucked.

The only thing left for my family to do was put me to work doing something completely unrelated to technology. And so, I was apprenticed to my godmother's bakery, a hole-in-the-wall on Dundas Street West, specializing in Filipino pastry.

I did not dislike it. The smell of hot and humble pandesal bread was comforting. They had me shredding purple yam and young coconut, and soon I was helping fill the front window with pastries. We sold buko pies, pillowy mamon rolls topped with a snowstorm of grated cheese, and even made a fancy ensaymada by filling sugar-glazed brioche bread with macapuno, a jellied coconut cultivar. But my godmother's leche flan, with its smooth golden caramel topping, was the neighbourhood showstopper.

Using my hands meant that I had to concentrate. And that meant no room for Wheat Bump to enter my head. I started experimenting with extract made from ube, the ubiquitous Filipino purple yam. Four years at an arts high school meant I knew how to paint and draw. Only now I was using flan as a canvas. With the tip of a wooden skewer as my brush, I taught myself how to stencil vibrant purple designs in the bottom of the flan tin before pouring in the hot syrup.

The result was portraiture in caramel. My work was meticulous; I could create still lifes on custard, landscapes in liquified sugar. Once a week I hand-painted a tray of flans with deep purple crows, so that when they were displayed together, a flock of birds seemed to careen across a caramel sunset sky. My godmother made a sign in the window that read, *New Baker in Residence.*

One day I was scraping down baking sheets in the back when I heard a customer arguing with the cashier.

"Not. Just. To. Buy." A woman stood there, over-annunciating each syllable in a loud voice she clearly reserved for immigrants. "I want the person who did that." She was gesturing to the front window. The cashier held open an empty cake box and a sheet of wax paper.

"I fill box, no problem."

"You don't understand what I'm asking." She planted both hands on the counter like she might vault over and take down the cashier. "Who made *those* pastries?"

"I did," I said, snapping off rubber gloves. "The leche flan are mine."

The woman spun around and looked at me. She was gorgeous, intense. Her eyebrows were raised as though scored to the timbre of her voice. I didn't recognize Sabine because I didn't watch *Wake Up Canada*, wasn't into baking celebrities, and had been travelling through Europe when the gay wedding cake story hit the news. But with her made-up face, cropped mink bomber jacket and scuffed motorcycle boots I knew she was someone.

"Who are you?" she asked me.

Five minutes later she was pulling down her pants and showing me the tattoo on her lower back. A flock of black birds arranged in a remarkably similar formation to the ones I'd painted.

"I'm having a party tonight. They're kind of my symbol." She hiked her pants back up. "You don't think it'll be too matchy-matchy?"

I shook my head, unable to imagine a dinner party where dessert and buttocks would be on display at the same time.

She wanted all of the tarts, so I took out a larger cake box. She followed me down the length of the counter with her phone out, snapping photos of the refrigerated halo-halo.

"I have a bazillion followers on Instagram. If I post a couple of—" She stopped and pointed at my hands. "You have strong baker's hands. Like me."

I looked from my hands to hers. The slender but firm knuckles, the slightly fan-shaped nail bed, the olive skin tone, even the faint, blue-veined etching across the backs were similar. In fact, nearly identical.

She looked up at me, eyebrows once again rising in crescendo. Then she took in the greasy little bakery storefront. "How would you like a real job?"

Nineteen

Wanda

"We're going to miss the flight." Paul smokes one of his thrice weekly cigarettes while we wait under the hotel portico for our car to arrive.

"The airport's fifteen minutes away. We could basically walk there," I say, looking out at the lake. The view from the hotel entrance is impressive. The harbour is still a working one and dotted with both large ships and sailboats. Beyond the breakwater, in the nautical distance, lies the Sleeping Giant. For a moment it really does resemble a man asleep on his back. But when I blink it turns back to rock.

"That's the world-famous Sleeping Giant."

Paul stares into the cobalt leagues and grunts. I want to tell him that he needs a proper haircut, someone to level the dark hairs at the back of his neck with a razor. But there's nothing sexy about grooming advice. Instead, I nudge him playfully in the ribs. "You sleep like a rock too."

He says nothing but shifts away from me ever so slightly. I instantly regret my reference to sleeping together. It's not like I'm always trying to take things to the next level with Paul, but once in a while I'd like some acknowledgement that we see each other's naked bodies on a regular basis.

I sigh and pull my laptop out of my bag. "Let me find out what's going on with this car." Truthfully, I don't want to go home. I'm tired of getting my father out of jams. I'm tired of being parent to a parent. It's clear I'll have to spend the day tomorrow in the bank branch trying to convince some mortgage officer of an oversight on our part. That a letter was lost in the mail. That a phone call was not received. I've got a list of excuses. Then the whole wasted day will end with me dipping into my remaining savings to extract us from this mess and clear our account for the next month.

I crouch down and open my laptop, searching for the tab where I'd placed the taxi order this morning. The other reason I'm lukewarm about our departure is that I'm leaving without seeing our storyline through. Even though our original course got skewered by Sabine's father's death, I think I came up with a pretty impressive workaround. And the footage from the bakery looks great. The uncle looks like a character drawn from a Mario Puzo novel, the line-up around the building is crazy, and the highly photogenic Persian has all the makings of a small-town unsolved mystery.

As I shut down tab after tab in search of the cab company information, I come across one that I should not have opened in the first place. It contains Collette's Outlook calendar. And it makes me wonder again, why she hasn't returned my emails, texts or voicemail messages? My fingers pass lightly over the keys as I toggle from calendar to email inbox. I glance up at Paul, but he's examining his camera case. I still have a strong hotel Wi-Fi signal because Collette's inbox refreshes instantly. I don't know why I do this. I've snooped on various people in the past and it has never left me feeling right. Probably because it's a betrayal enacted in order to discern a deeper betrayal.

And eight messages down I find it.

Dear Collette,

Britt, Brett and I met last night and wanted to get our thoughts down immediately. We know we owe you a response document for your pitch, *What's in Your Pantry.* I think we adequately expressed our reservations over lunch last week and want to kick off by saying how impressed we are with the strides Sabine has taken to address our comments. You already know we find her compelling and, as an on-screen personality, appealing. But the vulnerability she displayed today on the sad occasion of her father's passing is really tracking for us.

We will be issuing the team a formal document and it is our recommendation to green-light your pitch!

However, there is a condition we want to present to you— informally—here. It is not a small ask. But you know best how to manage your creative talent and we want to give you every opportunity to do so—in advance—to ensure this is a positive experience for everyone.

While we appreciate Wanda Ocampo's finely drafted pilot script, as a team we don't envision Wanda co-hosting this program alongside Sabine. We believe that Sabine's current subscribers will be puzzled by Wanda's billing as co-host, since she is in no way featured on the YouTube channel, *Sweet Rush*. The addition of Wanda as a lead role is superfluous. From our dealings with Wanda, we perceive her role to be that of support personnel to Sabine. This works for us. We can extend to her an on-camera role assisting contestants and whatnot.

Collette, won't you join us tomorrow morning for breakfast here at our offices? We know you front a tightly knit group and we'd be happy to help you find the words to manage Wanda's expectations about the months ahead, thus ensuring a happy outcome for all.

Sincerely,
Brie Heberts
Netflix Joint Head of Unscripted Development

"It's here, let's go." Paul taps my shoulder but every part of me that has external kinetic power is paralyzed. Meanwhile everything inside is set in motion. I kneel on the pavement and feel my heart plummet a dozen stories into a pool of stomach acid. Paul doesn't even see this. He's already circling the car to throw his duffel bag in the trunk.

"I'm not going," I say.

"What?" Paul is hidden behind the car.

"I said, I'm not going!" This time I shout. He shuts the trunk and looks at me on the ground, surprised.

I know better than to wait for him to help me get up. I push my spine against the brick wall of the building and slowly inch the whole enterprise of backpack, laptop, carry-on bag and myself into a standing position.

"What's wrong with you?" he asks coming around toward me.
"We've got to move."

The weight of it all nearly knocks me down again, but I use
the fluidity in my knees to dodge Paul and lunge at the passenger window of the taxi instead. "You're late!" I shout, startling the
driver. "You were supposed to be here half an hour ago!"

The driver looks confused but lowers the window an inch.
"Airport?" he asks with some sort of accent.

"Go fuck yourself!" I scream, and spin around, still holding my
suitcase, laptop and backpack. Just trying to keep it all together.

Twenty

Wanda

"I can't believe this is happening again," I say and gulp my second gin and tonic in the hotel restaurant. I despise gin and that's why I ordered it. I need something loathsome going into my body to challenge the loathsome feeling already there. "They want what I created but they don't want me."

Paul nods but says nothing. I'm grateful, at least, that he's agreed to stay behind with me. He's got the editing software open on my computer and is transferring some extra footage he shot this morning.

"I already suffer from PTSD, so I know it when I feel it coming on," I continue. "There's no fucking way I'm going to let them get away with it." I slam my fist down on the bar which draws the attention of people around us having lunch. It also causes the head on Paul's beer to slide off sideways.

"Fucking Collette!" I say it loudly because I'm feeling it strongly. "What kind of fucking agent sells you down the river like that? I should have gotten my own representation. I should have insisted. I should have gotten a goddamn lawyer. Fuck!"

Paul wipes away the displaced beer foam with a stack of tiny cocktail napkins.

"Collette is basically an out-of-touch, old-as-fuck alcoholic clinging to Sabine for her last dying breaths. All she does is make dinner reservations and order champagne. I'm the one who's done all the work and now she's just going to let them tear it all down. *While we appreciate Wanda Ocampo's fine contribution, we don't want her anywhere near the show!*" I grab Paul's arm. "We can't go back there like obedient dogs. We're the ones who are going to be jobless once this thing goes into production. Have you thought about that, Paul? Have you realized you're not going to be the one filming *What's in Your Pantry?*"

He seems to think this over. "I've been shooting *Sweet Rush* for three years and the work looks good."

I ignore Paul's confident approach. He'll learn the hard way once Netflix tosses him aside for a big name DP. Meanwhile, the bartender has brought me a third drink. God bless these northern people who ask no questions. The gin still feels like fire, but I take it down in one shot because the hole inside of me is getting bigger, not smaller.

"And fuck the flights!" I say, remembering that I've forgotten to cancel them and that we'll surely be charged. "I'm not budging from Sabine's side. Collette is only going to listen to—" I stop.

Oh my God. What a fucking fool.

"She knows." I turn back to Paul. "Sabine knows." Of course she does—the look on her face this morning. How she was rushing me on a plane just to get rid of me. Collette must have called her right away. "Sabine knows and didn't have the balls to tell me."

"Not to interrupt, but did someone say they should have gotten a lawyer?"

I look up. Three barstools over a man sits with fork and knife poised over a steak. He's looking at me with eyes that are so icy grey I get the taste of a menthol lozenge in the back of my mouth.

"A lawyer? Who told you that?" My voice is shrill, defensive.

"You sort of announced it," he says, cutting into his porterhouse. He's about forty but has silver hair and wears a very expensive suit. I must be watching with feverish unease as the fillet begins to bleed out on the white china because he looks down at his plate. "This is cattlemen's choice right here."

"Are you one?"

"What?" He folds the slice into his mouth and chews the bloody pulp.

"A lawyer?"

He swallows and nods. "I am. What sort are you looking for?"

"Entertainment law."

"Ah, well. I don't do the fun stuff."

I roll the highball glass between my palms and realize that I am finally drunk. But the realization doesn't offer any solace. I'm as angry as ever.

The man lays down his knife and fork, folds his cloth napkin and slides two bar stools over toward me. "Duddy DuPierre," he says, extending his hand.

I have to put down the glass to shake it. "Wanda," I say. "And this is Paul." I gesture over my shoulder.

DuPierre's sleek brows rise toward his metallic hairline. "Was Paul."

I turn and see my computer, the empty pint glass, but no Paul.

"You're fierce, Wanda," DuPierre signals to the bartender. "I wouldn't want to be on the other side of a lawsuit from you."

The barkeep comes around holding the bottle of gin that I've been steadily putting away. But DuPierre puts his manicured hand over the rim of my glass. "Get us the good stuff, would you?"

When the man leaves in search of the "good stuff" DuPierre leans back on his stool. "I'm not prying, just bored out of my skull here. And you, young lady, happened to be having the most interesting one-way conversation I've heard in a long time."

"Paul doesn't talk much," I explain. That's part of his charm. "Why are you here, bored out of your skull?"

"I'm just waiting." He shrugs. "Flew in yesterday. I represent one business that's trying to buy another business."

The bartender returns with a bottle of cognac. DuPierre nods and guides his pour into two snifters. "Drink that," he says handing me one. "And then *you* tell *me* what you're doing here."

I sniff the amber fluid and don't mind it. It somehow pairs nicely with the man's voice. "I came here to film a celebration, which turned into a funeral."

DuPierre's eyes glint like quartz in his angular face. "Fascinating. Is that what you've got up on your computer?"

I turn to look at the screen. I have my script open. Every episode we create I transcribe into standard manuscript format and add it to our production bible. Beside it is an exterior shot of Bennett's Bakery. The big sign over the parking lot is frozen mid-rotation displaying the little genie on the flying carpet and the line, *There's Nothing as Magical as a Persian!*

"Making a movie?"

I reach up and shut the laptop. "Not exactly."

"I heard that baker died."

I nod. "I work for the baker's daughter. She's a social media influencer. A celebrity, really."

DuPierre gets this look on his face that older people get when you try and explain the complex social media landscape that is all around them but which they cannot see. "And what exactly do you do for this baker's daughter that's got you so worked up, Wanda?"

"Why do you assume those two things are linked, Duddy?"

"Did I do that?" DuPierre's smile burns at a low, steady voltage. "My apologies."

I pick up the cognac and sip at it smoothly, without the desperation of a drunk. "I create content for her. She's the top food influencer in the country."

The bartender materializes and places a bowl of mixed nuts in front of me. This kindles a little spot of warmth deep inside. Collette is still in my head, but I imagine her now as three inches tall and trapped in a sticky amber.

"How is it that the bartender knew what you meant by the 'good stuff'?"

"I've got bottomless expense account written all over me." DuPierre chuckles. "Now tell me, Wanda. What has the baker's daughter done to you?"

Twenty-One

Sabine

I return to the scene like all good murderers do. The grey house in daylight is not nearly as criminally inspiring as it was last night and, after scanning the local police report online, I'm confident that I didn't actually hit my stepmother. In fact, I'm willing to bet she didn't even recognize me. But Enzo and I park the car around the corner just in case.

In the front lawn a pair of white elms sway in the late afternoon breeze. My father hated them. He'd grown up tending to a stocky, productive chestnut grove and maintained that North American trees did nothing of value but fan their branches and drop their leaves. Still, he never cut them down. He couldn't. The house—everything inside and out—belonged to Julia.

Enzo gives me a shove from behind and we go up the short flight of steps to the front door. I don't have time to worry about whether we should knock; the door is open and suddenly I'm standing in the foyer, my eyes blinking rapidly trying to adjust to the darkness. I see that no efforts have been made over the years to enliven the dark craftsman woodwork. The only natural light comes from the rose window up above the entrance, but it's feeble light, split apart by the lead mullions and tracery. Whatever's left over is absorbed by the Persian rug underfoot.

"I don't think I've been here in ten years," Enzo says under his breath. Though he'd worked with my father every day, Julia wasn't exactly an entertainer. The place is just as we left it. Living room to the right of the foyer, staircase up the centre, the grandfather clock standing sentinel beside it. My father chose to locate his study down here, to the left of the foyer, opposite the living room. The *paesani* who came to see him on business tended to assume an old-world spirit of informality and made for the living room. But they'd always be ushered back to the study where my father could keep the walnut desk between them. This was opposite of Zia Stella's house where all guests were funnelled into the living room, treated to the best room in the house.

Enzo takes my elbow and steers me into the living room where his parents have already gathered. Zia Stella is in heels and black lace and holds a wine glass with a napkin wrapped around the stem. She's wearing some sort of defiant shade of red lipstick. Dante is positioned in front of the cold hearth, hands shoved in the pockets of a well-tailored suit. I imagine that he's been rehearsing his pitch to Julia all day.

"Jesus Christ," Enzo says under his breath. "It's Mrs. Peacock and Colonel Mustard in the library with the candlestick."

I'd like a glass of whatever it is my aunt is drinking, but when I look around the room, I see neither bottle nor spare glass. Just the same olive-green sofa and matching drapes, the notched dentils of the oak mantelpiece with crystal sconces lit on either end to illuminate the late Tom Thomson sketch of a heavy-limbed pine in between. Julia came into this marriage with money, the house, and the sketch. Meanwhile my father, I'm willing to bet, went his entire life not even knowing what the Group of Seven was.

I tug Enzo's sleeve and he follows me across the room. I run my hand across the bookshelf. "Look," I whisper. "The Shepherdess and the Harlequin!"

Enzo follows my eye to the built-in shelving flanking the fireplace where two Royal Doulton figurines stand flourishing their skirts. I recognize them immediately, their garish paint, so at odds with Julia's chilly aesthetic.

Enzo's face lights up. He steps closer to the bookshelf to examine them. I glance around the room to make sure we are unobserved. Stella has taken her glass of wine to the window while Dante stares at the sofa. He stares but doesn't sit. To sit would be to cede advantage to whoever enters the room next.

Confident no one's watching, I pick up the Shepherdess. "Enzo, she was my first." The lighting is too dim to find the seam along her neck but I tip her backward so he can see her.

"You sweet serial killer, you," he breathes.

I can't recall exactly when the particular predilection took over, but I know for a fact that by the time I'd outgrown it, I'd managed to break the heads off of every single figure in Julia's porcelain collection. I realized early on that if you flipped the statuettes over, their names were stamped on the bottom. For some time, I kept a mental scorecard of the victims. The first decapitation (the Shepherdess with a white lamb poking out from the folds of her cornflower blue skirts) was an accident. I remember knocking her off the end table where she usually resided. The sound brought Julia rushing into the room. She knelt down to pick up the two pieces. It was an amazingly clean break, but the destruction brought tears to her eyes. It was fascinating to watch emotion colour that white, impassive face. To see tears break off the stony promontory of her cheek and jaw.

Then she looked up at me, and the tears turned into something else. Julia reached out—I remember this clear as day because it was the only time she ever laid a hand on me—and pinched my cheek. She grabbed the skin and gave it a painful twist. It was such a quick gesture, something that, an hour later, might have been forgotten if it wasn't for the pink butterfly that rose under my cheekbone. I walked around with that mark for a week. The pink turned to purple and then receded. But it lit something inside of me. Within months, every single one of Julia's figurines had a checkmark beside her name: Shepherdess, Carmen, Eliza, Montclair, Bathsheba, Wendy, Harlequin, Clara, Belle.

My grandmother, perhaps guessing the source of the mark on my face, somehow managed to acquire a tube of Krazy Glue. It was her role to protect me from Julia, to keep some semblance of order in a house where, it seemed, none of us was happy. As quick as I could break the figurines, she would put them back together. Her work was immaculate. Julia was never the wiser. Thirty years later and you'd have to really know what you're looking for.

"No, no—not here. In the study."

I nearly drop the Shepherdess. Enzo grabs it from my hands just in time. Then we knock heads trying to get it back on the shelf before anyone looks at us. He puts a hand on my back and gently pushes me away from the bookcase. I turn around slowly. Standing in the entrance, in a faded blue Chanel jacket, is Julia.

"Please, we want you in the study." It's the same voice I remember, carefully articulated but hollow. It seems to float in the air above our heads for a moment before vaporizing.

Zio Dante turns from the sofa and steamrolls across the carpet toward her. "Julia," he says. "My condolences."

I realize this is the first time they've seen each other since the death. She looks at him, her eyes unyielding in the folds of her parchment-fine skin. Her white hair is pulled back in a ponytail. She doesn't bother with make-up anymore. Or maybe she doesn't bother because it's us. She nods at Dante, then her eyes pass over him, over the room, over me without stopping.

"He's setting up in the study," she repeats. "Let's not keep him waiting."

The four of us look at each other as Julia turns and walks back out into the foyer.

"Oh my God, Julia's as sympathetic as ever." Enzo shakes his head.

"Do you think she recognized me?"

"Now? Or when you tried running her over last night?"

"Both."

"One way to find out," he says and sweeps his arm in the direction of the study.

The "he" that we have kept waiting is not the priest, as Stella may have been hoping for, or even Julia's minister, but my father's long-time lawyer, Gianni D'Abruzzo.

"My God, Sabine, is this you?" He both pumps my hand and kisses me on the cheeks, Italian style. "Mamma mia, you're a gorgeous one, you turned out alright!"

I smile weakly and see that D'Abruzzo has opened up his briefcase on my father's desk.

"Why we have to meet under these tragic circumstances, I do not know. What is he thinking, the man upstairs?" D'Abruzzo points to the second floor. "Taking a man such as your father and leaving other, less worthy ones to roam the planet, eh?" I notice he glances at my uncle as he says this.

"Are you saying a few words?" I ask as he pulls a stack of papers out of the briefcase and squares them neatly on the desk.

"It's pretty straightforward, don't you worry." He licks a thick finger, divides the stack of pages and pulls my father's chair out from the desk. "Your father told me you published a cookbook, eh? And you got some baking shows you do on the computer? Just fabulous."

Before I can ask him what exactly he's doing here I catch a whiff of the past. It's the Oscar de la Renta perfume that trickled down steadily from the third floor and clouded up my childhood. I turn and find her planted squarely behind me.

"Hello, Sabine." Julia puts her hand out. She's not looking at me like I'm someone who recently tried to kill her, so I can't help but feel relief. However, what she is levelling in my direction is a look of complete apathy. He was still my father, my last living parent. I did live here in this house with them for fifteen years. None of that is reflected on her face.

"Ladies, let's take a seat." D'Abruzzo cuts in, thankfully, so I don't have to shake her hand. "Francis would want us to expedite this process, eh? Dough's a wastin'."

Enzo and Zia Stella take two of the dining room chairs that have been brought into the room. Dante stands at the doorway, confused.

"What's D'Abruzzo doing here?" he asks no one in particular. "Where's the priest?"

"Sit down, Dante," Julia points to a chair beside Zia Stella. "We have more important things to take care of."

"I will stand."

"No priest?" My aunt pulls a tissue out of the sleeve of her cardigan. "*Dio mio*! If only Francesco had stayed in Italia instead of coming to this country of *dannati*!"

I sit beside her. "It was his heart, Zia. It would have still happened, no matter where he was."

"But he would be safe under the wing of Gesù Cristo. Instead, not even a priest to say a few words?"

"Francis didn't care about that," Julia lowers herself slowly into an armchair on the other side of the room. Away from us.

"And no viewing—not even a casket?" Zia Stella presses the tissue to her nostrils. "Instead, they will burn him like they do the Indians. *Che vergogna!* How do we know for sure he is dead?"

"He's dead, alright." Julia tells her. "I found him on the dining room floor myself."

"Let us put the emotional aside for now." D'Abruzzo says. "I know it's hard for you ladies to do that, but let's carry out Francis's wishes tonight, eh?"

Is this a will reading? Enzo and I look at each other over Stella's head. Dante seems to realize this at the same time that we do and comes fully into the room. He grabs a dining room chair and drags it noisily toward the window.

D'Abruzzo settles heavily at the desk and shows us a sealed envelope. "Being the attorney of Francis Rose, née Francesco Rosetti, I have his final wishes. This is a sealed copy for the family to peruse at their leisure." He puts the envelope down and spreads out a document.

"Julia Rose, you will keep the house on Summit Avenue, its title, contents, and vehicles." D'Abruzzo nods to himself. "You will acquire full ownership of all liquid assets registered jointly at the

Canadian Imperial Bank of Commerce as well as retirement and investment holdings at Edward Jones and Associates. You see," D'Abruzzo interrupts himself, "Francis was a man who took care of his wife."

Julia remains impassive. She has both hands planted on the chair and stares at D'Abruzzo as he hums and shuffles the papers in front of him. "Okay, here it is." He picks up one of the pages and taps it with his finger. "As we all know, Francis loved his family first. His work second."

I try to catch Enzo's attention again over his mother's head so we can exchange some eye-rolling glances. D'Abruzzo is a little off the mark; I'd flip those two great loves, if I were writing the speech. But Enzo is wiping at his cheek and gripping his mother's hand in her lap. Their grief is like a quick little slap in the face, a shame which I feel more than any actual loss.

"It's a business Francis built around his great skill," D'Abruzzo continues. "He was a Michelangelo in his workshop." The lawyer glances around at us. "Francis Rose, as co-owner of Bennett's Bakery, leaves his one-half ownership of the building, its contents and the business to his daughter, Sabine Rose."

I'm still looking at my aunt and cousin when I realize D'Abruzzo has just said my name.

"You see, Sabine?" D'Abruzzo says over his glasses, his face falling into the soft dewlaps of a basset hound. "Your talent with your cookbooks and baking show did not go unrewarded in your father's eyes. He left you his share of the business."

There's dead silence in the room. The lawyer is looking at me, maybe expecting something profound, at least approximately reciprocal to what he's just laid out. I look at Julia but she's examining her fingernails with great intensity.

"Let me simplify the jargon for the ladies, eh?" D'Abruzzo sniffs, realizing his news hasn't quite landed as he'd anticipated. "'As for intellectual property associated with the aforementioned business,'... yada, yada ... 'I leave this to my daughter, in special conjunction with the ownership of the bakery.'... yada, yada ... 'Ownership of either entity is conditional upon the other.'"

Stella and Enzo are looking at me. Julia is straightening her wedding ring. Dante stands up. "What the devil does that mean?"

D'Abruzzo cracks his knuckles and smiles. He reaches behind the desk and brings up a second briefcase, this one made of metal with a locking combination pad on either side of the handle. He looks at me as he slides the briefcase across the dark marled surface of the desk.

"It means, Sabine, he has left you the recipe of the Persian pastry."

Twenty-Two

Sabine

Upstairs in the bathroom I splash water on my face in an effort to fend off the hangover that's making a sudden return appearance. I feel around for a towel but find only doily-edged handkerchiefs draped over the rod. They look like they might dissolve if I actually get them wet, so I just look in the mirror and let my face drip into the sink. It's the same mirror I stood in front of as a child while my grandmother got me ready for school. I remember the arduousness of those cold, northern mornings, bracing myself against the sink, my grandmother working a wet comb through the hair that grew in uncultivated abundance.

Never mind. She'd swat my hands away and fix a ponytail so taut my eyes wept. *It's going to come loose during the day.* And she was right. Painful as the morning corral was, by mid-afternoon hair tufted from the sides, wisped around the ears, giving me the gauzy appearance of sideburns.

I crack open the bathroom door and scan the hallway before I emerge. The brass lampshades cast a gloomy light. The same wild turkeys trot across the burgundy wallpaper. There are two bedrooms on this floor which had been my grandmother's and mine, while my father and Julia's suite occupied the entire floor above.

I stand there for a second, stuck between the past and the present. Then I follow the turkeys to the left, even though the staircase leading down to the foyer—to the front door, to the airport—is on the right. Then I push open my bedroom door.

"It's going to rain in here?" My grandmother stands in the doorway of the bedroom frowning at the new pink brocade canopy while I bounce up and down on the mattress. The dressing table and highboy are a rose-stained oak that probably looked dainty in the showroom but now, under the dominion of a giantess, seem fated for kindling. My father ordered the whole set after our arrival, when it became apparent I couldn't share a bed with the old woman for long.

"Julia chose this for you," he lies. It's early days and he is still hoping to overcome his wife's resistance to having a young child in the house.

I don't answer. I am pretty, but thick. My belly strains against a pullover and my skirt is twisted backward. The hair, dense as a helmet, holds the kink of an old braid. My knees are dimpled, fat and powerful so that with each rhythmic landing the bed's metal frame squawks like an abused animal.

"*Smettila, disgraziata!*" My grandmother takes a threatening step toward the bed.

"*Lasciami.*" I cry to be left alone without breaking in the metrics of my bounce. My head, at the apex of each jump, narrowly misses the roof of the canopy. "*Strega!*"

"You see?" she says to my father in Italian. They will always speak only Italian to each other. "I'm a witch. But am I going to hit her? It's Sunday." The old woman holds up her hands, a Pontius Pilate gesture. "The nuns at that school were too liberal."

It's only when my grandmother turns away to inspect the new furniture that I stop my assault on the bed. The coils and springs and painted wood frame settle down. Father and daughter stand face to face. Though I've been under his care for nearly a month, he's barely had a good look at me. I am always moving, always twisting, contorting or scowling. Can he blame me? I've been ripped from the only home I've ever known, with the most unsatisfying explanation. *I am your grandmother. Your mother is dead. We are going to live with your father.*

"Sabi," he smiles weakly. He's looking for a trace of my mother in my face. Or maybe he's looking for himself. After all, he'd left before I was born. "Do you like the new room we bought for you?"

I scratch at the fuzz of a sideburn. Then I stick out my tongue.

"You forgot this downstairs."

I look up from the little pink bed. D'Abruzzo stands at the bedroom door, his large girth filling up the frame. He's holding the metal briefcase.

"Ah. My bad."

He glances around the room, which, surprisingly, is in archival condition. "I know you're strolling down memory lane, but give me your ear for one minute, okay?"

"Okay," I say casually as he makes his way to the little secretary desk. I worry that the slender legs of the chair will snap under his weight, but when he sits, they hold strong.

"I don't think you expected this great gift of your father's legacy?"

"I did not."

"So you are surprised. Fine." He rests the briefcase on the shag rug by his feet. "But it's important you know Francis had motivations for doing things."

"Such as?" I don't bother editing the impetuous tone in my voice. This gesture—leaving me his entire business—is so out of the blue that it feels strategic. And immensely inconvenient for me.

D'Abruzzo sighs and reaches into his breast pocket, pulling out a slip of paper. "You know, us immigrants, we come here for a better life. And we want to pass that better life on to our children."

God, the immigrant speech.

"Your father was a . . . conflicted man. Conflicted about being here. I don't believe this world was ever his dream. All the time I know him, he never finds his place here."

"I think he found it pretty well." I hold my arms out to the room.

"About a year ago he comes to me and says your uncle is talking to some company about selling the Persian recipe."

I glance at the attaché case on the floor. It looks bulletproof with its reinforced corners. "Dante doesn't own the recipe."

"He does own half of the bakery where it is produced. Dante likes doing business deals, he goes to these trade shows to meet people. He thinks he's doing your father a favour." D'Abruzzo glances at the door. "Francis asks me to look into it. How does he go about selling an intellectual property? How much could he get for it—that sort of thing."

"How much could he get?"

"We never got that far. I start making inquiries, but a week later he says, forget it. He changed his mind. Instead, he comes to my office and puts it in his will that you get the bakery and the recipe. He wants it so if you sell them, you have to sell them together."

See what I mean? Strategic. I get the sense that D'Abruzzo is trying to tell me something without telling me directly. Which is the worst kind of business dealing. I know from my sponsorship contracts that everything should be spelled out at a fifth-grade comprehension level.

I smile. "Like you said before, put it in words so that even the ladies can understand."

D'Abruzzo nods eagerly at this request. "In other words, he put guardrails in place in case anyone asks you to simply hand over the recipe. It is officially intellectual property with a real dollar value—to be determined by you—and tied to the ownership of the bakery. They are part and parcel. He does this, Sabine, assuming you are going to sell his half of the bakery and therefore to ensure you walk away with the best possible price for his life endeavour."

I nod slowly. "So my uncle doesn't rip me off?"

"I've known this family for twenty-five, thirty years. Your father and uncle worked well together." D'Abruzzo tips his head to one side, as though weighing the complexity of his words. "But Dante's got to buy the cow if he wants the milk, eh?"

"And what's that?" I point to the scrap of paper he's rolled into a cone.

The lawyer holds it up between his sausage-like fingers. "The briefcase combinations. I'll hold on to them to ensure the recipe remains under lock and key. When you sell it, you will hand the recipe over in this virginal state, so to speak."

I slide off the bed and go to the window. It's still daylight but the moon is visible, hanging like a fingernail paring on a cover of cloud. "So why did he leave me this?"

"You don't seem happy."

"Enzo was his baker—my father and I weren't even that close."

"He still was your father."

I turn from the window. "But what am I supposed to do with it?"

D'Abruzzo shrugs and replies, "Follow the truth? Isn't that what you're after?"

I'm annoyed by this suggestion, the inferred intimacy. "What do you know about me?"

"Very little. I know your mother died. That you didn't meet your father until you were four or five years old. That must have been hard."

I go to the other side of the bed where the framed photo of my first Communion still hangs on the wall. I lean in and look at my six-year-old self at the altar of St. Anthony's, hands folded under my chin in a fit of angry prayer. Julia had ordered the Communion dress from Eaton's a size too small and its lacey sleeves had cut gashes into my armpits. "It was what it was," I tell him. "Nobody had time to indulge me and my feelings, that's for sure."

"As I said, Sabine, I've known this family a long time—as an outsider with certain privileges. But my feeling is they did indulge you. Or perhaps protect you, keep you out of things."

I can't stop the burst of laughter. "What sort of things? That's a very dramatic statement."

He holds up his hand to stop my laughter. "I don't know from what, Sabine. All I know is there was something."

Yes, her name is Julia.

But the lawyer's looking down. I follow his eye to the briefcase on the carpet. "The Persian?" I laugh. "You think he was protecting me from the secret recipe?"

"There is a reason he put a lock on it, no?"

And then I think of my last day on the job as the Persian Princess, driving home in the delivery van with my father as he put an end to my reign. How he'd called the Persian "a mistake that began a long time ago." And how I couldn't shake the feeling that he was really talking about me.

But D'Abruzzo clearly believes there's some sort of folklore surrounding the pastry. He also clearly believes women need special guidance when it comes to business. I see how both of these opinions might actually dovetail nicely to my advantage.

"Since you've been taking care of my father's business for thirty years, you won't mind one more task?" I sit back down on the bed and put on my best, helpless smile. "I need to return home tomorrow. Can I count on you to handle the sale?"

He looks hurt. Or, at the very least, disappointed. "Sabine, you should be here."

"You can just send me the stuff to sign when Dante makes an offer."

"You need to get a proper evaluation done, do a walk-through with an insurance agent. Get an accountant to look through the books. You give me some time and I can find the company that was interested in the recipe last year. Maybe that gives you an idea how to set a price."

I'm shaking my head before he even finishes his sentence. "I don't have time. I'm right in the middle of a very big work deal. I need to focus on that."

He presses his lips together sympathetically. "Legacies are not easy money, that's for sure. But what if your father had said that to Don Ernesto all those years ago, 'I don't want the Garibaldi!' Can you imagine?"

I need to focus on the show. Doing a walk-through with an insurance agent is not on my agenda—whether or not I was on the cusp of a life-changing event. I'm so overwhelmed by the thought that I nearly miss what he's just said.

"Who's Don Ernesto?"

D'Abruzzo gives a belly-jiggling laugh. My eyes go to the little chair absorbing the impact.

"Who? The genius who saved your father from a life of checking prostates!"

I must look confused because the lawyer's face changes. "You really don't know?"

I shake my head.

"The Garibaldi?"

"What's the Garibaldi?"

D'Abruzzo is looking at me so intently that his brows knit together into a prehistoric bird over the bridge of his nose. "The Garibaldi," he says slowly, "is the Persian."

Twenty-Three

Francesco, 1983

He finally realized a life of medicine was not for him in the middle of an anatomy lab in the basement morgue of the University of Napoli. They had just dissected their first cadaver. The professor was showing them how to remove the lung when Francesco stood up from his lab stool and walked out of the room. Up the stairs and out of the building, through the ceremonial campus gates and up Corso Umberto I until he came to the *pasticceria* where he stopped each morning for his espresso and panino. The girl behind the counter was surprised to see him at this hour. "You look like you've seen the Devil."

"Worse," he told her. "I've seen inside of him." Francesco was quiet, his face eternally preoccupied. He spoke only to the counter girl and after receiving his espresso stared into it as though it might be his last. The staff in the bakery secretly referred to the medical student as Dottore della Morte. Doctor Death. They weren't that far off with the moniker. Looking into the body that morning had confirmed what, for some time, he'd suspected to be true. There was nothing sacred, holy, spiritual. No soul, no God. Just matter. And he wanted nothing to do with it. He could not imagine a life of service to the body, its upkeep. For what? To end up a heap of cold muscle on a table? He was not young—it had taken his family years to save enough to send him to medical school—and he had a wife and mother at home, but none of this was enough to persuade him to go back to the university.

This, of course, would be impossible to explain to his mother who'd put all of her energy toward turning Francesco into *un dottore*. She still lived, as peasants had in feudal times, on the *latifondi* of the rich and shady Toti family in the hillside above the town of Palatino. Assisted by her daughter-in-law, she tended to their beehives, chestnut trees and small livestock in exchange for a cottage near the road. She wanted desperately for Francesco to rise above this station and take them away from there.

"Listen," he said to the girl who made his espresso every morning. "Is Don Ernesto hiring? I know my way around a bakery." He looked down at his hands. They had been inside another man just an hour earlier.

She smiled. He was handsome. "Always room for you."

His father had been the village baker in Palatino, so it did not take Francesco long to find the rhythm of the place. He could knead dough at an impressive pace and felt a thorny hit of pride when his boss, Don Ernesto, used his Christian name. The little man was something of a mystery to Francesco, who had no access to the upper echelon of *la vita napoletana*. It was said that the don whispered his confessions directly into the ear of the monsignor and advised *il consigliere comunale* on civic matters. He dined frequently with the mayor and was driven home in his *auto privata*. It was odd that a baker—a labourer—should rise to the ranks of the elite and be given the titular honour of "don." But for this, Ernesto was in debt to a pastry called the Garibaldi.

The Virgin Mary was good for business. Every town in Christendom knew the value of a Marian apparition, the foot traffic and trade it generated. But in the 1950s Mercato neighbourhood of Naples, it wasn't the Blessed Mother, but the lean and heroic figure of Giuseppe Garibaldi who appeared to the baker Ernesto.

Because the story had been told countless times, its angles had been modified, the way a book softens at the edges. Years after the war, when both the Germans and Americans had gone, Ernesto, who rose early with a perpetual hangover, came down the alley adjacent to the piazza and saw a man waiting in front of his bakery. Tall and willowy, the stranger stood in a vaguely confrontational *contrapposto* while leaning on the hilt of a sword—a ceremonial piece whose point was staked between the cobbles. His eyes were fixed on him.

The little baker stopped dead in his tracks. He knew the visitor by the *camicia rossa*, the moustache with its unpruned edges growing into the great sandy beard, a face held in place by the downcast eyes he'd seen reproduced a thousand times in both schoolbooks and statuary. It was the nineteenth-century patriot, war hero, and crusader for Italian unity, Giuseppe Garibaldi.

Ernesto pressed himself against the darkened window of Caffè Firenze in fear; Garibaldi had been dead for over seventy years. The figure, still barring the door to the bakery, raised a hand and signalled for Ernesto to approach. He didn't dare disobey; the visitor's physique and forceful gesture made it evident he would brook no opposition.

"Do you know who I am?"

Ernesto came forward, nodding. Garibaldi was Father of the Fatherland, the Sword of Unification. A hundred years earlier his Expedition of the Thousand had swept through the peninsula, fusing disparate states into the country of Italy, ensuring the perpetuity of the Italic race. Now, standing in front of the Neapolitan bakery, he appeared to waver in and out of existence, as though he were a radio signal that Ernesto couldn't quite capture.

"The fatherland has been broken," the hazy figure said. "Our own soil"—he pointed down the alley—"has run with the blood of our brothers."

Ernesto glanced down the quiet street. The Germans were gone, the Allies too. But years later and Naples was still ravaged. A shithole.

"Make a sign, Ernesto. Men must remember the lives their fathers have sacrificed."

The little man fought for his tongue. He was a drinker, just past thirty, and not a likely candidate for any grand gesture. "I am only a baker."

"And cannot a baker show love for his country?" Garibaldi stepped out of the doorway. He raised his sword to the sunrise. "Do it today, Ernesto. History waits for no man."

The baker felt he should bow but didn't dare take his eyes off the spectre. As Garibaldi turned and walked down Piazza Mercato, he began to emit a strange green light. He was limping. This detail in particular survived the thousands of retellings and authenticated the story, for Garibaldi had been shot in the foot during his campaign in the Aspromonte.

Before the central figure of the Risorgimento disappeared around the corner of Caffè Firenze, he turned once and called back to Ernesto. "We shall meet again before long to march to new triumphs."

In history texts, Garibaldi's great quotations were often read with a spirit of motivation and *fraternitas*, but what Ernesto heard that morning was a rumbling threat.

There was only one thing a man could do with such a prescriptive, Ernesto later told the newspaper *Il Mattino*, and that was to bake. In appearance it was simple: two multi-layered loops of laminated dough joined together in the shape of a figure eight. The carefully wrought dough was laced with fruit butter and spice, then baked until the golden layers separated into the flaking pages of historical parchment. Ernesto chose the symbol of *infinitas* as an expression of the continuity of Italian heritage; a thousand individual layers brought together as one *in perpetuum*. In the 1950s, the nation struggled with tepid government leadership, impermeable corruption and ill-advised blood bonds just as it had before the war. But in Naples, this popular symbol of solidarity gained gravitas. The little baker began to be featured in all of the country's important newspapers and even managed to find a wife.

Don Ernesto jealously guarded the details of the Garibaldi recipe. In his youth, he'd received training from a French baker and continued to use the language in reference to his work. He would make the *détrempe*, the dough packet, and *beurrage*, a butter inlay, at home and then assemble it into a *pâton* at the bakery. The Garibaldi required a day, six *tours*—the process of folding and rolling—and six cycles of chilling before it could be shaped, panned, and allowed to rise. As a result, Don Ernesto was perpetually at some stage or other in the Garibaldi process.

By the 1970s, RAI TV would come down to the waterfront each year on the Feast of Garibaldi to cover the daylong celebration and procession which began at the church and ended outside the bakery with a blessing of the pastries. The televised interview with the baker and the namesake pastry never failed to score high ratings. While Don Ernesto was still a drinker, he tried his best to keep it behind closed doors so only his wife and daughter bore witness. And when they did, it was from a large, newer house with a view of Vesuvius, away from the stinking harbour.

Francesco grabbed his brattice cloth and went into the courtyard. It was the hunchback Scaletti's job to unload the Garibaldis before they opened their doors in the morning, but the old man chose this time each day to shuffle out to the latrine with a copy of *Il Giornale* under his arm. Francesco didn't mind picking up the slack. It had been four months since he'd left the medical school, and the relief still filled his body like helium. He floated above his tasks and took pleasure in working with his hands. He could knead dough at the same pace as the heavy-duty electrical mixers. He worked silently whenever possible and told himself it was much cleverer to create than to dismember a man just to see how he'd been created.

Of course, he hadn't told his wife or mother back home in Palatino that he'd dropped out of school. That he'd become a baker. His mother blamed their relative poverty on the fact that her husband had followed this route after the war. Even though the days that his father had let Francesco follow him to the bakery and assist with the bread were some of the happiest of his childhood, it would mean nothing to the women who were waiting for him. Nor would the excuse that he was suffering a crisis of faith. That he had no desire to resurrect men from the dead.

Now from the wood ovens came a fleshy heat followed by the haze of fruit and butter that made Francesco's mouth water. He slid a palate in and began to remove the hot trays, carrying them inside to the cooling rack. There were twenty pastries per tray, each the size of two small fists joined at the knuckle, ready to be pulled apart to share. Don Ernesto made only enough for one run per day. By the time the line for bread began inching forward, the Garibaldi tray would be cleared.

In that moment, Francesco wanted nothing more than an entire Garibaldi to himself. He took one off the rack and slid it into his apron pocket.

When he turned from the rack, he found Don Ernesto standing in the doorway, a cigarette tipped between his lips, two canvas sacks over his shoulders and an oilskin-wrapped package in his hands. Each morning he arrived in his Fiat with the dough he'd made at home. Early on, Francesco had tried to help him by taking the sacks, but the man had reared back, hands raised to show that he alone was sanctioned to bear such a load.

The little baker was not looking at him now, nor at the searing hot bulge of the Garibaldi in his pocket, but at the worktable. Francesco's face coloured. He'd left half-formed dough while he unloaded the oven. He was not a pastry apprentice. His job was strictly to scrape trays and bake uniform loaves of utilitarian bread. But he'd helped himself to flour, yeast, a tablespoon of anisette and, even more unforgivably, to sugar, milk, and six eggs.

The old man turned and left the room without speaking. With unspecified humiliation, Francesco approached the table where he was attempting the braided sweet bread ring his mother made each year at Easter. Though he did his best to remain guarded, he was drawn to pastry, and often found himself flouring the work-table reserved for its creation.

Don Ernesto returned. His packages were gone, and he held a bottle of grappa with a rag for a stopper and two glasses. He pulled up a stool, nodded at the work in progress. "Easter is months away."

Francesco cleared his throat. He looked at the eggs he'd placed in a bowl. "Yes, but this tastes good any time of the year."

"It's my daughter's favourite." The don motioned for him to continue with the sweet bread then sank down on the stool. "I used to make Lucia one every year. She would sit here and watch me for hours, begging me to teach her to bake. Now she just begs for money, vacations, a car."

The young man floured his hands lightly and began punching his dough into elastic compliancy as the don watched.

"They say you left medical school to come work in this dungeon."

Francesco raised his chin but said nothing.

"That you left a body split open right on the table."

There was no use confirming or denying this. Instead, Francesco began to braid his three lengths of dough. Every third cross-over he paused and nestled an egg into the dough. It would bake in its shell along with the bread.

"The plaits will hold the egg as gold prongs hold a gemstone," Don Ernesto said, pouring them each a few ounces of clear fluid.

"Your body makes you fit for bread, Francesco. But perhaps you are a man of philosophy? The sort who does not believe in shortcuts?"

"My father was a good baker. He taught me some things."

The old man looked at his hands. "It's hard to look at dead men when you have an artist's intuition."

"Tell that to my mother." Francesco pinched the ends of the braid together to complete the wreath. "This will not satisfy her, I'm afraid."

"No, it likely will not." The don held the second glass out until Francesco wiped his hands on his apron and took it. "But will the alternative satisfy you?"

He put the shot back in one hot swallow and looked at his boss. "I'm here instead of there, aren't I?"

Don Ernesto nodded. "As I said, I could do worse than keeping you on as bread maker. But pastry is the most exacting and delicate skill a baker can have. The French have some intelligence in these matters. They keep these things separate; at the boulangerie they make bread, a place of hot work. But at the patisserie the artisan works in cold materials—icing, fruit, *la crème*. As there must be bricklayer, there must be architect."

Francesco put the glass down on the worktable. "And which am I, do you think?"

"You have the talent and desire to create, yes?" He nodded his small, whiskered head as if to elicit the young man's response. "I am sixty-five this winter, likely dead before I find another man of substance I can properly apprentice. It would do my heart good to instruct you in the art of the pastry. La patisserie."

Twenty-Four

Sabine

"My father didn't believe in the ghost of Giuseppe Garibaldi, did he?"

"Of course he did," D'Abruzzo says when he sees the look on my face. "In the new world, ghosts are given the rough edge of one's tongue. But in Italy, people believe that the dead come back to settle unfinished business."

"And for some good PR."

"That doesn't mean he made up Garibaldi's visit." The lawyer removes his glasses and folds them into his breast pocket. "The point is, your father was looking for something greater than himself to believe in. A reason to follow an unprescribed path."

I sit down again on the bed and run a hand over the coverlet. I can still remember how the waffle-weave texture felt tucked up under my chin at night. "He was really studying to be a doctor? He told you all of this?"

"In bits and pieces over the years." D'Abruzzo nods. "Imagine, Sabine. Your life could have turned out completely different."

For the better? I let the idea slide. "He must have worked hard to keep up the charade. My grandmother could sniff out a lie a mile away."

"She was a character, I recall." He chuckles. "Your father would go home to visit once a month. But these trips were not something he relished, poor man. Before seeing your mother, *buonanima*, he had to prepare his lies; that the money he'd sent her was from his graduate stipend, that his rounds kept him from communicating more. Each visit he swore that on the next visit he would tell them the truth; after all, even medical school would have to end sometime. But always, he put it off."

I can just imagine the women back in the village, waiting for the young *dottore* to finish his studies, dreaming of a time when they would buy a big house and fill it with beautiful things. Meanwhile my father was pounding dough and sweating like a dog in the back room of some filthy Neapolitan bakery.

I look at my father's old friend. "I don't see him apprenticing under anyone." Let alone some con artist baker. "To me he was born knowing how to bake."

"There's no such thing! You young people are in such a rush to break from the past, eh? You miss the most valuable lessons." The lawyer puts a foot on the briefcase and pushes it across the floor toward me. "Try to be smarter than that, okay Sabine?"

I blink. "What are you saying?"

"You know that painting with the dogs playing poker?"

"Yeah?"

"Sometimes there's a Picasso painted on the other side."

Twenty-Five

Francesco, 1984

One by one, Francesco's skills flourished as Don Ernesto's pastry chef. The old man was turning him into a craftsman, immersing him in the French technique that made his bakery the most well-regarded in Naples and applying it to the native pastries. From Francesco's hands came the crisp and complex sfogliatella, the rum-soaked babà and the lacquered sheen of the pasticiotti's egg-washed shells. The old man praised Francesco's marzipan fruit (an excellent representation of his technical skill) and criticized his crostata (the enriched dough lattice too thick and melting into the hot apricot tart). But for all of his generosity in allowing Francesco to cup his palm at the fountain of knowledge, Ernesto had withheld the secret recipe of the Garibaldi. The novice wasn't surprised; it was a weighty piece of knowledge with transformative power. It had turned the alcoholic bread maker into Don Ernesto, a man of wealth and honour.

At the forefront of Francesco's mind, always, was the fact that he hadn't told his family that he'd left the university. And so he was bound in a perpetual lie, selfishly following his heart while letting down the women who depended on him. He took some refuge in the fact the other men who made the bread were now under his direction. Instead of looking at him as competition, they brought forward their dough for inspection and followed his direction when a particular alteration to yeast or flour was required. They always invited Francesco to have a drink in the piazza after work, the men dragging out chairs from Caffè Firenze and forming a circle around *il dottore*. It might have stung Francesco to hear himself called that, the reminder of the status and life of comfort he'd tossed aside, but he believed the men he worked with respected him. And if he could make a living doing something he was good at, wasn't that enough?

On Christmas Eve 1984, a snowstorm carpeted Mount Vesuvius and turned the dirty streets of Naples into a rare white place of beauty. The storm also shut down the rail lines, and the trains coming in and out of Napoli Centrale were suspended until enough men could be hired to dig out the tracks.

There would be no Christmas for him in Palatino this year. His wife and mother would have to go into town and attend midnight Mass without him. In his small apartment near the university, Francesco was unpacking the suitcase he'd filled with presents for them when there was a knock at his door.

He lifted the lace curtain the landlady had tatted and saw his padrone through the square of glass.

"Don Ernesto, what are you doing here?" Francesco stepped aside so the man could enter. He stood dressed in a straw hat and a suit the colour of eggshells, stamping his pigskin shoes on the mat. "You're dressed for Ferragosto, not the dead of winter."

"Boy-oh-boy, as they say in America." Don Ernesto slid a thumb under his trouser brace and snapped it against his chest. "The last time it snowed on Natale, it was before the war." His face was lit in a way that told Francesco he had been drinking. He allowed himself to be ushered into the small flat and went to stand by the radiator. "I'm sorry you missed your train home after all the good work you did for me this past year. Just now I came from the bank. I'm telling them how each week I get bigger orders from the markets. Each day I'm sold out by noon."

"It's a good problem to have."

"I've got to lock myself up like a monk just to keep up." Don Ernesto showed him his soft white hands.

"You need to rest," Francesco told him. "It's Christmas Eve, go home and let your family take care of you."

"Christmas will keep for the morning." Don Ernesto removed the hat and adjusted his hair, which had been combed to disguise the widening patch at the back of his head. "What I would like from you tonight is a promise."

Francesco looked at him. He was a jovial drunk, but something in his tone told the younger man to pay careful attention. "What's that?"

"Tell your mother that you have given up medical school."

"With respect, what business is that of yours?"

"Soon I will be done with the bakery," Don Ernesto said. "I want you to take over."

Francesco had skipped ahead to this possibility many times before, entertaining what might come from his apprenticeship and devotion to the bakery. But now that it was upon him, he felt both a forward motion and a flattening of his heart.

"It's your life's work." Francesco shook his head. "I'm not a worthy man."

Don Ernesto ignored his false modesty. "You must promise to tell your family." He was quiet for a moment watching the snow drill against the window. "Hide behind a falsehood for too long, Francesco, you will never recognize yourself again."

On Christmas Day, Don Ernesto taught Francesco how to make the Garibaldi.

They began by sifting salt, sugar, and yeast into several kilos of flour that the old man had measured into a great mixing bowl. Into this, he had the apprentice pour a crock of cream and beat it into a wet batter. The baker's face, though decorated with drink blossoms, was solemn as he added more flour, coaxing the damp mix into a shaggy ball of dough.

"Give it a light taste of your hands," the old man told him. "Then into the cold."

Francesco began kneading the *détrempe*. The old man watched, then took it away from him before he could abuse it too badly in his eagerness.

"Now to make the *beurrage*. Pay attention here." He scooped a kilo of spiced, boiled fruit into a linseed sack and squeezed it so that it released a thick syrup known as mosto cotto. "A French woman taught me a special way to make this," he said. "Her people were scientists. You hear of Marcellin Berthelot?"

Francesco shook his head.

"A famous chemist in France." The old man gazed at the hot mosto. Into this emulsifier, he dropped a ball of his own churned butter, allowing it to dissolve like a milky lozenge. "In addition to beauty, she had some of her grandfather's ingenuity, that's for certain."

Francesco stood at his side, pulling a wooden spoon through the butter. He watched it liquesce into a slick surface. If only he could make his joy in this moment concrete, so that he could hold it up and show his family this was the sort of science he was meant for.

"You make the mosto in advance—anytime you find fruit about to spoil. No matter what you use, you follow my formula." The old man took the pot off the heat and showed Francesco how to pour the new, spiced butter into shallow pans. "Now put it in the cold room."

"And after this?"

"It's all rolling and folding."

"That sounds easy."

"An entire day of it."

It was nightfall before Don Ernesto was ready to tinker with the first *pâton*. With a sharp knife point he made one continuous cut, tracing the quadrilateral pattern around until he reached the heart of the rectangle. He pinched each square corner on the strip into a curve.

"You cut at a ninety-degree angle with only a sharp blade," he told Francesco. "A dull knife will pull the layers apart and the butter will escape. If the butter leaks, it's going to catch fire in the oven. If it stays sealed, it'll steam the dough from the inside."

He lopped off a piece as one might a length of rope and, on a baking sheet, began twisting it into the signature infinity loop that was the Garibaldi. Francesco understood that a man with a wrinkled map of shortcuts could never make the pastry. It required a devotion to process, a craftsman. He himself had done nothing special in his short life. He had not made any glorious sacrifice for art or tradition that might have induced Don Ernesto to share his last secret.

The man looked up from his dough suddenly. "One's calling in life, it can come in surprising ways, yes?" he asked as if privy to Francesco's thoughts. "Some people don't believe that Garibaldi came for me at the bakery that morning."

"Did he?" Francesco stopped what he was doing. He looked at the old man and was suddenly filled with a burning desire for reassurance, with an almost childish need to believe in something greater than himself. The unseen. He had left medical school for this. He'd abandoned a profession of respect for a sack full of sugar or a miracle. The difference between the two was a light switch turned on or off.

"Yes, he did." The old man didn't waver. "Of course he did."

Twenty-Six

Wanda

I stare at the cuticles on my left hand, realizing that at some point during this interminable wait, I've bitten them ragged. My first thought, of course, is that Sabine is going to kill me for doing this. But then I quickly remind myself that I'm the one with an inalienable right to be angry.

When she finally comes into the lobby, she's holding a metal briefcase and for a second I wonder if it contains the ashes of her father. I stand up. When she sees me, she freezes. She's expecting me to not be here, to make things as smooth as possible for her.

Because that's my job, isn't it?

She keeps her sunglasses on and skirts around the pods of armchairs and coffee tables to the empty concierge desk where I'm standing. "What are you still doing here?" she asks, clicking her ring anxiously against the briefcase handle.

I am hoping to take a logical, calm approach here. To point out how Netflix had, in a matter of days, mowed a wide swath through the carefully crafted pilot that had taken me an entire year to conceive, plot and write. To not disguise the blow dealt to me by my demotion to errand girl—there is no hiding my displeasure in that of course—but to frame it as an opportunity to rally together and sell this project without compromise.

Instead, I open my mouth and ask, "When the fuck were you planning on telling me?"

Sabine stares at me but says nothing, which confirms that she knows. I feel my throat constrict. I wonder if you can go into anaphylactic shock from grief.

"How did you find out?" she asks finally.

"If your email gets hacked and you're too stupid to change your password, you can't blame someone for hacking it again."

Sabine puts the briefcase down, shoves the sunglasses to the top of her head and looks around the lobby. "Look," she says quietly. "I know this feels disappointing right now—"

"It feels like a betrayal."

"But it's not! It's just a business move, Wanda. It's what Netflix needs to keep our show as a contender. Isn't that what we've worked for?"

"No, we were working for *our* show. Not *your* show alone."

Last year Sabine and I signed up for lunchtime kundalini yoga. We were expecting a good stretch and an excuse to buy Lululemon tights but instead found ourselves hunched on all fours in a nearby church basement, panting rapidly like dogs. The Breath of Fire was supposed to relieve stress. It seemed ridiculous at the time, but I find myself doing it now. I drop into one of the lobby armchairs, resisting the urge to put my head between my knees. That would be complete defeat.

"It's still your show, Wanda. You wrote it." Sabine sinks into the chair opposite of me.

"And they're going to make me write myself out of it."

"It's just less on-screen dialogue for you, really," she says. "Netflix has the right to change anything they want. I mean, we're lucky they've taken this as far as they have."

I look up suddenly. "Then let's shop it elsewhere. Someone else will buy it. As is."

Sabine's face falls. "It's taken us a year to get to this point with the development team. You said it yourself, this chance isn't going to come around again."

I can see how this is all my own stupid fault. When I wrote *What's in Your Pantry*, I knew how appealing it would be for her to be judge and jury—to not have to do any of the baking herself. I might not be a character on *Sweet Rush*, but I am essential for our channel's success, and she knows it. She's relied on me for so long. But here, with Netflix, I've written her a set-up where she doesn't actually need me anymore.

"You tried to put me on an airplane so you wouldn't have to tell me yourself."

She finally looks away. "I just thought it would be easier if Collette took you through the new offering."

"New offering? Is that how you see it?"

"Everything that's happened here, with my dad, it just felt like too much. I thought if you and Collette could sit down face to face you could probably figure things out. She's the professional, after all."

I nod my head. "Then let's do that."

"Do what?"

"Let's get Collette to figure things out. Let's get her on the phone."

Sabine untangles the sunglasses from her hair and goes through several intricate steps in order to fold them back in their case and return this case to her purse.

"Sabine, get Collette on a call," I say again. "Tomorrow morning."

"Collette didn't make up the terms. She's just a messenger."

My phone starts to ring. For the first time I'm glad to see my father's name on the screen.

"But she's a negotiator." I stand up, hoping she gets that the responsibility is squarely on her shoulders. "Which is exactly what we need right now. Because there's no way I'm going to agree to these terms."

Twenty-Seven

Wanda

"Hey, lard-ass."

"I thought it was Dad calling," I tell my brother Manny.

"Nope. Just me. I would have used my line, but you forgot to re-up my phone account."

I have to swipe my hotel card four times before it unlocks my door. "What do you want?" I ask impatiently. There's nothing worse than seventeen-year-old boys.

"Dad wants to know when you're coming home."

I get into the room, throw my wallet on the desk and sit on the bed. "I just got here. I'm working, okay?"

"Some guy keeps coming to the door."

"What guy?"

"I don't know, fart face. Some guy in a dark SUV. Dad says it's nothing, but this is the third day in a row."

I fall back on the bed and groan. It could be anything. The truth is, we live in a double whammy household, with my father neglecting to make mortgage payments while my aunt and uncle neglect to return to the Philippines even though their tourist visas have expired. "Did he ask for Tiyo or Tiya?"

"Why?" my brother asks. "You think there's going to be an immigration raid? That would be so cool."

"Are you a moron? You want them to get deported?"

"Bitch, please. Do I give a shit? We'll get the living room back."

"Maybe it was just the mortgage officer."

"What the fuck's a mortgage officer?"

"Did this guy in the SUV give Dad any papers?"

My brother snorts deeply. "He gave him jack shit because Dad didn't open the door. He just told me to tell you to come home."

"Like I said, I'm working." It's got to be the mortgage problem he called me about earlier. Despite holding a solid job as produce manager at the No Frills, last year he missed three months of payments because he was sending money to help restore a church in Quezon City. "Tell Dad I'm going to transfer some money to his account. He needs to pay whatever's outstanding."

"I need a couple hundred while you're at it."

"What for?"

"Nintendo."

I hang up and throw the phone against the wall. It hits the padded headboard, bounces on the mattress and lands right back where it started, by my head.

I pick it up again and navigate to our YouTube channel. The comments are still coming in for the video shot at the bakery. Sabine ended with a terrific mystery—the missing Persian recipe.

Rising Yeast Girl   just now
Persian dough—see Domenique Ansel's Cronut. Looks like your dad did the same, only decades earlier.

Muriel Blaze 520   just now
Classic whodunit! You sure your dad wasn't killed for the recipe? Stranger things have happened.

I roll my eyes. And then a name I recognize pops up:

ZiaStellaVasco just now
Sabine, tomorrow I make bomboloni con crema de pasticcera. Be at my house 11 sharp to help.

⌣⌐

Two years ago, when I was on King Street West with an hour to kill before a doctor's appointment, I walked into a Starbucks near the Odin offices in the Ping-Pong Factory. As I waited for my matcha latte I heard someone say "Wanda," and it wasn't the barista. Two young women stood at the pastry display case. I didn't know their faces, but I did recognize the bright purple Odin lanyards around their necks.

"*That* was her name? You're sure?" one of the girls asked the other as she tapped at a cheddar scone behind the glass. "Not Geraldine?"

"It was Wanda."

"What happened to her?"

The taller, thinner of the two let out a masculine grunt. "Crawled under a rock and died."

"I would have put a gun in my mouth," the other said, taking her cheddar scone from the barista. "Much quicker."

They both stood giggling as my body caught fire. I don't remember leaving the shop but the next thing I knew I was staggering across King Street, waiting for something to run me over.

But nothing did. I limped over to the streetcar stop and chewed down the cuticles of my entire left hand. I couldn't even cry. I was dismayed that this could still happen to me—that remorse could persist at such a high frequency.

It's funny that such a seemingly inconsequential action as ordering a matcha latte could bring about such enormous change. Because you know what I did? I got on the next streetcar, went home and started writing the pilot of *What's in Your Pantry*. It was, perhaps, the most courageous act I've ever performed. Sabine and I had been talking about a TV show for a while. Since I tracked viewers' comments, I knew what worked and what didn't. Then I just added the competition element. Fans constantly sent recipes hoping we would feature them, swearing their doughs, frostings, and fillings were simple enough to be made with ingredients found in the most basic pantry and fridge.

What struck me about other baking competitions was how many stupid contestants were unable to pull off what was required of them. They were given the ingredients, the recipe and calibrated kitchen equipment—what else was there to do? In my mind the real challenge was making something out of nothing. The stone soup of baking shows. We wouldn't give our amateur bakers any ingredients or recipes. We would just shove them into their cupboards and challenge them to make miracles out of thin air.

When I started writing the show, I thought I was after simple catharsis. But Wheat Bump—and the kind of money attached to it—had sailed. What I really wanted was to get off of the Whatever Happened To list. I didn't want to be on TV because I craved the spotlight like Sabine, but to prove I existed.

Twenty-Eight

Sabine

The phone beside my bed starts to ring just as the vodka and soda starts to work. I roll onto my stomach to answer it.

"Come down to the bar for a drink," Zio Dante says.

"What for?" I glance at the alarm clock. It's 9:20 p.m.

"A toast to your father."

"You want to buy the bakery," I say, closing my eyes. "I get it."

"They have a good cognac down here. Thirty years old."

I open one eye and look at the decimated mini bottles of Smirnoff lined up on the dresser, each one running me ten bucks. "Are you buying?"

"Yeah," he says. "Who else?"

The bar of the Mayfield Hotel is a comfortable place to get bombed out of your mind—which, of course, is not what I'm going to do. The east side of the room is a wall of windows looking out over the lake that, as the sun sets, reveals the twinkling lights of boats and buoys. The designers had enough good sense to eschew the nautical design and went for gentleman's club instead, with deep leather armchairs and panelled walls. My uncle and I

sit at the bar, our images reflected in the mirror between tiered
bottles and pints. He smells like cigarettes and is still wearing his
suit from the memorial-turned-will-reading.

"Your father sets up the deal the way he thinks is best. I am not
offended," Dante says. "He wants to make sure you get top dollar."

"So, you're here to offer me top dollar?"

"Sabine, I know my bakery. I know its fair value and what I am
able to pay—but don't think this is some fancy place in Toronto,
eh? This is a small town."

I've nearly finished my cognac and it's not sitting well. "What's
a fair offer?" I ask, realizing it's kind of ridiculous to be asking the
buyer to set the price. I should have run the numbers in my own
head. I am, after all, a single woman of a certain age without a nest
egg to speak of. The money I made modelling is long gone. And
all those years when Reynolds largely footed the bill, well, let's
just say I was more grasshopper than ant. The world's image of an
influencer is one of wall-to-wall glamour, but swing that camera
around and you'll see the place where the wallpaper ends. I know
firsthand how easy it is to create an illusion. All you need is five
feet of clean countertop, a blank wall or, when all else fails, some
decent Photoshop skills. For years I've convinced the public that
a rented studio is my kitchen. In reality, the last time I turned on
the oven at home, I may have incinerated the family of mice living
inside of it.

Dante takes a sheet of paper out of his jacket pocket and
unfolds it. I'm expecting to see a drawn-up contract, but it's just
a blank page. Then he reaches into the other pocket, takes out a
pen and, with wide penmanship that gallops across the page, he
writes: *300K.*

"Over four years," he says. "I'm sure you can put the money to good use, eh? It can't be cheap to take a camera crew wherever you go."

My uncle watches my face for a spark of excitement. Does the amount feel commensurate to the lifetime my father poured into the place? Am I conjuring images of myself up in cottage country, wrapped in a chinchilla throw while swishing an '89 Bordeaux between my teeth? No. However, it's a pretty decent amount for having done nothing but show up at a will reading.

"What are you thinking, Sabine?"

In fact, if I do the rough math—taking what I netted from last year's baking product sponsorships and subtracting Wanda's and Paul's salaries, the studio space, materials, equipment, wardrobe and travel—each month I'm left with just enough to keep from defaulting on my mortgage. In this light, Dante's offer is a modest but effective buffer between me and destitution.

Of course, I'm not counting any potential earnings from a Netflix show.

"What about the Persian?" I ask. "What's the recipe worth on its own?"

Dante laughs and finishes his drink. "I don't care for the Persian like your father does. I spent almost forty years making bread and delivering bread, first for Mr. Bennett, then as a padrone, you know? If the Persian brings people in the door, then so be it."

The tiny bell tinkling in my head tells me he's lying.

"D'Abruzzo said there was some company you were trying to get my father to meet with last year. That they wanted to make an offer on the recipe. It must be worth something."

My uncle stares at me. "D'Abruzzo says that?"

My eyes sweep the room. I'm not sure how much to say to Dante; maybe I've said too much already. And how many times have I told myself not to get involved? I glance again at the mirrored barback and realize there's a man seated in an armchair by the window watching me. He has laser-cut silver hair and is impeccably dressed, down to the pocket square and tie in two coordinated shades of blue. I know the face, somehow, but can't quite place it. When I meet his eye in the mirror, his smile is quick and fox-like.

Then I remember. The man in the sauna.

I look away, back to my uncle. Fuck it. If D'Abruzzo knows, Dante knows. "He told me how Nonna sent my father to medical school and that he quit without telling his family."

Dante extends a pinky finger into his ear and gives it a vigorous toggle. "Yeah? And what else?"

"He went to work for a baker instead. Don Ernesto? And that it was this baker who actually invented the Persian. Well, it was called something else—"

"The Garibaldi."

"Yes. It was already some famous Neapolitan pastry." Then I look up. "Well, I guess you know all this?"

"D'Abruzzo should learn to keep his mouth shut."

"Why did you change its name? What does Persian mean, anyway?"

Dante's not watching me anymore. He's busy running a fingernail along the wood grain of the bar. "You ever see *Ali Baba and the Forty Thieves?*"

"As in 'Open sesame'? It rings a bell."

"The first TV I buy in Canada—I turn it on and this is the movie playing."

Definitely not as inspiring as the ghost of Giuseppe Garibaldi.

"Look, Sabi, the Garibaldi is an idea. The Persian another idea entirely. Your father makes many changes."

And for the first time it strikes me that my father, the celebrated baker, inventor, visionary, might very well have been a thief. I place my snifter back on the bar, barely able to contain my smile. "Sounds like my father came to Canada and started producing his own knockoff version of this Garibaldi."

Dante says nothing. Which is probably a first for him. It's kind of sweet that he wants to protect my father's reputation, and I should leave it alone. But it's also not every day you get a bully like Dante in the hotseat. "Why did he and Don Ernesto part ways? Did the old man know he was taking the recipe to Canada? Or did my father steal it?"

My uncle's face has changed again. His brows have flatlined. The skin around his mouth is taut. "You should watch how you talk about your father, *buonanima.*"

He's definitely getting angry, and I'm definitely enjoying taking a run at him. "You know what just occurred to me? I've got subscribers in Italy. I should post about it on my channel, see if anyone knows this pastry from Naples called—"

"Leave it alone!" Dante slams his palm against the bar. For a moment all sound in the room stops, all eyes turn our way. I sit immobile. The violence of the sound, the humiliation, plays between my ears. I look up into the mirror. The Silver Fox is gone.

I think of D'Abruzzo staring at the briefcase. *There's a reason he put a lock on it.*

It's only at this moment that the idea comes to me; what I've been told about the past and what actually happened is not necessarily the same thing. And that, as far as family members go, Zio Dante is probably the least concerned about keeping that truth from me. "Why did my father leave Italy in the first place?"

Dante is about to answer, but I cut him off, just in case. "And don't tell me 'for a better life.'"

Twenty-Nine

Francesco, 1985

The Neapolitan calendar was decorated with a number of non-canonical celebrations, but the upcoming Feast of Garibaldi made Don Ernesto temperamental, which drove him to drink more than usual. At the end of his shift, Francesco found the baker asleep on a cot between the warm ovens. He left him there and went out through the front of the bakery to the piazza where merchants were decorating their storefronts in anticipation of the crowds that would come. The annual feast had risen to prominence after the Second World War once the blackshirts were gone. Even La Fraternità di Garibaldi, one of the most venerable old organizations in the city of Naples, would dust off their service baldrics and coat-of-arms to join the procession in the Mercato district.

As it had in the old days, the procession would end at the bakery, where the Father of the Fatherland had made his last documented appearance. The fraternity had long ago sent Don Ernesto a Tricolore, upon which was the fine needlepoint head of Garibaldi surrounded by a laurel wreath and flourished with the apothegm, *Dio e Popolo*. Each year the old man waffled over where to mount the flag, and inevitably he would drag in a ladder from the courtyard and hang it over the pastry counter. The hope was that after a brief salute, God and the People both would move along the counter and buy pastries to take home.

To meet demand, the don had installed an extra oven in the courtyard. Two new counter girls were brought on and taught how to make change and wrap pastries in anticipation of a line-up. And after seven months of training Francesco had, by the don's own admission, perfected the pastry's butter-crisp finish. Among the other bakers and staff, the housewives and children who came to the bakery, he was acknowledged as heir to the Garibaldi tradition. He'd received a written invitation to dine at the mayor's home during Carnevale. Even the hunchback, Scaletti, would leave Francesco his newspaper when he was done reading it.

Though his body had been toughened by work, his hands cured into leather balls, underneath Francesco had never been closer to anguish. He still hadn't told his family the truth. Each day since he'd walked out of the morgue classroom had been an opportunity to tell them he wasn't prepared to live their dream, but he let them slip away, one by one.

How could he change course now, when the women were prouder than ever of him? In their minds, he would be graduating as a real doctor at the end of the calendar year. Each month, he caught a train south to Palatino and spent the two-hour ride preparing himself with stories and lies of medical school acquaintances, of patients. He created exotic illnesses, miraculous recoveries, tragic deaths. He was glad they didn't have a television in the cottage because most of the stories were creative embellishments of the RAI program, *Un Dottore Nella Casa*.

Anxiety overtook him with increased frequency. Even though Don Ernesto's bakery had, for the past two years, served as a refuge, he had begun to question his mentor. Francesco saw how heavily the old man relied on his staff. Left to his own devices, he regularly burned the crostata and under-proofed the bread. He still drank until blacking out, or worse, stumbled out across the square on the arm of his hunchback, got in his car and veered up the mountainside to his home. The only thing he tended to with any consistency was the Garibaldi.

In Naples, the pastry was an institution. It didn't matter that the Garibaldi was the don's, Francesco didn't need creative accolades—he simply needed to be present at creation. He was realizing that he had no professional business ambition, that this would not be the generation in which his family left indentured servitude, and that he was fine with it.

But they would not be.

"Why are you still here?"

Francesco turned around. Don Ernesto had roused himself and stood in the doorway of the bakery. The old man looked like commemorative statuary. His hair had receded into a silver ring that he wore just above the ears like the *corona civica* of the Roman Senate. Beneath a filthy apron were shoes of soft leather. Francesco remembered his own father's hobnailed boots and how they sparked on the cobbles of Palatino.

"I need you back in the morning for deliveries. We have a new route."

"In the morning I have an appointment," Francesco reminded him. Although it was more of a reminder to himself, one that filled him with dread. "Scaletti can cover, no?"

"Of course, I'd forgotten." Don Ernesto stretched his tired chaff of a body. "Even the young deserve a break now and then."

"A medical appointment," Francesco corrected him. "Not a break."

Don Ernesto looked at him so carefully the young man was sure he could read through the lie. "Have a drink with me? Before you go."

Francesco sat down at the worktable and waited as the don brought out a bottle of grappa. "We would run out of Garibaldis in the first hour if it weren't for you," he said as he pulled up a stool. "You were made for this. How did we get by before?"

Francesco watched as the old man poured a few ounces of clear fluid into a finger bowl and a shot glass with a clear fissure down its length.

"My fondest wish, Franchi, is to stop all this business and go back to the Calabrian Sila. That's where my mother's people are from. There's nothing like mountain air when you're ready for the sunset."

"You're too young to retire," Francesco said, accepting the glass. But the labour in the bakery was intense; backs were strained, toes were crushed, strong hands were at a premium. Don Ernesto could carry out few of these functions now.

"Who said retire? I mean death."

"Birth and death are two events we cannot schedule for ourselves." Francesco caught the sobriety in his own voice and wondered how he'd come to sound like such an old man.

Don Ernesto was watching him, his pinky finger ringing the mouth of the bowl from which he sipped grappa as though it were steaming soup. "You came to me before you knew you were talented. All you had, I suspect, was the desire to create something?"

Francesco had better manners than to offer the self-aggrandizing response which his question seemed to be eliciting. So he drank and said nothing.

"You've been a good soldier to me," Don Ernesto said. "I think of you as a son. In that spirit I must tell you about something that weighs on my mind."

He had the spirit of an elegant drunk in his voice. Francesco wished he could say something to assuage the man's concerns—before these concerns were made known to him.

"Francesco, did you keep your promise to me? Did you tell your family you left school?"

He looked up. "Of course. Months ago."

Don Ernesto smiled. He raised an index finger and shook it gently. "We're similar, you and me. We don't want to disappoint people. But fabrications, they serve no one in the long run."

Francesco looked at the clock. Instead of the shame of being called out on a lie, he felt the low, mealy sensation of anger stirring. "If that's all, consider yourself free of the weight."

The old man looked at him for a moment. "Very well. My own truth, this time," he said. "Of when Garibaldi came to me."

Something loud rang inside of Francesco. "What about it?"

"Garibaldi did not appear as a man to be gazed upon by the living," Don Ernesto swivelled the cracked rim of Francesco's glass away before pouring another shot of firewater.

"He was a horrible spectre. The red shirt of the revolution—it was a white shirt soaked in blood. Behind the intelligent eyes was not compassion, but terror. Instead of kneeling in adoration, I fouled my own pants. You see, I was a wastrel when he came to me—not fit to be a soldier, a father, or husband. He did not tell me to make a tribute to my country. He came to show me how little I mattered."

"But he did come to you?" Francesco heard how his voice had

turned this into a question. He was looking at the old man across the worktable, but at the same time he was back in the basement morgue, watching the professor remove the lung from a corpse.

"He came. And then I woke up." The old man sat back on his stool and folded his hands in his lap. "It was a terrifying and glorious dream. One I spent months trying to re-enter. I looked around my rented room and asked, 'Where is Giuseppe Garibaldi now, eh? Where is the Sword of Italian Unification?'"

Francesco glanced around, noticing how dirty the corners of the bakery were. He saw the mess of pans that had accumulated in the wash basins.

Don Ernesto was pointing to the bottle in front of him. "In vino veritas, Francesco. I could not let the idea go. When I began to make money and important friends on the back of this lie, I said to myself, 'Well, I've turned my entire life around!' But look at me. I am still a drunk, still a wastrel."

"What are you saying to me?" Francesco asked.

"I didn't give you the recipe to hide behind. I gave it so you might take the path forward."

"I'm not a liar and not a wastrel."

The old man looked at him. "Not yet."

In the morning he waited on the platform at Napoli Centrale until he saw the little figure that was his mother debark the train. Francesco pressed his back against the stucco wall, full of a strange and shameful inertia. He loved his mother; she'd raised him singlehandedly after his father died, but there was nothing she believed in more fervently than her own will.

Francesco told himself to get in motion. He pressed off the wall, broke out into a wide smile and moved down the platform toward her.

"*Figlio mio!*" The little woman came and put her hands on his; they were like two small terns perched on his fingers. She kissed him on both cheeks. She was here for her annual visit with the cardiologist. Her frosted whip of hair was coiled and jabbed here and there with pins. It made her look frail, but Francesco knew the specialist would measure her arrhythmia, write her a prescription for medication and send her off with the assurance that she had another fifty years ahead of her.

"Look how handsome you've become."

"I was home to visit three weeks ago! Surely I'm the same," he said. But as he spoke, he noticed a crust of dried bread dough on his sleeve and felt a minor panic. He manoeuvred her to his left arm so that he could bury the dirty sleeve in his jacket pocket. "How are you and Lucia getting on? How are the Totis?"

"Crooks as usual," Maria replied. This was not an exaggeration. The family she'd spent the last twenty years working for were bookies, forgers and loan sharks, a family of professional thugs whose clientele list was said to represent a cross-section of southern Italian society.

"Luckily, they don't pay much attention to the old lady who keeps their beehives and weeds their orchards," Maria sighed as they walked toward the taxi stand. "Besides, a few more months won't kill us."

Francesco raised his hand to hail a car. "Oh no? What do you mean?"

Maria looked at him, then reached up and slapped him gently

on the cheek. "Soon we'll leave the cottage and move into town. You're going to have to live close to the hospital."

The doctor's office was close enough to the university that his mother, as she stepped out of the examination room, imbued with the fifty years of life the specialist had just issued her, decided she was due a tour.

Francesco looked at his watch and frowned. "We don't have time. You hate rushing for the train," he reminded her.

Maria threaded her arm in his. "God willing, I will be your very first patient, Francesco. And I'll never have occasion to come back to this armpit of a city. So show me your school."

As they walked along Corso Umberto I, Francesco forced an elasticity in his limbs which he hoped she would interpret as familiarity. He hadn't been on the campus in nearly two years. "This is the main administration," he told her, pointing to the triple-arched entrance of the university's Romanesque façade. "That is the bursar's office. Beyond those gates are the classrooms." He was keeping her safely on the opposite side of the street lined with shops and restaurants, hoping she wouldn't ask to see inside the buildings.

"It is grand, isn't it?" She stopped to admire the monumental façade that took up a whole city block, her nostrils flaring as though she were inhaling the architecture, or somehow was responsible for it. "I dislike the city, but it takes a city to house such a tremendous institution."

Francesco's tongue itched with irritation, though it was unclear to him just who he was irritated with. Don Ernesto's accusation yesterday haunted him in its accuracy.

He glanced at his watch. "Up ahead on Mezzocannone we can get a taxi to Napoli Centrale." He just wanted to put her on a train and send her home. Separate that life from this.

But his mother had turned and was staring at the trattoria a few doors away. "Francesco, that man is looking at us. Do you know him?"

He turned too. In front of the Caffè Tarantino stood Don Ernesto and the counter girl, laden with deliveries. The young woman was handing stacked pastry cartons to the barista in the doorway, but Don Ernesto met his eye. "Francesco!" he called.

"You know them?" his mother asked.

He shook his head.

"He just called your name."

"But I've never seen them before." Francesco gathered up something that passed as a smile and put a hand on his mother's back. "You know what? God willing, this is your last trip to Napoli." He barely waited for a break in traffic before ushering her across the street toward the university gates and away from Don Ernesto. "Let's see if we can't look inside."

Thirty

Sabine

Dante has forgotten about me. He sits hunched, an elbow on the bar and one foot on the ground, his empty snifter turned upside down. "If only Francesco went straight home the next night, once the Processione di Garibaldi is finished. Maybe none of this comes to be. But he cannot leave things alone. He has to be forgiven."

"Why?" I break into his thoughts. "What happened after the procession?"

My uncle sits up, frowning. He looks like he might grab my chin and give my head a shake. Instead, he reaches for the sheet of paper and shoves it at me. "Take this money I'm giving you, Sabine. In the morning say goodbye to your aunt and go back to Toronto. Just like you wanted, but richer."

I push as far away from him as I can on my stool without falling over. "What happened between my father and Don Ernesto?"

"You still ask questions like a foolish child," he says.

I can take his insults. "Tell me. What do I find at the end of the Garibaldi trail?"

Dante looks at me, the short skeins of muscle in his neck bulging. "You find that your father is a murderer."

Thirty-One

Francesco, 1985

The morning of the feast day the old man tore around the back room like the *levante* that brought clouds and rain. "Don Ernesto," Francesco called over the stack of pastry trays he was carrying to the wash, "can I talk to you for a minute?"

"We have a line fifty customers long out front and the procession hasn't even arrived." The red tendrils around Don Ernesto's nose dilated. "The last thing I have time for is a chat."

"Dottore," Scaletti said from his stool in the corner when Don Ernesto had flown from the room, "have you been a bad boy? Does Papà not want to talk to you?" The four other men in the back room who'd witnessed the exchange snickered.

Francesco dropped the trays into the wash station. He was sorry as soon as he'd done it. The clatter just punctuated his anger. He wasn't even sure what he wanted to say to Don Ernesto. Offer an apology? But for what? He had behaved childishly perhaps. With disrespect, for certain. But the don wasn't his father. He had no agency over him.

Francesco screwed the faucet handle the whole way until the sinks brimmed with scalding hot water and lye. Then he sank his hands in and began to scrub.

—

Once the bakery doors were locked, he bought a bottle of grappa and slipped in with the crowds of the night market. The air was redolent with putrefying greens and tanned leather, fresh basil, shit from the fields, urgency and sea air. It suited his mood. He drank straight from his bottle as he walked around the piazza, but the drink served only to heighten his senses and, as he approached the stretch of restaurants, he became convinced that it was his own body emitting these odors. There was a game of *calcio* being broadcast and some of the bars rolled large TV sets out front so patrons could sit and watch and lose count of the drinks they ordered. Though the procession had ended, many of the participants had lingered here in the piazza where the restaurants were open late. The Christian Democrat marching band was made conspicuous by their uniforms and the large brass tuba someone had propped up between chairs. There was a cleric or two in the crowd, plus the standard bearers. Members of La Fraternità di Garibaldi, who'd borne the palanquins of the Virgin and Garibaldi on their shoulders earlier, had had the good sense to return both statues to the church before joining the crowd.

Don Ernesto sat at the Caffè Mezzo-Mezzo with Scaletti and two of his bakers. He had put on the same straw hat and suspenders he'd worn the night he showed up at Francesco's flat, offering to teach him how to make the Garibaldi.

Now the old man's eyes widened as Francesco pulled up a fifth chair to their table. The others looked up at him with amusement that they made no move to disguise. It occurred to Francesco that they had always been laughing; he had just failed to notice.

"Someone invite you?" Scaletti asked.

"You don't have room for one more?" Francesco sat down. He had the idea that if he faced Don Ernesto's scorn now, everything would go back to normal.

"A table only has four sides, Rosetti," the hunchback said.

Don Ernesto was watching him. "Tell me, how did your mother enjoy her day in Napoli?"

Francesco didn't answer.

The trim little moustache danced drunkenly under the baker's nose. "Listen to this." The old man slapped the arms of the two men sitting closest to him. "I see this *papagallo* and his mother on the street while I'm making his deliveries for him. I'm five metres away, calling his name. He's looking right at me. What does he do?"

Francesco saw how his approach had been all wrong. First and foremost, Don Ernesto was not his father. He was a drinker with an ego that had been trammelled.

"He pretends not to know me! Rushes the old woman away in case I infect her."

"Well, Don Ernesto, he is *un dottore*." Scaletti smiled and scratched an armpit. "He knows the diseased like us can be dangerous."

The baker raised his glass and drank to these words.

"I'm sorry if I offended you, Don Ernesto," Francesco concentrated on ignoring the others at the table. "I didn't want to burden my mother with my circumstances."

The old man shoved his chair back and stood up. "Your circumstances? Have I done you a disservice by allowing you to work at my bakery?" The don's voice broke over the sound of the soccer game on the TV. People were turning to stare. Francesco looked around the piazza, wondering how to exit without humiliating himself further.

"I came to apologize—"

"Your apologies mean nothing to me." Don Ernesto interrupted. "What I care about is that my bread and pastries are made and my floor gets scrubbed. But I guess you're too good for that in the eyes of your *mammina*, eh?"

"Okay," Francesco rolled his large shoulders back. He rose slowly from the table, attempting to ballast the situation. "I see how things are. Maybe I'll talk to you tomorrow."

"There won't be any work for you tomorrow." Don Ernesto was gripping a shoulder of each of his bakers in order to keep steady. But both they and Scaletti were silent. The laughter had died from their eyes. "See if your mother wants you back. I hear the Toti family have made her their very own *reginella della montagna*."

Francesco lunged across the table. The old man had just called his mother "little queen of the mountain." He might as well have called her an old town prostitute. In some sped-up corner of his mind he watched himself plucking the old man's suspenders and crushing the ridiculous straw hat, but he stopped himself short of making contact. The old man's reflexes were both automatic and delayed. He jumped back at the exact moment a waitress carrying a tray of beer passed behind him. Don Ernesto slammed into her, sending the woman and her beverages crashing into the cobbles.

The entire square fell silent. Even the commentators on television seemed to go quiet while the bakers helped the woman off the ground. Don Ernesto leaned against the table. He looked at his protégé with confusion, then turned and walked away.

The rational side of Francesco's brain told him, *leave it alone.* You can't reason with a drunk. Besides, he had no reasonable argument to present anyway. But a moment later he was backing away from the table and following the old man.

Knowing that Scaletti and the others were watching him, he made his way through the crowd of tables and chairs with a palpable, bow-legged purpose. A man looking for horses to break. He trailed Don Ernesto down one of the narrow streets that funnelled from the piazza, keeping a dozen metres between them. It was a neighbourhood in decline. Many of the buildings here were left empty, the glass removed from their windows and replaced with pasteboard and masonry. The road was also in bad repair, full of loose stones. Given his drunken state, it was a miracle that Don Ernesto was still on his feet up ahead. A speeding Fiat swerved across the road and Francesco had to jump back between two parked scooters to avoid being hit. He watched his mentor pass a house stained by sea mold and disappear into a covered arcade. Francesco paused a moment before starting down the damp corridor. It was true that he was a coward who didn't want his mother to know the truth. But in that moment, he realized what was causing his strange sorrow. It was what the old man had confided in him. That there was no Garibaldi. That the spectre was a lie he'd enacted in effort to change his desperate situation. Was Francesco such a child that he needed to believe in these chimeras?

When he emerged, he saw Don Ernesto standing against a guard rail looking out over the Bay of Naples. Moon illuminated the harbour and beside him, a series of steep flagstone steps led down to the deserted wharf district.

"Don Ernesto?"

The old man spun around. He was always fastidious about his appearance at the bakery, but now his straw hat was gone. His shirt was untucked.

"You! What else do you want from me?"

Francesco stepped out of the darkness. "I came to explain myself. You were right—about my lie. It was disrespectful, what I did."

Don Ernesto regarded him impassively. "You think I care about your respect? About an introduction to you mother?"

Francesco took a step forward.

"I chose you as my successor. But you were a coward all this time."

"Why did you tell me about Garibaldi?"

The don looked at him, incredulous, his head wobbling unsteadily. "Did I offend you? I gave you my recipe, the keys to the kingdom."

Francesco thought about this for a moment. "It's true, you let me in. But the room was empty. The bakery was just a bakery."

"Of course it is! Fool. Did you expect the corpse on the mortuary table to reanimate as well?"

The old man took a step and his ankle twisted under his weight. His hand gripped at the guard rail, but Francesco saw he was in no state to be left alone. "Let me walk you back." He came forward slowly to show he was not a threat.

The don shook his head and took a proportionate step backward. "I made a mistake with you, Franchi. I thought you would do better than me."

Francesco had come as far as the metal rail. "Let's go back. I can drive you home."

"I built my entire life on falsehood." The don raised his hands to his head and smoothed down his hair. "Now I see it will continue. Tell me, what will you do with the Garibaldi?"

To avoid answering, Francesco reached for his arm. Don Ernesto pulled away from him, shuffling on the lip of flagstone stairs where his left foot found no purchase. His equilibrium was already impaired, and before Francesco could react, the old man tipped backwards. His hands flailed for the guardrail, but he'd already begun to tumble, palms up, useless.

For the second time in one night Francesco lunged for him. He was strong, but the old man's stout little frame was caught up in its own velocity, something Francesco could not predict and therefore could not outwit. It carried Don Ernesto headfirst down twelve stone steps, then left him on the landing in a crumpled heap.

"Ernesto!" Francesco would never know how long he stood immobile at the top of the stairs. How long it took to shake himself free of the torpor and gallop down to the bottom.

He kneeled beside the don. There was, miraculously, no blood. But the old man's head was turned at an unnatural angle and he'd landed with his left leg and right arm trapped beneath him. Francesco had trained as a doctor, but all of that knowledge vanished. He had to resist the urge to straighten out limbs, to align the neck and head and return normalcy to the body.

He moved around so he could see the man's face. His eyes were open. Was he breathing? The reeking proof of his own breath caught in the shell of the old man's ear and wafted back at him. He placed the palm of his hand over Don Ernesto's mouth and felt nothing. But his palms were hardened by work and it was a crude estimation. He placed his fingers on the temples. Don Ernesto's head felt like the skull of a plover, an origami of plates and fissures. His pupils were wide in the dim light, his eyes bulging. They reminded Francesco of black buttons, sewn down with thick, looping stitches.

Francesco kneeled closer. Placed his ear against the man's chest. For a full minute he leaned hunched like that, listening. Sometimes he was convinced he heard a wild heartbeat, just to realize a moment later it was his own. Finally, his legs caved under him. He sat down hard and fixated on a point of light in the harbour.

When he turned back, the old man's face had changed. The stern little bones of his nose and chin had turned to paper. His eyes were open, but the light was gone.

Thirty-Two

Sabine

The moonlight stays with me all night. I don't dream but I wake up over and over, wrestling to rid myself of the old man's face. On my third attempt I get out of the bed and go to the hotel room window. I think of my uncle's words. His description of the moon over the water all those years ago is so much like what I see tonight over the lake that I can't say for certain which part of the story he's told me and which part I filled in myself. I think of my father, who I never knew. Who I never suspected capable of such strange depths. I see him crouched in a stinking harbour with blood on his hands. The very same man who'd rejected the responsibility of life and death finds it forced on him nonetheless. I think of how one falsehood leads to another, and another. Leads to this moment now. I think these things and I don't sleep again.

When I get to the rental car in the morning, I find Wanda and Paul already in it.

"What are you doing here?" I ask, opening the door. I expect this sort of efficiency from them on workdays, but today it annoys me. "I'm going to my aunt's house."

"We know that." Wanda is in the passenger seat. She reaches over and clips her seat belt defiantly. "We're coming with you."

I'm holding the stupid briefcase. I'm not sure why I brought it except that it suddenly seems to hold so much more than a recipe. I get behind the wheel and glance at Paul in the back seat. "You want to film?" I ask.

"It's our job, isn't it?" Wanda answers for him. "Unless you've fired us?" She smooths a braid over her shoulder, and I notice her fingernails have been bitten down considerably, the polish chipped and cuticles raw.

I sigh, stowing the briefcase by her feet. I'm finding it especially difficult this morning to pivot between her emotions and my own. "I just don't know how necessary it is anymore. To get more footage."

"You mean, because Netflix green-lit you, you feel it's no longer necessary to provide your subscribers with content?"

I consider her words and decide it's best not to answer. Instead, I feel around my pockets for the key fob.

Wanda hands it to me without making eye contact. Then she spreads her chewed-up fingernails on her lap, as if daring me to comment. "What's in the briefcase?"

"The Persian recipe." I start up the car, lower the windows and let the lake breeze flow through. It's hard to breathe with so many bodies in the car. Wanda and Paul. My father, Don Ernesto. "My father left me his half of the bakery. The recipe goes with it."

"Congratulations." She nudges the metal case with her foot as if to see if it's awake, then crosses her legs. "Have you thought over what we talked about yesterday?"

I pull out of the parking lot. "Sure."

"Good." Wanda raises her left hand and chews at the pinky nail. "And what is your view of the situation?"

I try to control my breathing. I've read that for some people, sociopaths in particular, empathy has to be learned. In the case of Wanda, I am clearly the sociopath because it's so difficult at times to see things from her perspective. Yesterday I was sympathetic. But today, her peevishness over losing co-star status leaves me cold. I'm one step away from my dream career, from headliner status, from the sort of relative professional security that I have never known in my life. And she refuses to just let me have it. I want to remind her that I'm her boss, that she—just like Paul—is a gun for hire. But I know that in truth, we are much more deeply entwined.

"Collette says she can get on the phone with us tomorrow," I tell her, and make a mental note to actually arrange this call with Collette.

"I said today!"

"It's the soonest she can do. Hack her calendar if you don't believe me," I bluff. "We can tell her all about your reservations with the—"

"They're not *my* reservations, Sabine. They're *our* deal-breakers."

"Okay," I say in my calmest voice. "That's what we're going to say to Collette. She's the best in the business. We're going to get her to sort this all out before we sign anything."

My eyes are on the road but from the corner of my eye I see Wanda turn to look at me for the first time.

"You mean it?"

I nod, I even slap the wheel for added emphasis. And when she curls up her fingers and buries them in her pockets, I know I've bought some time to figure out what might persuade her to let me do the show without her.

Thirty-Three

Wanda

The aunt is waiting for us in full make-up, hair curled, and a frilly apron wrapped around her small waist. "I did not think you are all coming," she lies.

"Of course," I tell her. "You're perfect for our show."

"Now you will get a real lesson in Italian food!" She kisses me on both cheeks with a magnanimity that truly personifies "turning it on for the camera." But then I detect the alcohol on her breath and the cheery welcome makes sense. I don't dare judge; after all, I know a thing or two about processing grief.

Paul skirts around us, setting up the equipment in Stella's kitchen. "Let's just use a couple of space lights," he says. "We don't want it to look too premium."

He's right. The bit from the living room has been tracking well. People bought Sabine's plight and I think the handheld aspect played a big role. I'm all for these caught-on-film, largely unscripted pieces in combination with our sponsored segments.

While we're getting ready to shoot, I don't ask myself what I'm doing here. The mission is always just the next shot, the next set-up, the next post to feed the seemingly endless appetite of our followers. If I stop what I'm doing I become another person. Addled and pacing, worried about what Sabine will say to Collette. That she won't be able to get through to her.

"Where do you want me to stand?" Stella asks as I arrange the canister of flour, the eggs and the butter for the bomboloni on the kitchen island. "Beside Sabine?"

I glance at Sabine who's waiting for the espresso to percolate as though her life depends on it. "She'll come in and out," I say. "Like your helper. You move around however you need to. Paul knows how to get the right angles."

Stella nods and dips beneath the island. When she emerges it's with a bottle of vermouth. She unscrews the top and pours a generous amount into each of our espresso cups. Sabine lifts the percolator and drizzles a bit of the steaming black chaser over the booze.

"Okay, Zia. Ready to get famous?"

Bomboloni are the original deep-fried doughnut hole, popular in the overly indulgent pre-Lenten season. They are sprinkled with sugar, filled with cream and best served warm. I take notes on my phone in order to add a succinct summary at the head of the post.

Stella is a champion on camera, with an instinctive sense of when to make eye contact, when to explain her technique of injecting *crema pasticcera* into the small balls of dough, and when to simply let the audience follow. Sabine's role is kept to that of host. She throws questions to the aunt when a voice-over is lacking, and steps clear out of the way when it's time to deep fry the round fritters. It's a simple little recipe and to cap the segment we have the two women seated at the island behind a plate of sugar-kissed bomboloni. The effect is that of two morning show anchors gossiping over coffee.

"The taste is the Italy I remember from childhood," Sabine lies, and bites through the sugary crust to reveal the cream silk interior. She was four years old the last time she was in Italy.

"Your father loved these." The aunt's smile wobbles slightly. She raises her tiny espresso cup which is now pure vermouth. "To Francesco and Italia," she says.

When we cut, Sabine's face turns off. She slides off her stool and wanders around the peripheries of the kitchen as though seeing it for the first time. She glances at her own cookbooks on the buffet, then moves on to a collection of plates commemorating Pope John Paul II's visit to Canada.

Stella unties her apron, carefully folds it into a square, and turns to her niece. "So, is your uncle going to pay you a visit today?"

"He already did." Sabine sits down at the kitchen table. "He made me an offer."

"He wastes no time." Stella opens the cupboard as though to return the bottle of vermouth, then changes her mind and brings it to the kitchen table. "But is his offer good for the business?"

Sabine shrugs. "This is a lot to have dumped on me at once."

The aunt puts the bottle down with a strong thud and then sits. "Then let me make it easy."

"Be my guest."

"Sell the bakery to me and Enzo."

Sabine looks at her. Then she reaches for the vermouth, unscrews the top and places it on the table where, I have a feeling, it will remain.

"Your uncle offers you three hundred thousand?"

"How do you know that?"

"We still have the same accounts. When I was at the bank this morning I saw he moved some money." The aunt is sitting erect, her face bright, her voice nearly strident with pride. "Sabine, I did a reverse mortgage on the house. I will give you four hundred thousand over two years for the bakery your father built with blood and sweat."

The niece sits back, her face perplexed. "Why?"

"For Enzo!" Stella throws her hands in the air. "He is never free as long as he works for his father. If he is a partner, Dante cannot control him."

Sabine's lashes flutter for a moment. "So, what you're asking," she begins slowly, "is for me to take your house out from under you?"

"It's just a mortgage," the aunt says naïvely. "Nobody takes the house from me."

"You don't have an income, Zia. I can't take your only investment."

"When Enzo is a partner, he can marry who he wants. He can have children. I can become a grandmother. There is some reason for me to go on living."

Sabine shakes her head. "I don't want to get involved in your family business."

"Enzo is an excellent baker. We will honour your father each day."

Sabine should take the offer. Her life may look like a shiny round orb from the outside, but women her age with no fixed income are just disasters waiting to happen. I watch as she looks around the Tuscan-inspired kitchen, her eyes coming to rest on the briefcase that she set near the back door. "And what about the Persian recipe?"

"What about it?"

"Dante was trying to get my father to sell it to some company last year. I have an idea what he wants to do with it. What will you do?"

The aunt unfolds her hands. "Who tells you Dante is trying to sell it?"

"D'Abruzzo."

Stella nods slowly. "Don't pay attention to that. Your uncle's head is full of fantasies. He thinks he's going to get rich since the day I met him." She leans forward conspiratorially. "The business is of value, but the recipe is worth nothing."

"I used to think so too," Sabine says. "Except he told me an interesting story last night. About the baker my father used to work for in Italy?"

Stella's face sharpens.

"And the Garibaldi. And the real reason my father came to be here in Canada." Sabine picks up the vermouth cap, rolls it between her fingers. "Zia, is it true my father was wanted for murder?"

Murder? Paul looks up from a tripod stand he's folding into submission. His eyes go to the camera that he's placed on the kitchen counter, then to Sabine. As I watch, she ever so slightly shakes her head at him. Without even looking my way, Paul turns back to the tripod.

"I'm sorry, *figlia mia*." Stella's eyes are shimmering at the bottom of a pool of tears. "It's a terrible history."

Sabine inhales deeply. "Why didn't anyone tell me?"

"Tell you? I wish to God you never have to learn it."

I stare daggers at Paul, but he's busy looping extension cords around his forearm. The camera remains out of reach on the counter.

"This is why he didn't come back to Italy? When my mother died."

The tears have broken and streak down Stella's face. "Yes," she says. "He could never go back to Italy."

"Tell me what happened."

The aunt says nothing.

"He's safe now, you know." Sabine reaches across the table and squeezes her hand. I see her rake her teeth over her bottom lip before delivering the words the other woman needs to hear. "He's safe in the arms of Jesus."

Stella nods.

"No one can come after him now, right?"

The aunt buries her face in her hand.

"Then tell me what happened after Don Ernesto fell."

I give up on Paul and sit at the island, right in front of the plate of bomboloni.

"What happens?" Stella's face has turned the colour of birch bark. "He runs away. He wasn't thinking right. Your father took the train home to Palatino that very night—it was stupidity or cowardice, I don't know. Maybe I would do the same thing. That night of the procession, everyone sees him chasing after Don Ernesto. The old man was a drunk, but your father knew he would be blamed."

"But it was an accident," Sabine says.

"How could he prove that? Of course, by running away, it made him guilty. Who would stand by him after that?" Stella pulls the vermouth toward her, jiggles the bottle but finds it empty. "It was your grandmother who convinced him to come here to Canada. 'You did nothing, you saw nothing,' she tells your father. 'You go visit your cousin Dante in Canada and you forget about Don Ernesto.'"

Sabine's face grows ruddy with this information. "So, just like that, he comes to Canada and starts a new life? What about my mother? He just left his wife?"

I don't know if Sabine sees it, but there's real hesitancy on the aunt's part to divulge information. I can't tell if it's because she's overwhelmed by the history herself, or because she's deciding, on the spot, what to relinquish and what to hold back.

"What nobody knows yet, Sabine, is that your mother is pregnant. It probably doesn't change anything even if he knows. Nobody is thinking straight, you understand? He gets on an airplane the next day and arrives to us a mess. We pick him up at the airport and he's wearing the same clothes for two days. He does nothing but sit in his room for a month." Stella glances at the ceiling. "In Napoli and in Palatino the carabinieri are everyday questioning, searching his apartment, your grandmother's house. The women think he's studying medicine to be a doctor. The police tell them no, he is a baker, *un manipolatore* with no further use for Don Ernesto once he gives to him that cursed recipe. And we sit here with Francesco thinking any moment they find him."

"And no one did?"

There's another pause before Stella picks up the storyline. "Your grandmother, she is a caretaker for the Toti family for many years. You know who they were? Here they call them mafia. Two months after your father arrives, we get an envelope to our door. Working papers, you know? For the name Francis Rose. Through a Toti *consigliore* in Napoli your grandmother makes Francesco Rosetti . . . disappear."

Sabine stares at her hands as this invisible piece of the past falls into place. "What kind of life did he live here?"

"One of falsehood."

"So Zio Dante got him a job at Bennett's Bakery?"

The aunt nods.

Sabine gets up and walks to the window where a jaybird sits perched on the sill. "And this is where the Garibaldi became the Persian? Why would he use that recipe in his new life?"

"Kindness," the aunt says.

"Kindness?" Sabine wraps on the window, startling the bird into flight.

"Okay, stupidity."

Thirty-Four

Francis, 1985

"We need a night baker." Arthur Bennett walked quickly, the papers that Francis had brought in case of a language mix-up fluttering from his clipboard. "Shift starts at five p.m., goes till five a.m. and includes clean up." He paused to make sure the young man was following. "We'll talk as we walk, yeah? There's no sitting down in this job."

"*Sì, sì*. I can do. No problem." Francis kept up; he'd spent two years in Don Ernesto's bakery and hadn't set his backside down once. Why would he start now?

"By the time the rest of the world wakes up you'll have already made two hundred loaves of bread." Bennett pointed out a line of mixers. "I need a fellow to operate each step here."

The young man was impressed. The stainless-steel vats with their interchangeable paddles and blades eliminated the grunt work. Although Don Ernesto's bakery was fully automated, the machinery could only work small batches at a time. Here, in a room that seemed as large as the airport arrivals hall, were wire whips and spiral dough hooks large enough to disembowel an elephant.

"Where'd you get your training, uh ... Francis?" Bennett glanced down at the clipboard.

"Italia."

"Where in Italy, I mean? Where'd you learn to make bread?"

Francis stopped. He was unable to commit Don Ernesto's name to paper.

"You do know how to make bread, right?" Bennett sighed. "We need an experienced baker—not to teach a baker."

Francis nodded.

"*NO—TEACH—THE BAKER,*" Bennett said loudly, as though the young man suffered a hearing ailment.

"*Sì, sì.* In Italia, I work in the bakery, I make the bread."

"That's what your cousin said, Francis. That's why you're here. But Dante talks a lot, you know? We deal in mass bread—*commercial.*"

It wasn't the first time Francis felt frustration inch up his neck. He'd had some English training that first year at the university, but the rest he'd picked up from television. It was no surprise that he was unable to express himself in detail.

"Not a couple loaves on Sunday," Bennett continued. "I need a man to take over the whole night shift on his own."

"Okay, I do." He bowed, then instantly regretted the gesture. This was a simple exchange: labour for money. Not extreme gratitude.

Bennett put down his clipboard in order to heave a sack of flour into a mixer. Francis watched him for a moment, then stepped up, took the sack from Bennett's shoulder. "I make it just how you want."

The older man allowed him to tilt the sack into the mixer, then leaned over to inspect as his steady pour disappeared into the machine's centripetal swallow. "I don't want to be down here all night. I have other responsibilities, yeah?"

Francis shook out the corners of the sack and then folded it carefully.

"Okay, let's keep walking." The man pointed in the direction of a metal staircase.

This Bennett didn't look like any baker Francis knew. Even Don Ernesto, who'd been small, had a stout aspect. There was nothing potent in this man's stature. He might have been anywhere between fifty and sixty and looked like a bundle of kindling held together by cobwebs.

"I'm working on the pastries. *PASTRY*? Sweets? *Dolci*, I think, in your language?" He surprised the younger man by ascending the staircase two at a time. "Quality pastry is essential to the status of a bakery. Of course there are some people who think I'm better off just churning out white loaf, getting more contracts. I've got a wife who lobbies for bread." Bennett shook his head. "How do you explain creativity to a philistine?"

Francis started up the stairwell behind him, understanding neither the question nor its rhetorical nature. Halfway up, he could see the massive metal ceiling joists. They were the same cold steel as the northern lakes. Then, a step later, the steep angles of the oiled wooden rafters came into view, as though the architect had looked to the pyramid of treetops for inspiration.

"The truth is, I've been experimenting." Bennett grabbed his arm and pulled him up the remaining steps. "I've created a new sort of process for pastry. Started with the dough—an egg and yeast formula. Years of trial and error—ten or so—and I'm nearly there."

The attic was used to store pallets of sugar, but it also housed Bennett's office. Beneath the two dormers, which were punched out of the sloped ceiling, stood a desk heaped with aluminum braziers, stockpots with spigots, cones of twine, rolling pins chiselled to leave impressions of eyelets, angel hair, or fleur-de-lis in rolled fondant and gum paste. There was an overhead light dangling by the desk, but Francis felt in this attic the darkness of the smithy.

"I looked into it, how to file for the patent and everything." Bennett approached the desk. On its surface was a plate with a glass dome that Francis hadn't seen for the clinker and ash. Beneath the dome, a golden bun.

For a moment he felt borne up on a great wave of astonishment. Francis took a step back. Could it be? Had the Garibaldi boarded the flight with him in Napoli? Followed him to Bennett's Bakery in Thunder Bay, Ontario?

The man reached for the dome and raised the lid. "I don't mean to get ahead of myself, but I think this is going to change the world." He lifted the plate and held it out with religious ceremony. "I call it the Pershing."

The younger man felt the adenoidal pinch in his throat release; the sudden return of oxygen rich air was dizzying. It wasn't the Garibaldi after all. Bennett's creation was a tight snail, wound around a core, approximately one-half the size of Don Ernesto's sigma knot. It was the same russet colour, though, and given the distortion of the glass dome, he saw how he might have been mistaken.

Francis's fingers trembled as he accepted it. Against the Wedgwood-blue hatchings of the plate, his hands were those of a peasant. He picked up the Pershing, ten years in the making, and was surprised by its weight. A mere ounce or so, though he'd expected the heft of a cake doughnut. Bennett took a step back and tipped his chin, indicating to Francis that he should bring it to his mouth. His eyes were moist.

Francis bit and chewed. He'd tasted cinnamon for the first time as an adult. The warmth of it was an intrusion that he distrusted. But as he turned the soft dough on his tongue, he saw that this job offer hinged on his response. He needed the work, he needed to start sending money home and to pay Dante and Stella for his room.

And yet, he could not give credit where none was due.

"Is nothing special," he said to Bennett.

The older man made a choking sound in his throat.

"But you put the cream over, no?" After all, there were to Francis's knowledge only a handful of things that couldn't be fixed. "*Mettere la crema* on top?"

Art took a step toward him. For a second Francis thought he might have to fend off slender white fists. But Bennett just clasped him at the shoulders.

"You're right." He sobbed a faint vanilla essence. "It's no good. All this time and it's no good."

This was a sort of anguish Francis understood—a distress that had nothing to do with poverty, death or women. Whose tortured disquiet was caused by an idea, an *ossessione*. But to spend ten years on one pastry—imagine!

When Art Bennett looked up again, the dwindling light cast an oxidized patina across his cheek. He collected himself and smoothed his apron. "So, then, Francis. You'll start tonight?"

Bennett, Francis would learn, was a war buff who carried around a childhood obsession with General John J. Pershing. Pershing was the commander in chief of the American Expeditionary Force in

World War I and, thanks to his overseas efforts, the thrilling the-
atre of war was, for the first time, brought to the wider world,
turning it into a spectator sport for young men. With Black
Jack Pershing there was enough guts and glory to fill elemen-
tary school children's scribblers and keep men like Art Bennett
dreaming. He wished to make some tribute to him.

"A cinnamon fritter, perhaps. A pastry with a story. I'll call
it the Pershing," Art had told his new wife when he toured her
around his bakery on Memorial Avenue. "Something with frills
and reason."

"You're better off making bread than selling doughnuts,"
Mrs. Bennett replied. "Bread puts food on the table."

"It's not a doughnut," he told her. "It's a pastry."

From that very first day, it was apparent to Francis that the
Pershing was Bennett's deepest plight. The baker suffered the particular misery of the artist whose work couldn't quite catch up to
his ambition. In the year that followed, Francis made every excuse
to go up to the attic and check on the soft bun under glass. Every
few days, Art made a new prototype, slid it under the domed plate
and stared down as some god might have through the oculus of
the Roman Pantheon. He hadn't been able to perfect the dough
which hovered somewhere between cake and doughnut, and
being a purist, he'd rejected the idea of an icing.

"Like putting lipstick on a pig," Arthur said one day when
Francis found him sitting at his desk holding his grey head up by
the ears. "I'm all out of reasonable ideas. In the literary arts, one
might call this 'writer's block.'"

Francis pointed toward the desk. "You mean the Persian?"

Bennett let go of one ear. The cartilage held its fold like a crimp in a buttered furl of strudel dough. "Persh-ing. You bit off the *g*."

"Easier to say that way."

"Young man. You won't get anywhere with shortcuts."

Thirty-Five

Sabine

"General John J. Pershing?" I slap the kitchen table. "Dante told me he named it after the movie, *Ali Baba and the Forty Thieves*."

Zia Stella wrings a dishcloth in the sink and shakes her head. "And you want to sell your father's greatest achievement to that liar?"

"To be fair, this Pershing doesn't sound anything like the Garibaldi," Wanda says licking powdered sugar from her fingers. She and Paul are seated at the island, polishing off the plate of bomboloni.

"I am coming to that," Stella says as she returns to the table and begins wiping figure eights on the clean surface. "In the early days, Francesco *è disperato* when he thinks of the old country. He curses what Don Ernesto did to him, then a moment later he curses what he did to the old man. Only when he is working— busy—he forgets.

"It takes many months, but Francesco comes to run the night shift at Bennett's Bakery. He enjoys the labour, the responsibility. Bennett's is more *moderna* than Don Ernesto's, but Francesco's judgement is still required at every turn, and in this he finds a calm."

My aunt makes a second pass with the dishcloth, "By then he learns you would be coming into this world, Sabine. And there was no greater *motivazione* than that."

I fold my arms across my chest. "Are you saying he remade the Garibaldi for me?"

She nods. "For your family. He says to Dante, if we put our money together, could we not buy the bakery? They would be padrones, owners. In time they could bring in more money than they did as labourers. It was your father's greatest wish, Sabine, to bring you over from Italia."

But my aunt's not looking at me while she says this. Instead she puts one hand at the edge of the table and into its cup sweeps invisible crumbs.

Thirty-Six

Francis, 1986

O ften, when the attic was empty, Francis visited the Pershing under its glass dome.

One day, nearly a year into his employment, he brought up a broom and began manoeuvring it around the pallets, sweeping up a renegade trail of sugar. In addition to his bread duties, he was learning the ways of the American pastry. He always remembered how Don Ernesto had drawn a line between the cool artisan of the patisserie and the hot brute who toiled in the boulangerie. Art Bennett had a similar perspective and had realized that in Francis, he had an eager student. A bread maker with a sweet tooth lodged in his heart who was worthy of his tutelage. Arthur had given birth to the Lemon Basket, to which Stella would later add a strawberry and rename the Butterfly. He'd snapped out the perfect Coconut Ring with the rim of a water glass, and taught Francis how to take the classic Italian sfogliatella, flatten it, and call it a lobster tail. Even the regional cream-pot delight, the Sally Ann, born of Bennett's hand, was passed along to Francis once his compulsory duties were through.

Now he swept carefully around Bennett's desk. It was the usual headache of invoices and ledgers. Francis couldn't help but notice the numbers and balances, some of which were circled in red pencil. It was Dante who first told him how close the bakery was to bankruptcy. His cousin had heard it from the machinery repairmen who grumbled about how long it was taking Bennett to pay them. The rumour seemed to build after that. When Francis rode the service elevator up with the men from Ogilvie Flour to make sure the regular, enriched, and pastry sacks were stacked apart, they said if he knew what was good for him, he'd look for work elsewhere.

The Pershing sat in its usual spot, on a corner of table, under the glass dome. Francis had been mistaken the first time he'd told Bennett there was nothing special about the Pershing; he hadn't known anything about the process. Since then, he learned that Art used a yeast-leavened dough similar to bread as a base, coiled it to resemble a cinnamon bun, and then deep-fried it like a dough-nut. This sort of interdisciplinary handling was unheard of and helped explain why the Pershing tasted like a bunched-up Kleenex. But why a baker like Art, skilled in the popular dough and batter processes, had choked on the recipe for so long—Francis could not imagine.

The young man leaned the broom against the desk and lifted the glass dome. The Pershing still weighed a few ounces. He raised it to his mouth, took a bite, examined the cross section, chewed slowly, considered things. There was a resemblance he'd noted from the beginning. But just as obvious were the differ-ences. Don Ernesto had baked a spiced butter inlay right into the dough, whereas Bennett sprinkled his with cinnamon, then rolled the sticky sheet like a rug and lopped it into buns. The tight coil was necessary to prevent the pastry from coming apart in the deep fryer. The Garibaldi, which cooked in the oven, was formed into a looser, figure-eight weave. Don Ernesto knew that when baked at the correct temperature, the butter sealed within the Garibaldi's seams would steam the dough and cause the laminated layers to puff and separate.

Francis respected the deep fryer for its incredible cooking speed and ensuing flavour, but submerging Don Ernesto's dough in oil would be messy business, leaving him with a sodden lump of grease. He ate the rest of the Pershing. There might be a way. What if he could manage to modify the dough? What if he used Don Ernesto's recipe for the Garibaldi as a base? If it was going to make it through the deep fryer, the coil would have to be tight like the Pershing, but the dough would have to carry the near-savoury and layered quality of the Garibaldi.

Up until now, Francis had done his best to guard against self-betrayals. He hadn't the heart or stamina to revive a pastry that only reminded him of all the things he'd lost. For the longest time he'd convinced himself that the recipe had died that night with Don Ernesto.

But his thoughts were changing. He was changing. An ocean, a language and a culture were between him and the past. He'd always carry the sorrow and guilt he felt over Don Ernesto, but he had a living family to support, a household to contribute to, and a future to plan for.

Though he was not a businessman by nature and did not delight in transactions the way his cousin Dante did, it was clear to Francis that Bennett desperately needed the sort of cash infusion that a partner could bring. Much better if it was someone who could match his craftsmanship while not being taken for a ride by creative fancy. Arthur might be amenable to the idea. He hadn't started a bakery so he could calculate numbers at the end of the day. Francis understood something about his boss;

what he needed to survive and his reason for living were two different things.

Francis just happened to be the man who could provide both.

He lowered the glass dome, spun it carefully on the empty plate as though to summon inspiration, as though to summon Don Ernesto. He wanted to ask his old father figure how to proceed. He wanted the implicit understanding that passed between men who did what they had to do to survive. But the don was in the unseeing place. And even if he were alive, Frances had failed him. A fact from which he would never recover.

It came out pink. Back in Napoli, the men he worked with would have found the colour to be a handicap, but Francis embraced the hue as a tribute to the livelier tastes of his adoptive country. He knew something of the American preference for tart raspberries and strawberries with their pitted, showy flesh to the dusty figs and pears of the old world. Francis made a berry compote, laced it heavily with cinnamon—for he was anxious that Art Bennett recognize his original vision in the creation—blended it with butter and watched it thicken into a pleasing, pink *beurrage*. Where Art's cinnamon paste had been too austere, the berries infused moisture through the inner layers of the laminated dough, giving it the surprising pink hue.

Before he could fold this new inlay into the *détrempe*, he had to alter the composition of the laminated dough itself. Each day, after working at Bennett's Bakery, he sat hunched in Stella's basement kitchen, surrounded by the tools and instruments of alchemy. A scale and flask, a burner, mortar and pestle, two crucibles, a glass-bottom dish and several other bits from a child's chemistry kit he'd bought at Zellers. It took weeks to perfect the ratio of flour, yeast and cream to ensure the dough could withstand Bennett's deep fryer.

Once the adjustments held, Francis began the process his old master, Don Ernesto, had taught him, utilizing the "roll-in" method with its sequences of folding and chilling. Then he settled on the tight single-coil formation and brushed it with a soft pink icing to compliment the blush radiating from the centre.

Often during this process he thought of his apprenticeship to the Garibaldi and wondered what the devil was he playing at here. But he reminded himself that many of his countrymen had come over for a better life, bringing with them the tools of their trade. Did farriers and masons cry every time they had to pick up an anvil or trowel? Besides, the Garibaldi had not been given to him for free. He'd paid for it with his whole identity.

Francis had weighed the situation correctly. A short month later, in exchange for the contents of his and Dante's bank accounts and the completed recipe that had eluded Arthur for over a decade, the cousins extracted for themselves a 50 percent share of Bennett's Bakery.

Thirty-Seven

Sabine

That night, after entering a dozen different combinations into the attaché case locks, it dawns on me that I'm going about this all wrong. I crawl over to the minibar and feel around the top for the corkscrew. Part of me knows the answers I want aren't inside the case. But the other part—the large, angry part—refuses to be shut out like this any further.

"Open sesame," I tell the briefcase and jam the pointed tip of the corkscrew into a lock. I twist it with one hand while depressing the button with the other.

Nothing. The lock remains solid, impervious even, and I end up throwing the corkscrew across the room.

The fact that my father was a fugitive helps explain why there was no one there to rescue us when my mother got sick. It might also explain why it took so long to bring my grandmother and me to Canada. Maybe he was waiting for the trail to go cold.

What it doesn't explain is why he'd snapped up a new wife so quickly. Why he never once spoke to me about my mother. Why, in my memory, the most basic fatherly gesture he'd ever made was later rescinded.

The last day that I reign as Persian Princess seems to me the last day of childhood. I get out of the van, my costume torn and dirty, my forehead bleeding, and follow him inside the house. It is one of the rare occasions when Julia is sitting in the living room, flipping through a magazine, no doubt comparing her life to those pictured in its pages.

"What happened?" She's looking at me but addressing my father, and I know better than to answer.

"An accident." He takes his bloody handkerchief from my hand, folds it to a clean patch and presses it to my forehead again.

"Oh," Julia says, and turns back to her magazine.

I will remember this moment, the two of us standing there on the expensive hallway carpet, staring into the living room as though we are hired help.

My father breathes deeply. "Julia!"

She looks up again, this time startled by his tone.

"What do I use? She is bleeding."

My stepmother throws the magazine on the coffee table and stands up. "I have peroxide in my bathroom." I smell her perfume as she swishes past us to the staircase. I take hold of the handkerchief and begin to follow her up the stairs.

Julia stops and turns around.

"You can wait here," she says.

When I go to bed that night, I hurt all over. From the still undiscovered broken rib, from the cut on my forehead, and from Julia's words. The one thing that is okay—the one thing that glows—is the way my father took care of me. He swabbed my forehead with cotton, his face grim. I secretly hope it will leave a scar to show him that I am human, that he still needs to pay attention to me. It will be a reminder of what I had done for the bakery business that means so much to him.

I am in my little pink bed, when I hear voices outside my door.

"You can't sleep or what?"

Through the slit of my eyes, I see my father and grandmother in the doorway. They have both come to check on me. My nonna is holding a water glass in which, I know, are her dentures. Without the frame of her teeth, her mouth is a collapsed soufflé and her words have none of their fiery articulation. A couple of years later, when she suffers her last stroke, my father will wrap her dentures in a handkerchief and bring them to the undertaker.

Now he follows her into the bedroom and stands at the foot of the little bed. "I would sleep if my wife would let me into our bedroom," he tells her in their Campanian dialect.

"Your father wouldn't have let me get away with that business." My grandmother shrugs. "Things must work differently here between a man and a wife."

"She says it looks bad for the business that we let her go out dressed like that. Stella should have stopped with this princess garbage a long time ago."

"At least Stella is more like a mother." Nonna hands him the denture glass and picks up the coverlet that I'd kicked to the floor. "If Julia loves you, she should love your daughter."

It is strange and thrilling to hear my grandmother talk this way about Julia. And oddly gratifying to learn I haven't been making things up—my stepmother really doesn't care for me.

"Julia is not strong of mind," I hear my father say in his wife's defence.

"She's strong enough, alright. She is just unwilling." My grandmother snaps the blanket over the foot of the narrow bed with the same agile force taught in the army.

"And what should I do about that? She wasn't given the choice of whether she wanted to be a mother."

I hear the old woman punch a spare pillow into shape instead. "Most women are not."

Still holding the water glass, my father sits down on the little bed. I feel the mattress sink near my feet but keep my eyes closed. "Mamma, you made a decision a long time ago that affects everything we do today. Sometimes I wonder—"

"You wonder what?"

"Who you did it for?"

I squint again in the darkness and see him pick up a stuffed rabbit from the bed. What did my grandmother do?

"For you, Francesco! Who else? Your family should be together. And this child is your family. Your blood. That woman upstairs is not."

"It's not right." He throws the rabbit back on the bed.

Nonna is silent for a moment. "How was I to know you had a frigid wife?"

"You put me in an impossible position." He stands up suddenly, my whole body bounces as the springs uncoil but I try to lie still. My heart is pounding.

"And you put me in one twelve years ago! Have you thought of that?" My grandmother's voice flares and then drops. "Should I have left the child behind in Italy, Francesco? To be raised by nuns?"

My father hands her back the glass. "You know very well that neither one of you should have come."

Thirty-Eight

Sabine

It's Monday afternoon by the time Collette can get on a call with us. I realize things are going to go downhill the moment she answers her phone.

"Collette Blanche—Holland Weiss Fortitude," she snaps, although she knows it's Wanda's number.

"It's Sabine," I say quickly, glancing at Wanda across the room. She's leaning against the dresser, her arms folded, hair tied into a top knot. I know she expects me to lead the conversation, to strong-arm Collette into meeting her demands. To that end I did send her a note ahead of time, reiterating how important it is that we listen to Wanda, see things from her perspective, try to find a solution. Collette never wrote back.

"I've got twenty minutes, ladies," Collette says in a voice I do not like one bit. She's never set a time limit with me before.

Wanda unfolds her arms, takes two long strides toward the phone. "Then let me get to the point," she says. "I'm not taking the deal. *What's in Your Pantry* is not for sale unless I am co-starring and get co-production credit."

Collette is silent for a moment. "Well, based on a call I got this morning, that's not going to be a problem."

Wanda looks at me and raises one eyebrow. "It's not?"

"The dev team has been instructed by their steering committee to recommend an alternative program platform to what you have pitched."

"Alternative?" I drop down on my knees beside the coffee table where the phone is. "Collette, what's going on?"

I can hear her sifting through papers on the other end. "It's more of what I told you before, but worse."

"How the fuck can it get worse?" Wanda shouts. She too gets on the carpet in order to be closer to the phone. It's strange, this feeling that we can affect the outcome with our proximity.

"I told you to sign as soon as they sent the revised offer," Collette sighs. "Neither of you did. In the meantime, Netflix leadership has had the chance to step in and examine how dear Britt, Brett and Brie have interpreted viewer research and plan to spend their unscripted development dollars. Turns out, upper management doesn't want another cooking competition with no-name, relatable, empathetic contestants. They want to pit real chefs against one another. Think *Top Chef Masters.*"

Wanda's voice is a whisper. "What's that have to do with *What's in Your Pantry?*"

"It has nothing to do with it. And that's where you are suddenly shit out of luck."

"What?"

"There is no more *What's in Your Pantry*. Instead, it's being green-lit as a Netflix original: *On Your Toes with Sabine Rose.*"

Wanda looks up at me, terror in her eyes. "They can't do that."

"You bet they can. They can do whatever they want. In fact, let me read what Brett sent me this morning." Collette clears her throat. "'We actually prefer *On Your Toes with Sabine Rose*! Our branding director believes in using Sabine's full name both for

SEO optimization and to easily convert existing channel subscribers and social media followers. We've already got interest
from Anna Olson, François Payard, and Paul Hollywood.'"

Paul Hollywood!

But then I glance at Wanda who sits on the edge of my bed,
elbows on her knees, head cradled in her hands and temper my
reaction. "What does this mean?" I ask.

"It means you'll be hosting a heavily scripted studio show,
Sabine. And when I say scripted, you can bet that those celebrity chef contestants show up with their own producers who
comb through every last line of dialogue." Collette sighs, but it's
an I-told-you-so kind of sigh. "It also means Wanda's co-creator
credit is going away. As will the paygrade associated with that title.
However, each chef will be assigned a sous, so she can still be on
camera." Collette pauses. "Because we know how important that
is to her."

Wanda gets to her feet and heads for the door. "We need to get
back home. I'm going to switch our tickets."

"That would help," Collette says. "I'm emailing you the new
paperwork as we speak."

"Their idea is complete and unoriginal schlock. Sabine, your
brand is going to disappear next to big-name chefs and I'll be
nothing but an errand girl." Wanda comes back to the table and
stands looking down at me. "We need to get back so we can talk
to Netflix. In person."

"You need to sign right the fuck now!" Collette yells through
the phone. "You waffled on the original offer and they took the
opportunity to scale you back even further. I've seen entire deals
disappear this way in hours. You'll still be on the show, Wanda,
and you'll get some production credit."

"This isn't the show we want to be in." Wanda holds my eye and points at the phone. "Tell her."

I look at the phone but say nothing.

"Sabine!"

I flip my hands over on my lap. "But I do." I say quietly. "I want the show."

Wanda's eyes go as wide as pie plates. She sits down again. "What about me?"

On the other end of the line Collette clears her throat. "Wanda, I believe this is what you call 'looking after one's best interest.' The operative word being 'one.'"

Thirty-Nine

Wanda

There are a thousand things I could say to Sabine right now, but words alone cannot adequately convey my fury and sense of betrayal. Instead, I grab my computer from my room and go sit in the hotel bar. I order a double Hennessy on her tab.

Only because she's a complete narcissist has Sabine been able to overlook the fact that you don't fuck with the fucker who knows everything about you. The fucker who has every move you've made in the last three years on video.

The cognac gets to work right away because I don't even notice Paul enter the bar until he's standing right beside me, looking at the laptop over my shoulder. I slash at the track pad and switch screens.

"What are you doing?" he asks.

"Drinking."

He picks up my glass, sniffs the contents, then gives me a look.

"What?" I ask, irritated by his appearance, the look, everything. "Haven't you heard? Our boss came into money."

The bartender has spotted Paul as well because he comes over, magically producing a glass out of thin air.

"You joining her?"

"A drink for my friend," I answer for him.

"Single or double?"

"Oh, a double for sure." I change my mind and touch the track pad again, brushing back to the editing suite where Sabine is frozen with her mouth open, arms raised and holding a mixing bowl over her head. "And charge it to the same room, Sabine Rose."

I tap play, then, and watch as Sabine smashes the mixing bowl to the floor, marvelling at how well it times with the musical track I've chosen, a symphonic crescendo in *Eine kleine Nachtmusik*. I have dozens of these moments. It's turning out to be the easiest sizzle reel I've ever assembled.

Paul is leaning over and looking at the screen again. I let him. In the next clip she's screaming at someone off camera while Paul tries to pin on her microphone. That someone is me. I make a mental note to lower the soundtrack mix here so viewers can get the full impact.

"What is this?" Paul asks. It's a lot of questioning for someone who barely talks.

"Greatest hits, babe."

I shot the next clip myself on the sound stage at *Wake Up Canada*. The make-up artist had dipped into frame one too many times to blot Sabine's forehead before they started filming. As a result, Sabine rips the brush out of the woman's hand and feeds it into the whisks of the stand mixer on the counter.

"I love this one," I murmur drunkenly.

"What do you plan on doing with these exactly?" Paul asks as the bartender sets down sixty dollars of alcohol in front of him.

"Just sending a reminder to Sabine that perception is reality. Or maybe, reality is perception?" I scrub proudly through the whole reel, four minutes of Sabine throwing tantrums and bowls, insulting me, shouting at Paul, and storming off the set. I'm so glad I've kept these nuggets over the years in my Not for Public Consumption file.

"Are you out of your mind? You can't trash her like that."

"They're trying to push me out of *What's in Your Pantry*, the show I created and wrote," I say, closing the laptop. "Which, by the way, is no longer called *What's in Your Pantry*, and features a rotating crew of mostly male chefs baking it off."

Paul looks hurt. Or maybe confused. It's hard to tell as I've so seldom seen him display any emotions. "I shot most of that footage—I don't even think it's legally yours."

"Listen, you don't want to debate ownership with me right now." I pick up my glass. "By the way, that was a massive fail on your part yesterday. At Stella's house. That camera should have been on the whole time."

"Sabine didn't want it on."

"Since when does Sabine know what makes good content!"

Paul shakes his head. "Wanda, you're out of control. You need to go home."

"I'm perfectly in control." I try to hide the fact that when I raise the glass to my mouth I miss and dribble about thirteen dollars' worth of cognac onto my shirt.

"What you're doing there is fucking suicide," he says, pointing to the computer.

"It's a wake-up call. A chance for her to make things right."

"No, you want Sabine to pay for something you messed up years ago."

I grip the edges of my computer. He does not get to throw Odin back at me like that. "Why are you blindly supporting her like this? I thought we were friends!"

"Friends? Christ, I'd hate to see what you do to enemies." He stands up. "Just don't come to me for help when it's too late."

"And don't come knocking at my door at midnight," I snarl as he turns and walks away.

I don't need him anyway. I raise the lid on the computer and find the YouTube screen. I title the video, "Diva Set" and program the compilation to post tomorrow at noon, which is our proven sweet-spot hour for follower engagement. Of course I need only one view for it to work its magic, and that is Sabine's.

However, knowing her as well as I do, I've also accounted for the margin of self-interest that often overrides her common sense. Which is why, in addition to the sizzle reel, I've also started assembling a second compilation video. This one I'm calling "My Safety Reel."

When I close the YouTube tab I see the small pop-up screen that had been hidden beneath. It reads Upload Complete. I find the external drive icon on my desktop and drag it to the trash in order to safely eject the flash drive from the computer port. It's old technology, but some days you need a tangible advantage. I wait for the Japanese kitten's raised arm to stop waving, then I pull it from the port, give it a brandy-streaked kiss and snap it back onto the chain around my neck. I drop the chain inside my shirt, feeling the beckoning cat settle between my breasts.

I call it a safety reel, but it's really a cyanide tablet.

"Had a feeling I'd find you here."

Duddy DuPierre startles me. I slam the computer shut, even though there's no evidence visible on the screen.

"Jesus, you know how to make an entrance."

His grey eyes widen at the reproach and I find myself drawing a mental triangle between them and his lavender tie.

"What private function have I interrupted this time?"

"I'm writing in my diary, what does it look like?"

"Ah, sarcasm."

Before I can tell him that I want to be alone, he sits down on the stool Paul has vacated. "By the way, I just passed your friend, the quiet guy. Every time I show up, he leaves. You think he doesn't like me?"

I shrug. "You haven't come up in conversation."

DuPierre picks up his glass. "Is this what I think it is?"

"Look, I'm kind of busy here," I say, taking the glass out of his hand and putting it down beside my own empty snifter. "Why are you looking for me? I thought we'd established that you're not the kind of lawyer that can help me."

"I'm actually here in self-interest. A twist on the old you-scratch-my-back routine."

"You want me to do some scratching?"

"Exactly," DuPierre says. "I am completely in receiving mode." He takes a business card from his breast pocket. I watch as he deals it, face up on the bar. "We used to exchange these, back in the day."

My phone starts ringing beside my computer. I glance down and see my father's number.

"Go ahead," DuPierre says. "Take it."

I hesitate, then reach for the phone and switch it to silent mode. "I'm good."

"In that case, let's get back to me." DuPierre pushes the card toward me. "Corporate counsel for Brighello Foods."

I pick up the card and recognize the carnival mask logo. "The cookie company?"

"That's right." His smile is a shot of silver in the darkening room. "Although we prefer 'biscotti.'"

"I take it from the heavy cardstock that you're a pretty big deal?"

"Last time we met I told you I was the boring kind of lawyer. But since then, I've realized that you could make my job a whole lot more interesting."

"This the part where I scratch your back?"

"I'm here in Thunder Bay to acquire the Persian pastry recipe."

I blink. It takes me a second to process the link between us.

"To be honest," he continues, "I was here last year to do the same thing and failed. Which is unusual for me."

"You're a closer?"

DuPierre's face illuminates. "Exactly. And I hate to say it, but I feel that the baker's death, while tragic, is going to improve my odds this time."

My phone starts vibrating now. It creates a seismic ripple in the cognac. I feel my temper flaring. "So this is your incredibly circuitous way of asking me what?"

"For an introduction. To your boss."

I grab the phone and shove it in my bag. "What for?"

"See, last year, I met her uncle in hopes of offering a bid for the recipe. He promised me all sorts of cooperation, but then cut me loose. Here we are a year later and he's making the same promises, but says he needs a little time to sort out bakery affairs."

"Sounds like you don't need Sabine then."

"I'm starting to think your boss is a more reliable scoop."

Now I sit back, smiling faintly. "You have good intuition."

"It's part of the job." He pats his tie against his chest. "I've been watching her YouTube channel, you know."

"So?"

"So, who exactly has the recipe? Did her father take it to the grave? She posed the question and inquiring minds want to know."

"Sabine has it." I look at the business card again and then slide it into the crack of the laptop. "It's in a locked briefcase that even she can't open. Whoever she sells the bakery to gets the recipe. She's currently fielding multiple offers."

He nods slowly though clearly stumped by this piece of news. "And who are the contenders?"

I pick up the glass of amber fluid and rotate it slowly in the dim light. "There's the uncle, the uncle's estranged wife. A cousin."

"Then there's a chance she'll consider my offer."

"I doubt it."

A sharp crease appears in DuPierre's forehead. "Why not? I'm pretty persuasive."

"I have a feeling the sale will be a family affair." I put the glass in front of him, then gather my computer and stand up.

"That's it?" He looks mildly astonished. I don't know why this pleases me so much.

"Still itchy?" I ask. "Too bad." Then I walk away.

Forty

Sabine, 2000

There is a time when I am interested in the mystery of the Persian pastry. I am fourteen, living in a large, rambling house with an ancient grandmother, a workaholic father and a wraith-like stepmother who now spends days in bed. In English Lit, I'll learn there's a name for this grainy version of childhood, an entire genre devoted to tales of the mistreated child: Victorian Gothic. But for the moment I am alone in the feeling.

One afternoon while the house is empty, I open the door to the basement. It's been two years since the end of my flying carpet days, but I am still looking for a way into the pastry, which, I intuit, has some fundamental hold over my father. Even though he comes home exhausted from work, he heads straight to the basement workshop and attends to the dough. He does not allow company.

The stairs are bare plywood dotted with blunt nail heads. They sound like they may splinter and crack, but as I descend, I tell myself if they can bear my father's weight, they'll hold mine. The basement itself is a maze of rooms with a low-slung ceiling and faux wood panelling. I walk through the laundry room, past the boiler and a cold storage until I reach the terminus of the maze, my father's kitchen. It is without windows and, apart from the door I've just entered, has no source of egress. It is the very definition of utilitarian, straight down to its metal storage shelf, bare-bulb lighting and cement floor. You have to pull a cord in order to make the light go on, and when I do, it fills the tight square of a room with a buzz I can feel at the root of my molars. Just like at the bakery, there is a massive worktable at its centre.

This is where the Persian gets its start. At Bennett's there is actually a small fleet of men who shepherd the dough through the assembly process, who regulate the torpedo roller on the Moline machine, operate the guillotine slicer and adjust the temperature of the proofing cabinet and deep fryer. But these men are no more than wrists to the hand of God, their knowledge limited to single, isolated aspects of the Persian. The dough envelope and butter paste filling are prepared days, even weeks in advance, and only one living man knows how it is done.

I walk along the storage shelf, running my hand down the incline of a mixing bowl, poking fingers between the whisks of eggbeaters, until I reach the commercial refrigerator. It's the sort of appliance that requires you to pull the handle down hard, disengage the lock and then swing the door open. I like the effort this entails and imagine myself unlocking a submarine portal to flood its ballast chamber.

Inside are four glass shelves stacked neatly with bundles of dough. I take one out and carry it to the worktable. It's about the same dimensions as a laptop computer. I've already decided that there's no harm in just having a look. I lay the package on the table and carefully peel away the cellophane. There are six little notches running along one edge of the tablet of dough and I puzzle at the hieroglyphs' meaning. The tablet is chilled, not frozen, and when I stroke it, it feels like human flesh. I sniff it. I knows there's a cinnamon berry butter inlay inside but it's so neatly sealed that all I smell is the yeasty dough. For some time, the idea has been in my head that I, too, will be a pastry chef. That I will work alongside my father in his bakery. And to that end, my intention is to examine the pastry, try to glean some insight, then rewrap it in its tight little cellophane jacket and return it to the refrigerator.

Instead, I poke my finger into its heart.

The dough slowly gives way. I watch my finger disappear in the moist and cool centre—right up to the first knuckle—and then feel it come out the other side and strike the table below. When I pull it out, I imagine I hear a pop of suction. My index finger is greasy and pink-tinged from butter and berries. I sink my thumb in next. Then the ring fingers of both hands. The weaker pinkies struggle a bit but eventually puncture the surface. Before I know it, there are a multitude of holes in the dough. Ten to be exact, too many to smooth over.

I came down here wanting to know the magic of the Persian. But now, as I raise each finger to my mouth and lick it clean, I just feel disappointed. Like there's nothing to learn from the dough, as though the mystery flew out the second my finger went in. Or maybe it wasn't there to begin with. And what should I do with it now that it's riddled with holes? It's not safe to dispose of it in the kitchen trash. I could bag it and dump it in the backyard bin, but the garbage is my father's domain and there's no guarantee he won't sort through it before taking it to the curb.

In the end I tuck it under my sweater and carry it up to my room. I wrap it in a towel, put it under my bed and, after a few days, forget about it.

When I come across it again a month later it's completely green. The ten finger holes are perfectly obvious; it hasn't been able to heal itself and therefore not the magical entity I spent my childhood peddling. After that I realize it doesn't really matter how it's made if it can be so easily destroyed.

Forty-One

Sabine, 2002

My aunt stands at her stove and lifts a lid to inspect her tomato sauce. She waits until I take a seat across the table from my father, who's paging through Dante's copy of the *Chronicle Journal*.

"Franchi," she begins casually. "I was thinking we could use an extra hand in the bakery a couple times a week."

"What for?" he asks from behind the paper.

"The Christmas orders are going to start in a couple weeks and every year it's the same thing—short staffed," she says, just as we've planned. "Why don't you let Sabine help?"

"She's got to go to school," my father replies without hesitation.

"On the weekend, then," she suggests, whisking at the red froth as it lathers up the side of the pot. "And over the holidays she'll be off school."

"Sabine doesn't know how to bake. And I don't have time to be a teacher." He says it like I'm not there. At age sixteen, nothing infuriates me more. My aunt has cautioned me to be patient, silent, resigned even. She's told me to let her do the talking, but I can't help myself.

"Enzo gets to work at the bakery."

"Enzo's a boy." My father hasn't looked up from the paper. I suspect he's not actually reading it but using it as a shield.

"So what? That makes him better at making bread?"

"It makes him stronger."

"Stronger? He's only fourteen." I'm working hard to keep the sneer out of my voice. "And isn't it traditionally a woman's job, baking and stuff?"

My father flips one edge of the paper down. "You want to wake up at five every morning to make bread and deliver it with your uncle?"

"I just want to learn how to bake."

You would think that being raised by bakers would naturally put me in line to also become one. That I would count among them somehow. But my family has come to disassociate me from the business, even from my eight-year-old image that still rotates high above Memorial Avenue. The Genie, they call her. My face, co-opted.

"You're going to learn nothing working one day a week."

"Franchi, it's good for her to learn even a little bit," Stella says.

My father places the newspaper on the table finally. But his jaw is a boulder that not even the Angel of the Resurrection can roll. "You see her report card?"

Stella doesn't reply but gets very busy twisting the knobs on the stove.

"The letter C everywhere. One letter B. No A."

"That was last semester!" I have no idea how he got that information. I burned that report card in the fireplace when no one was home. "I'm doing better now. Besides, I'm going to be a baker, so what does it matter?"

My father doesn't seem to register what I've just said. "You'll go to school, to university and be a teacher. A nurse. *Una farmacista.* Something with value."

Stella puts down her spoon with a clatter. "What do you mean, 'with value,' Francesco?"

He looks at her, realizes his mistake, but it's too late.

"The bakery is not good enough for Sabine, but it's good enough for my son?"

"That's not what I said, Stella."

"That's what I hear. Enzo is allowed to waste his time learning at the bakery, but Sabine is going to university to have a real profession?"

I trace the rosettes on the tablecloth with my finger. Stella is going off-script but it's pretty fucking brilliant, and even I know enough not to interrupt.

"Enzo does good at the bakery," my father says weakly.

"Good thing. Because he's too stupid to go to university, eh?"

Stella yanks the oven door open and leans over to peek inside. She's down there for a long, uncomfortable stretch. But when she straightens up again both her voice and face are placid. "You both stay for dinner, okay? Sabi, set the flat plates for pasta."

For a minute I am once again eight years old, and Stella has just convinced my father to let me be part of the bakery. We all know it. I am going to be the Persian heiress.

But when I'm finally allowed to work part-time at the bakery, it is in the limited role of cashier.

"I might as well work at the mall selling bathing suits!" I say to my aunt when she brings me what she thinks is good news. "I don't want to be a cashier."

Zia Stella's face collapses like a woman reeling from a backhand. "Do you know what we pay the counter girls?" she asks.

"I don't care. The point is it's not what I want."

"Gesù Cristo! Why can't you just be happy for once?"

"Because!" I hear the word rise from my belly and am horrified that these two syllables are all I can muster.

"You listen to me, Sabine." She takes a step toward me, wagging her finger in a gesture she must have learned from Dante. "You'll take what's given to you and show your father you can do a good job. Without acting like a *disgraziata*. Prove that first, then we talk about baking."

"That's a shit deal."

"That's the only deal you got."

It does not take me long. A couple weeks in, and I've learned how to fuss over the delicacies, carefully stacking the Neapolitan bars on the rack so that the calligraphy of chocolate in their fondant tops appears to run together like one italic scroll. I can work the bread slicer with little fear of losing my fingers, though I prefer customers who buy their bread whole and who know that real Italian loaf should be torn. It's true, I have a lazy bone. I have some ideas regarding efficiency, mostly about packaging items that people tend to buy in bulk anyway, but no one has time to listen to me.

Only Enzo is taken seriously. He's two years younger than me but has already developed a moustache and a barking voice that rises over the machinery.

"Give me your five bones," My father lavishes on him, extending his hand for a shake when my cousin comes back from his delivery rounds. "You wash up and come see how I make the sfogliatelle dough."

Enzo has failed grade nine accounting but has managed to create a side hustle stocking a few of the city's high school cafeterias with Persians. Once a week my father makes an extra run of pastries for him. During lunch hour Enzo borrows the Bennett's Bakery van and makes the rounds of the schools himself. Never mind that he's still two years away from getting a driver's licence. He has what matters; a sharp tongue, a love of attention and the ability to hawk pastries like nobody's business.

After months of bagging pastries and making change I come to see ugly licks of desperation presenting themselves just beneath the surface of everything. In the five-armed swastika carved into the top of each Kaiser bun. In the torta al limone which looks as innocuous as a pierogi but oozes a yellow cream. The lewd French dinner rolls—which are slit with a razor before baking—come out of the oven looking like the engorged lips of a spraddle-legged woman. I use double wax squares to handle these.

To slow the misery of spring, I begin sampling freely from my sweet and savoury chattels. I pluck olives from the heart of Tuscan bread, grind flecks of aniseed between my teeth, place my mouth against the injection site of the Jambuster and suck out its raspberry innards. Once, Zia Stella catches me with my tongue lodged halfway into a crispy cannolo shell. "You!" she cries, throwing a pencil at me. "You're eating all the profit!"

Forty-Two

Sabine, 2004

For two years I range with an unhappy sense of dominion over the counter of Bennett's Bakery. By the second Feast of San Giuseppe (a day Italians celebrate by bringing home a half dozen or so of the traditional zeppole puff pastry) I have an idea to prepare the bakery so that my father's workday can go as smoothly as possible. To meet demand, we have to run triple batches of zeps (or "led zeps," as Enzo likes to call them when a tray goes bad). But the over-production of zeppole requires display space usually reserved for the native pastries.

Without anyone having to tell me, I take it upon myself to act as a sort of refugee coordinator. I survey the territory; the hanging racks behind the counter are considered the Eastern Wall of the bakery and had been given over to the Persian since the days of the northern forest fires. A tier below is the Sally Ann pastry, its matte chocolate glaze announcing a challenge I am not prepared to meet. Instead, I move the Danishes in next to the brownies. Tighten the space between the rows of Nanaimo bars and relocate the éclairs to the glass-top display case, so that customers can stare down into their deep, cream-filled channels. Due to their fragile ricotta and mascarpone contents, the torta di ricotta and tiramisu are removed to the refrigerators in the back room. It's not their feast day, after all. Finally, I take the showstopping sfogliatelle, which look like Bibles that have been dropped in the tub and then dried into ruffled stacks, and display them on a wicker platter in the window.

Then I wait for my father to come out and notice.

He never does—notice. Instead, to kick off the feast day I'm called into the back room. All the staff is. I find my father in high spirits, pouring everyone a glass of his homemade grappa. On the worktable is an enormous platter of zeppole. Behind the platter stands Enzo in a clingy T-shirt and cut-offs, though mid-March is still the dead of winter in Northwestern Ontario.

My father claps a hand on his shoulder. "Myself, I could not have done better with the zeppole. We have a true baker among us."

Though the zeppole is crafted of cream puff dough, Enzo has squeezed them from the crenellated nozzle of a pastry bag so that they've emerged from the oven whorled like a sandy-blond snow cone. He's then cored them, filled them with a specialty custard, sprinkled them with sugar and finished each with a pitted maraschino cherry that, under the glare of fluorescent lighting, looks as ludicrous as a split nipple.

"A toast to a job well done, Enzo," my father continues, raising his shot of grappa, "You have mastered the zeppole just in time!"

Enzo's shit-eating grin grows more flamboyant than his outfit.

"For chrissakes," I hear myself say out loud. "Someone get Golden Boy a pair of pants."

It's become clear that when my father passes on the recipe, it will be to Enzo, not me.

So, fuck my family. And fuck the Persian.

I leave the bakery then, although it's only two hours into my shift. I don't care that it's one of the busiest days of the year. When

I get home I just sit there, letting the car idle in the driveway. The sky is pebbled grey and has settled low over the rooftops. There's a big snowfall in the forecast that will blanket this dirty little town once more before spring and cut the sour stench of paper mill smokestacks.

The house is silent and dark when I go in. I am, in a way, already living alone. There's a light on in the kitchen that, in the old days, meant that Nonna was making food. But Nonna is gone now and the kitchen is empty. Julia's laptop computer is open, the screen lit as though she'd been sitting looking at something and then evaporated on her stool. I take a step toward it. In the browser window is an array of colourful pastry. I get closer. It's the website for the Marcon School of Culinary Arts in Toronto.

Find your voice in Cuisine, the home page promises.

I turn and glance around the kitchen. I don't like the idea of Julia walking in and finding me poking around her computer. But I am alone.

Our alumni prosper in all areas of Culinary Arts, Pastry and Baking, Oenology, and Restaurant and Culinary Management. Choose your specialty and learn from the Masters in one of the most dynamic cities in the world!

But it's the last line of copy that makes me stop.

You can change your life in as little as two years.

I understand, of course, that Julia has left this on the screen for me to find. What I'll never know is if she's doing me a favour, or simply one for herself.

Either way, it's the moment I begin entertaining the idea of attending college in a faraway town. Somewhere metropolitan and clanging. In this dream I am a skinny wisp of a creature in a chef jacket and molded clogs. It's true I can never see myself clearly in these reveries. My face is obscured, angled away as I hurry into the peripheries, turn a corner.

"I don't like it, Sabi." In her kitchen, Stella drops the flaking slab back on a plate. "It tastes like something went wrong."

This is not what I want to hear.

I have, after months of writing and rewriting, managed to produce two kick-ass essays about growing up in an Italian bakery. I have not written about the Persian because I have, for some time now, realized that I'll never be in on the secret. But it turns out that I don't need it. I've somehow convinced the Marcon admission staff to invite me for a baking trial.

There's one little hitch, of course. I have left the tougher job of actually learning how to bake until now. I have two weeks to perfect a signature dessert recipe if I am really going to get on a plane and fly to Toronto for my trial.

To that end, I've skipped a week's worth of Grade 12 classes trying to recreate recipes my father has already perfected. My most recent attempt is to breathe a new vibe into his eighties-style jelly roll. That afternoon I had chopped the unsold rolls into slices, dipped them in a stiff pancake batter and put them through the deep fryer. Then I sprinkled each with shredded coconut, plated it and brought it to Stella for an honest appraisal.

My aunt unravels a slice for a better look at the cream-lined spirals. "It's soggy like a diaper. Who would buy this?" she asks, looking at me.

I edge around the kitchen island and look at the roll. It actually tastes good if she'd just give it a chance. I raise the torn edge of the discarded pastry to my mouth instead. It's a habit now, the eating. In the past two years—since they'd put me to work behind the counter—I've gained weight. Stella's had to thread the sewing machine multiple times, rearranging the plackets, zippers and slits in my clothing to allow more positive ease.

"What can I do to make it taste better?"

"Throw it in the garbage," Stella says. She takes a bottle of vermouth out of the pantry and splashes a little in my espresso, a lot in hers. "You need to watch what you put in your body, Sabine."

I chew slowly on the fried jelly roll, as if decelerating the motion might disguise the crime. But when she looks at me, I know she's having a hard time reconciling the eighteen-year-old in front of her with the beautiful little girl who posed cross-legged on a flying carpet.

"The real shame is you have one of the best bakers in the world for a father and here you want to go away to learn," Stella says, stirring her espresso with the tiniest spoon ever forged.

"He won't care one way or the other."

My father had missed the first four years of my life, and these past fourteen haven't been much different. To her credit, my aunt has done everything she could for me, intruded where it was appropriate without triggering a family war. But it's just not enough. I suppose nothing can replace the constant harping of a mother.

"You know how it is with Italian men," Stella says. "They don't have the soft ways of the *inglese* husbands who change diapers and wash dishes."

"I don't need my diaper changed. I just needed some of his time."

She nods.

"He has enough for Enzo."

Stella says nothing. Because this too is true. Then she leans forward, takes the fried jelly roll plate by the rim and pushes it away. "You know what you need, Sabi?"

I shake my head.

"A good recipe. If you want to do well on this test."

I look up at her.

"Something that shows *dettagli precisi*. Ah—my cannoli!" She slaps the marble countertop excitedly. "With the cioccolata e ricotta di pecorino."

"You mean it?" I don't care if it's pity, I'll take it. "You'll get me ready?"

She sighs. "But it doesn't mean I like it—you going to go live in a big city by yourself. Who will watch over you? You'll be alone in the wilderness."

I smile. In fact, I'm liking the idea more and more.

"It's just school, Zia. Two years and I'll be back."

Forty-Three

Sabine

On Tuesday morning I'm crouched at the minibar pouring out a clear slurry of vodka when Enzo arrives.

"For chrissakes, Sabs," he says, "it's nine a.m."

"That's what the cranberry juice is for." I pick up the carton and dash juice over the vodka. I've got a legitimate need to take the edge off early. After our call with Collette yesterday, Wanda has either cooled down or is preparing to blow up my life. I'm just stuck in minibar purgatory waiting to find out which. "Besides, you're the one who looks like he can use a drink." His face is haggard, and his moustache needs pruning.

"In that case, make me one too," he says, flinging himself dramatically on the bed.

I remember him as a bit of a lampshade drunk, so I take care crafting his vodka cranberry. When I hand him the glass, he tips his head back, pours the concoction down and winces.

"Woah! When did you become a heavyweight?"

"It's your shitty influence." He hands the tumbler back to me. "It's Marcus."

I take the glass, but I don't mix him a second. "What about Marcus?"

"He took the job offer."

I've got no clue what he's talking about, but I do have enough experience with drinking and the wide gaps it creates in my memory to arrange my face in a way that mirrors his own expression. Shock, outrage, sorrow; one-third of each.

"I thought it was a bluff. Vancouver is on the other side of the continent. But it was a good offer and he signed."

"I'm sorry," I say, using my foot to shuck a path through my dirty laundry and take a seat at the desk. It's coming back to me now. Marcus's impatience with Enzo, his desire to be open about their relationship, to get married, and Zia Stella's insane offer yesterday.

Of course, the offer. It's the reason he's here. "So how is buying the bakery going to make a difference now?"

"It'll stop him from going," Enzo says. "It'll show him that I'm stepping up into a position where my father has no jurisdiction over me."

I understand how Enzo sees my father's death. It is a breach, an open window out of which he is meant to climb. But I look at ownership differently, as something that'll have him tied to Dante Vasco tighter than ever.

"Do you know your mother got a reverse mortgage approval on her house? That's how she's going to pay me four hundred thousand."

Enzo crosses his legs. "That's her prerogative."

"She doesn't have an income. I can't let her do that," I say. Although now I wonder if I reacted too hastily.

"You can't *not* let her do it." His face flashes angrily. "I'm going to take care of my mother, okay? We're all adults here."

I walked away from the offer yesterday, but the truth is, $400,000 over two years would make a far greater impact on my life than $300,000 over four.

"I'll level with you, Sabs. We talked to D'Abruzzo about it."

"You did?" I'm taken aback and a little bit hurt by this. Suddenly I'm imagining mother and son plotting to get what they want from me. "Isn't he supposed to be my lawyer?"

"You give him the word and he can get the paperwork ready."

"Jesus, Enzo. There are things beyond that goddamn bakery!"

"You can say that because you got out. But I'm still here."

I glance around the room, my clothes strewn about the place, the bed unmade because I keep forgetting to remove the Do Not Disturb tag from the door. Collette's flowers are already dead, the water in the vase brown, and the remaining stalk heads have grown hairy with algae.

"You went to that fancy pastry school. You know what I did?"

I don't answer.

"Woke up at five every morning to make bread. To deliver bread. To follow your father around the pastry so I could pick up whatever scraps of knowledge he'd throw at me before my own father would slap me across the head and make me get back to the bread."

"It's more than I got," I say quietly.

But Enzo's not listening. He gets up and goes to the window. "I can't do anything else. You got an education; the bakery has been my whole life."

"I didn't get a real education," I say. The words are out before I know it.

"I'd say the best culinary school in the country qualifies as an education, Sabine."

Fuck it. We both deserve another drink. I go back to the fridge, choose two tiny bottles of amber tincture. "I only got in because your mother coached me. But the reality was hard—very hard.

I dropped out after first year." I have never told another living soul this fact.

Enzo sits back down on the bed and looks at me.

"One silver lining, I lost thirty pounds from the stress. I started making good money modelling. When I got in at Along Came a Blackbird—well, at least I was in the food industry." I walk Enzo's glass back to him. "One day I met the right person who gave me my big break."

He watches me twist open the rye and empty it over ice. "Reynolds?"

I shake my head. "Wanda."

Forty-Four

Sabine

Sweet Rush has posted over one hundred and fifty videos in the past three years, which averages out to one video per week. This sort of consistency makes us a go-to for all the big sponsors of the baking world. It's how I'm able to keep squeaking by.

Producing the videos is a full-time endeavour. We choose a theme, script it and rehearse the bake in advance. We set up the cameras, do a lighting and sound test and then lock the studio doors. Because everything about Sweet Rush is predicated on a lie.

The green tea mille crêpe cake that is sliced apart to reveal twenty razor-fine layers of French pancake is a lie. The rhubarb-and-grapefruit tartelettes that I featured on the cover of my second cookbook? A lie.

The cherry blossom mochi? Big fat Japanese-inspired lie.

The wildly successful video of the chocolate cannoli piped with sheep's milk ricotta is a double lie. The more excusable part being that Stella is the one who actually invented it. The venial part is, well, much more venial.

On my laptop there's a password-protected folder innocently named Rough Cuts. In the beginning I would parse through it nightly, both fearful of the content and marvelling at our ingenuity.

These days I open that file very infrequently. Falsehood has a way of becoming inconspicuous and essential at the same time.

In that folder is our last studio video, filmed the day after our lunch with the Netflix team. I appear sufficiently recovered from the blood-orange martinis. My hair is pulled back in a tight, high ponytail and gold hoops large enough to double as bracelets swing from my ears. I'm wearing an ivory silk blouse with a black stitch ruffle. The first three set-ups are me behind the kitchen island set introducing the day's bake, an opera cake with hand-piped peonies and marzipan succulents. If I tap the video button and scrub forward, I see myself holding up the piping bag, pointing to the nozzle and explaining how to hold it at a forty-five-degree angle while applying even pressure and rotating the cake base rather than the bag of icing.

When you watch the video on YouTube, you see a cut to a close-up of my hands as they expertly squeeze the piping bag and twirl the cake tray until a shaggy hothouse peony spirals to life on top of the opera cake.

Only, they aren't my hands.

The Rough Cuts folder holds the truth. Watch the takes and you'll see. There I am pointing to the nozzle, explaining how to hold it at a forty-five-degree angle. There's Paul's voice calling "cut." There I am putting the piping bag down and walking off camera.

There's Wanda walking on.

Paul is still filming as Wanda, with an identical manicure, dressed in an identical ivory silk blouse with a black stitch ruffle takes her mark and picks up the piping bag. Then he pulls focus so that we're in tight on her hands as she spins and squeezes peonies from icing.

Scrub ahead to the bain-marie, a double boiler method used to melt chocolate for the *croustillant*. For a minute I almost believe those are my hands folding the *pailleté feuilletine* into the chocolate and stirring. But here Paul pulls out into a medium shot in order to keep the entire pot in frame as it's raised from the burner and carried over the counter. Only it's Wanda raising the pot, swinging it over the counter and pouring the *croustillant* over the sponge cake, her expression grim and confident at the same time.

She will trim out the frames containing her face later.

That's what Wanda does. Takes what Paul gives her and removes herself from the picture. Wanda is the real illusionist. She creates the magical motion picture effect of me, alone in a studio kitchen, creating one frosted masterpiece after another.

I wasn't kidding when I said the reason I hired her was because of her hands. Well, that and the artistry she displayed on the top of a caramel flan. And her glazed sweetbread. And her rolls filled with cashew dacquoise and rum buttercream.

When I first spotted the blackbird leche flans in her godmother's storefront window, I was still riding the wave of my gay wedding cake heroics. The newly married couple, Max and Gregory, were launching a high profile civil court case against the baker who'd refused their cake commission, and this translated to an uptick in my media bookings. My first cookbook hit the bestseller lists around this time, and Collette began urging me to post instructional videos on YouTube. "These days you need to be your own marketing agency," she told me in her posh downtown Toronto office. "Put that face in front of the camera."

I had chosen the name *Sweet Rush* and envisioned owning my own business—online sales to start, and then progressing to a real brick-and-mortar shop. To that end, I hired a company in India to create a website while I put an enormous security deposit on a commercial kitchen space in Liberty Village. It was the most productive use of caffeine and cocaine I have ever made. I bought the best ingredients and equipment I could afford, and thanks to my Instagram page featuring thirty-two different views of Max and Gregory's wedding cake, new requests were coming in. At some point during that crazy time, I realized I couldn't bake.

I'm not saying that I had some sort of creator's block. I literally mean I had no talent. My brulé was runny, my cakes would collapse, my icings were either wet, stiff or rubbery. The pastry came out chronically claggy. My flavour profiles were uninspired. Dough was under-proofed and overbaked. Or over-proofed and underbaked. It's been so long since I attempted a yeast dough that I forget where my handicap lies.

It seemed that every once in a while I could turn out a winning pastry. Even a stopped clock is right twice a day, right? The gay wedding cake was one such example. As was the weekend I flew to Toronto to perform the technical portion of my application to the Marcon pastry school, although by this point I had even lost Zia Stella's cannoli technique. I'm sure there were other times, too, when my work was adequate.

I grew up in a bakery family and had expected to acquire the knowledge by osmosis. Failing that, I once read that cooking is artistry, baking is science. Which suggested that all I had to do was follow a recipe closely and reap consistent results.

No such luck.

Three months in, my Liberty Village kitchen lease draining my bank account, I found myself refusing most commissions. I just couldn't turn out a quality product. It quickly became apparent that there would be no online shop—and certainly no trendy whitewashed storefront—in my future. At night I lay awake, counting my heartbeats and imagining people like Reynolds waiting in the margins of social media for news of my collapse.

In came Wanda with her Filipino ube paste and dashed dreams of the tech world. Her talented hands could paint exquisite fleur-de-lis on top of petit fours, braid silver birch into rustic wedding toppers and roll a cardamom jelly spiral out of even the most fragile genoise sponge. At first it was simple. She filled the order, I photographed them, posted them to the website and Instagram, and took credit.

Every baker out there seemed to have their own baking channel, and yet none had the sort of momentum that was still behind me. "You need to get back in front of a camera, address your audience," Collette urged. "You've done scores of interviews. This isn't the time to get shy."

Wanda set up the YouTube channel and filled it with clips from various interviews. But when it came to creating original content—showing people how to actually bake—things got tricky. I thought of my father, how simple pastry dough sprung to life in his hands. How even my uncle could give rise to legions of uniform bread loaves. In my hands, a simple hot-water pastry dough turned into an unappetizing lump.

"Let me try that," Wanda said, stopping the video we were attempting to record. She took the brown dough and in seconds had smoothed it flat with a pin. She used a ruler to measure the vertical wall of the baking tin, then placed the ruler on the dough and trimmed it with a crimping wheel. Not only did the strip fit the pan wall with precision, but there was no hesitation in her hands.

I looked at my phone sitting on the counter. "Maybe," I started, "you can do the prep work while I record. If I stay tight on your hands no one will know."

I said this as if the idea had just come to me. But it had been there all along.

Wanda nodded. "It's really like being your sous chef."

"You prepare the mise en place."

"Then you hop back on camera to show us the finished product."

"Those celebrity bakers on TV don't actually do any of the baking."

"That's what production teams are for."

Our thoughts crisscrossed like a plaited loaf. It was one thing to post photos of recipes already completed on Insta. But to create an intentionally false video was something else. It took strategy, cunning and matching manicures.

A short while later, Max and Gregory lost their civil court case against the baker who had refused their cake commission. But the public outcry led them to an even bigger victory—their own TV show. My subscribers and Instagram followers climbed past the two million mark. We couldn't keep up with the online shop, and as soon as the sponsorship offers started rolling in, we realized that we didn't have to. We shuttered the bake shop and hired Paul, a real cameraman who knew how to quickly light a set, mic for sound and who brought his own equipment into the equation. Instantly we looked professional. Larger sponsors took notice and offered us thousands per episode to mention, use, or prominently feature their products. Others bought up ad space around our videos, helping to drive *Sweet Rush* to the top of search results.

I handed the reins over to Wanda. That included choosing the recipes, creating the themes, scripting the shows, keeping a detailed production bible, and handling all the social. I had other stuff to do. There was the Quick Bake segment on *Wake Up Canada*, a second cookbook to envision, tattoos to burnish into my skin. There were drinks and party invitations and more drinks. And somehow, three years and six million followers later, here we are. Ensnared.

Knives at each other's throats.

Forty-Five

Sabine

When the phone rings at noon I trip over myself to answer. I've been watching television with the sound off, waiting for some sign of life from Wanda. Some acknowledgement of our conjoined treason and her ongoing loyalty to it. But even as I pick up, I know she wouldn't call on the hotel line. In fact, I know she won't show up or even message. She's waiting for me to make the next move.

"I gather you're still reeling from the other night," the voice says. No introduction, no pleasantries.

"What night are you referring to," I ask Julia, hoping I've matched her ambiguity.

"I think it's important you realize the context of your inheritance. He didn't know he was sick. Your father wasn't ready to have that briefcase handed over to you without a conversation."

Julia's voice is a hot puff in my hair. I switch the phone over to the other ear. "When was he planning on having this little father-daughter chat?"

She doesn't answer. I hear her lick her lips nervously but then remind myself that the heightened acuity I get from vodka is imagined.

"I don't know, Sabine," she says finally. "But I do know it's not right to just leave you with this burden and no context."

"Interesting choice of words."

"That recipe has been little else."

I go back to the television and take a sip of the drink perched on the arm of the sofa. I'm sure Julia can hear the ice cubes clink. "I know all about the Garibaldi already. His fugitive status. My aunt told me."

"Oh? Well, that's a surprise."

"I gather a lot of energy has gone into keeping the truth hidden over the years."

"Yes." Julia ignores my sarcasm. "Your father was certainly guilty of leading that charge."

"Why did he leave me this stupid thing if it could unravel his past?"

"In his mind, he still had years to go. Time to explain things to you." Then she clears her throat. "I can, if you want, try to do that for him?"

It's the first time in my life that Julia has offered me anything. And I don't like it.

"Like I said, I already know all about the dead baker."

"Both of them?"

It's only after I've arrived at Julia's house that it occurs to me, I'm once again over the blood-alcohol limit. I ring the bell and turn to look at the rental I've managed to pull up wholly on the driveway but at an odd angle. The front bumper is leaning aggressively toward Julia's old Mercedes.

When she answers the door, she's wearing camel-coloured jodhpurs and a white button down open enough to reveal an oversized sapphire necklace. She looks like she's come straight from the Southfork Ranch stables in *Dallas*. I breathe through my mouth, having no wish to be transported to the past by the scent of her Oscar de la Renta perfume.

The other thing I realize while I stand there is that I'm actually taking the advice of my father's lawyer. *Follow the truth*. I wonder if D'Abruzzo knew what he was doing when he slipped me the glorious but highly inaccurate history of the Persian? Who is the second dead baker? And what did it have to do with my father?

I suppose that's why I'm here. Julia, like Dante, is not keen on sugar-coating.

"Have you been drinking?"

See?

"A little," I say. "But just for fun."

Her face doesn't crack. "Were you drinking for fun the night you tried to run me over?"

I weigh my options. Wait out her unnatural blue gaze or turn and run. I summon up some nearly forgotten kundalini fire breaths and raise both hands in the air. "You got me." It's all I can manage by way of admission.

It's enough. She steps aside and lets me in.

Forty-Six

Francis, 1985

She was the first thing he saw the evening he reported for work at Bennett's Bakery. He made the mistake of entering through the front door near the pastry counter. No one had told him that employees parked in the back and used the chipped metal door next to the loading dock.

She wore a light blue apron that looked stonewashed compared to her eyes. While he waited for her to finish ringing in a customer's sliced loaf, he stared at her, thinking he'd only ever seen that blue before in the sea and sky, in the cloak of the Virgin Mary.

"Yes?" She gave him a tight smile, mistaking him for a customer.

He put out his hand. People were always shaking hands in this country and he just wanted an excuse to touch her. She was exquisite with that heavy sweep of lashes and painted mouth. He could have carved that face out of marzipan, dusted the freckles on the fine bridge of her nose with a sable brush.

She took his hand briefly. He was handsome as well, for a moment they could silently agree on this, their beauty. Then she pulled away and ran her fingertips over the keys of the cash register. "Are you picking up an order?"

Francis remembered where he was. "I'm here to work," he said through his thick, new accent.

The girl narrowed her strange eyes. He knew he'd suddenly sunk in her estimation. "You work here?"

"That's right." He wasn't fazed by the rapid cooling her voice and posture underwent.

"Then you have got to use the back door. The front is for customers only."

He nodded but didn't move. Stood there shamelessly taking her in until she turned away.

For the next three weeks, he came in to work through the front door. Each time she looked up from the till, smile on her face. Then, realizing it was him, her face would flatline, her cheeks flush. Her northern complexion made it hard to hide anything for long.

He was always surprised by this tough little town, so ready with her natural beauty and wide-open lake vistas. It was once the largest grain-handling port in the world, a massive transportation hub at the intersection of waterway, rail and road. Grain came in from the west by train, was loaded into freighters and began a fabled journey down the chain of the Great Lakes. Men were needed to do these jobs, the loading and unloading, and so it had drawn large populations of Italians looking for something better than they had been left with in Europe after the war. Francis took some comfort in the fact that others had come before him, faced the incredible white winters, mourned their lost histories, lived to tell about it.

He turned off Water Street and climbed up through the downtown business district until the metal glint of lake was visible in his rear-view mirror. He'd just started working and was careful about every dollar that passed through his hands, but owning a vehicle was a necessary condition of the place. He had traced the lineage of his lucent blue Dodge back through at least three men before him. The interior was stripped bare as a train station bench, but the seats were sturdy, and it handled well enough. When he purchased it he was aware that he was outfitting a new life. He'd been away from everything he'd ever known for months now and it was unclear if he would ever go back. It was easier instead to focus on what was immediately behind him, like the northwest shore of Lake Superior winching tighter in the cold. Or the salted road immediately ahead of him. Or, on this particular day, the blonde on the sidewalk staring at the display window at Ziegler's Furniture.

As he swung the car to the curb a peach rolled out from under the passenger seat. It must have escaped from the bag he'd brought home for Stella. "Peaches in November!" she'd cried and kissed his cheeks when she learned he'd paid a whopping five dollars a pound for this little luxury. Francis stretched over the console now and caught the renegade with one hand, bringing the peach's soft skin to the divot between his nose and upper lip.

Then, in three steps he was out of the car and clumsily scaling the snowbank.

She stood in a parka staring at the display window where silk damask curtains—the same tempera blue as her eyes—moved by themselves. The crunch of ice underfoot must have startled her because she turned quickly, almost angered by his sudden presence. She was smoking a cigarette, something he'd never seen her do, although he'd never seen her outside of the bakery.

"You like?" He gestured to the automated curtains.

Now that there was no cash register between them, they had the opportunity to take each other in. She drove her eyes over his good white teeth, the hair that stood up like a brush. Hazelnut skin and dark eyes. He couldn't tell if she liked what she was looking at.

"They're just curtains." The exhaust of her breath and cigarette smoke created a blue cloud between them.

"But they move." He glanced in the window and imagined what sort of house she lived in if she wasn't impressed by the display.

She shrugged and stomped her white, fur-capped snow boots. Francis felt himself grasping for words again. Television and radio were helping his English language education, but the words he wanted to give this woman eluded him.

"You don't tell me your name," he said, finally settling on an introduction.

He watched her take a final puff on the cigarette and drop it to the pavement. Francis admired how she made no move to crush it underfoot. "Julia."

"I am Francis," he said, touching his chest. He regretted this immediately. He had seen a gorilla on television performing the exact same gesture.

"I know," she said.

"You do?"

She smiled at his stupidity, revealing one slightly crooked incisor, the sight of which filled him with music. "I know everyone at the bakery. There's not much that gets by me."

He would later write this sentence down and try translating it to Italian in order to understand it better. It was one of his first mistakes in this new country. He was already attempting to parse her meaning when all he needed to know was right there. She was young and an *inglese*. He was the sort of suitor her father would chase off at rifle-point.

Francis put his freezing hands in his pockets and felt the peach. He drew it out, dimpled and perfect. They both stared at it without speaking. Then he placed it in her hand.

She rotated it between her fingers as if she, too, were surprised to see something bloom in this weather. He watched as she unzipped a pocket and placed it carefully inside. Then she turned and began picking her way gingerly uphill.

Sometimes, the only indication that Art was still knocking about the bakery building was the sweet draft of pipe smoke that circled down from his attic perch. Francis took the stairs two at a time, catching the faint curl of tobacco. It was now only a month into his employment, but he and Bennett were going to discuss adding Italian pastries to the sweet trays for Christmas. It had been the young man's idea. There was a market for amaretti, the delicate cookies piped from almond meal and sold by the pound. He might also urge Bennett to add cannoli with either cream or custard centres to his holiday repertoire.

"Ah, there you are!" Art raised his pipe and beckoned him to the dimly lit desk where invoices were pinned under the weight of a great adding machine. "Let's talk pastry."

The younger man came forward nearly tripping over a stack of double-strapped hearth pans which appeared to have not yet seen the rough side of a cleaning brush. There must have been thousands of dollars of dirty equipment and unopened packages up here.

"What pastry?" a woman's voice asked.

Francis turned. She sat at the far end of Arthur's desk, her elbows planted on either side of an accounting ledger, a pencil knit between her fingers. For a moment he stood in a vacuum. He heard the November wind howl outside. Then Art Bennett released him by rattling some change in his pocket.

"Francis, meet my wife, Julia."

Forty-Seven

Sabine

"You were married to Arthur? You were Mrs. Bennett?"

Julia nods. She's an old woman now, but the admission sets her jaw trembling.

"What happened?" I ask. "To Arthur?"

That's when she gets up and leaves the room. I sit by myself and listen to the grandfather clock tick off the seconds in the foyer. Julia comes back with two cans of Coke. One goes on a coaster in front of me. The other she cracks open and chugs. When she's done, she burps delicately into a fist and puts the can on the floor by her feet.

"Well, he died," she answers, finally.

I can tell this is not a complete summary, so I wait.

Forty-Eight

Francis, 1985

Francis started using the employee entrance. He felt humiliated that the connection he'd formed with this woman was all in his mind. There was plenty to occupy him in the bakery, he reminded himself. No need to add Arthur Bennett's young wife to this list.

In early December, he found men in the bakery workroom calling to one another in Greek, a language he did not understand but which he thought lyrical. They were attempting to hoist a large wooden crate on end, but, faltering, had to lower the load.

Art stood at the worktable in front of a mixing bowl, eyes closed, knuckles locked on the rim at ten and two. His face was as beaked and sharp as a gargoyle's. Francis approached slowly, found himself watching the man's chest, waiting for the rise and fall which he knew to be evidence of life. But there was no stirring, no assurance of breath. He reached out and tapped him on the shoulder.

Bennett opened his eyes. Slowly, as though waking from a dream that he knew well. He looked up at the young man and nodded. "She's displeased with me."

Francis knew who he was referring to. But since that day in the attic, he'd avoided talking to Arthur about his incredibly young and beautiful wife. Instead, he pointed to the men and the crate. "What's this?"

"A proofing cabinet. A nice one," Bennett murmured. It was where raw dough would be allowed to rise before being baked. The Greeks had finally gotten the crate upright and were prying apart wood slats with a crowbar. "It has a forced-air heating system and everything."

Francis had heard of his boss's wild expenditures, after which, it seemed, Arthur applied himself with considerable effort to the task of avoiding his wife. But there was no hiding the glass case that appeared to him to be roughly the length of a storefront window.

"As I told Julia, you need to spend money to make money." Bennett said as though reading his thoughts. "I'm going to produce the Pershing in volume."

Francis felt a quiet pity for the old man. First of all, there was no Pershing. Second, it was no secret the bakery was in dire straits. "Is it very—*necessario*? So big a machine?"

"It's not the size of the equipment—that's an incidental benefit. It's the quality output." Arthur gestured to the cabinet. "Quality, quality, quality. Once I get this pastry off the ground there's no telling where it'll go."

The Greeks eased a glass panel from the packaging and leaned it against the back wall of the bakery.

"That's what Julia doesn't understand," Bennett squeezed his knuckles to crack them, but no sound came. "She couldn't possibly, she's not a creator."

———

The Christmas season rolled in quickly, and with it, the Bennetts' annual holiday party at the Moose Hall. To Francis, Christmas in North America seemed a largely commercial affair, bearing little connection to that particular phase in the life of Jesus Christ he'd celebrated back home. Finding himself thus unencumbered by religious obligation, he began drinking heavily during the banquet. By the time the band started playing, he and Dante were at the bar keeping the whisky company.

He had avoided Julia Bennett so thoroughly during the hour their work shifts overlapped that he found he could now even ignore the thought of her. And since Dante was attending the party with him, Francis thought the night would make no emotional claims on him.

Until he saw her cross the dance floor.

Her sleek hair was pinned back, and she wore a blue silk dress that crossed over her breasts in a trim of velvet. He had to look away from the sharp bones of her sternum, her bare shoulders.

"That woman," he said to his cousin. "What's she doing married to an old man like Arthur?"

Dante scanned the dance floor. "Julia?"

Francis turned back to watch her float across the floor. She was a woman created for gentle splendour, he thought. For silk dresses, fragrant gardens, music, gems.

"Talk to her once and you'll know why," Dante snorted. "She's a shrew."

"Maybe she's a shrew to keep away guys like you."

Julia stopped then and turned slowly on one heel. He watched her blue gaze skim over the crowd until it fell on him.

Francis had already been warmed by scotch and invigorated by the effervescence of sparkling wine. Around him there was the glint of Christmas lights, female laughter, the music of water glasses. It was a simple thing to imagine that Julia had been dropped into the middle of all of this for his pleasure alone.

"She can't be happy with him."

"I like to see you in good spirits, Franchi." Dante smiled and pushed another drink at him. "But stay away from the boss's wife."

He understood he was trapped somewhere in the whisky's ebb and flow and not quite himself as he roamed the dance floor looking for her. The party was just lifting off the ground, but she seemed to have vanished. All around, spots of candlelight bounced between crystal and silverware, obscuring faces. He wandered downstairs to the entrance. Francis leaned against the glass doors wondering what would he even do if he found her? He knew nothing of dancing. The footwork, the tempo, the position of arms—these were all progressive contortions of a society that had excluded him.

"You're leaving?"

He looked around the dim foyer until he made out a female figure leaning against the deserted coat check counter.

Upstairs the band was playing "Fools Rush In" but Francis shook off the song's implication. He could feel the glass door giving him the push he needed until suddenly he was standing in front of her.

"I was looking for you," he said.

Julia stepped close to him, tilted her face up so that he could smell the perfume in her platinum hair. "Well, here I am."

—

They found themselves: Each morning he slipped out of Dante's house, drove up to Cornwall, left the car there and scaled the rest of the hill on foot. He let himself into Arthur Bennett's house through the back, climbed one staircase, then another, until he reached the bedroom on the third floor where she waited for him. Something buzzed in his chest every time he opened the door and crossed the bedroom floor toward her. Julia, like every other miracle of perspective, enlarged as he approached. He kissed her fingers, her lips, the lidded crescents of her eyelids, milk-blue and trembling. It was not an upward journey to reach this woman, but an ascension.

They forgot themselves: This thing they were doing filled them both with a sickness. When she took off her blouse, he could see the purple bruise of her erect nipples through her brassiere. He pulled off the straps so that they hung below the small swells of her breasts. Then he fell back from her. The vulnerabilities of her naked body drew off his anger. When he reached for her again his hands were softened.

"Don't." She slapped him away. "Don't be tender. If you're going to do it, do it fully." She pulled him by the hair to show him how, manoeuvring his mouth this way and that. Harder, until he grazed her nipples with his teeth. He pushed her down on the bower of her clothing and knelt on the bed. Only then did he hear the sound of welcome deep in her throat. She raked his pants down his hips, so eager to feel his bones through her skin once more, anxious for the discomfort this layering brought. In the dim light filtering from beneath the door, he saw where he'd scraped her breasts raw with his incisors. He wondered how she'd hide this from her husband. But the thought was one of curiosity, not concern.

—

Francis watched for a moment from the top of the attic stairs. Art stood by the desk, his narrow back to the entrance, bent as though listening to a direct address from the small television. On the screen a vigorous funnel of smoke puffed out of the sea, overpowering a tiny Portuguese island.

"Looks like World War Three." Art acknowledged the younger man's presence without turning around. "The war to end all wars."

The sun filtered in through the dormers and cast a spotlight on the attic floor. Francis stepped around it. His eyes flicking at the mushroom cloud. "I brought this." He held up a paper lunch bag.

Arthur pointed to the screen but did not turn. "That volcano is under the sea. The water around the island actually reached the boiling point—a complete destruction."

Francis had lived in the shadow of Vesuvius; he could not give credence to every natural disaster. "Try," he said, unpleating the crisp fold and standing the bag open on the desk.

The old man remained at the far end of the desk, patting his silvering scalp. He had yet to take his eyes from the screen. "What is that?"

"*Una soluzione.*"

"To which problem, exactly?"

Francis looked around the cumulative sprawl of the attic, the chair where Julia often sat pushing around nonsensical numbers. He had an earnest desire to save Art Bennett from bankruptcy. He also had an earnest desire for his wife. Somehow, over the last several months, these two endpoints had merged. He'd nearly convinced himself that one could be given in trade for the other.

"You need help with the Pershing, no? So, there it is."

Bennett turned finally, slow as a berthing ship in contrary winds. Francis pushed the bag toward him, then watched as he took the lip of it between finger and thumb, dragging it across to his side of the desk.

"I use your recipe," he heard himself say, "and I make some changes."

Art's forehead clouded as he stared into the folds. "Then it's your recipe, isn't it?" He pushed the bundle back across the tabletop.

The young man itched with anxiety. "It's some of it yours, and some is mine."

This would be true, of course, if the Garibaldi had been his to begin with.

Arthur stood eyeing him like a large, suspicious child. He was blocking the entire television set from view. Francis moved away from the desk, sat on a chair against the wall. "Taste it." He nodded to the package. "You decide."

Art picked up the bag again, his hands vibrating slightly as he shook the little bun out on the desk. While it was possible to unwind Don Ernesto's bun to get at the soft double core, a properly constructed Pershing did not unwind. This one felt weightless, though it was a pleasing insubstantiality. As Francis watched, he brought the Pershing to eye level. He gave it a little pinch and watched as the bun puffed back, filling the indentations made by his fingers. Art sniffed it, turned it over on his palm, then took a bite.

While Bennett chewed he held the bun at arm's length, frowning at the colour revealed inside. Francis's heart raced. He bit into his upper lip, imagining the impassivity of pine-rimmed lakes and cold iron. He wanted to present the same hard, flat face he and Julia wore when they passed each other in the bakery to cover the explosions inside.

"You see, the taste is the same cinnamon—"

Arthur silenced him with the spiking of one eyebrow. He took another bite, this time chewing vigorously, as though to get to the end of things. With his free hand he crumpled the paper bag. Bennett was already giving his opinion, it was the quick hammering of his jaw, up and down.

When his right hand was empty, he looked up. There was a hard light in his eye.

"It's pink," Art said.

"Yes."

"What kind of charity is this?"

Francis did not flinch; he hadn't expected the man to concede gracefully. "I have no interest in charity."

"Thievery then?" Bennett stepped to the side and the small screen came back into view. "Francis, are you a thief?"

He had not set out to be. Francis understood then that there would be consequences he could not yet see. But he had come too far. "The Pershing, it belongs to you," he heard himself say. "But the business, part of it will belong to me."

On the TV the same scene as before. A mountain blowing, over and over.

Forty-Nine

Sabine

'm perfectly sober by the time she finishes the story.

"Is that why my father finished the recipe for Arthur? Was it, like, a trade for you?"

"No." Julia leans forward. "Yes, perhaps. It is entirely possible to love someone and still stab them in the back. Francis loved Arthur. He legitimately thought he could help him. If he solved the recipe, Arthur wouldn't have to chase ghosts all day up in that attic. He could focus on the bakery as a whole. He'd already eaten through most of the money my father had left me. This is the house where I was raised, and the bank was coming after it next. I told Art I would leave him if we lost the house—" Julia shuts her eyes for a moment.

"He took the deal?"

She sits back on the sofa and crosses her legs. "Your father and Dante each bought a quarter share of the bakery and Arthur let everyone think the recipe was his. Funny enough, all of Art's predictions were right. The damn thing was a hit." Julia's face works against its natural creases and folds itself into a smile. "There were terrible forest fires that summer. It was Dante's idea to bring free Persians to the firefighters every morning. It was on the local news, then the national. Well, you know your uncle's character—everyone wanted to interview him. Pure bombast and entertainment. He's the one that changed its name. Pershing was too hard to pronounce with his accent. It made Arthur furious. But then everything made him furious. He should have been pleased as punch. He'd just resolved the greatest creative challenge of his life, but in the months that followed he became . . . morose. Aggravated. It didn't make sense."

I'm beginning to grasp the undercurrent here. "Unless he knew."

Julia nods. Exhaustion breaks across her face. "One morning, your father went in ahead of the morning shift to clear storage space in the attic. We were getting a big sugar delivery. At the top of the stairs, he sees a pair of rubber boots tipped over. A chair on the ground. He looks up and sees Arthur hanging from the rafters."

"Jesus Christ." I press my palms to my cheeks. "He killed himself?"

"We were fools to think it was a secret. Everyone in that bakery knew. Arthur knew. If it was a trade, I think he felt he got the short end of it."

Her matter-of-fact admission has sucked the air from the room. I lower my hands to my lap and look at the blue veins, trying to make sense of the blood running there. "How could my father keep working there? He set up his office in that attic."

"I suppose it was another way to punish himself." Julia clears her throat. "I sold Francis and Dante the other half, but we had to keep making the Persian—and more of it. It was bringing in all sorts of business and publicity. We were trapped by it. Your uncle was like a dog with a bone when it came to publicity. But after the death, your father . . . changed. He lost his shy delight in the work.

He looked around and all he saw was machinery and men relying on him for a paycheque. Favours to ask for and to grant.

"The two of us were also trapped together. It's difficult to explain but nothing could stand up to the misery we'd created for ourselves. We'd essentially pushed a man to his death. When I think of the years I went through, unable to get out of bed in the morning. Do you know, I was fifty before I learned about anti-depressants?" She stops, looks out the window. I turn, too, and can see the branches of the white elms sift against daylight.

Just when it seems like she's slipped into the past and is going to stay there for a while, Julia straightens her shoulders and slides one snugly cuffed ankle over the other. "Of course all of this business with Arthur was a lifetime ago. History has rearranged itself since, sliding from one side of the room to the other."

I admit, this glimpse of the fallout of her affair is sad, romantic in the retelling, and quite possibly a little too neat. There are details she has neglected to mention, enormous consequences she has overlooked. Like the fact my father was married the entire time. That he had a child.

I stand up, walk around the room and stop at the bookshelf holding the Shepherdess figurine. My grandmother's handiwork was so good it's impossible to spot the decapitation line. I pick her up, turn her carefully in my hand, run a fingernail along the back of her neck. Nothing.

"We replaced it."

I turn around slowly. "What do you mean?"

"After you smashed it. Your father bought me a new one."

"I thought—" I slide over to the shelf where Carmen and Bathsheba stand in three-quarter pose. They are all alabaster skin and flawless necklines.

"Your grandmother tried some business with glue. It was a big mess." Julia comes over to the shelf. "One night your father came home with a big wooden crate. He had replaced every single one of them. Well, except for Wilhelmina. She'd been discontinued."

"I don't remember Wilhelmina," I say quietly, clutching the Shepherdess to my chest.

She levels her eyes at me. "I don't expect you would." Then she holds out her hand.

"Did he feel guilty?" I hand over Shepherdess and watch as Julia returns her to the bookcase.

"Of course. Arthur had started that collection for me."

"I don't mean Arthur. My father had a wife and child in Italy. A *dying* wife."

My stepmother finishes arranging the figure and turns. She looks at me, not with sympathy but with frankness. "When he left Italy the way he did—a fugitive—all bets were off."

"What does that mean?" I've asked this question a hundred times, it seems. A plea for clarity. I'm disappointed in Julia. She had promised to lay out the truth without compromise, but what I'm starting to hear is a faltering narrative.

She returns to the sofa, lowers herself into its centre. "He had to forget part of that life to get on with this one."

"I was part of that life!"

"Sabine, I never wanted children. Not with Arthur, not with Francis."

"So why did you agree to bring me over? Did he force you?"

"Not him," she says. "Your grandmother had some strong opinions about what was best for everyone. Her choices made it very hard for me to live with her—and you."

"Once again, I don't understand."

"I didn't at first either." Julia looks at me, her skin translucent, the complex intersection of veins visible at her temple. "He wasn't without honour, your father. It's just that your grandmother kept him in the dark about what had happened in Italy after he left. When you showed up on this doorstep at age four—neither one of us knew you existed."

Fifty

Sabine

To say that I drive crazily across town for the next twenty minutes is an understatement. I've forgotten my phone at the hotel, so if I want to sate my immediate need to yell at someone, I've got to do it in person.

No one answers at my aunt's house. I go around to the backyard and kick at the kitchen door until my foot hurts. I take a saucer out from under a potted geranium and whisk it angrily across the backyard like a Frisbee. I watch with some satisfaction as it smacks into laundry hanging from the clothesline, leaves a Rorschach of dirt in the centre of a clean bedsheet and drops to the grass. Then I hobble back to the rental car, recalculating my route.

Who else knew?

I'm backing down Stella's driveway when it strikes me that there are only three surviving members of this conspiracy. It's Dante's turn.

He's just reached the part of the afternoon Persian demonstration where he uses a dowel to tap the pastries bobbing in hot oil so they'll flip. I push through the late afternoon crowd, perform an ungraceful leap over the stanchions and swing around the glass divider.

Dante spins around, startled. "You're not wearing a hairnet!"

"You didn't know I existed?" I grab the balsa dowel from his hand, snap it in half and throw it in the vat of hot oil. "Start talking."

We are in the same attic where Art Bennett's fate was written. Standing under the same succession of iron joists, one of which he had roped like a steer and ridden to his death.

How sweet that my father has left me one half of this good luck charm.

"Your Nonna Maria, she does the right thing," Dante says, ripping off his hair net and throwing it on my father's desk. I don't like the litter of sticky tart tins he's been using as ashtrays, the way they're strewn across the metal surface that had always been so organized.

"Maria knows that if Francesco learned his wife was expecting a baby, he would return to Italy."

"As he should have."

"To be arrested?"

"There had to be some in-between. For her to keep me a secret for four years—that's psychotic."

"What's this mean, 'psychotic'?"

"She was crazy."

"No. She sees the big picture."

"She was manipulative."

"She saves her son's life."

"And ruined mine." This is when I see wet splotches on my shirt. I have to touch my face to fully realize I'm crying.

"How does it ruin your life?" He looks genuinely confused. "The way I see it, Sabine, you ruin it all by yourself."

I wipe at my face and take a step back.

"The little performance you gave downstairs? You ruin an entire trough of Persians when I only got two days' worth of dough left." Dante comes around my father's desk, shimmying an Export A into the crack of his mouth. "You are the one who needs to get your head checked."

I tell myself I will shove him if he takes another step toward me.

"You will not find your father here." He holds his arms up, gestures evangelically. "Too late. The best thing is to take my offer, get on a plane and go home."

Crawl back under the rock you came from. Then it occurs to me.

"Who was trying to buy the recipe last year?"

Dante stops cold on the tongue-and-groove flooring. "It doesn't matter. Your father, he is not interested."

"But you were." This is why he wants an uncontested negotiation. "Once you own that briefcase, how much are you going to hand it over for?"

My uncle fixes his eyes on me, attempting to bore a hole through my skull. That's when I see things from his perspective. He's put in his time. He's done with the toil of bread. He is, and always has been, Dante of the smokejumper era, the same man who welcomed the northern fires and sold the country back its own ash. He is the one who created the slow churn of the Persian assembly line out front, who drew the line-up of people that bent and kinked three times before snaking out the door. I see that in his mind the Persian is his. It's as if the great Giuseppe Garibaldi had leaned to earth and whispered the recipe into Dante's ear.

And it doesn't mean a lick to me.

"I'll go back," I tell him, wiping my nose with the back of my hand. "But first my share is going to Enzo."

Fifty-One

Sabine

It's late in the day by the time I get back to the hotel. I locate my phone in the bunched-up bedsheets where it's whizzing and illuminated like a sleek little time bomb. There are about a thousand texts and voice mail alerts, all from Collette.

"Where have you been?" she shouts when I call her back. And without waiting for me to answer, "What the hell is that last post about?"

I don't know what she's talking about. But I'm guessing it's not good, so I stay quiet. The last thing we posted was the nice, Italian-spiced video of Zia Stella making the bomboloni.

"Don't tell me you haven't seen it?" Collette's voice trails an electric crackle. "You've let that little weasel go too far this time."

My palms are slick. I lower the phone to the bed, switch it to speaker and scroll back to the home screen. Right behind Collette's barrage of messages are all the alerts from my analytics app. *Sweet Rush* has had 12,000 unique views in the last four hours.

Zia Stella is good, but she's not that good.

My index finger is shaking so badly I have to stab at the YouTube app a half dozen times to engage the haptics. The screen opens and there I am in the static frame of a video I've never seen before.

My mouth open, I'm holding a bowl in the air. The caption reads: "Diva Set."

I shut one eye, tap the video and watch myself smash the bowl to the floor. The jaunty classical music soundtrack scores the trajectory of the bowl perfectly. Cymbals crash as it smashes into a thousand ceramic pieces.

"Sabine, are you there?"

The next clip is of me in the airplane on our flight here. I'm right up in the flight attendant's face. Here the soundtrack cuts out for the five seconds it takes me to shriek, "*What's highly dangerous is what the two fucking morons in the cockpit are doing!*"

"Sabine!"

But I can't answer her. I'm afraid my heart will jump out of my mouth. The third clip changes pace somewhat. I appear flat-out tranquilized as two PAs walk me off the set of *Wake Up Canada*, my feet barely skimming the ground. My head swivels on my neck like a pumpkin balanced on a bean pole.

I fast-forward. Here I am back in the studio kitchen. Paul is trying to mic me but can't get the clip to attach to my collar. I remember this, losing my patience. I reach up and shove him roughly with both palms. *"Jesus Fucking Christ! I'll do it myself!"* In the next clip I'm smiling, addressing the camera as I pull on oven mitts and take a cake out of the oven. But when I place it on the cooling rack, the entire thing collapses in on itself. Like a reflex, I slam a fist into the top of the hot cake. Then I jump back, howling, blowing on my scalded hand.

"Sabine, this is very bad for you."

"No shit," I whisper and hit pause.

"What's going on there?"

Then I suddenly think: What other footage has Wanda pulled out of the archives?

"Oh, no, no, no," I chant as I scrub quickly through the remaining scenes of smashed platters, sour faces and abused assistants. But it's me, just the worst of me brought to light.

"There's no Wanda," I say, tapping my chest in order to restart my heart. "Thank God."

"This is all Wanda!" Collette snaps. "I don't know what she was hoping to accomplish, but she's basically torpedoed any chance of being on the show. And she may have sunk your shot as well."

"I think that's the point." I'm still breathing in waves of relief. Am I going to rip her to pieces once I get off the phone? Yes. But this diva reel, this is not the worst possible scenario.

"Listen to me, Sabine. Get on a plane right now, okay? You get back here and we'll put you in front of the dev team tomorrow. You make sure you are beautiful and sober. We assure them, face to face, that this was a prank. That you are mentally fit for this role. That we're on board with their changes—excited even. That Wanda is not going to be a problem."

"How can I promise that?"

Collette doesn't answer right away. I imagine her moving around her desk, closing her office door, sitting down on her tufted rose sofa, picking at one of the copper-headed nails that hold the upholstery in place. "I am going to take care of Wanda personally."

Normally I'd be on board with some old-school reckoning. But Collette only knows half of the story. I may be the face of the enterprise, but Wanda is the hands.

"The thing is," I start quietly, "Wanda may have other, worse footage."

"Of what?"

I press my thumbs against my eyelids, glance at the hotel room door and take the phone off speaker. "Of the way we film *Sweet Rush.*" I can tell this is going to be a struggle to explain. "Wanda is the, uh, body you see doing the actual decorating, the details—well, basically any of the baking."

"Sabine, what are you talking about?"

"I can't actually bake."

Fifty-Two

Wanda

"Open the goddamn door before I kick it down."

Inside the room I brace for impact, but Sabine must be barefoot because her kick registers as a dull thud, followed by a groan. I'm not surprised by her reaction to the diva video, I'm just surprised it took her so long to discover it.

"Wanda!" She starts slapping the door with both palms. "If you're not going to talk to me then take that bloody video down."

So, she doesn't know how to remove videos from our channel. This is valuable information considering what I have programmed to appear on *Sweet Rush* tomorrow morning.

For a minute there's no sound. I slide up the door and press my eye against the spy hole. Sabine is standing there, eyes narrowed, hair slick as though she ran a pair of greasy hands through it. It doesn't occur to her that she's done anything wrong. She's unfazed by the fact that, in the matter of a few short days, I've been robbed of my raison d'etre and reduced to a silent-on-camera character on the show I created for myself! She could have changed the outcome. If she had stood up to Collette like she said she would, she could have stymied the tide against me.

We stare each other down, two feet apart with a door between. This is how we are. Seeing each other and not seeing each other.

I touch the flash drive around my neck. Doesn't she realize I have her entire fifteen-year career in my hands?

Her cheeks puff out and I hear her doing the rapid kundalini yoga breathing that once upon a time we thought was bullshit. *You fucking traitor,* I think.

"You fucking traitor!" she shouts.

Once Sabine retreats to God knows where, I slip down the hall to the elevator hoping to catch Paul in the bar. I have some unfinished business with him and his sanctimonious attitude. He knows full well how much I do for Sabine, and yet he's made me the Judas here.

Instead, I find DuPierre in the lobby. He's wearing flip-flops and swim trunks and not much else.

"I'm starting to think we're the only two people staying at this hotel," he says.

I size him up; his lack of clothing practically demands it. Unlike his completely depigmented scalp, his chest is lean and grizzled. He looks like he could dive from a ten metre board and slice through the surface without creating a single ripple. He is not unattractive, although I question the judgement of anyone walking around a hotel half-naked.

"Shouldn't you be out knocking down doors?" I ask. "Last time we spoke I gave you some pretty good intel."

"And what was that?"

"All the players in line for that recipe you're after."

He smiles. "The brass has waited years. Another few days won't make a difference."

"And here I mistook you for an ambulance chaser."

He scrapes his room card against the silver needlepoint stubble on his cheek and looks at me. "Come for a swim."

I shake my head. "I don't have a bathing suit."

Before I know it, he's grabbed my hand. "Perfect."

Fifty-Three

Wanda

'm not someone who just strips down to their skivvies in front of strangers, but that's exactly what I do by the hotel pool. The lights are low, the saltwater pool is warm and DuPierre is watching me from the other side of the deck. Not in a sleazeball way. More like he's impressed. Admiring of my shamelessness. Which makes slipping out of my clothes an easy matter. It's been a long time since anyone's been enthralled by something I've done.

I take off my glasses, forego my usual cannonball, and slip into the deep end. Across the pool Duddy sinks below the surface, flashes like a Pacific herring, then emerges a moment later a few feet away. I can hear his hair squeak as he sluices water from it.

"So, now that we're alone, tell me why you've taken this tact to sabotage your boss?"

"Are you referring to the new video on *Sweet Rush*?" I stretch both hands out over the surface of the water and create a half-moon ripple around me.

He floats up the side of the pool. "I'm an official subscriber. One of many."

"It's more of a rally cry. A reminder about, well, loyalties."

"That's quite a nudge. Is this about the TV deal you mentioned?" I hesitate but then nod.

"How much money do you stand to lose?"

Of course he thinks it's about money. What compels men to drill down to this expected bottom line?

"Boy, you've got me all figured out." I push off the side and slice across the pool. The saltwater feels good against my skin and burns my eyes. When I surface at the shallow end, Duddy is somehow already there.

"I do know a thing or two after twenty years in this business," he says to me as I plant both feet at the bottom.

"The cookie-lawyering business?" I'm glad I'm wearing a black bra because the water here only reaches partway up my chest. "How did you get into this line of work, anyway?"

"Corporate law?" DuPierre frowns. "There were family reasons."

"Like what? Your father gave a ton of money to the law school?"

"Actually, my mother raised me." He leans against the pool tile. "Drove a school bus her entire adult life to do it. Eventually it was my turn to take care of her."

I squeeze out one of my braids. "So much for rich, white guy generalizations."

"Sometimes they're correct," DuPierre says slowly. "And not always pleasant."

"For example?"

He shrugs. "For people like you and me? It almost always comes down to money."

"Really? What kind of people are we?"

"The kind that don't have everything handed to them."

"Good thing we're generalizing, because that's most people in the world." I flip on my back and swim away from him. I can hear him paddle after me, but I keep my eyes on the trussed ceiling. "I don't care about cash."

"You would if you knew how much my client is ready to offer for the recipe."

I tip my head to look at him and feel the rush of water enveloping one ear. DuPierre rolls onto his back so that he is floating next to me. His sharp profile is like a submarine surfacing.

"I want you to help me buy the recipe—and the bakery shares —from Sabine."

Something in my chest dampens with this information. It really is about business. What did I think was going to happen? That he'd try seducing me in the pool?

"I've got one chance to make this deal happen, then the brass is going to take it out of my hands. It's fair to say your boss is . . . touchy right now? My gut says I go to her myself and it won't go over well."

I feel my shoulder blades begin to constrict under water, so I kick myself upright and begin treading lightly. DuPierre does the same. For a moment our legs tangle together underwater. I pull away and make it to the side in a few short strokes.

"It won't go any better with me involved."

"I think your vision's a bit myopic, Wanda." He swims in my direction but keeps his distance this time. Without my glasses he's a mercury blur. "You have enormous sway over Sabine, but for some reason, you're choosing not to use it."

I watch him swim to the side and hoist himself out of the water. "Or, I should say, you're using it in a petty way."

That stings. Probably because it's true. It alarms me that he's discerned this much about me from a couple of drinks and a video post. I trace the pool tile with a fingernail. "You don't know my situation with her."

He sits on the ledge and sniffs chlorinated water. "Then tell me."

"She can't bake."

It just falls out. That happens to me sometimes. I get worn down by inquisition and demand, flattery, and appeal. Suddenly, I hand over years of secrecy and effort to a stranger.

I let go of the side, point my toes in an underwater elevé and pump my shoulders until I reach the bottom. I flutter my arms to keep myself pinned to the tile while a steady stream of bubbles rushes past my eyes. It makes no sense. Why should it be so hard to stay afloat, but even harder to sink? I think about this until my lungs have nearly exhausted their oxygen supply. When I shoot to the surface Duddy is waiting for me.

"Make my deal part of your deal," he says quietly.

"Now I know why you're not out there kicking down doors. You've got a battering ram right here."

He doesn't deny it, the role he's plotted for me. "I'm going to offer her a lot of money, Wanda. You get her to take my deal and from that, you name your commission."

Fuck it. Fuck the slanted biases of his face and grey eyes all focused in my direction. I never bought it for a minute. I thumb the water from my nose, pick my underwear from my butt. "Why does Brighello want the recipe so badly?"

He shakes his head. "Can't break client confidentiality. But I will tell you it's a human interest story."

My fingers are pruning. I pull myself to the ledge a few feet away from him and let water stream from my bra cups. "A human interest story might be what convinces me to help you."

"I can't say a word, Wanda." It's one of the only times since I've met him that he sounds serious.

I lean over and look at my reflection in the water. "This human interest story, have you got a draft form of it somewhere in your email?"

He looks down at my reflection and then nods slowly.

"And that particular email address is the one on the business card you gave me?"

DuPierre nods again.

"Well then." I smile. "Who needs words?"

Fifty-Four

Wanda

It's an article, an old one in an Italian newspaper called *Il Mattino*, from the days before the internet. The courier font is fuzzy, like someone rooted through a microfiche file, printed it on a copier, then scanned it with their phone.

As the file downloads from DuPierre's email account and uploads onto my computer, I turn on the blow dryer, aim it at my hair and attempt to ease apart the knots the little bottle of hotel conditioner has missed. DuPierre's offer is just sitting there in my brain like an unwrapped present. I think of how I nearly lost myself when I lost Wheat Bump. Back then it was impossible to see beyond the money—the millions of dollars I could have had some part in. I kept telling people that I had been robbed, because for me, "robbery" had somehow become shorthand for giving in to stupidity. I had been stupid-ed out of millions of dollars. But the truth was I had happily sold Wheat Bump for $200,000. Before Odin switched the playing field on me by tweaking the app, repackaging it and peddling it off to Microsoft, I was over the moon. I'd given half of the money to my father for the house and that made me happy. The rest I carried off with me overseas so that I could explore some of the most historic countries in the world in style.

Then, just like that, a windfall became pocket change.

Maybe DuPierre's right. For some people it always comes down to money.

I switch off the blow dryer. My hair is still damp, but the file is ready, and I'm interested in learning why Brighello is so interested in this rinky-dink Persian recipe. I save the file as a PDF and then disconnect from Duddy's browser. The article itself is in Italian, which means I'm going to have to feed it through some translation program. I was hoping to copy and paste the text directly into a browser but it's a scanned article and my computer won't recognize the characters. I'll have to type it in by hand if I want to decode it.

An hour later I sit back in my chair and feel two parallel bolts of pain tear through my shoulder blades, just east and west of my spine. I've sat hunched this entire time taking only shallow breaths. Anything deeper and the room would have surely imploded.

"My God," I whisper, and close my computer, carefully pushing it to the edge of the desk, as if that might make the story go away. As if I might unlearn it.

Fifty-Five

Sabine

I wake up well past noon on Wednesday having lost count of the number of consecutive days I've been hungover.

Is this a problem that needs to be dealt with?

Sure.

But right now there's a whole whack of issues buoying around me like a tub full of turds. The hotel phone rang on and off through the night until I knocked the handset from the receiver, kicked it into the bathroom and shut the door. I knew it was Dante. Other than Julia, he's the only one that doesn't have my cell number. The only one who believes in the unalterable certainty of his wishes.

The first thing I see when I actually open my eyes is the Persian recipe sitting on the dresser. The briefcase looks menacing, like something an assassin might carry. Funny that it should still be locked tight when so many other things have been spilled open.

When I told Collette about my baking problem yesterday on the phone, there's no denying she got all cold on me. I tried framing it in a way that was advantageous, explaining how my lack of true skills is the *very reason* I'm committed to hosting a cooking competition; I'll never have to bake on camera again! But Collette wasn't in a mood to riff. She told me again to get on a plane—something I have obviously neglected to do—and get in front of the Cerberus, get in front of any other ammunition Wanda may possess.

Have I been disingenuous to my subscribers? Yes. But if you want to talk real, life-altering lies, take a look at the ones my father and grandmother spun. They built entire lives on cobwebs and shifting sands.

My head is throbbing as I sit up and scan the bedside table for any fairy-sized bottles of booze I may have overlooked last night. Someone needs to raise a toast to them, the Schemers and Thieves. But there's not a single intact bottle in sight. Which means I'll have to execute the days' first Herculean task, swinging my legs over the side of the bed, unassisted.

I rise, gingerly, transferring my weight to my feet, give an ever so slight bounce to make sure they hold before taking a step to the dresser. When I pick up the phone my face unlocks the home screen and wakes the analytics app. There's a new spike in activity. I put the phone down. For the second time in my life, I'm terrified of what's being said about me.

My purse is on the floor, so I get down on my knees, dump it out and catch the Xanax bottle before it rolls under the dresser. I count out two pills and swallow them dry. Then I chase them down with a third. I slide the phone down to the floor beside me. The simple knowledge that those little pills are in my body, advancing on my anxiety like a slow but effective militia, is enough to prepare me to try again.

One new video. Posted two hours ago. Ten thousand views.

I skip our sponsor's ad, ready for some highly compromising footage of myself. Instead, it's a video of a small orange monkey sitting on the counter of a modern, white kitchen. The monkey stares at the camera with its enormous, lovable eyes, makes a chirping sound, then hops to the far end of the counter.

He leaves a small pile of shit behind.

The camera follows as he jumps from the counter to the white range and deposits another load right between the front burners. The circus-inspired soundtrack seems to be keeping time with the creature's bowel movements. When the music hits the bridge, we see the monkey walk on all fours to a dinner table set with white stoneware. I hold my breath. Incredibly, the animal jumps from plate to plate, stopping to squat on each one and serve up a runny amuse-bouche.

I don't know where Wanda found this footage. More importantly, I don't know how to get rid of it. I press the back of my hand to my temple and scroll down past the video to the comments.

JoJo Bean 2 hours ago
Is she having a mental breakdown? Puts yesterday's weird video into context.

^Hide reply
Sarah Eddie 1 hour ago
She's been hacked by Russians

LocandTania just now
russians scraping bottom of barrel!!

ReynoldsWhitakerII 2 hours ago
Finally, Sabine shows us her true self and skills!

Reynolds's comment is followed by at least a dozen thumbs-up icons.

Vic + Jonny 22   1 hour ago
What happened to all the other videos??? Looking for the rough puff one but entire channel seems blocked?

^Hide reply
BarStoolBakes   1 hour ago
Monkey sh$t on them??

What happened to all the other videos? I scroll up and down frantically, but the right hand column dedicated to related content is now entirely populated by monkey videos. I go to the *Sweet Rush* home page where the shitting monkey sits in the cued-up position. But the videos below it—all 150-something of them—have been replaced by black boxes and the words, "Video Not Available."

The phone slips from my hand. I let it go. The briefcase stares me down from the top of the dresser. That's when I know what I have to do. Or, more accurately, that's when I know I can delay no longer. I pick up the phone again. Even though it only fell a foot or so, a large crack spiderwebs diagonally across the screen. It's the sort of moment made for smashing mixing bowls.

Instead, I call Enzo. I need him to turn that briefcase into money. Fast.

I might as well be holding one-half of my skull in each hand as I stand in front of Wanda's room. Fortunately, she opens the door this time because I would not be able to tolerate the sound of my fists pounding for long.

"What?" She stands with her feet planted, arms akimbo.

"I get it." I lean one arm against the doorframe. I'm doing some big-cheeked standard yoga breathing to basically keep myself from throwing up. "You're angry. You have every right to be because it's not going to happen the way you want. That's the honest truth. But I'm going to make it up to you as much as I can."

To my surprise, Wanda steps aside.

I creep past her and scan the room—ten times neater than mine—for a chair, or a hospital stretcher. I settle on the sofa by the window. She has the same view of Lake Superior that I do, the water and sky just shades apart.

"I'm taking the offer from my cousin. We're signing on Friday. You heard it yourself—four hundred thousand over two years." It's difficult, but I need to get this out as quickly as possible before I lose my thread, before I lose consciousness. "That's two hundred grand a year, gross. I'm going to pass it directly to you."

She is still standing at the entrance, blinking at me. I lower my head to the throw cushion while she takes her sweet time closing the door and walking over to the bed.

"How do you know that's the highest offer?"

The sleepy torpor of the Xanax is kicking in. "What do you mean, how do I know?"

Wanda opens her mouth to answer, then changes her mind and sits on the bed, smoothing her denim skirt over her lap as though we're at afternoon tea at the King Eddie.

"Four hundred thousand over two years in exchange for what?"

Good, we're getting somewhere. "In exchange for your silence."

"Wow," she says in a deadpan voice. "That's dramatic."

"I've got nothing but drama to offer."

"You must really value my silence. That money could do wonders for you."

I squeeze my eyes shut. I can't believe I'm handing her this windfall.

"You still have a fair amount to pay on your condo mortgage. Your retirement savings are practically non-existent and your combined bank account balance barely qualifies you for free chequing."

I swallow back a wave of bile imagining how she's accessed this information. "So, the condition is this." I push myself up on one elbow. "You need to sign the contract. Now. While I'm still here." I roll on one hip and reach into my pocket for the pages I printed in the business office. "You sign, take a picture and send it to Collette."

I watch her take the contract and leaf through it as though she's never seen it before.

"And CC me on that email." I get up. Fortunately, her bathroom is in the same place as mine. I start toward it, each step slow and considered, as though I'm walking on the sloped and irregular surface of an alternate reality. I make it as far as the desk and grab the wastepaper basket. The one thing I tell myself as the vomit rises in waves, *now comes the relief.*

Fifty-Six

Wanda

I book a flight departing late Friday afternoon and swear that this time, I'll be on that plane. Sabine will sign the business over to Enzo at noon, I will make sure it happens, then get the hell out of this place. The key is to just sit here until then. I can do it; it's already Wednesday night. Avoid the lobby, avoid the bar, avoid Duddy DuPierre.

I think about how the flight home will be the complete opposite of our flight here. I think about how we've all come undone, how much we've lost. Of course there are other, bigger losses I could make Sabine aware of. But I've decided not to. I can't bring myself to implode someone else's world, even hers. Sabine will never know what I've done for her; it's an invisible act of loyalty. She doesn't deserve it, but she doesn't deserve to ever find out what's written in that article.

I'm changing into pajamas covered in cartoon ponies when my phone dings. I lean over the screen and read the message from Collette.

Zoom me now.

—

When she lets me into the meeting, she is a white, disembodied head floating in a dark room. I've been granted audience with the Great and Powerful Oz.

"Oh good," she says. "I wanted you to see my face when you hear this. Just so you know it's real."

My hands are face down on either side of my laptop, the palms wet. When I raise them, they leave two patches of perspiration on the dark wood veneer.

"Wanda, you're off the show." She says it quietly, neutrally. Not with glee or sympathy.

"What?" That's impossible. I signed the contract. I laid the broomstick of the Wicked Witch of the West at her feet.

"No sous chefs, no assistants," Collette continues. "They've decided to bring in a co-host for Sabine after all. Antony Oberfleet. He's South African. What they call a 'paper craft' star. Three and a half million YouTube subscribers. Gorgeous, gay, global. Basically, he checks all the boxes."

"Paper craft?" It's all I can manage to say over the trumpeting wail that fills my head.

"Apparently people who like baking also like making things out of paper. Centrepieces, wall art . . . Well, you can look him up yourself."

"But I signed!" I finally spit out. "You told me to sign and I did."

"That was yesterday afternoon. Completely irrelevant now."

"You can't do this to me."

"You did it to yourself!" Collette's face is a ripple of green phosphorescent. "The diva video alarmed the dev team. It was pretty clear to them who posted it—who had access to that footage. But to stupidly follow it up with that monkey stunt this morning? That sealed your fate."

I am crying and I don't care. "Does anybody want to know why I did it?"

"Again, irrelevant! Has anyone ever told you that you're shit at reading the room?"

I can feel tears inside my nostrils. I must be sucking them up with every sob. "You were in those meetings too—you could have said something."

"I'm not only talking about Netflix." Collette presses her temple with an index finger. "I mean with Sabine. You insinuated yourself into her life like a little cling-on assistant."

"I'm not just an assistant."

"Right, I know all about it. You're the keeper of her career secrets." Collette's smile is stuck to her eyeteeth. "But think carefully—how badly do you want to be the whistleblower? Is it worth me personally destroying any career you try to make for yourself in Toronto?"

"You're making me out to be some kind of monster. All I've done is help Sabine."

"Believe it or not, I know that's true." Collette switches on a desk lamp and her office and torso come into view. She sits back, folding her fingers into a power teepee. "Which is why I'm taking the time for this tête-à-tête. First, you've got to realize that your part in any TV deal is dead. Once you've acknowledged this, I think I have a way for you to move on."

I wipe my cheeks with my pajama sleeve. "Move on to what?"

"Wheat Bump is looking for someone to sit on the board of directors. Holland Weiss Fortitude happens to manage their PR.

If I walk down to the eighth floor and ask for a favour, I can make you a shoo-in for the spot." Collette is staring right into me across a thousand kilometres. "Wanda, I know you have a history you want to mend there."

But the tears go cold in my lashes. It's as though she's speaking a language I once knew but can now barely comprehend. The way she laces back and forth between threats and favours makes me want to put my head between my knees.

"Does Sabine know?"

"She can't help you." Collette breaks her hands apart and starts shuffling papers on her desk, a signal that this particular tête-à-tête is over. "I haven't told her yet about this latest evolution at the network. But she won't have much say. They nearly kicked her to the curb with you."

Fifty-Seven

Wanda

Paul is not answering his door. I even do our special triple knock which I jokingly used to call the *booty call tap*.

"Paul," I say into the crack of the doorframe. "It's me, Wanda."

Who else would it be?

"Paul," I raise my voice. "I'm going to knock louder and louder until you open up."

Seconds later I hear him unlock the bolt. I knew the threat of embarrassment would work.

"What?" He stands blocking the doorway with his body. He's wearing the complimentary hotel robe and I can hear a violent gunfight playing at low volume on the TV.

"I just—can I come in?"

"No."

I pick at a chip in the paint of the door frame. "Collette says I'm out of the Netflix deal. Completely. They're replacing me with some guy that makes centrepieces out of paper."

"I don't care, Wanda."

The edge of the paint chip comes loose and stabs me under the fingernail. I take a step back. "Why are you being such an asshole?"

"Actually, you're the asshole." He's got the door handle in a white-knuckled grip. "You took private footage I shot under contract—compromising footage—and made it public."

"It was all fake to begin with!"

"I was happy, Wanda." Paul is looking at me as though I'd run over his dog, then backed up over it for good measure. "I liked being with you. I liked working with Sabine. But you didn't get what you wanted so you had to blow it all up."

"Jesus." I wipe my eyes. It's not clear if this is a new batch of tears or a continuation from the Zoom call. "That's rich. If a person stands up for herself, she's suddenly—"

He closes the door quietly in my face.

Fifty-Eight

Wanda

On Thursday morning when I remember who I am, where I am, and how I got here, I'm flooded with a hopelessness and regret that have somehow become hallmarks of my career. Back in the Wheat Bump days I had a faceless corporate entity to blame. This morning I lie on my back and begin to spread the black gel of culpability much closer to home.

For three years I've served as Sabine's stunt double, always believing I meant so much more. You can't help but forge an intimate family bond in a company as small as ours. As pedestrian as it sounds, the workday was—well, fun. When you take into account the fact that she couldn't bake, it's pretty astounding that she built an influencer empire from nothing. Took her looks and a bit of charisma and turned it into a six-million-strong movement. I admired her shit-talking brazenness. People really do think twice before messing with a tough-as-nails bitch, and as someone who'd been messed with big-time, it was an attitude that I aspired to; something I thought I'd learn under her wing. But the truth is, I built a shrine to an unwilling mentor. She wasn't taking me in, she was keeping me close. That's skill as well—being a parasite. Taking without the other person realizing you're giving nothing back.

My phone rings. My father's name lights the screen, which means it's my brother calling.

"What do you want, asswipe?" I yawn. "It's too early to be calling."

"Wanda?"

"Yeah?" I sit up. Anytime Manny doesn't lead with an insult, it's time to worry.

"Did you get my message last night?"

"What happened?"

"You need to come home, Wanda."

Behind him I hear my mother and father arguing. Otherwise, it's my aunt and my father arguing. Or my uncle and my mother. "What's happening, Manny? What are they saying?"

"Those guys from the bank are here—like really here this time. With a sign and shit?"

Another man's voice now in the background. It's not my father or my uncle.

"They're saying we're in default? They came with a power of sale notice. It's like, stapled to our front door."

"They can't do that." I scramble to my knees. "Put Dad on the line."

"They said we've ignored all the court documents."

"What court documents?" I slip off the bed and fumble with my computer.

"We have thirty days to . . ." His sentence hangs there unfinished. I hear him page through some sheets. "Here—'to bring the mortgage back into good standing, paying the mortgage arrears and other penalties.' But Wanda? This was dated twenty-two days ago."

"Put Dad on the fucking phone!"

"Now he's outside arguing with the guy who's holding the staple gun."

I type "HOW BAD IS A POWER OF SALE NOTICE" in my browser and get served up a bunch of ads for law firms.

Manny is sobbing quietly, which is, I promise you, not what you want to hear a seventeen-year-old boy do. "Does this mean I'm going to lose my room? Are we going to live in a motel?"

I feel big pearls of sweat bulging along my hairline." Does it say how much we're in arrears for?"

"I don't know what arrears means."

"How much does he owe?"

Manny whimpers. "There's so many pages."

"Look at the back," I tell him. "Skip to the end."

I hear him thumbing through the document. "Okay, I'm at the end, Wanda."

"Take a breath. Read me what it says."

"It says lots of stuff."

"Look for dollar signs, Manny."

"Here! I found it. Right near the end." He sounds excited, sure of himself. For a moment I have hope that my father hasn't actually sunk us.

"'I hereby give you notice that the amount now due on the mortgage for principal money, interest and solicitor costs is, in total, $94,708 Canadian.'"

I don't know how I know DuPierre's room number, but five minutes later there I am, unwashed, unbrushed, still in my pajamas, and slumped against his door.

"Woah, what happened to you?" he asks, stepping aside so I can stagger into the room and collapse across the freshly made bed. I stay like that, face down, thinking, deciding, until my glasses begin to crush the bridge of my nose. When I roll over, he's standing over me, looking as sharp as a galvanized nail in a grey suit and a seafoam tie.

"You alright?" He smells as minty as he looks.

I sniff. "Who made the bed?"

"What?"

"It's too early for housekeeping." This has just occurred to me while face down on the duvet. "Did you make it yourself?"

DuPierre smiles. "Thanks for noticing. You know, I always say, a fresh start to the day begins with a freshly made bed." Then he looks at me, the shit-storm that's just plowed through his door, and the ridiculous smile fades.

"I'm going to go out on a limb and say you're not alright."

"If I was alright, would I show up at a stranger's hotel room at ten a.m. in *My Little Pony* pajamas?"

He reaches down and brushes hair out of my face. "Your real friends have shunned you?"

"Worse."

Manny sent me pics of the notice of sale document. I understood the upshot, which was about the same amount that his teenage brain had already deciphered. Our father had sat on this notice for over three weeks, hoping it was an empty threat. Now we had eight days to pay back $94,000. In full. Not only had he missed six months' worth of mortgage payments, he'd also defaulted on a home equity loan that he took out last year without telling me. Considering we don't have anywhere close to $94,000, it appears that we are full-on, furniture-on-the-front-lawn, evicted.

"My father's an asshole with money," I say.

"I'm sorry, kid." DuPierre sits down and offers me the pristine pocket square from his jacket pocket. "Mine was a drunk."

I sit up and blow noisily for a minute. He doesn't even wince. "He's lost us our house two times over." *The house we bought with my Wheat Bump money.* "We're out on the street."

He says nothing, and for a minute I think he's going to put his arm around me. Which wouldn't be the worst thing in world right now. Instead he gets up, crosses the room, and sits down at the desk. "So how can I help you? You know I'm not that kind of lawyer, right?"

The $400,000 Sabine promised yesterday works out to less than $8,000 a month. Then minus tax, legal fees and take into account when the payment cycle is actually set to start—the offer isn't going to cut it. I need a hundred grand in eight days.

"I'm going to help you buy the recipe from Sabine," I hear myself say.

He glances at his computer. "Wanda, did you read the article in my email?"

"Yes."

"You understand, then, what the stakes are for Brighello?"

"More importantly I understand what the stakes are for Sabine."

He runs a hand through his hair, then gets up, comes back to the bed and sits. "Listen, I thought about this all night. It was a bad idea to involve you. I wasn't clear with you that it's my job to make this happen regardless of people's emotions."

"Right. The cutthroat cookie business."

"Look, I care about you, Wanda."

I look up. He cares? Or he *cares?*

"And I don't want you to be responsible for whatever might happen to Sabine."

"Why does she even have to know?" I flop back down on the bed. "You do this kind of thing all the time. She takes the offer, signs some paperwork. You go back to your corporate head-quarters, she goes back to her life—never the two shall meet."

"I can't guarantee that."

I think of my family; the twins, Manny, my mom, my aunt and uncle, even my father. I think of every stick of furniture, every scrap of paper turned out on the front lawn. I have to take the chance of turning Sabine's world upside down in order to prevent it from happening to mine.

Fifty-Nine

Sabine

"Antony has created the most amazing three-dimensional paper banana!" Britt tells us.

"Nearly a metre-and-a-half long." Antony Oberfleet says in his funny accent. He spreads his athletic arms to demonstrate. They are out of the video frame, but we get the picture.

"We can suspend it from the ceiling during parfait week." Britt's video square has dominated most of the Zoom call this gloomy Friday morning. She's clearly the one who discovered Antony Oberfleet. Personally, I can't imagine François Payard agreeing to go head to head with Anna Olson while standing under an oversized banana, but Collette's instructions for this call were pretty clear: listen, nod, murmur encouragingly. Otherwise keep my mouth shut.

"What the fuck does paper have to do with pastry?" I'd demanded earlier when she called with the latest update from the Cerberus.

"Their research indicates that baking shows are losing in popularity."

"How is that even possible? In our last conversation baking was all the rage."

"A new hybrid model is emerging," Collette said. "Baking alone is out. Baking while crafting is in."

"That's complete bullshit."

"Look," Collette raised her voice sharply. "Two days ago they were ready to ditch you, right along with Wanda. I had to swear up and down that you weren't a total loose cannon. Stake my forty-year career on the fact that you weren't having a nervous breakdown. I said you'd been hacked. They weren't buying it— this was clearly an inside job. Finally, I had to throw Wanda under the bus."

This is why I'm not allowed to complain, even though I've lost solo-host status. Wanda is off the show. This Oberfleet character is in. I am next in the line of fire.

"How do we know Wanda won't . . . retaliate?" I asked quietly.

"She won't bother you," Collette replied. "I gave her a long-overdue career spanking that settled her right down."

I didn't mention it, but it's more likely that $400,000 in hush money is what settled her down.

"I just hope I'm backing the right horse here, Sabine," Collette continued. "A week ago, this show was the most important thing in your life. Now, you seem only vaguely interested. I've asked you repeatedly to come back and talk to these people in person, reassure them that you're committed to the project. This isn't a one-off—it's a series, and you're not giving off a series vibe. And those videos! Sabine, you don't seem to understand how damaging they are."

The me from a couple weeks ago would not have sat quietly through this harangue. Was she *backing the right horse*? I would have reminded her that I was the *only* horse she had in this race.

But the me we're dealing with now—exposed, a fraud—is at a certain disadvantage.

"I'm signing the sale of my father's business today," I offered weakly. "It's been ... distracting."

"The timing is terrible."

"Once it's done, everything will go back to normal," I promised. How could I make it any clearer? I was about to bankrupt my aunt and hand over every nickel of my father's forty-year legacy just to keep the project, my career and a giant paper banana afloat.

Now Brie, the friendlier head of the Cerberus, cuts into these thoughts. "Sabine, have you immersed yourself in Antony's channel?"

"Yes!" I lie, transmitting the positivity that is required of me. "It's so fun, Antony!"

"No, yours is so fun!" he insists. His flattened South African vowels almost make him sound genuine. "I'm a huge fan of *Sweet Rush.*"

"We've been scouting a partnership for Antony for over a year," Britt interjects. "When he mentioned that he follows your work, the idea just clicked."

I'll bet. "Paper and pastry." I nod, glancing at the time. "Who would have ever thought of that combination?" I'm due to meet my cousin and D'Abruzzo at noon to sign the paperwork. It's also when Enzo is set to bake the last batch of Persian dough that my father created. And Paul will help commemorate by filming.

"Antony has charisma. Ant—sorry to talk about you like you're not here!" Brett's chortle is alarming. "But you and Sabine as co-hosts and co-judges will make for some great streaming."

I clear my throat. "And will the guests have to, uh, fold things?"

There's silence from all of the squares, but I spot Collette's eyes bugging out of her head.

"I mean, will Jamie Kennedy have to make origami paper napkins along with a tart flambé? Or how do you envision this working?"

"So, paper craft is about a lot more than origami," Antony says through a decidedly dimmed smile. "If you've seen my paper garland video, Sabine, you'll know what I'm talking about."

"I love the paper garland video!" I assure him.

"So fun, right?"

"So, so fun."

Sixty

Sabine

'm drinking coffee, getting dressed and deciding whether to add a fourth sedative to my routine when there's a knock at the door. I'm half-expecting this. I didn't really buy Collette's cool assurance that she'd simply snuffed out Wanda's hopes and dreams with a stern talking-to.

What I don't expect is for her to show up at my door with a man.

I recognize him immediately. The Silver Fox from the bar. From the sauna.

"This is Duddy DuPierre." She jabs a finger in his direction then walks into the room.

"We've met," he says, following her.

I watch with disbelief as they casually saunter in. "Actually, no. We haven't."

"Sure we have." The Silver Fox takes in the hurricane path that is my room. "I gave you some friendly advice in the sauna."

I expected Wanda to come to me in tears or in a rage. But the woman leaning against my dresser has her arms folded coolly across her overalled chest. There's something very wrong with this scenario, but I don't have time to find out what it is exactly.

"Whatever you're doing here, I'm just on my way out." I slide my phone into my purse. "I'm going to be late, in fact."

"DuPierre is here to talk about the Persian." Wanda glances at the briefcase on the dresser beside her. "To make an offer, actually."

I blink. The pills must be working already. I feel a sweep of exhaustion at this latest bit of ridiculousness. "I don't even want to know what that's all about," I tell her. But I grab the briefcase in case she decides to pull a grab and dash.

"I represent some people who made an offer to your uncle last year," the Silver Fox says. "Which he promised to discuss with your father."

I look around for the car keys. "Guess it didn't pan out, huh?"

"No, but I did circle back, after your father died. I laid out a generous offer." He actually moves the pile of dirty laundry off the desk chair and sits down. "In fact, you might have seen me in the bar that night you met him for drinks? I didn't realize that all this time he's never actually been in possession of the recipe."

"And he never will be, so you're out of luck." I find the keys under the duvet and look up. "Who are you, anyway?"

"He works for the cookie company," Wanda pipes up. "Brighello."

"Biscotti company," he corrects her. "Italy's premium biscotti manufacturer."

"He wants to buy the Persian recipe and the bakery shares. But mostly the Persian."

The Silver Fox folds one leg elegantly over the other, brushes an invisible crease from his trousers. "Who needs the middle-man, right?"

I have no idea what Wanda's involvement is in all this. The best I can make out is that it's just another in a string of bizarre encounters engendered by that blighted Persian recipe, and the sooner I get it into Enzo's possession the better.

"Super sorry," I say as I make for the door, "but it's already in the works."

He's like quicksilver because when I reach the door, he's already there. I freeze mid-step. "Get the hell out of my way."

He's not exactly blocking my path, but he creates a formidable obstacle between me and the outside world. I turn and look at Wanda. She knows better than anyone how I feel about people foisting themselves on me.

But she's staring at the floorboards, playing with a chain around her neck.

The Silver Fox takes a document out of his jacket pocket and unfolds it carefully. "I'm offering you eight hundred thousand euros for your father's share of the bakery and all intellectual property rights associated with the Persian recipe."

I see now that this is a prank. "Get the fuck out of my room," I tell him.

He stands, fingering the staple in the corner of the document. "It's a legitimate offer, Sabine. The same your uncle would have received if he'd managed to bring me the recipe."

I glance down at the briefcase. I'm clutching the handle so tightly my fist is turning red. I should know better than to ask. But I ask anyway. "Why?"

"People like it." He moves away from the door, places the paperwork on the entryway table and puts his hands in his pockets. "Brighello specializes in grocery store biscuits. Stellinis, bambolettos, strombos, donarellas. We're looking to expand to mass-marketed cakes, doughnuts and pastry. Become the Vachon of Italy."

I look at him. "Bullshit." Then I look back at Wanda. The laminate floor is practically peeling under her gaze. "This is your doing, isn't it? Some sort of weird revenge play?"

"How is offering you eight hundred thousand euros revenge?" the Silver Fox asks.

Wanda snaps out of it and glances at him sharply. Something tells me I should figure out the connection between these two, but there's no room for that kind of sleuthing under the Xanax cloud.

"It's not because of the show," Wanda says quietly. "And even if it feels like it, it's not really revenge. Anymore."

She reaches behind her neck and unclasps the necklace. "You're going to take his offer. You'll keep half of it, the rest you'll give to me. Cash. No strings, no conditions. And preferably within the next forty-eight hours."

I smile. I can't stop it. A huge, shit-eating grin cracks wide across my face. I don't know what it means or where it comes from but when Wanda sees it, she steps forward and drops the chain in my hand. Instead of a pendant, it's strung with a flash drive in the shape of one of those massage parlor cats.

"What is this?"

"I think you know."

Oh.

I look at my open palm. The cat is painted in Japanese characters and its little paw actually moves. I see now. It's my entire career, boiled down to this.

"So, it's extortion?"

"Why put a label on it?" Wanda tries to smile but seems close to tears. "Just take the fucking money, Sabine."

Before I even know what I'm doing, my hand closes around the flash drive, flies across the space between us, and strikes her in the face.

Wanda cries out and stumbles backward. But that's all I see. I'm out of the room then, racing down the hallway, taking the stairs two at a time. Briefcase clutched in one hand, all of my sins in the other.

Sixty-One

Wanda

"Well, that didn't go as planned." Duddy brings a bucket of ice from the machine down the hall.

I say nothing. My mind and body are in shambles. I let him talk instead.

"The Brighello people are in town," he says wrapping a handful of cubes in a pillowcase and positioning it against my cheek. "My boss felt the need to be here in case things went south. Which is what appears to be happening."

I know what happens next. He'll tell me to pack my stuff, get on my flight and let Sabine wrestle with the fallout on her own.

"I thought Brighello doesn't want to step in." I shift the ice pack and test my jaw.

"They don't, Wanda. But they can't lose that recipe."

Sixty-Two

Sabine

Things are far too jovial in the bakery. D'Abruzzo is late but Paul has just finished filming Enzo putting the last batch of Persians on the cooling rack. My cousin is surrounded by co-workers who are just minutes away from becoming his employees. Someone's placed a gorgeous mirror glaze chocolate cake on the worktable in the back room. From the number of high-fives going around, it's safe to say the team approves of Enzo as their new boss.

At the very least they prefer the idea of Enzo to that of Dante as their sole overlord.

I walk up and down the row of upright mixers. D'Abruzzo was supposed to be here fifteen minutes ago with the paperwork. I try not to think of what just happened in the hotel room. Not about the man, the money or Wanda's face. Not about the Persian or what might drive someone to offer eight hundred thousand euros for it.

"Come and have a drink," Enzo calls as he peels the gold foil from a bottle of champagne.

Eight hundred thousand euros. That's over a million Canadian. It has to be a prank.

"When the ink is on the paper," I tell Enzo. "It's bad luck—"

But he's already popped the cork. The other bakers cheer as he starts filling small plastic flutes.

I tell myself I'm doing the right thing as I pace back down the row of mixers to the worktable and grab a glass of champagne before they're all snatched up.

"How did you manage to set this up without your father around?" I ask Enzo.

"It's his out-of-town delivery day." My cousin winks and shakes the last few droplets of champagne into my glass. "He should be making the rounds in Nipigon right about now."

"You mean you didn't tell him?"

Enzo drains his glass. "I'm so glad you agreed to rush this through."

I look at the briefcase lying flat on the worktable. "You know the Persian has an unsavoury history, right? Be careful with that thing."

Enzo follows my eye. "What do you mean?"

"Men have died over it."

He laughs. "Men are always looking to blame their stupidity on things."

I wonder if he knows about Don Ernesto or Arthur Bennett. Or my father and Julia. Or my non-existence until the age of four.

"You don't even want to know what's inside?" he asks.

"Nope." I swirl the ounce of fizz in my glass. "After this I'm getting on a plane and devoting myself to making lifelike objects out of paper."

Enzo looks past me and sniffs. "Looks like the other half of your entourage is here."

I turn slowly, the champagne still in my mouth. I squeeze it into my left cheek pouch and hold it there, feeling the slight burn. Wanda has found her way into the back room and stands with her back to the swinging metal door. The Silver Fox is with her.

I swallow. "Jesus Christ."

She spots me and makes her way over. There's something in her face that I've never seen before, like she's about to attempt some physical feat that her body's not equipped to handle.

"Sabine," she pushes past Enzo and grabs at my arm. Her cheek is red and slightly swollen where I've hit her. "It's legitimate."

I peel her hand off my arm and throw it back at her.

"DuPierre," she tries again. "You need to listen to him."

"Sabs? You okay." Enzo steps forward.

"We're good," I tell him quickly. The last thing I need is for Enzo to perform some sort of chivalrous act Wanda can later use to build an assault case against us in a court of law. "Call D'Abruzzo again," I tell my cousin. "Tell him to hurry."

"Okay." Enzo tucks the empty champagne bottle under his arm. "I've got another one of these on ice. I'll be right back."

"You haven't signed yet?" Wanda glances around as Enzo leaves. "There's still time, Sabine. You have to trust me on—"

"Trust you?" I back up against a storage cabinet. "You just tried to blackmail me for eight hundred thousand dollars that I don't even have."

"Euros!" she cries. "Eight hundred thousand euros! You're not listening to—"

There's a crash from the very back of the building. We turn and look down the hallway that leads to the loading dock. An entire rack of baking supplies is lying on its side.

Dante stands in the rubble.

He steps around the aluminum landslide of baking sheets, Pyrex shards, and a burlap sack of sugar that's split down the centre like a Christmas pig. Then he sees me.

His shirt is untucked and there's a greasy light in his eyes. I watch as he makes his way toward me, kicking a cake pan out of his path with such force that it shoots metallic sparks as it skitters across the floor. He stops at the worktable and looks at the mirror glaze cake. "Isn't this nice, what you and your cousin have arranged. You think you're pretty smart, eh?"

He's a good five feet away from me but I swear I can smell his sweat and feel his spittle on my neck.

"You know how long—how hard I work for this bakery?" Dante asks.

I clear my throat. "Forty years, apparently."

Wanda steps toward me. In my peripheral vision I notice Enzo returning with another bottle of champagne. Two or three of the revellers have put their glasses down and I see DuPierre pushing his way through them. Dante is surrounded. It doesn't occur to me to be afraid.

That's my mistake.

The pastry knife with its curved blade is meant to be used to slice the cake. No one else seems to notice when my uncle slides it from the table.

"You are what they call a good-for-nothing," he says quietly as he comes down the narrow aisle to where Wanda and I stand trapped between a sink and a supply cabinet. "Always you were, always you will be."

"Sure." I nod, my eye on the six-inch blade.

Dante mops his brow with his shirt tail. "Put on this earth to get in the way. I know it. Your father, he knew it too."

"All true." I raise my hands in the air, the international symbol of surrender. My uncle chooses to ignore it. With his free hand he grabs one of my wrists and twists the arm behind my back. I hear Wanda cry out as he shoves me up against the cabinet so that the side of my face is pressed against the metal door. The force brings a light shower of baking flour down over us.

Then he brings the knife to my face, just inches from my nose so that I see my own eye, wet and terrified, reflected. In this moment I understand that I was always meant for this, to be added to that list of casualties. Don Ernesto, Arthur Bennett, Sabine Rose.

Suddenly Dante grunts and slumps against the cabinet beside me. His right shoulder makes a dent in the metal just inches from my face. But he's still holding the knife. I manage to push away from the cabinet in time to see him spin and slash the blade through the air. The large glass mixing bowl Wanda has used to hit him over the head crashes to the ground. Then she does too.

Sixty-Three

Sabine

Enzo, DuPierre, Paul and I take up an entire bank of chairs in the waiting room of the ER. We sit in silence because it's easier than trying to piece together what happened back there. Between the blood, the bakers wrestling my uncle to the ground, and Wanda whimpering while DuPierre and I tried rolling her over, it was one shit-show of a compromised crime scene and impossible to tell how much damage Dante had done. D'Abruzzo arrived just in time to accompany him to the police station, but the cops made it absolutely fucking clear that we all have to go file a report once Wanda's out of surgery.

Now Enzo gets up, steps gingerly around the briefcase (I think he's catching on to what I mean about the recipe's unsavoury history) and approaches the vending machine. I watch him feed it loonies then take his sweet time deciding. He finally punches in the number of the Oh Henry! bar, which I could have told him he was going to do from the start.

It surprises me that I still know him the way I used to.

I think of his father brandishing that knife. The absolute, pathological conviction that he was being wronged. And it reminds me of something else I know about Enzo.

He'll never survive being pitted against his father.

He'll never get the equal footing or acceptance or whatever the fuck it is he thinks the bakery's going to give him. I watch him unwrap the chocolate bar and take a bite.

"Well, that was weird," he says thoughtfully as he chews.

DuPierre gets to his feet suddenly. His suit is stained with blood. He looks at me, his forehead creased into two perfectly symmetrical planes.

"I'm sorry but it's about to get weirder."

Paul already has the camera up on his shoulder as we watch DuPierre cross the waiting room in an elegant, foxlike tread. A woman wearing a dark, masculine pantsuit stands by the sliding glass entrance doors scanning the crowd. For a second I think she's a cop. But then Duddy approaches her, takes her hand, kisses her perfunctorily on both cheeks and starts talking.

She has a sharp nose that juts to the left and pebble eyes that narrow as Duddy continues to speak. I watch as his hands get into the action, his gestures growing larger, but her face remains impassive. Finally, she looks past him. Her eyes come to rest on our little huddle seated by the vending machines. On me in particular.

Paul squints into the viewfinder as she approaches us. Up close her masculine pantsuit is actually well-tailored. Too well-tailored for a cop.

She's still looking at me. "You are Sabine?" She has an Italian accent.

I nod.

"Daughter of Francesco Rosetti?"

I glance at Enzo. "Yeah, Francis Rose."

The woman shakes her head. Her dark hair is threaded with grey and cut bravely against her head as if she has nothing left to hide. "Francesco Rosetti, it's his real name."

I feel something unlucky click in my head. I think of Dante's story where my father boards a plane in Naples with one name, then walks into Bennett's Bakery with another. For forty years he'd done a good job of covering his trail. But I somehow know that in this moment I am responsible for it all coming undone.

"Who are you?" I ask.

"Lucia Amarone." She doesn't put out her hand.

DuPierre solidifies at her side. "Sabine, Ms. Amarone owns Brighello Foods. Like I was telling you, we are here to make you a once-in-a-lifetime offer for the Persian recipe."

"Who are you?" I ask again.

She is still staring at me, her face a stone. "Your mother."

I turn to Paul. "Turn that fucking camera off."

Sixty-Four

Francesco, 1983–84

She made his espresso every single morning when he arrived for work at the *pasticceria*, just as she had when he was a paying customer. But now, instead of spending a few minutes chatting with her before his lessons at the university, he simply downed the espresso in two swallows and disappeared into Don Ernesto's workroom until well after sunset.

Sometimes she'd try catching him up in a clever little intrigue, offer to read his future in the dregs of his espresso. Anything to keep him around a little while longer. He was aware that she took private credit for him being here; after all, she was the one who got him this job.

After Francesco's transition from healer to baker, it became his habit to join the other men at the Caffè Firenze after work on Thursdays. She was there when he arrived one night. Francesco had always assumed that she was sweet on him and had gone out of his way to discourage her. But that night she was smoking a cigarette and engaged in a conversation with one of the jazz musicians who played in the square for loose change. She barely glanced in Francesco's direction. He watched her down a thimble of grappa and tell a joke about the local police. He'd heard her tell it to a customer at the bakery that very morning but found himself laughing anyway. While her nose made it impossible to call her attractive, she was lean without her bakery smock, and her legs looked nice enough in a mini skirt.

He found a spot next to her, cocked the vintage newsboy cap he'd found at the *bancarelle* near the cathedral to the side of his head, and waited for her to comment on it. She had always noticed little things about him while he had his morning espresso. The various tags and badges he had to wear at the medical school, the patch of dough on his bakery shirt that had dried in the shape of Argentina. But now Lucia just glanced at his hat, sucked a front tooth and turned away to tell a dirty story about a horse doctor.

That night, despite her dismissal of him—or more likely because of it—Francesco fell over himself trying to win her attention. He persuaded the saxophone player to lend him his instrument so that he could serenade her at her chair. He called her Principessa, the best espresso maker in Napoli.

What she really was, however, was the daughter of Don Ernesto Amarone.

Francesco pushed away the crostata di marmellata and looked out the window. The sky from his tiny apartment was white and illegible.

"What's the matter? No good?" Lucia glanced at the pie.

"It's fine. My stomach's got acid these days."

"It's because you didn't make it." She spun the plate around. "No one bakes as good as Francesco."

He mauled at his chin. "Don't get offended, I didn't get good overnight."

"So why don't you teach me something?" Lucia put a finger through the tart's cross-hatched top and into the apricot jam. "Or are you old fashioned like my father?"

It was no secret that she wanted to bake but that her father prohibited it. "I should throw my own daughter into that back room with a half-dozen sweating swine?" Don Ernesto had once asked him. "The better job for a woman is up front, smiling and making conversation." Francesco had nodded at this intelligence. As long as the don considered him as one of the swine, he'd be less inclined to suspect Francesco of carrying on with his daughter.

Now he looked at the crostata. "Fine. You want an education?" He pulled the plate to him again. "Your jam is good, but the crust is too thick. You need to roll the dough thin as an earlobe." He tapped a spoon against the heavy lattice of dough which had sunk into the marmellata. "See how it collapses? Too thick."

"But taste it. It's delicious."

He shook his head. "Nobody's going to taste it if they don't like the way it looks."

Lucia's face hardened at this. Francesco felt ashamed suddenly, as though he'd spoken of her own desirability. "There's no short-cut, Lu," he said hurriedly. "Pastry does not forgive."

"Gesù Cristo, you sound just like Papà. Maybe you should marry him."

He felt a sharp itch between his shoulder blades then. Is that where she thought they were heading? Their nights together, the occasional weekend away, the entire affair was a secret. Which is how he preferred it. He'd told her from the start that he was a jealous attendant of his own privacy. That whatever happened between them, stayed between them. And she seemed to agree to those terms.

Now he looked at the cratered crostata and felt remorse. "Bring a knife and come sit." He pointed to the chair beside him, trying for a concession. "Let me taste."

"Don't trouble yourself." Lucia picked up the pie, walked to the corner of the room and dumped it in the rubbish bin. "You want an espresso?"

He knew her temper was feminine. Mercurial and attention-seeking, she was a girl who'd been given too much rope. It came in bursts and dissipated quickly, so the best thing to do was look away.

"Give me one with vermouth," he told her. "A short one—the train leaves in an hour."

"Let me clean myself up and I'll come with you." She untied her apron.

"Another time. Palatino is cold and ugly this time of year."

Lucia tossed the apron aside. "It doesn't seem fair that you know my father and I know nothing of your mother."

He got up slowly, went to the window. "I work for your father. It's different."

"Does she even know about me? Be honest. Or am I as imaginary as medical school?"

"You know I can't take you today."

Lucia's suspicions were, by and large, correct. How could he return to his mother in that cottage where she lived her solitary existence and tell her he'd dropped out of medical school to work at a bakery? That he'd taken up with the girl who made coffee all day?

Francesco turned, found her unfastening her dress in the middle of the kitchen. She pulled the garment over her hips and breasts so that she stood in a camisole and underwear. Then she came and put her arms around him, rubbing a hip into his groin. "I'll be here all weekend by myself. You know I hate that."

He pushed her back, gently, but enough to break the chain of her arms. Something told him it wasn't normal, the way his spine arched away from her in these moments. He preferred her in darkness. In darkness he could have his own thoughts. "You'll be fine," he said. "You always have a good laugh at work."

"Sometimes I think you've got another woman stashed away in Palatino."

Francesco started looking for his boots. He knew where this conversation was going. "Yes, her name is Maria Rosetti, and she hates it when I miss the train."

"I'm serious, Francesco. It's nearly a year like this. We need to talk things over." She folded her arms at her chest and leaned against the windowsill. In the filtering daylight he could see through her camisole to the slats of bone and gentle pulp that indicated a woman. "My father knows about us."

"What does he know?"

She looked at him for a moment. "Enough to assume that you're going to marry me."

Francesco felt his chest tighten at this precipitous leap. Marriage was the last thing on his mind. He had too much yet to prove. And if a time did come for marriage, something told him that Lucia Amarone would not be his first choice. "These days people get to know each other first."

She played with the strap of her camisole. "I'm curious, Francesco. Why do you think my father taught you the Garibaldi recipe?"

He sat down hard on the kitchen chair and began lacing up his boots. "I have no idea."

"Because of your incredible talent? Because you're such a serious and hard-working young man?"

"I think," he said without looking up from his shoes, "there's something in your voice that I do not like."

"Look at me, Franchi." She came and stood in front of him, took his chin in her hand and tilted his head back. "In the real world people do things for practical reasons. My father gave you the recipe because he expects us to marry. Because . . . I expect us to marry."

Francesco felt ashamed by her partial nakedness, by the impossibility she was offering. He stood and kissed her forehead.

"Get dressed. I have a train to catch."

Sixty-Five

Sabine

"Can you stop for a minute?" I race through the parking lot trying to keep up with the eccentric Italian woman who has just claimed to be my mother. "You've just laid some pretty crazy shit on me here!"

"Yes, come," she waves at me to pick up the pace then points to an enormous white SUV across the lot. "I must put money in for parking the car."

I follow her zigzag course between vehicles, trying to catch her words as she digs through her purse. "Francesco earned respect in the bakery before my father's death, but afterward, the workers remembered only his silence. We used to call him Doctor Death—I started that name." She throws me a dark little smile over her shoulder. "When Papà fired him in front of everyone, he decides to take his revenge. This was the story the police keep telling to us." She stops in front of the parking meter and looks at me. "Do you have any of the loonies?"

I shake my purse and can hear some change collected at the bottom.

"The weeks after they find my father, I refuse to believe Francesco could do this. I imagine any minute he shows up at my door with an explanation. I imagine hiding him from the police."

She takes the coins from my hand and starts dropping them into the machine. "He will take me away someplace and we will start over. I believe he is innocent. He, in return, is bound to me forever." She looks up at me. "Besides this, I also had a secret."

Sixty-Six

Francesco, 1985

I t was true that the night of the Feast of Garibaldi he had followed Don Ernesto out of the square and to the lip of the abandoned wharf to apologize. The day before at the university *campo* he'd pretended not to know him or Lucia so that he wouldn't have to present them to his mother. So that he could avoid telling the old woman that he'd dropped out of medical school. But most of all, so that he would not have to introduce her to a girl he had no intention of marrying. Certainly he wasn't without flaws himself, but once, in his apartment near the university, Francesco lit a candle and carried it into the bedroom. He leaned carefully over Lucia's sleeping face, shifted it this way and that, trying to find an angle where he could view her with some satisfaction. There *was* something formidable, wasn't there, in the way she smoked a cigarette?

That night of the feast, he emerged from the covered arcade and saw Don Ernesto standing against a guard rail looking out over the Bay of Naples. Moon illuminated the harbour, but it was an ugly perspective, full of cranes, metal shacks and the rusted-out hulls of boats. Beside him, steep flagstone steps crumbled down to a deserted wharf.

"Don Ernesto?"

The old man brought his small head around. His braces had fallen from his shoulders and he stood slouched, his pants sagging at the waist. "Not you again! What else do you want from me?"

Francesco approached slowly. "I came to explain. About yesterday, with my mother—"

"Your mother? You waste your breath. What do I care about your mother?"

"I was disrespectful to you." Francesco took a step forward. "And to Lucia."

"So you do remember my daughter's name!" The old man winced as though sucking a bitter clementine. "Do you know what she told me?"

He could only imagine.

"She said, 'Don't worry, Papà, he loves me. He's going to marry me.'"

Francesco saw the old man was in no state to reason. Or to be left alone. He raised his hands to show he was not a threat. "Let me walk you back to your car."

"I made a mistake with you, Franchi. I thought you were a son." Amarone shook his head and took a proportionate step backward. "I gave you my recipe *and* my daughter."

Francesco had come as far as the metal rail. "Let's go back. I'll drive you home."

"You took one—the other you threw aside, eh?" The old man rubbed the deep goal posts between his eyes. "You never had any intention of marrying her, did you?"

There was no satisfactory answer, so Francesco reached for his arm instead. Don Ernesto recoiled from the touch, pivoting away from the person who'd helped himself to the two things the old baker prized most. In trying to recapture some dignity for himself and his daughter, the don triggered the drunken shuffle of his feet. It was a backward dance into empty space.

Sixty-Seven

Lucia, 1985

Her father's funeral was a stately affair, and the statue of Garibaldi was promenaded ahead of his coffin by the eponymously named society. The Fraternità took it upon themselves to shutter the bakery on Lucia's behalf, selling what they could. Amarone had been connected, beloved by all, a mystic who'd communicated with the spirit of Giuseppe Garibaldi. But all this meant little to his debtors when it came time to collect. After Lucia paid off what was owed, she had nothing left. And when it was known that she was pregnant and unmarried, nobody wanted to know her.

She finally took that train ride to Palatino.

At the station she asked around until someone told her where Maria Rosetti resided. "But don't go poking around there," one of the baggage handlers told her.

"Why not?"

"That's land owned by the Totis. You know who they are, the family Toti?"

She did not.

"Good. Keep it that way, young lady."

—

An hour later she'd found a farmer who agreed to drive her up to the property. The mountain road rose half a kilometre and then branched, providing access to the Toti farm and its several fields and cottages. When they pulled up to a rusted gate, Lucia could smell the rosemary bushes and juniper berries that had reached their year of maturity, and in the distance, the soil of barn animals.

The man got out without a word and went to the gate. He took off one of his boots and beat it against the rail. Lucia slid out of the cab. Behind the tree line she could make out the shape of the farm-house, its tiled roof sloping down like the brim of a cap. A plume of smoke rose from the chimney. A thick tangle of rosemary ran in disorderly fragrance along the gravel road through the trees. A stooped woman came down along this path toward the gate.

"I'll wait for you," the old man told Lucia as he returned to the truck. "You won't be long."

Lucia approached the gate slowly, taking in the chiaroscuro acres of grass plains and rocky outcroppings that stretched along either side of the farmhouse. It was wild country, but it seemed impossible that it would ever get ugly here as Francesco had claimed.

The old woman humped around knots of juniper and broom until she reached the gate, then placed both liver-spotted hands on it. "Who are you?"

Lucia licked her lips. This was Francesco's dearly feared mother? She wore rubber boots and pants under a house dress that should have been cut to dusting rags a long time ago.

"My name is Lucia Amarone. You know that name, Amarone?"

"The baker that got himself killed. The carabinieri have been here enough times."

"Your son worked for us. He and I were . . ." Lucia had rehearsed this conversation a thousand times on the train, but now the words were coming out sideways. "Engaged."

Maria looked at her, the bones of her cheeks, intractable hemispheres. "He never mentioned you. I imagine my son would have told me about the girl he was going to marry?"

"It was still secret, I—"

"What do you want, Lucia Amarone?"

The girl poked her tongue at a molar, thought she could feel her pulse in it. "I want to know where he is."

"You and I both," Maria said.

"I'm expecting his baby."

Lucia could imagine the woman having any one of a thousand different reactions to this news. There was something appealing about the idea of her stumbling backward and grabbing at her heart, for instance. Instead, Maria raised one foot to the gate and with a stick began loosening some manure stuck in the rut of her boot.

"You want money, maybe? But I don't have any."

"No! I don't care about that."

"Then you want to lead the police to him? To avenge your father?"

Lucia realized she was now gripping the fence. "I love him! I know he's not guilty."

Maria threw down the stick and shut her eyes. She opened them again and looked around as if expecting to find the visitor gone. "I'm going to tell you something now that is very hard to hear, Lucia. But the sooner you accept it, the better it will be for you and"—she motioned to the girl's mid-section—"your child."

"Francesco's child," she insisted.

"If my son loved you in return, he would have told you where he was going."

Sixty-Eight

Sabine

"Three more times I go to see that *strega*. I am getting bigger and bigger with you each time. And, like Peter, three times she denies me." Lucia leans against the front bumper of the SUV. "Old witch." She's staring off into the tree line edging the hospital parking lot as if the past also resided there.

"After you were born, I became involved with a man, a horse rancher, and we went to live with him outside of Naples. *Grazie a Dio*, because otherwise we would have been dead in the street. But he never wanted children." She turns and looks at me. "Sabine, I never asked if you want to even hear this story."

I think of Stella then, and Dante, and even Julia, how their stories had dovetailed neatly into one another but had never quite expanded sideways to complete my vision.

"You're assuming that I actually believe you're my mother," I say.

She nods. "Skepticism. Is a good attitude. It's how I run my business—how I make Brighello one of the top ten earners in the Italian packaged food industry."

"Right now it's just a story, okay? You were at the part about the rancher."

"To be honest, I first made this decision to send you away when I saw I was abandoned by Francesco. The first year of your life—it was a chore to look at you, with that big forehead and small nose. It was a wonder I did not smother you with a pillow."

"Wow. You are blunt."

"Nazario was not a bad man, considering I never loved him. He didn't push me to give you up. But when you were two years old the horse trade began to take him across the country. North he went to Piemonte, south to Calabria, east to Puglia, and he wanted me there. When he travelled alone, he returned home a beast with a loose temper and sometimes a fist to match. That's why I sent you to the Ursulines. It left me free to follow Nazario. And when we were home in Naples, I would come to visit you."

"The lady in the coral suit," I whisper.

"What's that?"

"Nothing." I shake my head. "I just have this memory of a woman in a pink dress, with high heels. Nonna Maria said it must have been one of the sisters. But I remember she took me in a taxi one day—"

"To the fabric market."

The smile falls away from my face. I turn to her. We look nothing alike. It's unlikely that there's an ounce of truth in this. What's more probable? This is just an elaborate scheme to get the Persian recipe.

And yet.

"One day, when you were four years old, I get a phone call from Sacro Cuore. They said you disappeared. Just vanished. There was a woman who came to the school on Saturdays. They thought her a village peddler or poor tenant farmer and once a month they bought honey from her for the kitchens. The children loved her visits because she would bring honey and sweets. The Honey Mother, they called her—"

I push off the car bumper. I fumble through my purse looking for something solid to hold on to or else throw. I find my car keys.

"I have to go," I tell the woman. I pull the bag over my shoulder and walk away quickly.

"Wait! Sabine."

But I'm shaking both hands in the air, an "I've heard enough" gesture that I hope translates well in Italian. By some miracle I find my rental car in the parking lot, my own meter expired. I ignore the parking violation in the window and jab the keys into the ignition, then scroll the windows down as it's incredibly difficult to breathe. I throw the car into drive and speed down a lane of vehicles toward the exit. But instead of heading toward the mechanical gate I switch into reverse and back all the way around the parking lot until I reach the SUV. Lucia is still standing there.

"How did you find me?" I shout out the open window.

She looks at me as if it's the stupidest question in the world. "The internet."

Once again, I think of D'Abruzzo's cloak-and-dagger advice, which in my mind has become "follow the money." What he really said was "follow the truth."

And that's how I end up on Julia's doorstep.

"You have blood on your shirt," she says with distaste, but allows me inside.

I look around the foyer I first entered over thirty years ago. I remember my grandmother thrusting me forward, presenting me the way a cat might drop a dead mouse to the doorstep. I remember Julia's face blanch on the stairwell. The exact expression that my father wore in the airport.

"My grandmother kidnapped me," I gasp. "And you all knew."

Julia removes her reading glasses and presses the divots in the side of her nose. Then she gestures for me to follow her into the living room.

Sixty-Nine

Maria, 1990

Together, the children made a terrible noise. The leaden, ancient Abbazia del Sacro Cuore spat them out two, three at a time so that they were carried into the yard on a cloud of sound. Here and there the children were shepherded by the casually attired Ursuline sisters. From behind the gates, Maria watched them tumble through the bright day; imps and elves carrying balls and skipping ropes.

Maria looked for Sabine among them. The nuns aired out the children three times a day, taught basic instruction in between, and fed them their supper at sundown. Older girls were encouraged to keep watch over the younger and this blending of rank, height and age lent a homogenizing aspect to the schoolyard. With their drab blue uniforms, Mediterranean complexions and crooked haircuts, the girls were difficult to distinguish from one another.

Maria's heart rose when she finally spotted the child. She was in the company of another little girl today and this pleased the grandmother. Often, Sabine stood alone at the edges of the building, avoiding the crush of bodies chasing after a ball, waiting until it was time to be led back inside. The hem of her dark blue skirt had come undone and it dragged nearly to her ankles. It angered the grandmother that no one had thrown a few stitches on the border to keep the girl from tripping over her own feet. Maria put her hand on the gate but didn't enter. She watched Sabine and the other pallid creature hold hands, their backs against the abbey wall as though they wished to disappear between the cracks and chinks of the mortar. Their usual caretaker, a swarthy and suspicious girl of about ten—Maria recognized her too by now—had snatched away their skipping rope and was using it to lash at a fourth girl who was on her hands and knees, lowing like a cow.

That was enough. The grandmother swung open the iron rail wide enough to let herself through, but not wide enough to encourage a stampede of escaping children. She was very careful with the opportunity the school had allowed her. Maria had established a sizable bee colony in one of the Toti's clover meadows, and once a month she walked down the mountain road to Palatino, boarded the train and rode to Salerno with honey for the abbey kitchens. Employing the honey was a stroke of genius and her visits to the school had become legendary. The sisters would allow her to distribute sweets to the children before leading her to the storerooms to conduct her business with the cook. Sabine and the rest of the students knew her only as Honey Mother.

The usual tumult began as soon as the children noticed her. Maria couldn't help but wince as she prepared for the assault. The girls' cries rose like penny whistle screeches, changed direction and bounced off the walls of the schoolyard. Instead of forming neat lines, they clustered in pinwheels and helices, dirty hands outstretched, a few tugging at her black shawl. They had a certain unwholesome lean to their faces. Maria brought out the crate of small paper cones filled with honey, placed it down among the children and stepped back. She had reserved the larger one for

Sabine, who she knew would hang to the back of the crowd. Maria wondered if she'd picked up this painful shyness from her father. From all accounts her mother had no such inhibition.

She had to shut her eyes in order to shake off the thought of Lucia, that miserable excuse for a mother. She'd taken up with a horse farmer and, in order to follow him around the country, had put the child in the abbey. It had taken Maria considerable effort to discover her whereabouts. She wasn't thrilled to go to the Toti family with such personal requests, but when she approached the school two years ago and saw the little girl for the first time, her reluctance vanished. She couldn't say there was an outright resemblance to her son, but something in the child's bearing, her prettiness and colouring, convinced her Lucia had been telling the truth. It was a grandmother's intuition.

Lucia had proved herself a survivor, putting her own comfort ahead of that of the child's. This neglect afforded Maria the opportunity to see the girl on a regular basis. But the grandmother was not so callous. It was a terrible thing for a girl to be motherless, a trauma that could not be salved by either Lucia's occasional appearances at the abbey or even her own pilgrimages. She'd spent two years planning and saving for this day, and finally it was here. The tickets were purchased, the stone cottage swept clean. Her son was comfortably married and ready to receive her.

Maria bent away from the flock of children to retrieve a rubber ball that had been discarded in the mad rush. Sabine stood at the edges as if waiting for the larger animals to fall away, sated. She was bracingly dark, sturdy, with eyes as big as the ten-lire piece Mussolini issued during the war. Here is where she could conjure Francesco's face, the same unblinking gaze. Maria rolled the ball toward her, skirting it along the circumference of the crowd, attempting to demonstrate to the child the path she might take around the others. Sabine let the ball come to a stop at her feet, then picked it up, cradled it against her chest. Maria beckoned her over.

"Sabine." Maria bent down as the little girl approached. "I have something special for you." She was aware of the presence of a sister supervising the knot of children around the crate. From her canvas sack, Maria took out the large cone of honey, folded back the wax paper and held it out to Sabine. The girl looked at it with the same excitement she exhibited each visit. She had no idea why the Honey Mother chose to perform this act of kindness toward her. They had a quick, furtive routine by now, the grandmother nodding encouragingly until the child put out both small hands.

This time, Maria did not hand the cone over. She took a step toward the gate instead. The child followed. Maria felt the desperation of years since Francesco's exile rise to the surface. Sabine deserved a family, the protection of a father and a mother.

"The best place to eat this, Sabine, is just beyond there." The old woman gestured to the tree-lined avenue a dozen yards away. From there she had already mapped the quickest route to the train station. "So the other girls won't see that you have the largest treat."

The child seemed to understand this, the jealousy and meanness of other children. She made no complaint as the grandmother shielded her from view and slipped her through the gates.

Seventy

Francis, 1990

By nightfall, the entire family had assembled in his living room. They had been expecting his mother's arrival, of course, but even Dante had fallen into a stupefied silence when they saw the young charge that had accompanied Maria from Naples. The child had, since spewing the contents of her stomach all over Julia, inserted herself in the crack between the wall and the darkened television set.

Francis sat on the divan between his mother and Dante. Each clasped a hand or shoulder as though to keep him from flickering out of existence. Julia would not look at him. She sat in an armchair by the door, the furthest she could get from the group.

Stella sat her little boy, Enzo, on the floor, hoping his presence might convince the girl to come out from her hiding spot. "How did you—how did she come to be with you?" she asked the old woman.

Maria got to her feet. Francis saw that his mother was preparing to deliver a rationale that she'd no doubt spent the entire plane ride honing.

"You see how it is," she said, gently. "Nothing is more important than family. Francesco, you yourself know the great sacrifice you made coming to this country." She took a few steps, then stopped.

"But some people, they give up their family—they leave little girls with nobody to protect them. They throw them away when it's no longer convenient. The one that calls herself her mother? Maybe it's been four months since she's seen the girl. Two years since she abandoned her at that institution." Maria turned, looked hard at her son's confused face. "How could I tell you this, Franchi? I knew you would come racing back to Italia."

"She was at Sacro Cuore," he said. "Not abandoned."

"I should let a nun raise my granddaughter? What does a nun know about a child?"

"Ask her how she knows it's her granddaughter." Across the room Julia gripped her armrests as though she were the one travelling over the Atlantic. She didn't need to understand Italian to follow the old woman's righteous logic. "Tell her she'll likely be thrown in prison for the rest of her life for stealing that child."

Francis grit his teeth.

"What does the blonde say?" Maria asked.

"That the child already has a mother," he told her in Italian.

"Who, Lucia?" Maria threw her hands in the air. "Her face is like a slab of cake. And that nose! It hangs like a tangerine in the toe of a stocking. I don't understand how someone as handsome as you, Francesco, were led by her." She turned to eye her new daughter-in-law, Julia. "This one at least has looks to recommend her."

The child had pushed herself into the deepest recess of the space along the wall and was no longer visible; for the moment, she was a theoretical argument.

"How do you know she's mine?"

"Of course she is!" His mother exclaimed. "Just look at her— the spitting image of your father's mother."

Francis could see no such resemblance. He glanced at his cousin and Stella. Both of their mouths were open but for once, they made no sound.

"What I would have done if I knew earlier that her own mother didn't want her," his mother continued. "I would have raised her, walked her to school each day, put clothes on her back. Oh, Franchi, I just wanted her to know her father who loves her."

Francis stood and looked at his mother. At Julia by the doorway. "There's nothing left to say tonight." His eyes narrowed as though it was a chore to behold them. "Someone get her out from behind the television."

⌣

"We all kept the lie," Julia says as we sit in the same living room, thirty-something years later. "We told ourselves it was for your sake, but it was really *Murder on the Orient Express*. Your father couldn't bring himself to turn his mother over to the police. And because of that, we were all made accomplices. It was not an easy thing to live with, and I admit, I did a botched job of it all the time you lived under this roof."

I feel a flattening of my vision. As though I'm not looking directly at Julia, but at a reflection bouncing between several surfaces. "He didn't believe it? He didn't think I was his daughter?"

Julia looks up at me. She is twisting the rings on her right hand. "There was just no way to know absolutely. At first."

"At first?"

"When you arrived, he had to either agree to the act your grandmother had committed or turn you both over. On the spot. You understand?"

I press my palms against my cheeks to cool them. Then I stand and walk around the room. When I am close to the sofa, Julia reaches up and grabs my arm.

"Listen to me." She pulls me down so that I am kneeling. "At first he couldn't be sure. In time you came to look more like him, which made it easier to believe. By then, it was too late to change his ways. To show his affection. All he could do was try and shield you from the truth. It seemed that he always ignored you, but from the moment you walked into this house, Sabine— the moment he decided to keep you—everything your father did was designed to keep you from learning the truth. He thought the further away he stood from you, the more he was protecting you.

"And then last year, he got some inkling that your mother had tracked him down. This company, Brighello Foods, approached your uncle for the Persian recipe. When we learned who headed the company, we shut down talks right away. We told each other that it would disappear. But your father changed the terms of his will."

"Is that why he left me the recipe? Guilt?"

"Yes, that was part of it."

"What's the other part?"

Julia looks at me without pity. "You want me to tell you what? Something romantic? That he realized you had the right to know your true origins?" She shakes her head. "When your entire adult life is built on falsehood, you don't suddenly mellow into truth."

I stand up, shake the creases from my clothes and breathe. "Then what?"

"The lie was catching up."

When the child had been bathed of vomit and changed into a nightgown, he lifted her into the bed she would have to share with his mother and drew the covers around her. Her small, round head shone like an olive in the diffused light. Francis put a hand on her chin, tipping her head gently to the side so he could see her face. He studied the understructure, the tilt and distance between the nose and mouth, the mouth and chin, and wondered if she was his. If his mother was right.

"Listen." He settled on the bed. "Can I tell you about the farm where I grew up?"

She watched him adjust her sheets and fold the blanket with his great, pre-arthritic paws, perhaps recognizing in his efforts her own instinct to feather the nest of a new doll.

"It was a farm with cows and a white stone house in the centre. In the kitchen, my mother always kept a fire burning, and under the window was a pump where we got our water. A pump you had to turn by hand. It was the house where I was born. A cottage like in the fairy tales, with a big chair for my father. He taught me the alphabet—he would make me draw the letters for him, sometimes by the fire in the kitchen or sitting at the foot of his chair."

The child yawned but her eyes were still open, brassy and wet.

"Now that I am grown up in this house I sometimes wonder, *how did I get here? Was it all a mistake?* How did I go to sleep there and wake up here?" Francis held his hands out to the room around them. "I'll never see that place again. But every night before I fall asleep, I take a walk through it. I close my eyes and go from room to room, touching the walls, the furniture. I still go home, every night."

The girl squeezed her eyes shut, and in that moment Francis did not believe that she was his. But he also knew that it didn't matter. She was here and there was no good way to rectify it.

"You can do the same," he told her, smoothing the hair from her forehead. "You too can go home whenever you want."

Seventy-One

Sabine

When I walk into Wanda's hospital room, I see Duddy DuPierre standing on a chair, attempting to adjust the angle of a ceiling-mounted TV. There is a coffee percolator by the window, a pitcher of water and a vase of fresh mums. In the bed, Wanda looks like a bespectacled child in a bundle of hospital blankets.

They both turn to me. It's a weird sensation, being viewed from both above and below at the same time.

"I'm just going to sit," I tell them. I take the visitor's chair that Duddy happens to not be standing on.

"It's okay." Wanda looks at him. "I'm not in the mood for TV anyway."

"That's because they've given you some really good medication." He climbs down and looks at me warily. I can't tell if he's remorseful for having been part of this or satisfied for having done his job. My guess is somewhere in between.

"I think this is my cue to take a trip to the vending machine. Junior Mints, anyone?"

Neither of us answer but we watch him leave the room. When he's disappeared down the hall I point to her hand. It's bandaged and looks like a giant Q-Tip head.

"What did my uncle do to you?"

"My thumb," she swallows and holds up the wad. "It's gone."

I want to bury my face in my hands, but worry she'll think I'm flaunting my own perfectly attached thumbs. I sit on them instead. "I'm so sorry, Wanda. Were you—did you try to save my life?"

She shrugs. "Instinct."

For a long moment we don't say anything because there's just too much to cover and picking a place to start seems impossible. Finally, Wanda does her thing where she scrunches up her face in order to raise her glasses up her nose. Only the pain killers must have softened her facial muscles because it doesn't work. I reach over to push them up for her.

"I'd rather not wear them," she says.

I take the glasses, fold them and put them on the nightstand.

"I heard you met your mother."

I nod.

"I may have been responsible for that." She uses her good hand to reach for her water glass.

"I think it would have happened one way or the other." I stand and get the water pitcher. "You know my father and I had the same job?"

"Of course I know."

"No, I mean our other job—being big fat frauds?" I fill the glass. "But the long tail of transgression has finally wound its way back to me."

"I don't believe in karma."

I put the pitcher down, reach into my pocket and take out the flash drive. "Believe it," I say, holding it up.

Wanda squints. "What is it."

"The thumb drive." I dangle it so the beckoning cat waves his little paw. Then I realize what I've just said. "Oh, shit! Is it too early for a thumb reference?"

Wanda looks at it, then up at me.

"Post it." I tell her. "All of it."

Epilogue

9 Months Later

I t's best if we start off with the tragedies. There are plenty.

First, Wanda's thumb. It was recovered several hours after the attack from under one of the standing mixers in the workroom, having either rolled there or been kicked there during the scuffle to subdue Dante. As you already know, it was too late to attempt to suture it back onto Wanda's hand.

On the topic of Dante, he is currently serving a reduced sentence of one year for aggravated assault with a weapon. It could have been a lot worse if the judge hadn't happened to be a long-time customer at the bakery. D'Abruzzo represented my uncle and built his entire case around the fact that Dante had been a prominent member of the business community for the past forty years. Not just a labourer, but a padrone.

Speaking of padrones, Enzo never became one. This will sound obnoxious, but I made the decision for him. It would have been homicide to throw him in the ring against his father. And perhaps even more obnoxious, but true, it turned out to be the best thing for everybody.

This is where tragedy begins to turn on its heel.

Enzo left the bakery and moved with Marcus to Vancouver, where they said their vows during a small but tasteful wedding ceremony. A couple of months later Stella finally obtained her divorce from Dante (the fact that he was in prison was good motivation). She sold the house and followed her son out West where she finally made a well-advised investment: a glassy condo in Yaletown with a second bedroom that she's already turned into a nursery. She's going to be really busy when Marcus and Enzo's twin girls are born in the fall.

Which brings us to yours truly.

You might be surprised to learn that I've returned to the country of my birth for the first time since I was taken from it as a child, and that my travelling companion is Julia. But here we are, breathing our first lungful of this roiling city of filth and magnificence as we get out of an Uber on Corso Umberto I. If it were up to Julia, we would have walked to the city centre from the Naples airport.

This is her first trip to Europe, and she is completely embracing the experience. As the driver unloads our bags, we watch a tourist being relieved of his wallet by a swarm of street urchins dressed in rags and toting a baby bundled in veils.

"Little bastards!" the American shouts and beats at the oldest pickpocket with the very rolled-up newspaper they'd managed to dislodge from his pocket ahead of the wallet.

"How wonderfully authentic!" Julia cries, wrapping her silk scarf around her head and donning sunglasses. "I mean, just let the poor things have it."

I look around warily for any water fountains and hope she isn't going to pull a *Dolce Vita* on me. While I don't doubt that she loved my father, it's pretty clear that widowhood agrees with her. And despite her enthusiasm, I'm glad she's agreed to come to Naples with me.

Our feet clog along the pavement and cobble as we cross the busy thoroughfare and enter Piazza Nicola Amore. There we find ourselves surrounded by four identical neo-Renaissance palaces. Standing in the centre is my mother.

She doesn't exactly rush over to greet us—enthusiasm is not Lucia's style—but once she's kissed us both on either cheek, she insists on dragging all our suitcases to the arched portico of one of the buildings.

"Your apartment is on the fourth floor," she tells us, handing our bags to a uniformed doorman. "In Italia, fourth floor means fifth. You understand?" She looks pointedly at Julia.

"*Sì, grazie!*" exclaims the woman who spent the entire flight asleep with *Rosetta Stone Italian* open on her chest. She practically sprints to the entrance of the luxury palazzo that Lucia has rented for us. "Sabine, you go ahead. I'll see you at dinner."

My mother watches her go then gives me a funny smile. "*È certamente una bionda.*"

"Yes, blonde to the roots."

"Let's walk, eh? It's not too far." Lucia takes my arm as we cross the piazza. She's wearing a tweed suit and a bowler hat which, to be honest, makes me question her grasp on reality a tiny bit. But then I remind myself that nothing about this woman is expected, including her existence.

"Later I will take you by car to the factory, Sabine. You'll see how we are almost finished preparing to mass-produce the Garibaldi. The artist has made renderings for the packaging. There is a description on the back of how my father's recipe has been restored to its native home."

I smile, but I'm not here for the Garibaldi. While I know better than to lean too heavily into this mother-daughter thing—neither of us have training in that department—I do have some questions.

"So this is where I would have grown up . . . if things had gone differently?" I look around as we skirt pigeons and squint under the azure sky.

She nods. "I can never bear to be away from Napoli for long." She's silent for a moment, her thoughts curling away with the car and *motorino* exhaust. "About this topic, I want you to know something. When you went missing, it was not ignored. The story was in the newspapers in Salerno. Here in Napoli, *Il Mattino* did a long *articolo*.

"I've read it," I tell her.

"I hired an investigator after you and your grandmother disappeared. He went to her house on the Toti land outside of Palatino to ask questions."

"What did he learn?"

"I don't know—he came back dead. They say his car went off the side of the mountain." My mother shrugs. "That's when I know if one day, I was to find you, I would have to be rich as a Toti. But with respectability."

Which is exactly what happened, by her account. She left the horse rancher, returned to Naples and hit up every single one of her father's old compatriots to make an investment in reopening his bakery.

"I had to tell them it was my father's bakery, because Italian men in the 1990s, they are still of the Stone Age. But it was my bakery. I did not drink like my father did, so when I made a profit I reinvested in the business. I started to supply to the grocery stores until I had enough money to buy a factory. Then I hired the food scientists to make recipes with a shelf life." She flourishes a hand through the air as if to say, *the rest is history*.

There are things couched in this flash-forward that I want to back up and unpack. But I know this woman just enough to know that she is not used to being forthcoming. I can only give her pieces of my history to see what she does with them.

"You know, my father was never sure that I was his daughter."

Lucia laughs. "Of course you are. You can do a test for the DNA with your cousin."

"Maybe." I shrug and we walk on. "So why did it take you thirty-something years to find me?"

"I found your father first. They wrote about him in the *New York Times*. When I see your father's *nome inglese* and the picture of his Persian, I know exactly what it is—one half of the Garibaldi. From there I traced your name and voila, you."

"Then you sent DuPierre to meet with Dante?"

"That's right. Dante is—how do you say—the weakest link? Ah—here it is!" She stops us in front of what once was a Gothic church. The upper story has been completely sheared away and replaced by interlocking glass prisms. "La Scuola Nuova. Not so far, eh?"

I glance at the building but then turn my attention back to her. "There was an entire year between the first and second time Duddy came to Thunder Bay."

"Yes, *bella*."

"And you knew where I was for that whole time."

"There was just as much that I did not know."

I stand chewing my lip for a second. "Like what?"

There is a small dent in her smile; she isn't used to being challenged. "Maybe I worried that you would hate me when you learned who I was. Who knows what your father told you about me—*che fantasie.*" She nods to herself. "No, it was much better to keep these things separate: DuPierre comes to take care of the business first, I take care of the personal after."

The business first. I understand what she's telling me. If she had presented herself to me a year ago, I could have been a liability. An angry, estranged daughter standing in the way of her business dealings with the bakery.

My mother's smile is restored as she brushes some hair out of my eyes. "After all, Sabine, I had waited all these years. What was one year more?"

I kiss her on both cheeks and promise her that Julia and I will be on time for dinner. It doesn't even occur to me to ask her what she had been waiting for exactly. I already know.

The recipe.

Oh yes, the recipe. Lucia got it, but not the way you think.

Obviously my Netflix deal went belly-up once I revealed I was a fake. Kudos to Antony Oberfleet for showing up at the right place at the right time to clean up the spoils. What started as *What's in Your Pantry* became, in its final incarnation, *Rock, Paper, Scissors*, a department store window decorating competition which he now hosts. As they say in South Africa, *shame!* Incidentally, Paul was hired as DP on the show. By all accounts, his agent, Collette Blanche, got him a great package.

Netflix didn't just send me home empty-handed. They tried to sign me to a documentary project about being an online imposter.

The metrics were in my favour, they said. After Wanda posted the video on the flash drive revealing how she was my baking double, *Sweet Rush* climbed to the number one most visited YouTube food channel for three days in a row. Our subscriptions shot up past ten million.

And, because every dog has his day, I guess it's worth mentioning that one of the last comments posted to *Sweet Rush* was from ReynoldsWhitakerII and simply read, *Called it from the start!* (Actually, Reynolds's day ended up lasting seven weeks. That's how long his memoir, *Braised: A Snout-to-Tail Tell-All* was on the *New York Times* non-fiction bestsellers list. He somehow managed to mention me only five times, which, to my understanding of genre, makes his book a complete work of fiction.)

As you've probably guessed, I declined to participate in the Netflix doc about online imposters. And we closed down our YouTube account a few days later. Now, if anyone searches for *Sweet Rush*, they're served up a shadowy black box that reads "Video Not Available." I won't lie—it haunts me to this day. It always will.

But because of that enormous crash and burn, I'm now left with two other shadowy patches that I'm trying to understand. They are the reasons we've come here to Naples.

One is the story of my past. Of my mother, and the life I might have had if fate, in the form of my grandmother, hadn't intervened. I'm approaching this one with the cool distance of an ancestral researcher, which means it's really interesting but doesn't change much. The thing I've realized is that the people who were supposed to raise me were the ones who raised me. To learn that my father had been orchestrating my life behind the scenes—it actually meant something to me. Stupid as it sounds.

But I'm not going to honour his lies by living that way myself a minute longer.

Even though it makes me gag, Julia's right when she says, "It's time to live your truth."

The other shadow I'm working on is the story of my future, which is much more actionable. Funny enough, it's going to take place in my father's bakery. Because I actually never sold the share that he left me. Once my uncle gets out of jail, he's going to find he's got a new, tough-as-nails partner at Bennett's Bakery. I think it's going to work out well, despite the fact that he tried to kill me. And it's the reason I'm here; to prepare for it.

When I walk into the modern stone-and-glass courtyard at Scuola Nuova, Wanda is already there waiting for me. She looks very grown up and Italianate in her linen slacks and apron, her hair pulled back and thick-rimmed hipster glasses replaced by contact lenses. I think to myself that she finally looks like the pastry chef that she has always been. Until she starts rocking excitedly on her heels and throws her arms around me.

"How's the thumb?" I ask, disentangling myself and picking up her hand to have a look. It is a surprisingly clean cut, the thumb sheared away completely.

Wanda shrugs. "I'm officially in rehabilitation to teach my left hand what my right used to know. Duddy and I are taking a water-colour class: Thirty-Five Views of Mount Vesuvius."

Duddy stayed by Wanda's bedside until she was discharged, flew her back to Toronto and stopped the notice of sale against her parent's house. Turns out her father had been using the money to help an uncle buy a car wash business in Gatineau. And because there is no guarantee that he won't do it again, Wanda decided some distance was in order. She accepted Duddy's invitation to live with him in Naples, and if that's not the most romantic start to a relationship, I don't know what is.

I'm actually going to pause to take a little more credit here. When I decided to keep my father's half of the bakery, it meant that I also got to do whatever I wanted with the Persian recipe, a neat little loophole I dove right into. If you're wondering what the secret is, the truth is, I haven't got a clue. D'Abruzzo came with me to the hospital the day Wanda was discharged and together we presented her with the briefcase and the combination.

"You know what to do with it, right?" I'd asked her. She was still on some major painkillers, so it was best to be direct to her in these matters. "I know someone who'd basically kill for that recipe. Or pay you eight hundred thousand euros for it."

"Or more." Duddy said.

In the end, my mother paid Wanda one million euros for the briefcase and combination. She also agreed to be a primary investor in a new business venture Wanda was cooking up. I will say Lucia wasn't thrilled with me for helping to drive up the price, but I imagine she got over it once she snapped open that briefcase and disappeared into the Brighello Food laboratories for two weeks, reunited with the recipe that had been taken from her years ago.

"By the autumn you should be able to buy the Garibaldi in the *mercato canadese*," she had told me proudly on the phone.

I rolled my eyes. "It's just a doughnut."

"It is not a doughnut. It is a pastry."

—

Knowing Wanda pocketed a million euros has gone a long way to relieving my guilt about the fact that her thumb ended up under one of our mixers. What it cannot do is make me legitimate.

Only Wanda can help me do that.

"So, are you ready?" she asks and hooks her arm through mine, Italian style, leading me across the courtyard to the building entrance. She's going to teach me to bake, right here at Scuola Nuova, the pastry school that she and Duddy have started.

"This is going to be ugly," I warn her.

"Yes," she agrees, letting go of my arm to open the door.

I roll up my sleeves.

Acknowledgments

This book is a work of fiction, but the Persian is real.

If you travel to my hometown, Thunder Bay, Ontario, you'll find, along with a lot of outdoor beauty, a pink, frosted pastry whose origins remain shrouded in mystery. This book began as an endeavour to unravel that mystery, and consequentially to better understand the early days of my family in this country. This was a big endeavour and as such, there are a number of people to whom I am in debt.

First is my father, Ralph Mauro, who didn't talk much about many things, but fielded all of my questions about the bakery business as well as life in southern Italy. Although he passed away in 2017, this story has kept him present each day. Along with him, I thank my Uncles Vince Mauro and Mario Nucci. As Italian immigrants, they had the foresight, drive and opportunity to buy the real Bennett's Bakery from a widow named Julia Bennett in the 1960s.

Oh yes, the bakery is real. And in the 1950s, Arthur Bennett indeed took his life in the attic of the old Park Street building. I remember hearing stories about how no one ever wanted to go to the attic. There were noises up there that couldn't be explained. The freight elevator would travel up and open its doors without being called.

Before Mr. Bennett's final act, he created a pastry he named the Pershing—as legend has it—after his hero, General John J. Pershing. Someone, along the way, changed it to the *Persian*. The real Persian is made differently from the way Francis makes it in this book. That's to preserve the secret of the recipe, but the resulting pastry is as wildly popular as the one in these pages. This is due to the efforts of the Nucci family who took over the bakery business and made it into a multi-generational success story. I owe a big thank you, in particular, to Danny Nucci for a behind-the-scenes look at all that goes into bakery life.

Thank you to my brothers, Pasquale and Frank Mauro, who suffered through 5 a.m. bread delivery routes during their teen years so I didn't have to. Because I was too young to remember much, it was their memories that helped inform the description of the place. Thank you to my mother, Rita Mauro, who, years after hanging up her apron professionally, continues to amaze us with her baking skills. And a shout-out to Alexandra Mauro and Athena Provenzano for keeping the tradition alive on Instagram with @a__mangiare.

Thanks to the Canada Council for the Arts for their funding and support. To Jamie Brenner for all of her help, and to Laura Usselman for all to come. To my editor Craig Pyette at Random House Canada for his patience and enthusiasm. Thanks also to my publishers past and present, Anne Collins and Sue Kuruvilla, as well as Lauren Park and Pia Araneta for careful reads and helpful insights. Thank you to my friends Carla Olson, Laura Hemphill and Maura Kelly for taking part in endless plot scrimmages over the years.

A very special thank you to my husband, Josh Greenman, for helping me find the words. And to my girls, Lola and Sasha, for giving them meaning.

Finally, a nod to Mr. Bennett. His *Pershing* was, perhaps, not so much a mystery as it was a starting point. A reminder that stories are our deepest efforts to understand the things we'll never really know.

© Ken Jones

NANCY MAURO is the author of the critically acclaimed debut novel *New World Monkeys*. She grew up in Thunder Bay, Ontario, where her Italian-Canadian family owned the bakery that invented the enigmatic Persian pastry. She now lives in New York City with her husband and two daughters.